An Orphan's Empire

Tommy Brown

Order this book online at www.trafford.com
or email orders@trafford.com

Most Trafford titles are also available at major online book retailers.

Printed in the United States of America.

ISBN: 978-1-4269-5017-9 (sc)
ISBN: 978-1-4269-5018-6 (hc)
ISBN: 978-1-4269-5019-3 (e)

Library of Congress Control Number: 2010917734

Trafford rev. 12/15/2010

Trafford PUBLISHING www.trafford.com

North America & international
toll-free: 1 888 232 4444 (USA & Canada)
phone: 250 383 6864 • fax: 812 355 4082

ACKNOWLEDGEMENTS

I always wanted to write a book, but never took the time. In 1980, I began writing and in 1983 I had finished my first novel. It lay in a briefcase, handwritten, until 2009. I then allowed two people that are extremely close to me to read it. Through their encouragement and motivation and belief in me is why I pursued the publication of my dream.

So many, many thanks goes out to Merce Gillo and Patti Schiralli.

CHAPTER ONE

February 1980, the funeral had been over for a week. Now comes the vultures awaiting the reading of Jonathan Stuyvesant's will.

Martin Gold, Jonathan's personal attorney and executor of the will, was attempting to get started but the crowd was extremely unruly. The press, there were so many, acted like they were attending a convention instead of a will reading. This was going to be more news than Jonathan's death. Nobody except Martin Gold and William Tolliver, Jonathan's personal accountant, knew the exact wealth he held at the time of his death. It was rumored that the Jonathan Stuyvesant estate was somewhere around $2.0 billion. Martin Gold had told the press, at the funeral, that Jonathan "was no Howard Hughes, his affairs were very much in order. Everything would be explained at the reading of the will."

The crowd settled down and Martin thanked everybody for coming. As you looked around the room, you could see corporation presidents, university presidents, state political officials, Chicago city officials, people nobody knew, and people everybody knew. They all had two things in common, except the press – of course, they were all personally invited, and they all wanted a share of the BILLIONS.

Martin Gold was typical looking, 65-years old, short, plump, balding, and wears black-horned-rimmed glasses. He is also one of the most respected men in not only Chicago's hierarchy but throughout the nation. He is very wealthy in his own right. Martin had been Jonathan Stuyvesant's closest friend and confidant for at least 50 years. Jonathan had been Martin's best man 45 years ago and Martin's first son is named Jonathan Stuyvesant Gold. This would be the first time Martin has seen the will opened. Jonathan made a change in it only three months before his death, and Martin was not involved in the change. William Tolliver was also given a duplicate copy to avoid tampering, or at least the temptation to tamper. Jonathan kept the will in a bank vault to be opened by Mr. Gold and Mr. Tolliver at the reading and not before. The will is being delivered by the bank president and two armed guards.

As Martin opened the Manila envelope, you could see the guests mouths begin to water. Martin began to read, "I Jonathan Bernard Stuyvesant, being of sound mind, would like to express my gratitude to my guests. It has been rumored that I possess a wealth of over $2.0 billion. That is wrong; it is well over $3.0 billion. I have interests in steel, oil, textiles, rubber, coffee, sugar, computers, land, real estate, airlines, and communications. These interests spread to not only the United States but to over 20 countries around the world. My personal cash wealth is limited to $1.0 billion. This cash is in a Swiss bank. The Swiss bank president is present. Would you please come forward Herr Formunder and be seated with Messrs. Gold and Tolliver. Thank you! Now that you are ready for a very long and boring reading of my last will and testament, I am going to surprise you. It is going to be short and to the point. Let us begin with my interests in the aforementioned corporations.

1. STUYVESANT STEEL; Gary, Indiana: I am the corporation. All assets, cash, liability and operations I give to Mr. William Tolliver, my close friend and accountant. Mr. Tolliver will have total control of the corporation. It is his now – net worth $600 million! Good luck Bill!
2. OKLATEX OIL CO.; Tulsa, Oklahoma: Once again, I am the corporation. All assets, cash, liabilities, and operations I give to Mr. Martin Gold, my lifelong friend and personal attorney. Mr. Gold will have total control of the corporation. Do with it as you please my good friend! Net worth -- $1.0 billion.

These were the only companies I owned outright. All others I own stock in. There is an envelope with the name of each company and my net worth in each. Also, in each envelope is the name of the heir to that interest. Instead of opening each envelope now, I will just tell you that the total net worth is in excess of $500 million.

All of my stock in the rubber, sugar, and coffee industry will be sold and the cash will go to the Northwestern University Medical Center for research.

All of my stock in automobiles and airlines will be sold and the cash will go to Purdue University for research on engineering of the "great American automobile".

All of my stock in computers and textiles will be sold and the cash will go to the City of Chicago to build the most modern hospital possible.

Ever since I have known Jonathan Gold, he has expressed a great interest in radio and television. Johnny, here is your chance; all of my stock in WCHI radio and television. Sixty percent I leave to Jonathan Stuyvesant Gold.

The Stuyvesant mansion will go to the State of Illinois for use as a museum, one year after this reading.

All land holdings in the Chicago area will go to Northwestern University; all land holdings in Southern Illinois will go to the University of Illinois; all land holdings in California will go to Stanford University; all land holdings in Florida, I leave to Alfred Thatcher, my beloved butler, because he loves the sunshine.

The list went on, giving a piece of land to a lot of people nobody knew and ownerships of buildings to members of his personal staff. I am sure you are all wondering what I am going to do with the $1.0 billion in cash? I leave $100 million to the Cancer Society; $100 million to the Heart Fund; $100 million to benefit Birth Defects; $100 million to Muscular Dystrophy; and $200 million to the research of mental retardation.

Throughout my life, I have loved very few people. As you all know, I am a bachelor. I was not blessed with children so I was a very lonely person at times. Twelve years ago, another person without a family came into my life. That was a sixteen-year old boy named Tony – Tony Cole, an orphan who never knew his true parents. At first, Tony came to work for me, and after graduation from high school, he attended Northwestern University to study finance and play football. After graduating from Northwestern, he became my financial advisor. He became more than an employee. Tony, I never told you this, but I considered you as my son, and because I had never told anybody before, I couldn't tell you while I was alive, but

Tony, I loved you. Tony, you are one of the most intelligent people I have ever encountered and because of this, I have had a very difficult time on deciding exactly what to leave you. My decision is to give you a challenge. I am going to leave you some tools, many more than most men ever get. I am leaving you $400 million cash! Ah, but the challenge! I could have left everything to you, but that was wrong. I could have left you a lot more – period. But that was wrong. So, I leave you with the cash – ah, but the challenge! Tony, I challenge you to become the next man with a wealth of over $3.0 billion! I have given you something to start with, but my boy; you are a long way from three billion!

Thank you all very much. Have a good life. GOODBYE!

Tony Cole was bombarded immediately by reporters. It was as though, he was the only person in the room. William Tolliver had received Stuyvesant Steel, Martin Gold had received Oklatex Oil, but it was the CHALLENGE that Jonathan left to Tony, not even the multi-millions; they were clamoring all over him – "What are you going to do first?" asked one reporter. Another question, "How are you going to handle the challenge?" Tony could not answer any questions because they would not let him; they were firing questions so loud and quickly. Finally, when the reporters realized that Tony could not answer, it was quiet and Tony spoke. "Ladies and gentlemen, I truly can't answer any of your questions at this time, only because I am stunned. I expected Jonathan to leave something, but believe me; I never expected anything like this. Before you speak, let me say this, "Jonathan Stuyvesant said he considered me as a son." Tony seemed nervous and shaken for the first time. "Well, I have always considered him as much more than a mentor, he was my messiah, my teacher, my friend, and yes – my father. He will be the first person that I've ever missed, and I will forever be indebted to him. As for the "challenge", that is typical of what Jonathan would do to me. I realized why he did it, and I will accept the challenge but, as of right now, I have no idea of how. I am going to take a vacation and try to figure it out. Thank you, that's all I can say."

Later that day at the mansion – Martin Gold walked into the study, "Tony, may I speak to you for a moment?" "Of course, Martin, please come in."

"Tony, I just want you to know if I can do anything to help?"

Tony smiled, "First of all, would you like a drink?"

"Yes, scotch and soda please," Martin answered.

"Martin, what would you suggest I do?" Tony questioned. Martin was glad that Tony would ask for his suggestions. "First, I would not let the press force you into anything. They are going to build this challenge thing into big news. They will hound you, and watch your every move. Tony, you are going to be in every newspaper and magazine publication in the country tomorrow. You have really got to be careful; not only the press, but every shyster and crackpot around will be trying to get to you." Tony smiled again, "Martin, I am going to enjoy the press for a while and attempt to use it to my advantage. I am really going to take a vacation, starting tomorrow." Martin lit a cigarette, "Where are you going?"

Tony answered with a look of bewilderment, "I am not sure, but it will be somewhere warm. What do you think of California?"

Martin replied, "Palm Springs, it is quiet there – you could think and relax, and the media may not find you as easily."

"Palm Springs sounds good. Palm Springs it is," Tony saluted.

"Tony, I wish you the very best of luck in whatever you decide, and please allow me to assist you in any way I can," Martin hugged Tony.

"I will be in touch, Martin. Goodbye."

CHAPTER TWO

The plane landed with a bounce and screeching tires. The smog of Los Angeles was not noticeable today, the sun was shining brightly, and the temperature was a very comfortable 78 degrees. Tony thought "I'm sure as hell not going to miss the freezing Chicago weather." The tall blonde stewardess leaned down, "Mr. Cole, the airline will be more than glad to have a limousine for you if you would desire. We've been informed that you will be facing a horde of reporters upon departure."

As Tony looked up at her, he noticed her name, Lucy, and the look on her face. Before he answered, a thought ran through his mind, "I wonder what else she might offer?" With a grin, he said, "Lucy, I thank you, but I might as well get used to it. At least for a while, but I would like to wait until everybody else has left the plane. Would you walk off with me?" "Oh, of course, Mr. Cole." Lucy was truly excited!

"There he is! There's Tony Cole!" the reporters were yelling and flashes were going off like firecrackers.

The questions were going off as fast as the flashes. Tony was holding Lucy's arm, "Smile real big, you are going to be in pictures!" They both laughed.

"What about the challenge? Can you reach $3.0 billion?"

Finally, as Tony and Lucy were stopped and unable to move, Tony began to speak, "You know, I thought I was coming out here without notice, guess

I was wrong." Tony was handling himself like a seasoned actor instead of a brand new multi-millionaire.

The nation's leading papers had Tony's picture and the story of the challenge as front page news. Tony Cole is the hottest news around. He is being referred to as "the most handsome millionaire in the world", "pretty boy with millions", and "the richest and most eligible bachelor". There was a cartoon with huge letters spelling out CHALLENGE and Tony trying to carry them on his back. The captions read, "Can the billion $ challenge crush the million $ man?" Tony Cole was an overnight celebrity. People all over the nation were day dreaming of what they would do if they were given the challenge. Men dreamed of the sudden wealth, women dreamed of having Tony (and all that money).

"I am sorry, I don't have anything more to say than yesterday, other than thank you all very much for coming, and I'd like to introduce you to Lucy." Tony walked on with Lucy on his arm, "Can you get that limousine now?" "Yes, yes, let's go behind the counter and we'll call for it." Lucy grinned.

As Tony entered the limo, he looked back at Lucy and said, "Thanks. I hope you enjoy your pictures," and stepped into the limo. Lucy Allen will never forget Tony Cole, "Damn, is he gorgeous!"

"Could you drive me to Palm Springs?" The limo driver said, "I am at your disposal, Mr. Cole, so Palm Springs it will be. "Will this phone reach the Palm Springs area?" The driver said, "Sure will."

Tony called the Matador Hotel and asked for accommodations. They at first said there were no rooms, until he said he was Tony Cole – then the Presidential Suite was available. Tony asked for his arrival to be kept quiet.

He arrived and entered the hotel unnoticed, thanks to the manager, Victor Turner. Turner, in a very gracious manner, "Mr. Cole, the Matador and its staff are very pleased that you have chosen to spend your vacation with us. If there is anything you want, please call me personally – my extension is #111."

"I would like a bottle of Jack Daniels Black sent up, please."

"Would there be any tennis players available for a game tomorrow morning?" Why, yes. I will arrange a game for you." Tony turned to

Turner, "No, I mean, will there be someone at the courts looking for a game?" Puzzled Turner answered, "Oh, oh, yes. I'm sure there will be. Will there be anything else?" Tony shook his head, "No, thank you for keeping my arrival quiet. I am going to take a shower, have a drink, and try to recover from the jet-lag." "I'll have the Jack Daniels here immediately." Turner left.

Tony was standing on the balcony, looking at the desert. "Jesus, I am exhausted, he thought."

CHAPTER THREE

It was seven o'clock when Tony woke up. "Shit, I haven't slept this late in 10 years," he thought. He would have some ham and eggs and a Wall Street Journal sent up from room service.

As Tony was walking through the lobby, dressed in his tennis whites, a nervous voice spoke to him, "M- M- Mr. Cole?" Tony turned. She was cute, probably 22-23 years old, short, well-groomed, big busted, and bright red hair. "Yes." "Mr. Cole, I am Theresa Williams, and I- I- I'm with the L.A. Times. I don't want to interrupt your privacy, but would you please answer a couple of questions for me." Tony grinned, she's really cute. She didn't give him a chance to answer, "You see, I 'm just a staff writer, and if I could get just a short interview from you, it would do wonders for my career." The look on her face was pleading. She was sincere.

"Ms. Williams, I am going to play tennis right now, but if you would like to meet me here at, let's say, three o'clock, I'll answer any questions you would like to ask, okay." "Oh, gosh, oh, yes. I will wait." Theresa bubbled all over, "Thank you Mr. Cole, thank you!"

Tony sat at a table near the courts. The three courts were being played and only one other player waiting – an extremely lovely woman. Tony thought as he took a good look at her. As the lady looked around, and then at her watch, Tony realized that she was waiting for somebody. Tony could hardly take his eyes off her.

"Maggie, I'm sorry, I'm late, but I can't play this morning!" another woman walked up to her. "Why?" The other woman raised her hand and waved it in the air, "Of all days, I have to go back to L.A. John's mother is flying down from Seattle today. Just called and said she's coming. Christ, you would think, she'd give me some notice, but then she doesn't give a damn about anybody but herself anyway." "Maggie, I am really sorry, I will call you later." Maggie started to leave, "It's okay Angela, call later."

Tony walked over to her, "I am sorry, I wasn't eavesdropping, but I did over hear your conversation, and, well, I'm looking for a game, if you'd like? There's a court open now?" "Yes, I am anxious to play today." Tony had never felt the way he was feeling right then. It was as though he had to talk to her, he had to be with her at this moment. "God, this is strange." "I'm Maggie," she said as she offered her hand. "It is my pleasure Maggie. I am Tony." "How well do you play, Tony?" "I can hold my own with the average player; how about you?" "I play pretty good." As Maggie walked to the other side of the court, Tony watched her. She is the most exciting looking woman he'd ever seen. She had long black hair, well-tanned skin, weighs 110 lbs. on a five foot five inch body; she had well-rounded hips, just enough breasts, long thin legs, actually, an athletic-build for a woman. One thing that she had – Maggie is embellished with class, it's written all over her.

Maggie was modest about her tennis game. Tony played as hard as he could and she beat him 2 out of 3 sets. By doing so, she really had his curiosity.

"Fantastic, you play excellent!" Tony exclaimed as they walked from the court. Maggie, wiping her face with a towel said, "And you say you can hold your own?" They both laughed. Tony had been modest himself. There were very few people (week-end players) that could beat him on the courts.

"How often do you play?" asked Tony. "I play as often as I can. I'm the Matador Tennis Club Champion for both men and women, I might add." Maggie flushed, "I feel stupid, I was bragging about myself, and that's one thing I can't stand." "That's quite alright; after all you should be proud of your accomplishment." For the first time, Maggie took a good look at Tony. She said to herself, "This guy is not only a very good player, but very, very good-looking." "I wonder who he is." Tony's words broke her train of thought. "Would you like a cold drink?" Maggie said, "No, I've really got to run. I have a luncheon to attend, but thank you anyway." She turned to walk away and stopped, "Thank you for the game, also." "Thank you, Maggie, for the lesson. Have a good day." She put out her hand and Tony took it. "It's been a pleasure meeting you, Tony." "No, the pleasure was all mine, believe me." Tony held her hand a second longer than the normal handshake. Maggie turned and headed toward the parking lot. Her mind was immediately inquisitive, "Who is he? He seems special, he's so nice, he's good, he's handsome, plays tennis, too, stop Maggie!"

She turned around, he was still watching her. "That's what you wanted to know, now you know, he's asking himself the same questions you're asking." She sighed, "What the hell, I am glad I won't see him around much, whew!" She got into her yellow 250SL and drove away.

"Victor, there is a young red-head sitting near the entrance, correct?" "Yes, Mr. Cole." Tony grinned, "Would you ask her to come to the phone, please?" Turner answered, "Of course. Just a moment, please." Theresa picked up the phone. She was sure that Tony was going to cancel the interview. "Hello, Mr. Cole?" Tony spoke very bluntly, "Miss Williams, do you have a car?" He waited for her answer, "Uh, yes, why?" "I feel like a drive in the desert. Would you mind doing the interview while we're driving?" Theresa sighed, "No, no, that would be just fine." "I will be down in ten minutes, meet me in front with the car." Tony hung up.

Tony walked to the driver's side, "Would you mind if I drive?" Theresa stepped out and walked around to the passenger side of the red MGB as Tony slid under the wheel, he said, "I'm glad the top is off. I haven't driven like this in a long, long time." "You just start with your questions anytime, ask anything you like," Tony said as he drove away.

"God, I don't know how to thank you, Mr. Cole. Every newsperson in the U.S. would give their eye teeth to do this interview." Theresa was exuberant.

Tony: "You can thank me by writing it exactly the way I tell it."

Theresa: "I promise you that. I am ready now."

Tony: "Shoot!"

Theresa: "The media is really building up the challenge that Mr. Stuyvesant left you. Is it really that big of a deal especially since he did make you an extremely wealthy man?"

Tony: "Yes, the challenge is a big deal to me. As for the media, I can't answer why it's such a big deal to them."

Theresa: "What does the challenge mean exactly?"

Tony: "Jonathan Stuyvesant knew me better than anyone ever has. He's been giving me challenges and goals to reach ever since I've known him. Every time I'd meet the challenge, he'd come up with another one. When I failed, he would explain to me the reasons why I failed and recreate the challenge. I never failed twice on the same challenge. None of the challenges were easy, and when he left this world, he left this ultimate challenge to me."

Theresa: "So, you will attempt to meet the challenge and become the next man to be worth more than $3.0 billion?"

Tony: "Yes, I'll not only attempt it, I'll do it."

Theresa: "How do you plan on doing it?"

Tony: "To be very honest with you, I really don't know; I really don't."

Theresa: "Do you even have any ideas?"

Tony: "Not really. I'm continuously thinking, but I haven't put it together yet, but I will soon."

Theresa: "I'd like to ask you some personal questions, if it is okay?"

Tony: "As I said, ask anything you like."

Theresa: "Since you are, excuse me, very handsome, I'm sure that the female readers would like to know what you're really like, if you're married, engaged, or what your intentions are."

Tony: "Well, I'm 6 feet 2 inches, 185 lbs., 28 years old, never married – never engaged, in fact, I've never had much time for women. I've spent the last twelve years of my life learning how to be a billionaire. As far as intentions – and I expect you meant marriage – I have none. If I meet someone who is truly exciting, then maybe (Tony instantly thought of Maggie, the tennis player, she was exciting)."

Theresa: "It was stated that you were an orphan when you met Mr. Stuyvesant. Would you mind elaborating on that part of your earlier life?"

Tony: "No, I certainly don't mind. After all, it's not anything I am ashamed of. I was born to parents I never knew. I was left at the orphanage by a dark-haired man when I was eight months old. The man would not leave his name and told the nun at the orphanage to give me a name that she liked. He then walked away. The nun, Sister Carolyn, had a nephew that I resembled. His name was Tony, so she called me Tony. I didn't receive my last name until a year later because I was always playing in the coal bin. So Tony Cole was re-born. Life in the orphanage wasn't that bad. Hell, it was the only life I knew. I didn't miss my parents – Sister Carolyn was the only parent I ever had. She died about seven years ago. Honestly, it wasn't as bad as most people might think."

Theresa: "How does a 16-year old orphan boy get to know a billionaire as well as you did?"

Tony: "This is a story that I love to tell, because it explains that Jonathan Stuyvesant was not a calloused, egocentric billionaire. He was a man of heart. Theresa, you make sure this is written correctly. It was in the summer between my junior and senior years that we were told the school was not going to continue their football program because they didn't have the money to buy uniforms. This was devastating news to me because I was a pretty good player and was hoping to get a football scholarship. It was the only way I'd be able to attend college. I went to the principal to ask him if I could get a job and buy the uniforms if we could still have football. The principal said it wasn't only the uniforms, but we didn't have the money to travel between games or own our bus to take us there. He said it would take $10,000 to allow him to continue the football program. So, I started thinking - $10,000, he might as well have said the moon, it was as easy to get. But I didn't quit thinking. I was reading an article in the newspaper about this billionaire named Stuyvesant – he had given some institution millions of dollars – so I figured if he gave away millions, why wouldn't he give us a mere $10,000. I wrote him a letter, explaining our situation. It was the only thing left but in back of my mind I knew, he'd probably throw the letter away – after all, why should a man like him care about a bunch of poor kids. Three days later, Sister Carolyn called me to her office. There was a very rich-looking man with her. When I went in, she said, "Tony, sit down!" She held my letter out to me "Did you write this letter?" I looked at it "Yes, I did. It wasn't wrong, was it?" Sister looked at me with a grin, "No, no, Tony. It was very good of you to think not only of yourself but of others. This gentleman, Mr. Thatcher, is

Mr. Stuyvesant's butler. Mr. Stuyvesant would like to meet you. You have my permission." Well, I said yes, of course. Mr. Thatcher said there was a car waiting to take me to meet Mr. Stuyvesant right away.

It was the biggest car I had ever seen. It was real shiny black, not a speck of dirt on it. There was a chauffeur, a glass between the front and back seats. There were four seats back there. It was the most exciting moment of my life. Mr. Thatcher was very nice and answered all of my questions, which I must have asked thousands between the orphanage and the mansion.

The mansion was something out of a magazine. I couldn't believe that people really lived in that place. It was huge, just huge. You can't imagine what a place like that looks like a 16-year old orphan boy. Just awesome! So much for the mansion.

Jonathan Stuyvesant was at his desk in his study. Mr. Thatcher walked me in, "Mr. Tony Cole, sir." Jonathan leaned back in his chair, "Come in young man, and have a seat." "Yes sir." Jonathan looked at me, for what seemed to be hours, "So you are Tony Cole, and you want me to give you $10,000?" He was getting directly to the point – which I would learn later that he was always directly to the point.

I was nervous, but I was determined not to show it, "Yes sir, that's correct." "What makes you think I would want or should do that?" I looked him straight in the eye (the way Sister Carolyn always told me), "Mr. Stuyvesant, as I said in my letter, our school will not be allowed to participate in this year's football season unless we get the money." Jonathan also looked directly at me, and very sternly said, "Young man, do you think that I got where I am because I gave away money to everybody who asked for it?" I was beginning to get very nervous, but still determined not to show it. I leaned forward in my chair and said, "Sir, I haven't even thought about how you got so rich. All I've thought about is how I can convince you to give us the money, and I did say that I would work for you until I repaid the money, didn't I?"

At that point, he got up and walked around the desk and stood in front of me, "And what do you suppose you could do for me that could possibly be worth $10,000?" This question stumped me, "I, I, don't know, sir." Jonathan walked back to his chair, "Let me tell you, young man, rather Tony, you just answered that questions exactly the correct way. I like honesty. It is the only part of a person's character that truly means something, and I think – no, I am sure – that you possess that quality. Yes, I'll give your school the money, but I will have you work off the debt. You'll run errands for me, you'll do anything I ask of you – is that understood?" I was so excited, I couldn't speak, but somehow I managed to utter, "Yes, yes sir. Anything you ask." Jonathan stood once again – I stood also. "I'll see that the money is presented to the right people tomorrow, and you'll report here everyday immediately following football practice. Rodney will drive you home." "Mr. Stuyvesant, thank you, thank you!" "Goodbye Tony."

That was how we met – it was a meeting I'll never forget – not one word of the conversation.

Theresa: "You know, Mr. Cole, that's fantastic. But what happened after that?

Tony: "To make it short, I finished the school year, and I worked for Jonathan everyday. He arranged for me to attend Northwestern University. I played football for two years and decided to give it up to put all of my energy into my new interest – the world of finance. Jonathan made me his protégé. He would give me projects to do and then judge me on how I handled them. After graduation, I moved into the mansion and Jonathan gave me the title of "Financial Advisor" – the title I held at his death. That's it – short, but that's it."

Theresa: "Did you learn your trade well?"

Tony: "Yes."

Theresa: "You did think a lot of him, didn't you?"

Tony: "Yes."

Theresa: "Is that all, yes?"

Tony: "That's all that needs to be said."

Theresa: "How long is your vacation going to last?"

Tony: "I'm not sure, but I'm sure that we've ended the interview, okay?"

Theresa: "Of course, Mr. Cole. But could I please have another interview at a later date?"

Tony ignored the question. "Where the hell are we anyway? I've been enjoying driving so much that I didn't pay any attention." "I'm not sure either, but we're in the middle of nothing." Theresa turned off her recorder and stared at Tony. "Mr. Cole, you're a remarkable man, do you realize that?" Tony smiled – with his broad genuine smile – "I am not remarkable yet – but I will be if I can become the next man worth more than $3.0 billion."

"Would you mind if I asked you some questions?" Tony asked. Surprised, Theresa said, "No, of course not." "How long have you been a reporter?" Theresa wished she could say a longer time, but she answered honestly, "About seven months." Tony liked Theresa, "Do you like being a reporter?" Theresa said, "I think I'm going to like it a lot more after I turn in this interview. But to be honest, I have been very disappointed up to now." Tony grinned as he looked at her, "I'm not intending to be personal, but how much do you make at the Times?" Theresa was embarrassed to tell this multi-millionaire her meager salary, but did so, "You're going to laugh at how this half of society lives. I make a whopping $16,000 per year – plus expenses." Tony spoke to her without the grin, "Would you ever consider changing careers?" She said, "Well, I am doing what I've always wanted to do, but I am somewhat disillusioned right now." Tony thought for a moment, then said firmly, "Theresa, how would you like to be my personal secretary?" Theresa didn't know what to say. She was totally surprised, "Mr. Cole, I don't know how to answer that." Tony laughed, "Just say yes or no – but before you do, let me say that being my secretary will not be sitting behind a desk typing. It will be an interesting position to hold (Tony was very careful not to use the common word job)." Theresa's mind was running rampant, "Mr. Cole, you astonish me. You really don't know me. You are going to try to build an empire, and you are offering me a job as your secretary, why?" Tony answered immediately, "It's quite simple, you used your own initiative and ingenuity to get this interview, and you're intelligent, aggressive, anxious, single, and attractive. Is that enough answers?" Theresa now in shock – she didn't even think he had looked at her – all she heard was that he thought she was attractive (after all, ever since she first saw him, she thought about what a gorgeous human being he was). She said, "Mr. Cole, this is really exciting but I don't know what to say." Tony grinned again, "Theresa, if you decide to accept, I will expect you to move to Chicago – my headquarters will be there. I will pay you $50,000 a year." Theresa exclaimed, "My God!" This time Tony laughed aloud and said "Is that all you have to say?" Theresa laughed nervously but said, "I accept, I accept. I will move to Chicago and become your secretary!" "Great, just great! You start as soon as you turn in that interview and resign from the Times." Tony said as he pulled into the driveway of the Matador. Tony got out of the car, "Do what you have to do, but call me tomorrow afternoon, okay?" She had a grin from ear to ear as she walked around the car, "Whatever you say, BOSS! By the way, you're wrong – you're remarkable right now!" "Thank you Theresa," Tony grinned as he entered the hotel.

The desk clerk motioned, "Mr. Cole, oh Mr. Cole. I have a message for you from a Mr. Walter Devon!" Tony moved toward the desk, "Thank you, would you get him for me in about five minutes, and ring my room?" "Of course Mr. Cole."

Walter Devon was a lifelong friend of Jonathan Stuyvesant. He was about ten years younger but he had known Jonathan forever it seemed. Walter is now a very wealthy banker in Southern California. Jonathan put the money up for Walter to get a start in California, and he was genuinely grateful.

Tony picked up the ringing phone, "Hello!" "Tony, Tony my boy. This is Walter Devon. How are you?" Walter sounded ecstatic. "I'm fine Walter, and how are you feeling, and how is Eleanor?" Walter always pleasant, "We are just fine, just fine. Tony, I just found out you were in town. Could we get together?" Tony thought, "Yes, in fact, how's your golf game? Do you think you can get out tomorrow morning?" Walter speaking with a smile in his voice said, "My game is terrific. I'd love to play, just say what time and I'll have a foursome there." "How does eight o'clock sound, here at the Matador course?" "Great; I'll be there." Tony started to say goodbye but switched his words, "Walter, why don't you have coffee with me in my room, say at seven!" This pleased Walter, "Sure, I'll be there at seven. It is good we'll see each other Tony." Walter hung up.

Peter Weyland picked up his private phone, "Hello, this is Peter Weyland." It was Walter Devon, "Peter, are you available to play a round of golf tomorrow morning?" Peter answered, "I'm pretty busy, Walter. I don't think I can." Walter said baitingly, "Could you make the time if you were going to play with Tony Cole, the brand new multi-millionaire?" Peter excited, "Jesus Christ, yes, of course. I'd love to meet him!" "Well, meet us at the Matador course at 7:30 tomorrow morning." Walter laughed.

Peter hung up, sat back in his chair and said to himself, "God damn, this must be fate. This guy Cole can be just the right man for me to do business with." He went onto the patio. "You'll never guess who I am playing golf with tomorrow?" Maggie didn't look up but said, "No Peter. I'm sure I wouldn't." "Would you believe that guy that just inherited millions from Jonathan Stuyvesant!" "That's nice, real nice, Peter. Have a good time," Maggie wasn't very excited. She wasn't even aware of who he was talking about. As Peter left, he said, "This is going to turn out to be much more than a golf game for me."

CHAPTER FOUR

Peter was dressing, making sure that his clothes were perfect; everything had to be perfect if he was going to convince Cole to invest in him. "Peter," Maggie said excitedly as she carried the morning paper. "Is this who you're playing with this morning?" He looked at the picture of Tony, "Yeh, that's the man. Mr. Tony Cole…man of millions," Maggie was shocked. She had no idea who he was during their tennis match. Although she had thought about him off and on ever since that meeting, she was sure that she hadn't thought twice about another man in the eight years of her marriage to Peter; but this guy, this Tony Cole, sure has something no other men seemed to have – a certain excitable magnetism. She was sure he had women swarming all over him.

"Peter, did I tell you that I played tennis with one of the Matador's guests on Monday?" "No, I don't think so, why?" Maggie was reading the article about Tony and didn't look up or even hear him. Peter stepped from the bathroom, "Maggie, are you listening? Who did you play with – another one of the glitter people from Hollywood?" Maggie waved her hand as though to say wait a minute. Peter shrugged and returned to the bathroom. She finished the article and sat on the bed staring at the picture of Tony. She thought to herself, "I knew there was something special about him." Peter fully dressed now, "Are you going to tell me who you played tennis with, now?" Maggie looked up, "I feel so stupid, so ignorant, it was him and I didn't even know who he was." Peter said angrily, "Why didn't you tell me you played, Christ. What did he say, what's he like, how could you <u>not</u> know who he was?"

I didn't pay any attention to, who he was, just how he played tennis, he was nice and that's all I can tell you, except that I feel absolutely foolish, "Maggie said as she lit a cigarette nervously. "I've got to go, I'll apologize for you. By the way, who won?' "I did, barely," Maggie said softly. "See you later," he left.

While the phone was ringing, Maggie wasn't sure what she was going to say. The ringing stopped, "Hello." "Mr. Cole, I hope I haven't called to early, oh, this is Maggie Weyland—we played tennis on Monday," Maggie's voice was nervous. Tony felt a lump in his throat, he was excited at hearing her voice; but he spoke as though he was totally composed, "No, you didn't call to early, and I'm still smarting over my defeat, or rather your victory, and please, my name is Tony; Mr. Cole is much older sounding." Maggie was now embarrassed because she'd called him Mr., "I want to apologize for not knowing who you were Monday, I really feel foolish." Tony laughed, "Oh God, now we both feel foolish, because I didn't know who you were either." Maggie laughed and felt more at ease, "you're really nice and you've made me feel better. After I read the newspaper article about you, this morning, I just had to call and apologize." Tony could listen to her talk as long as she wanted to. She has a great voice to go along with the rest of her great beauty, "You really didn't have to apologize, but I must say it's very nice to talk to you again. By the way, I didn't tell you before, but you're not only a terrific tennis player, but an extremely lovely lady." Maggie flushed and thought to herself, "Oh my God, I've got to get off this phone!" "Well, Mr.-uh- Tony have a good golf game, Goodbye." "How did you know I'm playing golf today?" Tony was surprised. "Oh, you didn't know, my husband is playing with you," she was also surprised. "No, Walter Devon set up the foursome; I don't know who I'm playing with. Does your husband play golf the way you play tennis?" Tony questioned. She laughed, "He plays pretty good, but if you play golf the way you play tennis, you'll beat him. Before I hang up, I must say that was a very good and interesting article in the paper, the writer was right, you are a very exci-uh-remarkable man, and I really must go now." "Thank you, it was very nice talking to you, Goodbye," he said sincerely. She said "Goodbye" and hung up. Tony held the phone for a moment and thought, "She's got to be the most interesting and exciting woman ever!"

A knock at the door brought Tony out of his thoughts. "Come in, it's open," he said. Walter came in grinning and reached out to Tony, "It's great to see you, my friend, Christ you look terrific!" Putting his hands on Walter's shoulders, Tony said "It's really good to see you too Walter, and you're looking fit yourself." "Coffee will be up any second, have a seat, and relax. I've got to put my shoes on", Tony said as he went into the bedroom.

Room service arrived with the coffee, Walter tipped the waiter and he left. When Tony returned, Walter asked, "Have you seen the morning papers?" Tony shook his head. "Tony, you have captured the entire country, this morning's article pushed you right to the top of celebrities. People were already interested in you, but only because of the money and Jonathan's challenge, and now they're interested in you. Do you think you can handle the publicity?" "Walter, at this point, I'm not sure what I can handle. One thing is for sure though; I'm going to allow the publicity to help me get started towards becoming the next multi-billionaire, Tony stated flatly." Stirring his coffee, Walter remarked, "Tony whatever help or assistance I can give, just ask, it's yours." "Thanks Walter. So who are we playing with today?" Tony didn't let on that he knew Peter Weyland was one of them. Walter answered, "One is Bob Polski, a stock broker and investor who plays scratch golf, and the other is a successful lawyer turned real estate magnate, Peter Weyland, and he plays to about a three handicap. How's your game going?" Tony lighting a cigarette, "Well, living in Chicago and its February, my last time out was in October. So you guys have the advantage, but I'll be competitive. I was shooting par last year." Walter laughed, "Shit, you'll be competitive; the last time we played I shot my best round ever, a 71. I'll never forget it, and you shot a 69 to beat me by two strokes." "You ready to chase some birdies?" Tony started towards the door. Walter jumped up, "Let's go, I'm going to beat your young ass today!" As they left Tony remarked, "I hope you brought a lot of money."

Peter Weyland was on the putting green and Bob Polski was just coming on when Walter and Tony arrived. "There's the rest of our foursome, "Walter pointed to the putting green. Tony wondered which one was Peter, "he must be the one wearing the all navy outfit, seems to fit a lawyer." "Peter, Bob, it's my pleasure to introduce you to Tony Cole," Walter handled the introduction well. Bob was the first to extend his hand...Tony was wrong, Peter wasn't wearing the navy, in fact he was wearing a very fashionable golf outfit (one that Tony himself would have picked) "Very nice to meet you Mr. Cole," Bob Polski acknowledged. "My pleasure Bob, and it's Tony" Peter then shook his hand and said, "Tony, nice to meet you." Tony looked at him questioningly, he wondered if this guy knows what he's got at home, "same here Peter."

Once on the first tee, Walter said, "Okay you guys, I wanna take all your money today, and so what are we going to play for?" "Walter says that you're a scratch player Tony, so I think you and I will play pretty close, what do you say we give Walter five strokes and Peter three," Bob asked? "Fine, how much?" "Seeing as though you haven't had much time to spend any of that new money, Tony, why don't we play for a grand a stroke?" Walter laughed. Tony grinned, "Walter, are you sure you've got that kind of money?" They all laughed aloud and then agreed on the wager, $1000.00 stroke.

After nine holes the scores were, Walter 43, Bob 37, Peter 40, and Tony 34 (two under par). "Jesus Christ, Tony, the way you're hitting the ball, you should only be allowed to play every four months. I can't believe you; you always play your best against me. Walter was in disbelief. Tony grinned, "Walter I love ya, but I love your money more." "You had yours the first nine, the next nine is mine, I'm coming after you," Bob patted Tony on the back. Peter shook Tony's hand, "The greatest nine holes I've ever witnessed, Tony!" Tony just said, "Let's go to the back nine, okay guys!"

The back nine was no different than the front; final scores were Walter 86, Peter 79, Bob 74, and Tony a fantastic 69. Tony won $24,000.00. They sat at the patio bar. Peter handed Tony a check for $7,000.00, "Tony, I don't mind paying you this, because it was a joy to watch you shoot the eyes out of this course. You're a helluva player!" Bob was the next to pay up, "I have to agree with Peter, you are a helluva golfer. I'd hate to think what you'd do if you played all the time, great round Tony. I'd like to do it again sometime." He thanked both Bob and Peter. "Well, I'm not going to be as gracious as these two, you bastard; I don't lose $12,000 bucks that happily, but honestly, Tony, terrific round." Walter said admiringly. Tony shoved the checks into his pocket and said, "Well, I guess the least I can do is buy the drinks!" Walter threw his hat at him as they all laughed.

"Listen," Peter motioned, "I've got an idea, why don't we have a party in Tony's honor and introduce him to some of the Palm Springs people?" "Great idea," exclaimed Walter. "What do you say, Tony," Walter was excited? Tony was amused at the way these well-to-do businessmen were now going to attempt to get some of his new wealth. It was a game he and Jonathan used to play, and Tony had become a master, so he would enjoy it. "Hell, you never know, it could turn out to be profitable for me," he thought. "Gentlemen, I've enjoyed your company, and your money, on the golf course; so I'm sure I'll enjoy your company at a party," he said. Peter was the next to speak, "Okay I'll call Maggie right away and have her set something up for tomorrow night. Is that okay?" Everybody agreed, they'd have the party tomorrow night at Peter's.

Tony agreed to the party for another reason, besides playing the game, he could now see Maggie Weyland again. "You know," Peter broke Tony's thoughts, "My wife will be pleased about this, Tony, it will give her the chance to apologize for not recognizing you when you played tennis the other day, and she was truly embarrassed by that." Tony answered, "There was no reason for embarrassment, how was she supposed to know who I was, and why should it matter. She's one helluva tennis player, you know." "One of southern California's best, by God," Walter exclaimed!

Bob stood, "I've got to get back to my office, Tony it was a real pleasure meeting you and playing with you; I'll see you all tomorrow night." Peter was the next to leave, "The same goes for me, Tony, I'll call you later and give you the time. I'll send a driver to pick you up, okay?" "No, I'll bring my secretary, if that's alright, she has a car here." "Fine, but I'll call for the time." Peter shook his hand and waved to Walter as he exited.

"There goes a very bright, sharp, young man," Walter insisted, "He's going to go a long way." "Nice guy, yeh, a nice guy," Tony agreed. "Well, I've got to go myself, I got a God damned directors' meeting this afternoon. I hate the fucking things, but I guess they're a necessary evil. Tony, its great having you here, and I hope you enjoy my twelve thousand bucks. It was fun even though I lost. See ya tomorrow night," Walter squeezed his hand affectionately as he left. "Yes, Walter, tomorrow."

Tony ordered another Jack Daniels as he wondered about Peter Weyland. What is he into? What is his relationship with Walter Devon? What are they looking for? Tony had decided he would not like Peter, but he does like him. Why the hell does he have to be married to Maggie? Rather why does Maggie have to be married to anybody? Shit, I finally meet "the" woman and she's married, so, Tony Cole, forget about anything except friendships! But, shit, she's beautiful, no she's fantastic!

"Mr. Cole," the waiter said, "There is a miss Williams, Theresa Williams, on the phone for you, do you want to take it? She said she's your secretary." "Yes, I'll take it here, please," he ordered another drink. Tony picked up the phone, "This is Tony Cole." "Good afternoon, boss, this is your new secretary following orders," Theresa spoke excitedly. Tony grinned, "Very good, where are you now?" "I'm at my apartment in L.A., waiting for my next order," she quipped. "Go buy a new cocktail dress and then drive down here and have dinner with me, but don't wear the new dress tonight, it's for tomorrow night's party. Oh, did you resign from the times," Tony asked? "Yes, I resigned," Theresa gasped, "Oh, a new dress, a party, dinner, what is…" she stopped. Tony laughed at her excitement, "We have to celebrate our new relationship, and after all, you're the first person I've ever hired. See you later. Theresa, drive carefully." She said, "Of course, and Tony, thank you for everything, I'll be there around seven, okay?" "Yes, just call my room when you arrive, Goodbye," he hung up.

He picked up the phone and dialed Martin Gold in Chicago, "This is Tony Cole, may I speak to Mr. Gold, please," he said to the secretary. In seconds, Martin answered, "Hello, Tony, how's the vacation? Wow, what an article, the whole town is buzzing about "the" Tony Cole. What can I do for you, my boy?" "Martin, I would like a favor. Could your people get some information for me about someone out here," he asked? Martin, always happy to help Tony said, "No problem, just give me the name and I'll get back to you in a couple of days." "No Martin, I need the information by four p.m. tomorrow, can you do it?" Martin puzzled, "Well, that's quick, but yes, we'll get you the information." He wasn't going to question Tony on his intentions, he would just help him in anyway he could. Tony graciously, "Thank you, Martin, his name is Peter Weyland, an L.A. attorney and as of late venturing into real estate. Also, see if there is a connection between him and Walter Devon." "Walter Devon," now Martin was puzzled, he's known Walter for years, "Tony, Walter was one of Jonathan's closest friends, but you already knew that." "Yes, Martin, I know. I just finished playing golf with Walter. I just need to have some information, okay," Tony cut it off. "I'll have the information by four tomorrow," the phone went dead. Tony went back to his room.

The vacation's over, Tony realized it when he okayed the party. Just as well, he thought, I'm ready to start working.

Theresa arrived a little before seven, Tony had told her to come on up. As she walked in, Tony was fixing a drink, "Hello, Theresa, you look lovely, would you like a drink?" "Yes, a screwdriver please," she was still bubbling with excitement. She was dressed in a lavender chiffon dress that clung to her in all the right places. The lavender color accentuated her red hair perfectly. She's really a very pretty girl.

"So, tell me," he handed her the drink, "How did your day go?" She waved her hand in the air, "You wouldn't believe it, my whole boring life turned around overnight." Tony was watching her intently, enjoying her enthusiasm as he lit a cigarette. She went on, "I handed my editor, uh ex-editor, the interview last night and he was shocked, just totally shocked." She laughed, "He read the interview and said it was terrific. He then asked me how I got the interview, but said it didn't matter it was great. He'd get it in the morning paper." She gulped at her drink, then continued, "Now comes the good part," she imitated him, "Now, miss Williams, it seems as though your initiative is beginning to blossom. Let's see, you've been with the Times six or seven months and your salary is $16,000. Well, I think we'll just give you a nice increase, how would another thousand dollars a year sound to you?" Theresa laughed again, "I just looked at him and politely said, I must admit, I was grinning a little, "Mr. Adams, I quit!" He was astonished, all he could say was, "Why, now after this, this major story, why?" I turned to walk out and said, "I'm going to be his secretary and pointed at the article." "That was it. God, it felt good." She now looked serious, "What did you think of the article?" Tony took her glass, "I didn't read it." She looked hurt, "Oh, I thought you would read it, at least to see that I wrote the truth." Tony smiled at her, "Theresa, you told me you'd write it the way I told it, I believed you." He touched his glass to hers and said, "Here's to our new venture, together we'll kill 'em." She looked at him then leaned up and kissed him lightly, "Thank you, Tony; you'll never be disappointed, I swear." He took her by the hand, "Let's eat, I'm starved."

The dining room was half full. The Maitre' Di' rushed to them, "I have the best table for you, Mr. Cole, please, this way." As they moved toward their table, it was obvious that everybody was looking at them. Theresa was feeling uneasy; she forgot that she had a major contribution in the publicity that was beginning to surround Tony and whoever was with him. There was a buzz of conversation in the room. One person said, "So that's what a millionaire looks like." A woman remarked, "Wow, he's really something to look at!" The man with her added, "Maybe, but his lady is quite lovely herself." They had no more than sat down when a pretty teenage girl came up to Tony, "Mr. Cole, could I, please, have your autograph?" He looked at her with a grin that would've melted the hearts of all women. He took the pen and paper from her, "Why, of course, how could I not say yes to such a beautiful young lady; what's your name, honey?" The girl blushed, "Wendy." Tony signed a note and said, "Have a nice dinner, Wendy." "Thank you, Mr. Cole, thank you!" Throughout the dinner, people came up one after another each apologizing for interrupting them. Not once did Tony get upset, he acknowledged each one graciously. Theresa sat in amazement at how he handled every person with such grace. She was sure that anybody else would have become upset. Theresa had never been subjected to this before, and it was very exciting.

Finally, the dinner was over, they left amidst the same looks and buzzing as when they arrived. Tony looked at Theresa, "I'm sorry for the interruptions during our celebration dinner." Once again, she was surprised at him, "I don't believe you…you couldn't even eat for all the interruptions and you apologize to me. You are truly remarkable." He took her hand as they walked on, "I reserved you a room, why don't we get some sleep, because we're going to start working tomorrow." "Tony, you mentioned a party tomorrow night, what is it all about," she asked curiously? He smiled and said, "Young lady, you are going to meet the Palm Springs elite tomorrow night." He went on, "I want you to use your reporter's instincts and pick up remarks made by the elite. You never know, there may be a remark made that we can use later." She squeezed his hand, "Oh, wow, I'm really excited. I can't wait."

He walked her to her door and said, "Theresa, I'm very pleased with the selection I made on my first employee, we're going to work great together." As she opened the door, she looked at him, "Thank you, would you like to, uh, good night. Tony, what time in the morning?" "Whenever you get up, good night Theresa," he said as he walked away.

Theresa's room was fabulous, a suite very similar to Tony's, just slightly smaller. It was equipped with a bar and stocked with everything. She was somewhat fuzzy –headed from all the champagne she had at dinner. She was thinking to herself, "God, I don't believe I almost asked him to come in; but, oh Lord, I wanted him to. I wonder what it's like to sleep with him. He's the best looking man I've ever met. She was panting! Forget it, stupid, he's now your boss, if he'd have wanted you, he would have made the move. She undressed and slid into bed. Her last thought, before falling to sleep, "Shit, am I falling in love with him?"

It was eight o'clock when Theresa stepped from the shower and picked up the phone to call Tony. She thought as the phone rang, "Oh God, I wonder if he's up yet?" "Hello," Tony answered. "Tony, its Theresa, I didn't wake you did I," she questioned. Politely, as usual, Tony answered, "Theresa, my sleeping habits are most different, and you can call me at anytime. I'm up every morning at five-thirty, that's if I've been to bed yet. So don't worry about time with me, time is one thing that annoys me. Come over, whenever you're ready. See you then."

Tony was sitting on the couch with notes spread all over the coffee table. He was dressed in a jogging suit, he hadn't showered as yet, and he was drinking a large glass of orange juice. Tony had been doing a lot of thinking during the past few hours.

Theresa knocked. "Come in, Theresa, its open," Tony commanded. She was all smiles; this was one characteristic that impressed Tony, "Good morning, sleep good?" "Yeh, want some orange juice? How 'bout breakfast?" "I'll just have O.J., thanks, "She said as he handed her a glassful. "Well, Miss Williams," Tony leaned back on the couch, "You're going to start earning your pay today." She grinned, "Whatever you say." Yesterday, you were the secretary to Tony Cole, the man. Today, you're the secretary to Tony Cole, president of Cole Industries." Confused, Theresa questioned, "You never mentioned anything about Cole Industries before." "There wasn't any, until this morning, I've decided how we're going to tackle that damn challenge," he was excited. Theresa, once again, was amazed with him, and excited as well, "Wow, this is exciting, how, tell me how you're going to do it." First, hand me the phone." "You've got to tell me, please," she begged. Dialing the phone, he said, "This call will start the ball rolling." She started to speak when Tony spoke into the phone, "Derek Hill, please, this is Tony Cole calling." Theresa watched as Tony motioned for a cigarette. "Tony, you son-of-a-bitch, are you enjoying your millions?" Derek laughed. Tony laughed, too, "Not yet. Hey, did you know my mother?" Derek roared, "What the hell are you calling me for? I thought you had forgotten your poor friends." Tony hadn't mentioned Derek Hill before, but it didn't take long for Theresa to realize that the two of them were very close friends. She listened to the conversation, glad to see Tony so happy. Then he moved up on the couch and motioned for another cigarette, "Derek, I want you to join my staff, which right now consists of myself and my secretary, Theresa Williams. I want you to be my legal counsel and right hand man. Wadda ya say?" Derek sounded very serious, "Tony, I only have one question, how soon can I start?" With the laughter that erupted from Tony, Theresa knew Derek had accepted. Tony was ecstatic, "Just as soon as you can pack your summer clothes and get a plane to Palm Springs. I'll reserve a room for you here at the Matador. Just come up when you get here, I'll be in my room all day. Oh, fly first class, you might as well get used to it." "I'll be there, as soon as the friendly skies of United can get me there. Love ya, buddy."

As soon as Tony hung up the phone, he sighed and grinned from ear to ear, "Theresa, you'll love this guy. I sure as hell do!" Theresa was surprised at his statement. She was sure that he hadn't had much love by anybody during his life.

He stood up, clapped his hands, and said, "We're now going to get started. Call the desk and reserve a suite for Derek, while I jump in the shower." He pulled Theresa to him and kissed her, "Your beautiful lady," he said imitating Humphrey Bogart. She could feel her knees weaken; he had kissed her hard but gentle. She was so excited! "He's fantastic," she thought. She reached for the phone, and then looked towards the sound of the shower. She began to wonder, "What would he say if I stripped and got in the shower with him?" Her mind began to race and she said aloud, "Oh Christ, I'm dripping wet; I want him, I want him to take me. Her knees got weaker. She had an orgasm at the thought of Tony making love to her. Quickly, she began thinking of something else, "Uh, uh, call the desk, uh fix another orange juice; God damnit, do something!" She picked up the phone and made the reservation for Derek.

"Any phone calls," he asked as he came from the bedroom. He was dressed in khaki slacks and a navy pullover shirt. Theresa stared at him for a moment then said to herself, "Yep, I'm in love with him, shit!" "Uh, no, no calls, were you expecting one?" "Not really," he said.

They talked about the ideas for the newly conceived "Cole Industries" most of the day. Tony told her about Chicago and she told him all about Los Angeles. It was three-thirty when the phone rang, "I'll get it," he said as he picked up the phone. "Hello." "Yes Martin, boy you are quick," he lit a cigarette, "Shoot." Martin began, "Tony, you're talking to a real sharp one in this Peter Weyland. He's from San Francisco, family has money; graduated from UCLA; married a socialite from Cleveland, one Margaret Murphy, during their senior year in college. After law school, he joined the Parrot, Bailey, and Davis Law Firm in Los Angeles; immediate success. Began investing in real estate and within three years had accumulated enough money to give up his law practice, move to Palm Springs, and continue in real estate. Are you still with me, Tony?" "Yes, go on." "Peter then formed a company in Los Angeles. He would find a parcel of land, buy it cheap, and then find investors to build shopping centers, apartments, condominiums, or whatever on the land his company purchased. He would not put up any money of his own but was gladly taken in as a full partner for his services. The investors would gladly pay the price that was asked for the property, due to the profits that were possible. In most cases the investors would pay at least ten times more than Weyland had originally paid for the same land. So, he would make a bundle on the land and also be a partner in the new development. Tony cut in, "What about the new developments, have they made money?" Martin laughed, "That's the ironic part, and so far every one has been extremely profitable for all parties concerned. But, he has made some investments on his own, as of late, that has put him behind the eight ball. He can't make the payments on his purchases and he's overextended at Walter Devon's bank. It's rumored that the bank is ready to foreclose on him and he'll lose his shirt. So, there you go my boy, that's all I got for you." "Martin, I owe you a favor, thank you." "Be careful if you're talking to Mr. Weyland about investing, Goodbye Tony," Martin hung up.

Tony turned to Theresa, "I could use a drink, how 'bout you?" "In the middle of the afternoon?" she said, "No thank you." He stepped to the bar, "Well, I'll have one for both of us." Theresa walked behind the bar and put her chin in her hands, "You said you'd tell me about Derek before he got here, what about now?" "Okay" a knock on the door interrupted him. Theresa opened the door and there stood an awesomely handsome blonde man. "You must be Theresa, only a multi-millionaire has a secretary as lovely as you; hi, I'm Derek Hill." Theresa flushed, she liked him immediately and before she could speak Tony yelled, "Get in here and quit trying to hustle my gorgeous secretary, there's a drink waiting for you!" Derek and Tony hugged then toasted each other and in unison said, "Here's to the poor and lonely." They downed their drinks in one swallow and laughed heartily. Their closeness gave Theresa a warm feeling. Derek walked over to Theresa and put his arm around her, "Don't tell me, but Theresa is really going to be "my" secretary right? God damn, you're a helluva guy!" Tony laughed, "Bullshit, there is no way I'm giving up someone who's going to be the greatest secretary of all time. Let's have another drink." All this attention and flattery was just about more than she could handle, "Do you two always carry on like this?" Derek picked up his drink, "Young lady, you're in for the best times of your life, because your new boss is the best son-of-a-bitch in the entire world!" Before she could stop herself she said, "Yes, I know." Tony pointed toward the couch and acted as though he didn't hear her, but Derek noticed her emotions immediately, "Let me tell you about what we're going to do." As he sat down, "Theresa, would you call and order us a limousine for tonight."

Before she got to the phone, it rang. Theresa answered, "Hello, this is Mr. Cole's suite; I'm his secretary, Theresa. May I help you?" She looked at Derek and Tony and they all grinned. "This is Peter Weyland, may I please speak to Mr. Cole," he said in a very business like tone. "One moment please," Theresa handed the phone to Tony and said, "Peter Weyland for you, Mr. Cole." "Hello Peter, how are you?" Peter eagerly awaiting his chance to talk to Tony was anxious with his answer, "Just fine Tony, I hope you're still intending to attend our little party tonight. My wife, Maggie, is anxious to meet you again. I think she wants to apologize for your last meeting." Tony could see her in his thoughts, long black hair, beautifully tanned body, smiling face, "Of course. Oh Peter, would it be an intrusion if I brought along a friend and associate of mine?" Peter surely wanted to meet any of Tony's friends, "Why, we'd love for him to come, please bring him along. How does eight o'clock sound?" "Eight, we'll be there, thank you Peter, Goodbye," Tony hung up the phone.

Tony turned to Derek, "We're attending a party, this evening, that is to introduce me to the financial elite, and God knows who else, but I'm sure that I'm also going to be offered a business deal." "Good, we might as well get going," Derek insisted. "I want you and Theresa to be all eyes and ears, we may meet some people that will be able to help us later," Tony said as he went to the bar.

The phone rings again. Theresa answered in the same way. The party on the other end was quick talking with a deep southern accent, "Well, hello there missy, how 'bout putting your boss on the line. You can tell him it's that little 'ole oil man from Houston, Claude Benaforte." Theresa relayed the line to Tony. Tony looked at Derek, "Do you think it's a good time to enter the oil business?" Derek, "Hell, it's always a good time to get in the oil business." Tony took the phone, "Claude Benaforte, my good friend, how did you track me down?" Laughing, Claude replied, "Tony, you aren't hard to find these days. You're quite the celebrity now." He changed to a combination business joke-telling voice, which was a characteristic of him when he really wanted something, "Tony, when could you and I sit down to talk bidness, oil bidness?" Unimpressed, Tony spoke softly, "What makes you think I want to talk oil business?" "Because that's where the millions are and I'm the man who knows oil, my boy," Claude responded. "I'll tell you, Claude, my vacation is about over, and it's been a while since I've been to Texas. What would you say if my associate and I were to come down this weekend," Tony answered? "Great, super, terrific," Claude was excited, "I'll have a plane there to bring you down tomorrow, okay?" "That would be fine, Claude, we'll see you tomorrow, Goodbye," Tony grinned as he hung up. "Derek, Theresa, we're definitely on a working schedule now," he said as he poured more drinks. Theresa grabbed the phone, "Let me call for the limousine before someone else calls."

"Have you ever been to Houston, Derek," Tony asked. "Nope, never had the pleasure." Tony handed him another drink, "Well, you're going tomorrow. Claude Benaforte is going to attempt to hustle me into investing in Five Star Oil. He's been in trouble for some time now." "If you're truly going to be the next multi-billionaire, you might as well start with oil," Derek seemed sure of the statement. Tony sat down, "We'll see, we'll see tomorrow. Let me tell you about Peter Weyland." Tony and Derek spent the rest of the afternoon talking about possibilities for investments, and occasionally re-living some old times. Theresa went back to her suite to get ready for the Weyland's party.

Tony picked up the ringing phone, "Hello, this is Tony Cole." "Victor Turner, Mr. Cole, your limousine is ready." "Thank you, Victor." "Let's go, the car is ready. We'll stop by Theresa's room," he said finishing his drink. The door opened and Theresa came in looking like a model instead of a secretary. She was wearing a bright green cocktail dress with matching shoes and bag. She seemed to get prettier every time Tony saw her. "God damn, Theresa," Derek exclaimed as he looked at her, "You look absolutely gorgeous!" Tony just looked and thought, "I must be nuts, I should be dating this girl instead of paying her salary, "Derek is right, absolutely gorgeous!" "Come on, you two," she blushed, "You're just trying to make me feel good." Derek walked towards her, "Theresa, my love, when I tell a lady she looks good, it's strictly a compliment, but when I make a woman feel good, I take her in my arms and cover her with passion." Tony slapped Derek's back, "The bullshit in here is getting deep, let's go to the party."

The limousine pulled up to the Weyland residence, a large sprawling ranch, typical Palm Springs style, pool, tennis courts, the works. Tony, Derek, and Theresa were helped from the car by one of the servants. Peter Weyland was at the door to greet them, "Tony, punctual also. Good to see you." Tony replied, "Same here, Peter Weyland this is Theresa Williams and Derek Hill." Theresa was glad he didn't introduce her as his secretary. Peter shook Derek's hand firmly and took Theresa's hand in both of his, "My, but your lovely, I'm so glad you could come." As they walked toward the patio, where the party was being held, Derek whispered to Tony, "Well, he knows good female stock when he sees it. Did you see the way his eyes lit up when he looked at Theresa?" Tony nodded.

He saw her the minute they entered the patio. Obviously, the most beautiful woman there, and there were some real beauties. She had cut her hair to shoulder length, it's even nicer he thought, the black satin gown was perfect, it exemplified her nearly perfect figure, the small straps allowed her radiant tan to be seen. The black onyx necklace with matching earrings was just the right touch. Tony couldn't take his eyes away from her. She was, he now decided, the most beautiful woman he'd ever seen. Maggie was talking to two women when she looked at him, she could see that he was staring at her. Tony could hear Peter talking, but paid no attention to his words. He was watching Maggie walk towards him. She glided, she didn't walk. As she approached them, Tony's mind went crazy, "Take her hand, lead her out of there, get in a car, drive to the pier, get a boat, sail away, make love to her forever!"

"Tony, Tony," Peter finally got through to him. "Yes." "I would like to formally introduce you to my wife Maggie." They put their hands together, looked at each other for what seemed to be an eternity when Maggie finally spoke, "It is my pleasure, Tony, to finally meet you and know exactly who you are." Tony held onto her hand, "The pleasure is all mine, Mrs. Weyland, or would you prefer I call you Maggie," he said nervously. She was trying to control the feelings she was having, "What is it about this, this simply gorgeous man?" "I'm just plain Maggie to everybody, especially you," she uttered. "Margaret Murphy," Tony remembered, "Doesn't fit, but Maggie is perfect." Peter interrupted, "I would also like to present Theresa Williams and Derek Hill, Maggie." She hadn't even noticed them, embarrassed, she turned to them and put out her hand to Theresa first, then to Derek, "I'm so pleased to meet you, what are you drinking?"

Walter Devon bellowed from across the patio, "Tony, Tony Cole, come over here." There were about twenty people there and they all seemed to stop and turn to look at the "new money" they've all been reading about. Peter, aware of the awkward moment stepped in front of Tony, "ladies and gentlemen, I would like to present Mr. Tony Cole and friends Miss Theresa Williams and Mr. Derek Hill." The guests held up a toast in unison as Walter came forward, "They've already been told about your winning ways on the golf course, so don't be modest when asked." Maggie asked, "What would you like to drink?" Theresa requested a screwdriver and Derek preferred an old-fashioned, and Tony (as Walter was pulling him away) asked for a Jack Daniels on the rocks.

The guests were now busying themselves in normal conversation. A local restauranteur was frothing at the mouth while talking to Theresa. Two aristocratic snobby women had Derek cornered, and Tony was surrounded by a handful of inquisitive gentlemen. Maggie was attempting to talk with Eleanor Devon, but her mind was filled with her own questions about Tony Cole.

They had been at the party for about an hour, when Walter pulled Tony aside, "Do you think Peter and I could have a moment alone with you?" Tony thought to himself, "Sooner than if thought, they must need me pretty bad." "Yes, let me get another drink first, and I want Derek along, you don't mind do you?" Walter questioned <u>why Derek</u> to himself, but not to Tony, "Of course, bring him in. Peter, why don't you grab a bottle of J.D. and bring it in, while Tony gets Derek." Peter agreed, "Sure, but I'll get Derek too and meet you in the study." Walter, trying to apologize, but doing poorly, "Listen Tony, I'm sorry about dragging you away like this but," Tony put his arm around Walter "You need not apologize, I don't mind."

Peter and Derek came in a second after Walter and Tony. Peter closed the door behind them, "Can I freshen drinks?" Everybody was full. Walter was the first to speak, "Derek, I've never met you before, what is your connection with Tony?" Derek looked at Tony, then at Walter, "Friends, long time friends." Tony added, "Derek is my legal counsel, and he'll be my number one man in my affairs, whatever they may be." Walter responded,

"Well, congratulations, I'm sure you'll be a terrific team." Derek didn't like Walter, but he did like Peter. Tony had known Walter for many years, and he wasn't acting himself. "Why?" He wondered. Peter was still silent. Walter held out his glass for Peter to re-fill, "Tony, I'll get right to the point. Peter and I have a business deal to offer you." Tony sat unmoving, watching Walter and Peter intently. Walter continued, "You see, there is this piece of land out by Brea, that we, uh, Peter owns and it is ready made for a big shopping plaza. The area is growing in leaps and bounds and the residents need and want a shopping area like this. I know, you're not sure what you want to do but this could be a winner for you." He waited for Tony's response. Tony walked to Peter, "Could I have a refill please?" He sat down, no response. "Well, what do you think?" Walter insisting Tony answer. Tony took a long drink, looked at Derek, then at Peter, "Walter, if Peter owns the land, what do you have to with this?" "Well, I'm your friend, and I thought if I were able to talk to you, you'd be more acceptable to the situation, that's all," Walter stumbled through his answer. Tony didn't speak; he looked at Peter expecting something from him. Peter looked around, then picked up the bottle, walked over to Tony and poured him another drink, "Tony." Walter stopped him, "Listen Tony, this is a simple business deal that's all." "No, no it isn't," Peter interrupted, "Tony, let me tell you the situation." Walter sat down heavily as Peter continued, "You see, Tony, I've borrowed a lot of money from Walter's bank, well over my personal assets and I'm having trouble turning things over and Walter is in hot water from the board of directors to foreclose on my debts. Walter realizes the potential of the shopping center and wants me to be able to continue its development, but I've run out of resources. That's it, bluntly, that's it." He poured himself another drink.

Tony looked at Peter, "exactly what do you want from me? Do you want me to lend you the money to pay your debts or do you want me to invest in the shopping center?" "If you were to invest in the shopping center, I'd be able to pay the bank, which in turn would then advance me the money to begin construction on the center," Peter was answering honestly. Tony, talking in a calm soft voice, "how much do you owe the bank?" "Twelve million," Peter answered. "How much is your holdings worth, not your personals, just your holdings?" Peter squirmed, "Including the land that the center will sit on, around fourteen million." Tony looked confused, "I don't understand, if you have a liability to the bank for twelve million and the center property is close to that, why don't you sell that property and come out clean?" Peter answered, "Tony, if I sell that property and pay off the bank, I won't have anything left and besides, this center is my chance for the really big dollars. This is a real money making venture. I've dreamed how it's going to be. It will be like no other shopping center in the country." Peter dropped his head, "But it will never happen if I have to sell it. I guess, what I'm trying to say, is that it feels like a part of me!" Derek had said nothing, he just listened. He walked over to Peter, picked up the whiskey and said, "May I Peter?" "Please, please help yourself," Peter insisted. Tony rose, held out his glass to Derek, "How much are you asking me to advance?" Walter jumped up, "The bank would advance a new loan to begin construction on the center if Peter can pay two-thirds of the twelve million he owes and if you are the investor, they'll put an unlimited open account for the center." Tony quizzically looked at Walter. Why was he now so interested in the center? "Do you have a map of the area, and of the land itself where the proposed center will be?" Tony asked Peter. "Why yes, of course, right here," he pulled a tube from behind his desk and handed it to Tony. Tony handed the tube to Derek, "We'll look at it in the morning, and we'll give you a call tomorrow. Now, I think I'd like to enjoy your party Peter." Tony and Derek headed towards the door, "Give that to our driver, and come back in, okay," Tony directed Derek. "Sure enough, meet you at the party." Tony exited without looking back at Walter or Peter.

The party had continued without them and Theresa was having the time of her life. Tony caught her eye, held up his glass and smiled. She returned the gesture. He noticed Maggie; talking to the woman he saw at the Matador tennis courts. He went directly to her, speaking to the other guests as he made his way to where she was standing. He approached her just as her friend saw him, "If you turn around, you'll see your guest of honor. God is he good looking," Angela exclaimed! She turned and he was directly behind her. "Hello again, I'm sorry I was rude and left your party. I hope you'll accept my apology?" Shocked, Maggie said, "Why, of course, I accept, but there is no reason to apologize." "My, my, not only are you beautiful but courteous too," Angela remarked. He looked blushed. "Do you think I could talk to you for a moment?" He requested. "I know when to leave," Angela smiled as she walked away.

They strolled around the pool, Maggie first to speak, "Are you going to do business with Peter?" "I don't know, should I?" "That's entirely up to you, but I can I tell you one thing, Peter knows his business. He's made some mistakes, but he says the economy has a lot to do with it," she was sincere in her feelings about Peter's business judgment. "He's made a lot of money, not only for himself, but for a lot of other people, too," she continued. Tony asked, "Is Walter Devon one of the people who Peter helped make money?" Maggie didn't hesitate, "Walter Devon has made more money off of Peter's recommendations than Peter." Tony changed the subject, "I'm not one for telling what I'm thinking, but Maggie, I must tell you that I'm thoroughly intrigued by you. I think you're the most beautiful woman I've ever met." She was shocked, embarrassed. Flattered, and excited by his sudden change of conversation and unexpected statement. She stopped, turned to him, "I don't know what to say after that, except that I'm totally surprised and flattered." He looked her directly in the eye, "I don't expect you to say anything. I really don't know why I said it. I just had to say it to somebody, and so I said it to you. I won't ever mention anything about it again." Before she could respond, a very, very beautiful woman walked up to them, "Maggie, Maggie dear, I want to meet your guest of honor and you're keeping him from me," she said. "I'm sorry Roni, I wasn't aware that you had arrived. Roni Scott, movie star, may I introduce Tony Cole, millionaire and gentleman," Maggie looked affectionately at Tony.

Roni Scott was probably the most famous woman in the world, and probably, in most peoples eyes, the most beautiful. She's also considered an excellent actress. Her hair was a glistening auburn brown, shoulder length. She stood five feet, seven inches and 115 pounds. Her measurements were as well known as her name, and they are near perfect at 37-23-36. As Tony looked at her, he was amazed at her awesome radiance, "I'm certainly not disappointed in the "real" Roni Scott. You're very lovely." "Well, Mr. Cole, I'm not disappointed either, you're also lovely," she laughed. Maggie and Tony also laughed and Maggie said, "Well, I've got to see some of the other guests, will you please excuse me?" Tony now realized just what an impact Maggie has on him. He's left alone with the public's consensus of the most beautiful woman and he would rather be with Maggie.

Roni spoke in very soft voice, "You know it isn't often that I meet somebody who gets more press than I do, but I'm not jealous." Tony looked at her with his familiar charismatic grin, "I'm a novelty for the moment, but you are a living legend. My popularity will diminish very quickly, but yours will continue forever." He had done with that one statement, and grin, what very few people had ever been able to do in any way – he impressed

Roni Scott! "Whew, boy, do you know the right things to say. You know, I've just met you, but I'll bet, right now, that you win the challenge," she conceded. Tony took her by the hand, "Let's see if we can get a drink over there." He pointed toward the crowd. She took her hand from his, and slid her arm under his arm.

As they approached the rest of the guest, they were noticed by Walter... he was beginning to show the signs of too much whiskey..."Well, well, if that doesn't make a lovely picture; America's dream couple...the beautiful movie queen and the handsome millionaire." A few of the guests clapped their hands in agreement. Theresa looked at them, "Why couldn't I be the one with him." Maggie was standing with Peter and Angela. She thought to herself as she watched them, "I wonder if he's as sincere and honest as he lets on. He's not Roni's type. Whose type is he? Mine!! What did you say, Maggie Weyland? Are you out of your mind?"

Roni and Tony spent the rest of the evening together. Talking about films, actors, actresses, business, money, trips, and assorted other items including Roni's past marriage. They also drank heavily and were laughing a lot. On numerous occasions, Maggie would stop by and join in the conversation. The last time, while Tony was standing between them, he put an arm around each other and said, "This must be my lucky day, here I am standing between the two most beautiful women in the entire world!" Roni kissed him on the cheek and softly said thank you; Maggie just said "Thank you, Tony," and slipped away. He watched her go, and hoped that he hadn't offended her. He hadn't. Maggie was afraid...of herself.

The party was breaking up; everybody was shaking hands with Tony – wishing him well; thanking Peter and Maggie for a lovely party. "How would you like a ride in the desert to unfog our brains?" Roni quietly asked him. "Terrific idea," he agreed. Tony walked to Derek, who was standing with Theresa and Peter, "I'd like to talk for a minute"...they moved away from the others..."I'm going for a ride in the desert with Roni, you and Theresa can take the car back to the hotel. I want to get a helicopter, first thing in the morning and go see that property that Peter's talking about. I'll call you in the morning." "Right, good buddy, good luck. If you need any pointers...you know who to call," Derek laughed.

Roni and Tony said their Goodbyes to Maggie and Peter quickly but not before Tony could say to Maggie, "Thank you so much for a lovely party, and Peter, you have terrific taste in women. I'll give you a call tomorrow. Goodbye."

They were driving along a desert road silently. Tony with his head laid back and watching Roni, who was driving her Ferrari carefully. "You surprised me," he said. "I figured you for the hell-driver type." She looked at him grinning, "I'm very careful with everything I do and who I do it with. You see I'm not like most film people; they're mostly unhappy…I'm not. I love my life and I don't want to change it. So that's why I'm careful." "Well, I'm glad somebody else is happy, besides me. But I'd be a lot happier if I had one more Jack Daniels," Tony remarked. "I know just the place, but wouldn't you rather have coffee instead," she turned down another road. He laughed, "Hell, I guess I have had enough of ol' black Jack for tonight; where are you taking me?" She pulled in front of a well-lit ranch house, "A very cozy place; my house!"

Tony remarked at her taste incorporated into the house as they entered. "This house is my pride and joy. It's the only thing that is totally mine. I had it built out here for the solitude. I'm not a loner by any means, but especially after I finish shooting a movie, I really like to spend some time out here alone; how do you like your coffee?" "Black; are you making a movie now?" he said.

Pouring the coffee, she said "No, but I have to leave next week…we're starting a new film on location in Brazil." He picked up his coffee, "When, next week?" "Monday," she stared into his eyes, "Would you kiss me?" Slightly surprised, Tony put his hands on her shoulders and said, "I'd love to!"

She slid her arms around his neck, opened her mouth to accept his kiss. He pulled her tight against him. Their breathing was heavy. Her hands were running through his hair, she could feel his hardness against her. He pulled away, and kissed her face softly, then her neck. She nipped at his neck, then his chest – they were now panting. She put her hands on his face and whispered, "Oh Tony, let's make love!" Kissing her face, very softly he said, "I've already began making love to you." He kissed her hard on the mouth. Roni pulled away, "Come with me, I can't stand this." As they entered the bedroom, Roni slipped out of her dress – her breasts were visible as she turned to him and slipped from her panty hose. Tony began to unbutton his shirt; she stopped him, "Wait, I'll do it!" She stood in front of him, clad only in her panties; she unbuttoned his shirt kissing his chest after each button. She slowly pulled down his trousers and he put his hands under her arms and lifted her up and kissed her, "Oh Tony, Tony!" They fell onto the bed – groping for each other. Roni softly caressed his phallus while he was caressing her taught nipples with a loving mouth. Their bodies shifted in rhythm, her legs coming up and opening for him, "You're beautiful Roni," he murmured as he entered her and she squealed "Oh, Tony, oh God, you're terrific, your fantastic, oh, oh, oh, ……….."

Tony was smoking a cigarette on the bed when she came out of the bathroom, "Where do we go from here, Tony?" She asked as she sat down next to him. "You go to Brazil, and I go to Houston," he grinned, then pulled her to him and kissed her softly. They melted into one body, once again.

CHAPTER FIVE

It was seven-thirty when Tony picked up the ringing phone, "Hello." "Tony, Derek here, are you able to take a ride in a helicopter?" Derek laughed. "When is it going to be ready," he answered with a gravely voice. "Eight o'clock, I'll come over." Derek hung up, Tony made is way to unlock the door for Derek; then stumbled to the shower.

The helicopter swirled around, then back again, then returned. They flew over the land many times, Tony making notes. They flew over the general area, Tony continued to make notes. "We've seen enough, let's go," he told the pilot.

Tony picked up the phone, "Room service, send up a pot of coffee and a lot of orange juice." "Theresa, I want you to find out who owns the land surrounding the area where the center is to be," he commanded. "What do you think," Derek asked? I think Peter's right. I think he has a great idea. Did you see the new highway that's coming through the area? Did you notice all of the new construction? New housing? But most of all, the location; the easy access to the center acreage?" Tony was excited. "Yeah, I saw it all. I agree with you. But why do you want to know who owns that surrounding land?" Derek asked. "I have a feeling, there is more to this deal that we're seeing," Tony answered. "I've got it. You'll never guess who owns that land," an excited Theresa exclaimed! "Walter Devon," Tony said. Derek sat in disbelief, "Jesus Christ, <u>how did you know</u>? Tony pulled out the maps of the area. "Here is the new commercial construction, here is the new home sites…Tony was pointing to each site…here is a railway, here, right here is nothing, absolutely nothing; but it's directly behind the center land, it's bordered by the railway on one side, it's bordered by the new highway on the other. That land, is approximately 800 acres. After the highway is finished, and the proposed center is completed, that land will be worth at least ten times what it is today. When we were talking to Peter and Walter last night, I realized that Walter wanted that center built for some other reason than Peter Weyland's welfare. Also, Walter Devon doesn't catch "heat" about loans to depositors. I knew Walter had an ulterior motive." Derek stood up, threw his hands in the air, "You are a fucking…excuse me, Theresa…a fucking genius. I sat there, listed to them talk, and flew over the same area as you and God damn. I didn't pick up any if that!" "I told you, you're remarkable," Theresa gave her input. Derek turned to Tony, "so what are you going to do, invest in Peter Weyland's shopping center and make Walter Devon even richer?" Tony smiled, "Theresa would you please call Peter and Walter and ask them to come over here – right away?" Tony ordered rather than asked.

"Hello Mr. Devon, Mr. Weyland; would you please come in," Theresa ushered them into the suite. Mr. Cole will be in, in just a moment. Would you like a drink? Coffee, or orange juice?" Both answered, "Coffee, thank you."

Tony and Derek emerged from the bedroom, "Hello, Walter, Peter. I truly enjoyed your party. I'll have to return the courtesy some day. Walter was quiet…hung over really. Peter nervously noted, "I'm glad you enjoyed yourself. Tony, I presume you've taken time to discuss our proposition, with Derek, Do you agree that it could be a good investment?" The phone rang. Theresa interrupted, "Mr. Cole, the Five Star plane has arrived and would like to know when you'll be ready to leave for Houston." Tony looked at his watch…it was eleven o'clock. "Tell him we'll be there at one o'clock." Peter and Walter looked at one another but Walter was the curious one, "Have something going with Five Star Oil, Tony?" He looked at Walter, "Possibly."

Tony stood up, walked to the middle of the room, lit a cigarette, and then looked directly at Peter. "Yes, I agree with your evaluation of what that property could generate is accurate. As you heard, I don't have a lot of time today, so I'll be short with <u>my</u> proposition." Derek watched intently; he still doesn't know what Tony is going to propose. Tony went on, "Peter, I would like to not only invest in your shopping plaza, I'd like to buy the land outright. If you'll sell the land to me, I'll also take over the other holdings which you're having trouble paying for." He watched for a reaction. Peter took a long drink of his coffee. Walter grinned at Tony in agreement. Derek sat stunned. Tony began again, "That is one of three stipulations I require. Another is that Walter sells me the adjoining land to the proposed center site." He grinned as Walter choked on his coffee, "Walter, you'll be paid a good price for the land, you'll have the bank's money returned, and I'll deposit ten million dollars in your bank. Before either of you say anything, let me finish. The third and final stipulation is that you, Peter, come to work for me in the capacity of Vice President of Real Estate and Land Development. That's it gentlemen; I'd like a decision now. That is the way I intend to do business."

Peter looked at Walter who was wiping his forehead. Walter stood up, walked to Tony, grabbed his hand, and began to shake it, "Jonathan would be God damned proud of you, Tony. You're one smart bastard. I'm all for your deal." They both looked at Peter. He was very nervous, "I really don't know what to say." Tony lit another cigarette, "Peter, I'll answer some of the questions you have. You'll be working for Cole Industries, which as I said you'll be a Vice President; your salary will be $100,000 per year. Another company will be formed and you'll also carry the title of President for that company. You'll be in total charge of all real estate and land development within Cole Industries. I will want you to move to Chicago, which is where Cole Industries will be headquartered. Peter, you will be in control of the shopping plaza. "Hell, I've never even been to Chicago, but I'm sure I'll learn to like it," Peter shook Tony's hand, "You've got a deal."

Tony turned to Theresa, "Would you pour us a drink, so we can seal our deal with a salute?" Derek stared at Tony. He was amazed; Tony had just pulled off one helluva deal. They held up their glasses and Tony said, "To a good deal for everybody. Derek will work with your lawyers to draw up the appropriate papers."

After Peter and Walter left, Tony, Derek, and Theresa sat with a drink to celebrate Cole Industries first acquisition. Derek looked at Tony, "I am really amazed at how you handled them. Walter's right; you are one smart bastard. I'm proud to be a part of your team." "That goes double for me," Theresa gestured. Derek, once again "What do we do now?" Tony was quick to answer, "With this acquisition, and with what could happen tomorrow with Claude Benaforte, Cole Industries is definitely starting to take shape. So we've got to move fast. Here's what we'll do. First, I'll go to Houston now; Derek, you get in touch with Peter and Walter's lawyers right away, then go to L.A. or wherever you have to go and buy us an airplane – a Lear jet that seats at least eight. Then you get a flight and meet me in Houston. Theresa, you get your affairs arranged here over the weekend. I'll be in Chicago by Monday. You meet me at the mansion. We have to get a headquarters together. I guess we'll use the Stuyvesant Building, since it's going to be vacant now. We'll find you a place to stay; hell, you can stay at the mansion until we have to move. Let's go! Damn, I'm excited."

Tony dialed Roni's number, when she answered, he said, "Are you going to sleep the day away?" Roni grinned with the joy of hearing his voice, "Hello, you wonderful beautiful hunk of masculinity!" He laughed, "You flatter me but I must admit I enjoy it. I wanted to say Goodbye. I'm leaving for Houston soon." She sat up in the bed, "Can you come back to California before I leave?" "No, I have to go directly to Chicago from Houston," he said. "Hey, why don't I fly to Houston; we could spend some more time together before I leave Monday," she asked excitedly. "I wish you could, but I'm going to be tied-up in business the entire time. Good luck in your new movie. Uh, Roni, I really enjoyed the time we spent together. You're more of a woman than your fans will ever know." She began to cry, "God damn you! You walk into my life, lay all that damn charm on me, and then sleep with me. No, I'm wrong, you didn't sleep with me, all you did was fuck me. Now, you are going to just walk out. I'll be damned if you will. I'm going to Houston, if the only time we can see each other is to sleep, then by God, that's all we'll do, but we'll do it together at least one more time!" She was crying harder but continued, "You just aren't going to get away from me that easily. Now, tell me where you're staying." Tony stood in disbelief; he had no idea their one-night affair meant so much to her. He stuttered, "I, uh, I'm staying with a business associate, Claude Benaforte, but I'll get a reservation at the Galaxy. In fact, I'll get you a room there also. We'll have dinner with Claude tonight." "Oh, Tony, I'll take the next flight," she had stopped crying. "You know, you're really easy. You bit right on my crying act, or maybe I really am a good actress." Tony laughed aloud, "You're quite something. I'll look forward to seeing you, so will Claude. See you tonight.

As he hung up the phone he thought to himself, "I don't understand. Last night I made love to the most beautiful woman in the world. I'll probably make love to her tonight; she seems to enjoy my company, as I do hers. So, why do I think about Maggie Weyland all the time? Even when I was in bed with Roni? What has that woman got? What has she done to me? Is she the reason I hired Peter? Maybe Roni will get her out of my mind!"

Peter approached the pool where Maggie was finishing her daily 25 laps, "Maggie, Maggie, could you come out for a minute, I've got to talk to you?" Without missing a stroke, Maggie yelled, "One more lap." Peter fixed himself a drink while he waited for her. She stepped from the pool; her beautifully tanned body glistened as the beads of water sparkled like diamonds from the sun. She pushed the towel away and sat down on a chaise lounge facing the sun. Peter looked down at her, "Would you like a drink?" "No thanks. What do you want to talk about?" He pulled a chair next to her, "I've made a deal with Tony Cole, an excellent deal." Maggie looked at him, "If it's such a great deal, why do you look so down?" Peter freshens his drink. Maggie sat up, "Peter, what's bothering you?" Taking a large pull from his drink he uttered, "I sold everything, I sold him everything." "Darling, what are you talking about? You sold everything?" She was confused. "Maggie, Tony Cole Is a very smart individual. He knew that Walter owned the adjoining land to the center. Boy, he's sharp. I've never met anybody as sharp as him. That's why I'm anxious to work for him," Peter spoke enthusiastically now. She jumped up from the chaise, "What do you mean…work for him? Damn it Peter, explain what's happening!" "Well, first of all, I sold Tony the shopping plaza land," he spoke nervously, "He also took over all of my debts to the bank. The amazing part of this whole thing is that he wouldn't do anything unless Walter sold him the adjoining land, and to make sure Walter would sell, he said he would deposit ten million dollars in Walters bank. The final surprise came, when he said, that to culminate the deal, I would come to work for him as a Vice President of his new company, Cole Industries." Maggie lit a cigarette, "Peter, what does all of this mean? Do you want to work for him, or anybody else for that matter? Do you have any of your investments left?" He shook his head, "No, he now owns all of the holdings I had. Yes, I do want to work for him, because I believe he will be the next multi-billionaire. But, uh, Maggie, we're going to move to Chicago." "What!" She gasped, "Don't you think I should have been consulted about moving? What makes you think I want to move there?" He sighed, "Yes, you should have been consulted, but I didn't have time, he wanted an answer immediately. You've mentioned numerous times that you wouldn't mind living back east so that you could see the change of seasons." "I know, but I would have liked to have had some input in the decision." He took her hand, "Listen, we'll be able to spend a lot of time out here; Tony said I'll be handling the shopping plaza construction." She snubbed out her cigarette, "Peter, honestly, I think I'll enjoy living in Chicago. I just want you to be happy. When do we have to go?" "I don't know. Tony's going to call me Monday. Everything will work out fine," he kissed her lightly; "I love you! I've got to go; I have to see my lawyer." Maggie watched him as he left. She began to think, "A few days ago, he was just someone to play tennis with. Yesterday he was the guest of honor at our party. Today, he commands our lives. But worst of all, he commands my thoughts. What is it about this man? He's the only man that has made me even think about being unfaithful to Peter. I thought last night would be the end of it, I'd never see him again. Oh God, now I'll be exposed to him constantly."

CHAPTER SIX

The sound of the wheels dropping made Tony wince. He looked down on the sprawling Five Star ranch which Claude Benaforte owns. He let out a sigh of relief when the jet's wheels squealed on touchdown.

Claude was standing beside the pearl colored Rolls Royce when Tony stepped from the plane. "Tony, nice ta see ya son, nice ta see ya. Did ya enjoy my little jet?" Claude was his usually jovial self. Tony answered his questions as they entered the rolls. "We're gonna have us a whoppin' big Texas-style party tonight, Tony. I wanna introduce you to some big dollars that could help you in the future. O' course they're all gonna want you to invest some of your money in them," Claude was babbling. Tony interrupted, "Claude that bar right there wouldn't have any Jack Daniels in it by any chance?" Claude reached for the bar laughing, "Boy, boy, forgive my lack of hospitality. How would you like it?" "Neat," he replied.

The rolls pulled in front of the large plantation-style home. As it rolled to a stop, Claude said to his chauffer, "Bring Mr. Cole's bags into the house, he'll be stayin'." Tony stopped him, "No Claude, I've got reservations at the Galaxy. I appreciate the invitation, but I really have to stay at the hotel." "Claude, I appreciate the party you're going to have, but I have a request to make," Tony asked. "Whatever you want, you got it." Tony continued, "Well, not knowing you had planned this party, I made arrangements for a young lady to meet me in Houston tonight. Would you mind if I brought her to your party?" Claude slapped Tony's shoulder, "You young stud; can't even go away for a couple a days without bringin' in your own private stock. She must be kinda special, flying her in an all." Tony had heard about Claude's extracurricular affairs with some well-known beauties long ago. So he was going to enjoy dropping his bombshell, "Well, she's special to a lot of her fans, her name is Roni Scott!" Claude choked, "Mother fucker, boy, that's number one, number one of all the number tens. When you get one, you don't mess around. God damn, I can't wait to meet her!" Tony was elated, Claude reacted exactly as he expected.

"Let's go out by the pool, have a drink, and talk some bidness, that is if I can get my mind off of that gorgeous lady ya got comin'," Claude led Tony through the house to the pool.

As they sat down beneath an umbrella, Claude commanded his maid to bring out a fresh bottle of Jack Daniels. Tony waited for Claude to begin. "Tony, do you have any idea why I've asked you to come see me?" He was fishing to see if Tony was prepared. Claude knew that Jonathan Stuyvesant made it a rule to never enter business talks without knowing what hand his counterpart was holding. Had Jonathan taught this to Tony? "Claude, why don't you tell me," was Tony's answer. "Shit," Claude thought, he's smart just like Jonathan said.

"Tony, I'm sure that you are aware of the financial situation of Five Star Oil!" Claude made a statement sound like a question, once again for a reaction. Tony only nodded. Claude continued, "We tried to compete with the big boys, Exxon, Gulf, Mobil, all of 'em. They were buying up companies, so we bought up companies. They invested, so we invested. Only one thing wrong, we're small. We know the oil bidness, but we don't know the paper, clothing, or food bidness. Most of our acquisitions were total losses; most of our investments were total losses." Tony asked softly, "How bad is it?" He dropped his head, "Tony, I may be losing it all. I've got to do somethin' quick." "What do you want from me, Claude?" Tony was insisting that he ask him for whatever he wants. The reason, he wasn't sure how he could benefit from this situation. Tony continued, "Do you want me to give you advice or what?" Claude turned to Tony, "I want you to buy into Five Star Oil. We need cash. I'm willing to sell a large share of my stock." Tony, being cautious, knew that Claude personally owned 90% of the stock, asked, "How much of the stock do you own?" "I own 90%; my two brothers own 5% each. So you see I personally stand a chance to lose everything. Can you help, Tony?" "How much, how much do you need?" Claude rose and walked to the edge of the pool, "hundred and fifty million." Tony, wanting to be prepared had checked Five Star

Oil stock prices prior to arriving in Houston, asked, "Claude, are you telling me that you want to sell me that amount?" "Yes, exactly!" "What percentage of the stock would that give me," Tony pursued? Claude looked pensively at Tony, "that will give you 45%, me 45%, and, of course, my brothers will keep their 10%." Tony was surprised, Claude was being totally honest. He poured himself another drink, lit a cigarette, the asked Claude, "about your brothers, do they have voting power?" "No, they just hold their shares." Tony being inquisitive, "Who was in charge of your finances during your acquisitions and investments?" Claude seemed confused, "My V.P. of Finance Sam Parkinson. He came from one of those Ivy League schools, Princeton, I believe. Hell, he's smarter than any ten men I've ever met." "So he may be. If so, why has everything he's done failed?" Tony opened Claude's eyes. "Claude, I'll not invest the hundred and fifty million, but I will invest one-hundred and sixty million if you meet my requirements." Puzzled, Claude answered, "That amount would give you 51% and controlling interest. I don't want to give up my bidness. This is my whole life. I've built Five Star out of a hole in the ground. I'm almost 70 years old and I don't want to lose it after it's taken me a lifetime to build." He sat down. Tony moved directly in front of him, "Claude, I don't want to take your company. I don't know a damn thing about the oil business, but I do know finance. If I'm going to put out that kind of investment, I want to make damn sure I get an equitable return. If you consent to my proposal, we'll both win, but I must have control, without question or Five Star and my money will go up in smoke. This is how I want it, see if you'd agree. You would run the day to day operation; I'll not have any say. Either I or whomever I place in the position will handle all finance. It's that simple. Oh, one more thing. You have a will, I presume? I want it stated in your will that I will be given the choice to buy your entire shares (39%) of Five Star Oil at the price we have agreed on here today, not at the market price at the time of your death. What's your answer?" Claude sat and stared at Tony. Slowly, he stood up, "Tony, I'm about to pay you the greatest compliment I could give you. You are the shrewdest fucker I've ever met and that includes Jonathan Stuyvesant, and he was the God damned best.' Tony didn't respond. Claude stepped away with his back to Tony, and then turned around, "You know you've got me over a barrel. You've known all along that I've already exhausted every other avenue, and I was wondering if you were prepared for this meeting. Shit." He put out his hand, grinned, and said, "Hi ya, pahdner." Tony shook his hand and then said, "I'll go to the hotel now, and the formal transaction can take place sometime next week. Contact your lawyer. Have him at the party tonight. My lawyer will be here. They can iron out everything and they can make the change in your will, too. Shall we drink on it?" Claude poured the drinks, they toasted, and drank. Tony winked at Claude then asked if he could have his driver pick up Derek at the airport and take him to the Galaxy hotel?" Claude nodding, "No problem, then I'll have my driver wait at the hotel for you and your lady." Tony nodded in agreement then began to walk away. Claude called to him, "Tony? You'll meet the challenge with no problem. Jonathan would be very proud of you!"

As Roni and Derek stepped from the limousine, a horde of reporters and photographers rushed to them. "What the hell!" Derek exclaimed. "Hey, you're with a star, just grin and enjoy it," Roni said as she smiled and pushed her way through the press corps. "What brings you to Houston, Roni?" one reporter asked. "We understand you're here to attend Claude Benaforte's party tonite?" another asked. Derek stepped in front of her; realizing Tony was behind it, "Ladies and gentlemen, Miss Scott is here to relax with some friends before departing for Brazil. Please just let us through!" They made their way into the lobby where another rush of people converged on them. They were all saying the same thing, "Can I have your autograph, oh please, Roni!" Derek even signed a few. He really enjoyed it.

The manager finally moved them through the mass of people, directly into an elevator. "Your suite is ready, Miss Scott. I'll take you directly there," the manager spoke adoringly. "Could we go to Mr. Cole's suite first?" She asked in her actress voice. Of course, he agreed.

Derek knocked. Roni laughed, hiding next to the wall. Tony opened the door, "Ah, Derek, glad you're here; come in." Derek stood fast, "I come bearing gifts," he stepped back and Roni ran into the room, and threw her arms around his neck. They all laughed. "How did you two end up here at the same time?" Tony asked as he squeezed her waist. "We ran into each other at the L.A. airport, so I invited Derek to share my charter with me. By the way, why did you set up the press party in the lobby?" "What…press party…I don't know what you're talking about," he answered confused. "We are coy; aren't we? You know that we were swamped by the press and moviegoers when we arrived." She patted his face. "Yeh, if you didn't tip them off, who the hell did?" Derek said as he poured his drinks. "Claude Benaforte!" Tony reached for his drink.

"I told him Roni was meeting me here. He called the press for his own publicity. That son-of-a-bitch." "Oh , that's why a reporter asked me if I was here to attend Claude a…a…what's his name's party? Are we going to a party tonite?" Roni asked. Tony sat on the couch, "Oh, well, maybe it will turn out for the best. I'm sorry, if it upset you Roni." "If the media and my fans upset me, then I'm in the wrong business," she quipped. "Well, at least you're here. We can talk a little business and then have a good time at the Claude's party," Tony lit a cigarette.

"Roni, would you mind if Derek and I discuss business?" "No, go right ahead. Do you want me to leave, or can I stay?" She sat next to him on the couch. "Sure, you can stay." He kissed her cheek.

"So tell me Derek, how did it go in L.A.?" Derek opened his briefcase, then handed Tony a handful of papers, "These are temporary contracts; they're only contracts of good faith until the complete transaction can be written up legally. They're legal now, but we'll have to go out next week and sign the final contracts." Tony looked at them quickly. Derek handed him another contract, "This is Cole Industries' brand new eight-passenger Lear jet." Tony looked at Derek and smiled, "That's terrific. Do you like it? I certainly hope so, because I have a feeling you're going to be living in it for a while." Derek half-grinned, "Well, you do have to make a decision immediately. They want to know if you want any special paint or not. It comes in basic white with some blue stripes." Tony stood, ran his hand through his hair, "This is good. This will force us to design a Cole Industries logo. What do you think?" He looked at Derek for an answer. Derek was glad he asked, because he had already thought about the subject. "Well, I've got an idea. He pulled out a sheet of paper from his briefcase, and began drawing, "What do you think of this, Tony?" He drew out his thought, then looked at Tony for an answer.

Tony picked up the paper, walked around the room, looked down at Derek, "Derek, I love it!' He almost yelled. "Roni, look, this is perfect. It's truly unique." "Hey, that's terrific. Now you need to come up with a color combination that will make that logo explode. Like, uh, bright orange and blue!" She was getting as excited as Tony and Derek. Derek was all smiles. He had never been this happy in his life. Tony clapped his hands, "Okay, that's settled. You agree, Derek?" "Agreed." "Okay, call them back. The plane will be bright orange with our new logo in bright blue,"

Tony commanded. This is really exciting. I really enjoy you guys. There is no doubt that you'll make it big," Roni remarked sincerely.

"Derek, we've got to discuss the deal I made with Claude today," stated Tony. Derek got up to get a drink, "You mean you've already closed a deal? Christ, you continue to amaze me. Tell me about it!" Tony said, "Sit down; I want you to listen carefully, so if I've made a legal blunder, we can catch it now. Besides, you're working tonight. Claude's attorney and you are going to draw up something for us to sign." He went through the entire transaction, with Derek taking notes. When he finished, he asked Derek, "What do you think? Any legal problems?" Derek looked at Roni, then at Tony, he leaned back in his chair, "Tony, you have just pulled off the God-damnedest, shrewdest, most fantastic business deal of all time. Roni, you are looking at the BEST damned financial expert in this entire world. My compliments to the Master!" He held up his glass as a toast.

"Tony, the party was really enjoyable. You know, I shouldn't have worn clothes. Of all the people who looked at me. I've never known anybody with looks like Claude Benaforte. I honestly think he was licking his lips when he looked at me," Roni shivered at the thought. Tony pulled her to him, "I don't blame Claude, I've been licking my lips, too." He gently kissed her. She took a step back, reached behind her, pulled at the zipper on her dress; the dress fell to the floor, exposing her nude body. She wore no undergarments. Tony picked her up, "Since we won't see each other for a while, I'm going to make love to you in a way that you'll never forget." The rest of the night they spent in blissful passion. After making love, for what seemed hours, exhausted, they slept; engulfed in each others arms.

Tony slipped silently from the bed. He looked at the sleeping beauty, lying so peaceful. "It isn't fair to her," he thought. "I've used her. All I think about, while making love to her is Maggie. Roni, it's not fair. I'm really sorry, truly sorry." He went into the shower; his thoughts still were of Maggie. He grabbed a pair of jeans and his Northwestern sweatshirt, went into the living room area of the suite, closing the door to allow Roni to sleep. He poured himself a tall orange juice, lit a cigarette, and sat on the couch. He had been sitting for about an hour thinking about what was happening to him...Roni, she's beautiful, fun, and I think she'd fall in love if we kept this up...Maggie, she's also beautiful, married, happily married; I just hired her husband. I've always been against extra-marital affairs. What the hell is wrong with you, the only affair you've had with

Maggie is in your own head. Forget it...business, Claude Benaforte; Five Star Oil; shopping centers...Maggie...he got up, angrily snubbed out a cigarette. "Can't sleep?" Roni was standing in the door to the bedroom wearing Tony's shirt. "What's wrong; weren't you satisfied?" She smiled as she walked to him. He smiled, as he looked into her loving face. "Nothing wrong; I'm not much of a sleeper. I'm arranging things to leave." "When are you leaving?" She put her arms around his neck. "About an hour." Roni kissed him, then said, "Then I'd better get my little ass out of here. Christ, I've got a week's worth of packing to do when I get back to L.A." She started towards the bedroom, when she stopped, turned toward Tony, and softly said, "Tony, I think I'm in love with you!" She didn't wait for a reaction, just turned and entered the bedroom. Tony felt rotten, he really liked Roni, but "love" wasn't what he felt for her. He felt that for M...; he stopped his thinking; he wouldn't allow himself to say it.

Roni, Tony, and Derek rode to the airport together, since they had chartered flights. Roni to L.A., Tony and Derek to Chicago. The limousine stopped for Tony and Derek first. They stepped from the car, Derek said, "I'll go make sure the bags are okay. Goodbye, Roni. Make a great flick." He kissed her cheek. She got out of the car, "If I write you from Brazil, will you write back?" Tony grinned, as he put his hands on her shoulders, "That is the most ridiculous thing I've ever heard. Tony Cole, writing a letter. I'll call you. You let me know where I can reach you." She kissed him, "Good luck, Tony. Although you don't need it. You're just too damned fantastic to need luck. I'll call you." She began to cry as she climbed into the limo. Tony watched for a long time after the car was out of sight.

CHAPTER SEVEN

They didn't say much until the aircraft was airborne, then Derek asked, "Would you like to discuss her with me?" Tony grinned, "Some other time. But I would like to discuss some thoughts about the next few steps we're going to take in Cole Industries." Derek didn't push the Roni issue, "Hey, fine; I'd love to hear what the wheels in your head are saying as they spin." Drinks were served as requested.

Tony opened a leather-bound folder he was carrying, "I've been making mental notes and jotting them down when I get the chance; so let's see if we can make any sense out of this." Derek looked at the notes and laughed, "If you figure that out, Theresa will be right; you'll be remarkable."

"Listen, here are my ideas." Tony was enthusiastic, "We own the California land, of which we are assured of building a shopping plaza, correct?" Derek nodded agreement. Tony continued, "We're in the oil business. I've got an idea about the adjoining land to the proposed center. I think we should build an industrial/office park on the site. Derek began to speak, but Tony stopped him. "Wait, let me finish, then tell me what you think. Five Star had, at one time, plans to create a West Coast headquarters. I think now is a good time. They could be the first tenants of the industrial park, and if they were to build there, it would entice some other major companies to establish there as well." Derek, shaking his head in agreement, said, "Yeh, and Cole Industries would collect the monthly leases. I like it; but will Five Star agree to it?" Tony, "No problem there. Speaking of Five Star, I want to get a complete check on their finance V.P. Sam Parkinson. I have an idea we're going to bring Five Star back quicker than anybody expected, if my hunch turns out to be fact." "I'll get an agency on it first thing Monday morning," Derek assured him. "Here are some other ideas," Tony moved on. "If we are going to own a shopping plaza and an industrial park, why should we pay somebody to build them?" Easily answered, "We don't own a construction or building company," Derek said quickly. "Precisely right," Tony exclaimed. "But, I think we should change that." Derek raised his eyebrows. "Let's come back to this part. Derek, I want to go into real estate/land development along with building restaurants and department stores." This puzzled Derek very much, "When did you come this realization?" Tony looked at his notes, "When I was doing these. Look, if we had our own construction company and our own architectural firm, we could design, and build our own…wait. Look at it this way; we have the land development firm which finds the land. We have a real estate firm that either sells or leases the land we developed. So, add this to the Cole Industries tree. We buy an architectural company who would design any buildings for Cole Industries and would continue to do architectural work for the outside. We then buy a construction company who would build the Cole buildings. Do you see what I'm talking about?" "Cole Industries would pay its own subsidiaries to design and build everything for them. So in turn, Cole would get their total costs of building, returned through their subsidiaries," Derek answered eagerly! "God damn, that's beautiful. That's fuckin' fantastic!" Derek was so excited he could hardly stay seated. He stood up, ran his hand through his hair, and said with a broad smile, "When do we start moving on this?" Tony looked at him, smiled, and said, "Cole Industries will own a construction company and an architectural firm by the end of the week." "No, no, you can't do it that quick. Oh, oh, you've already made some deal. Haven't you?" Derek was dancing around the plane. "No, I haven't even made an inquiry yet," Tony said flatly. "Then how the hell…shit, I don't know how, but you'll do it. You know, I'm beginning to agree with Theresa right now!" They touched glasses and laughed. They talked, laughed, and drank the rest of the flight. Once they landed, they went to the mansion and spent the rest of the night drinking and talking about old times and business for the future. Tony Cole had is goal and Cole Industries now had a direction.

Theresa had arrived Sunday morning on the first flight from L.A. Her enthusiastic attitude overwhelmed both Tony and Derek. When Tony informed her of the Five Star acquisition, she was ecstatic, "Oil! My God, that's really big business." Tony and Derek laughed as Derek told her that Five Star was not Mobil Oil, but just a small oil company. Tony decided they should all take Sunday off and show Theresa the finer spots in Chicago.

On Monday, Derek and Theresa headed downtown to lease part of the Stuyvesant Building. Tony was also going downtown to negotiate a deal with a construction company and an architectural firm.

Paul Krug, President of Krug Building and Construction, was a strong looking, strong-willed German who built his company from the ground up, some 25 years ago. He's married to a lovely woman, Hilda, and the father of three daughters. One of which, Georgina, Tony had dated in high school. Hilda had always thought Tony was the man for Georgina. She was crushed when the relationship collapsed. Paul always liked Tony, but never thought he was good enough for his daughter, being an orphan had a lot to do with it. When Hilda read about Tony's inheritance, she told Paul, "So orphan boys all grow up bad, heh?" "I always knew he'd make something of himself." Paul shrugged, "You're right, Hilda, I was wrong about Tony."

The young girl behind the receptionist desk looked up at Tony, "Yes sir, oh yes sir, may I help you?" She was all smiles. "May I please speak to Mr. Krug, my name is Tony Cole?" He smiled as he spoke. The girl rose and opened the door to another office. She stopped to look back at him. Tony grinned once more.

The door opened and the large body of Paul Krug filled the entrance. For a moment he and Tony just looked at each other, then Paul smiled a broad smile and said, "Tony, Tony Cole, it's great to see you! Please come in, come in," he said as he put out his hand. Tony took his hand, "Mr. Krug, Paul, it's good to see you, too." The young girl gave Tony one last big – give—me—a—call—smile as the two men disappeared into Krug's office. Paul Krug motioned for Tony to sit down, "Please don't call me Mr. Krug; you're not asking if you can date Georgina again, are you?" They both laughed. "Congratulations, on your new-found wealth, Tony. How long has it been since I've seen you?" Paul offered Tony a cigar. Tony lit a cigarette instead as he said no to the cigar. "It's been two years, Paul; during the fund raising dinner for Senator Smart. How is Georgina and the rest of your family?" Paul Krug said okay but was now wondering why Tony was there. He told Tony that Georgina was the mother of three boys and happily married to a pharmacist in Evanston. His curiosity finally won, "What can I do for you, Tony? I'm sure if you wanted to know about Georgina, you could have found out from another source." Tony spoke to Paul without smiling, "You're right, Paul. I didn't come to ask about Georgina; although it's nice to know that she's doing well. I've come to see you about a business proposition." He waited for Krug's reaction. "What kind of proposition," he was curious. Tony got to his feet, "Paul, I understand your company can build just about any kind of building, is that true?" Krug was proud of his company, and was anxious to explain the accomplishments, "Yes, we began by building houses, then graduated to small office buildings, then came my big chance; I built the new wing at Memorial Hospital. We don't build cheap buildings, either. I'm very proud of the buildings we've put up. In fact, we're in the process of building the Northeastern Insurance structure on Madison Avenue." Tony already knew the Krug success story, but he allowed him to gloat. "You've been very successful, Paul, and that is why I've come to you," Tony complimented him. "So, I take it you want my company to do some building for you. No problem, Tony, we'll be glad to do whatever you ask." He wasn't prepared for what Tony was going to propose. "Paul, how would you like to dramatically expand Krug Construction?" He looked puzzled, "I don't see how I could expand. I have to turn down jobs now." Tony looked at him, "I'm going to show you, how. Paul, would you sell me your company?" He choked on his cigar, "What the hell are you talking about? Sell my company! Hell, what would I do then? No, Tony, I don't want to sell. That's kinda funny." He laughed out loud. Tony wasn't smiling, "Paul, I'm serious." Krug stopped laughing, and stared at Tony. "Let me explain," Tony now had Krug's undivided attention, "I have recently created a company, Cole Industries, which is going to have interests in shopping centers, oil, restaurants, department stores, and land development. We own a large piece of Five Star Oil, land in California which we'll build a shopping center and industrial park." Krug was following every word intently visualizing the prospects. Tony went on, "Look Paul, I don't want to j-u-s-t buy your company, I want to incorporate it." Paul stood up, "Go on, go on." Tony realized he had his curiosity at its peek, "I want Krug Construction to do all building for Cole Industries, but I want Cole Industries to be the end benefactor. Here is how both you and Cole can achieve ultimate profits and success. If you'll sign over your company to Cole Industries, you'll still be the President of Krug Construction, you'll have a salary of 1½ times what you now draw, you'll be on the Board of Directors at Cole while also carrying the title of Vice President of Building and Construction, you'll have a say in the rest of the Cole operations; also, I will deposit one million dollars in your personal account." He waited for Paul to answer. Krug walked around his desk, looked out the window, relit his cigar, then turned to Tony, "You've come a long way for a boy from an orphanage, but if I wanted to sell my company, I could get 100 million dollars for it. Why would I go for your deal?" "I've already given you good reasons, but money today, you'd have one helluva time getting anybody to put out a 100 million, but if you come in with me, we'll make Krug Construction one of the largest in the U.S. of which you'll be the President plus a director on the board of a company that will be worth billions in the near future, and Paul, you don't change one thing in your life except increased wealth and public stature. You'll be set for life. You can set up an office in Texas and California, as well as having an office in the Stuyvesant Building. Listen, Paul, you've got the best years of your life ahead of you, why not enjoy it to the hilt." "You've made a very good presentation," Krug was now calm, "You make sense in some ways. I'll think about it. Call me in a couple of days." Tony stood, "No, Paul, I need your answer now. That's the way I do business. Yes or no." The ball was now in Krug's court. "You're good, Tony. If we go together, when do you want to do it," Krug asked. Tony knew he had him. "This week, our attorneys can handle the particulars, and I'll write you a check for 1 million right now to seal it between us." Krug looked at him sternly, then grinned, "Write the check!"

They shook hands; Krug took out a bottle for a toast as Tony wrote the check. As Tony handed him the check, he said, "One other thing; the name of the company will now be Cole/Krug Building and Construction." Paul laughed, "God damn, you've thought of everything." They had their drink and Tony began to leave; he stopped, "Please give my regards to Georgina and Hilda. My lawyer will contact yours tomorrow. Goodbye Paul."

The restaurant was full as Tony entered, but Carmen, the Maitre di, whisked him to a table in the back that was available for VIPs. Carmen always sat him at this particular table. Tony had been frequenting the Golden Roman Restaurant for the past seven years. He and Carmen had become close friends during that period. "Tony, its been a long time. I'm a-happy for your inheritance. You make big news. I'm-a glad you still come see your old friends," Carmen said seating Tony. "Carmen,

I'll always come here. Hell, I feel like I grew up in this restaurant. How have you been, Carmen, and how's your family?" Tony asked. He was genuinely interested because he liked Carmen Lombardi very much. "Oh, everybody's a-real good. Thank you, Tony." "Carmen, I'm expecting someone to join me. A man, 30 years old, brown hair, good-looking, nicely dressed. Please show him back when he arrives. Oh, there he is, the one in the grey suit," Tony pointed towards the entrance.

"Mike, damn good to see you," Tony extended his hand. "Well, I must say, your new fortune hasn't changed your looks any. Nice to see you Tony," Mike remarked.

Mike Emerson was an old acquaintance of Tony's. He married Stephanie Alcott, the daughter of Alexander Alcott – wealthy stock broker and very close friend of Jonathan's. Mike also came from money, the Emerson Real Estate firm. He was appealing to women, and comfortable for a man to be with. He wanted no part of his father's real estate business. He attended Purdue University's School of Architecture. His life-long dream was to be an architect. He has fulfilled his dream, but not to the extent that he would have liked. He owns his own architectural company, but he's having problems financially. Tony was well aware of these problems. Stephanie had called Jonathan just prior to his death, asking for advice and money. Jonathan never provided the money; advice he did give. He told Stephanie to stay out of her husband's business affairs.

Tony had called Mike, upon leaving Paul Krug, and had invited him to lunch. "Well, Mike, how's Stephanie and the kids?" Tony began the conversation. Mike looked uninterested, "Ok, uh, fine, just fine." Tony realized that the small talk was over, "Tell me, how's business?" Mike shook his head, "Tony, it's never taken off. We can't seem to get the big jobs. To be very honest, I don't know how long I can keep the company afloat. If I could land one big job..." Tony ordered drinks, then looked at Mike, "Maybe, if you're willing, I can change things around for you." Mike looked interested, and smiled, "If there's anything you can do, Tony, I'd greatly appreciate it." Tony didn't hesitate, "Mike, I would like for you to be a part of Cole Industries." He allowed him to ask what he meant. "Be a part of Cole Industries. What is it? And, what kind of part?" Tony lit a cigarette, "Cole Industries is the name of the company I am forming. We'll be involved in oil, building and construction, real estate and land development, and some other things." Mike interrupted,

"Tony, I'm an architect. What could I do for you?" "Mike, we are going to build shopping centers and industrial parks. We own a large portion of Five Star Oil. Krug Construction Company will now be known as Cole/Krug Construction. Whatever Cole Industries builds, Cole/Krug will build it, besides continuing to take on other assignments. I want a complete architectural division. One that will have young ideas to design whatever Cole Industries builds. I want every Cole building to be unique." Mike was falling off his seat. Tony continued, "That, Mike, is what you can do for me; but I don't want to hire your company for the designs. I want Emerson Architects to become Cole/Emerson Architecture and Design, a division of Cole Industries." He waited for a response. "You mean, let me get this straight," Mike wanted to be sure he understood. "You want to buy my company, and you want me to work for you, uh, Cole Industries?" Tony was now going to ice the cake, "Let me lay it all out for you. Cole Industries takes over Emerson Architects. Mike Emerson, you, will become a Vice President of Cole Industries and President of Cole/Emerson division. You will be a director on the board of Cole Industries, of which, will involve you in all the other facets of our business. That's it, very simple." Mike just stared at Tony. "Mike, what do you take out of your business, money I mean." He looked at Tony, took a drink, then spoke, "Well, the books show my salary to be $60,000 per year; but I haven't been able to take $40,000 in the past two years." Tony squirmed a little, "Mike, I don't want to ask this question, but I'm going to. How is your personal finances, at home, I mean?" He took another drink, "Shot, Tony, I'm in deep trouble. I've borrowed from my father, and from Steph's father, and I don't know how I'm going to repay it." Tony dug deeper, "How much are you in debt?" Mike was embarrassed, "Oh, Christ, this is embarrassing. Oh, what the hell. I owe my father 100 grand in personal bills and Alexander 150 grand. Plus another 100 grand in personal bills." "Where are you living presently?" "We live out in the Overbrook section. Stephanie is always talking about moving to the Northern suburbs again. But…" Tony closed, "Mike, here's my proposal. If you'll accept the position I offered, I'll write you a check for $1 million right here. We'll call it, money received for the sale of your company and you can do with it whatever you like. Cole will also take over all your company's liabilities, as well. So you might say, the million is for you." Mike was flabbergasted, "Tony, I don't know what to say. I'm excited; but at the same time I wonder." "Wonder what?" "Are you offering this deal just out of friendship or for my ability as an architect?" Tony leaned onto his elbows, "You should understand one thing, right now I will do most anything for my friends. But If I didn't think you were the best damned architect around, we wouldn't be discussing this merger." Mike smiled from ear to ear, "I think I'll enjoy being Vice President of Cole Industries." They shook hands and Tony said, "Now, let's eat." They talked about the future and the past while eating. When they were ready to leave, Tony wrote out a check for the million dollars, handed it to Mike and said, "Pay off your father and father-in-law, then buy Stephanie a nice big house up North."

As Tony left the restaurant, he asked Carmen, "Would you be available to discuss a business matter with me this evening?" This is unusual, Carmen thought, "Well, sure Tony. This is my night off. Where?" "Do you know where the Stuyvesant mansion is?" "Of course, everybody knows a-where that is." Tony patted Carmen on the shoulder, "Good, why don't you come out around eight o'clock? We can talk there." Carmen was extremely puzzled, "Sure, Tony, eight o'clock. I'll be there. Chao."

Tony stepped into the limousine, "Let's go to the Stuyvesant Building, Rodney." He opened the bar, poured himself a Jack Daniels. He began to think about the events of the past week. He had acquired many prime acres of California land, become a major stockholder in an oil company, owner of a large construction firm, and an architectural company. He was now the President of Cole Industries – **Cii.** His best friend had become his right hand man and personal attorney. He hired a lovely secretary. He had met, and made love to one of the most beautiful women in the world. He had purchased his own jet. He had won $24,000 in one golf game. He had lost a tennis match to a woman…oh, but what a woman! Maggie! Maggie Weyland! "I wonder what she said about Peter's change in life. God, I can't wait to see Maggie again." His thoughts were interrupted as Rodney pulled in front of the Stuyvesant Building. "I'm not sure how long I'll be Rodney. Why don't you go have some coffee and then come up to Mr. Stuyvesant's old office."

Derek and Theresa were in Jonathan's old office – Tony's new office. He grinned as he looked at them, "Well, have you two accomplished anything today?" They both looked at him grinning. Theresa looked at Derek, "Go on, you first." Derek stood, "Tony, we've done it as you said. We leased part of the building, in fact, we leased four full floors because we're sure that we'll be needing the space by the time you're through building your empire. Also, we've found out quite a bit about Claude's boy, Sam. It wasn't hard either. It seems as though..." Tony interrupted, "Sam is also on another payroll, a competitor of Five Star, right?" Derek glanced at Theresa then at Tony, "God damn, how did you find out? We are the one's who know!" Tony smiled, "Nobody told me. It had to be something like that. That guy is too smart to make all of those bad investments. He had to be doing it for a reason. Money; it'll do it every time. Who's the competitor?" Derek sat down, "Aren't you going to tell us?" Tony laughed, "I don't know." "Jesus Christ, there's one thing he doesn't know. It was Colonial Oil in Dallas." "Derek," Tony said, "Is there any legal way to get our traitor?" Derek ran his hand through his hair, "Probably, but the only thing that would do is to get Sam. Colonial would fight it to the hilt, and if they're even half-smart, there'll be no record of his employment at Colonial Oil." "So, what you're saying is that Colonial can prove themselves clean and deny it, and Sam would be left out to dry," Tony wanted to be sure of the facts. Derek shook his head, "Yeh, that's about it." Tony stared out of the window for a moment then turned to Theresa, "Theresa, get Claude Benaforte on the phone for me." "We'll handle this matter ourselves, without a court," he said turning to Derek. "As soon as I talk to Claude, I'll tell you what I've been up to today. Is there any Jack Daniels in here?"

"Just a moment. Mr. Benaforte, Mr. Cole Is picking up," Theresa handed the phone to Tony. "Good afternoon, Claude." Claude bellowed into the phone, "Tony, ma boy, I wanna thank ya for bringin' that perty little Miss Scott to the party Sataday. Now what can I do for ya?" Tony was very deliberate, "Claude, have you told anybody about our deal yet?" "No, you said you wanted to wait a week. Well, I did tell ma Mrs." Claude was honest, that Tony was sure of. "Good, I want you to tell Sam, your V.P. of Finance. Don't tell him the whole deal, just inform him that I'm purchasing, controlling interest of Five Star. I want you to tell him we consummated the deal Friday. Tell him right now. I'm going to attempt to get back some of Five Star's lost investment money. I'll explain later. Whatever he asks shortly, you okay." "Sure enough, Tony. I'll do it right now. Talk to you later...pardner." Tony hung up, "We'll handle this situation shortly."

Derek moved anxiously toward Tony, "Okay; so now tell me about your morning travels." Lighting a cigarette, Tony said, "Derek, my friend, I've been out making work for you," Derek looked puzzled, "Oh, God, what now?" "You're going to be very busy, counselor. This morning, Cole Industries added two new divisions, to be known as Cole/Krug Building and Construction; and Cole/Emerson Architecture and Design." "Do you mean…yeh, you do," Derek was astonished, "How? God damn, that's terrific!" "Derek, we've now got one helluva great start. Emerson will design and Krug will build whatever Cole Industries builds and all monies returns right back to Cole," explained Tony. "Krug Construction, that's one of the largest construction companies in Chicago; but I don't know…Emerson?" Derek was asking for more details. Tony obliged, "I've known Mike Emerson for a long time. He's been trying to make an architectural firm grow but he hasn't done well. He's always had a dream to build the great structure. He'll make Cole structures unique, you can bet on that." He then informed Derek of both deals. Derek sat staring at Tony, "And when am I to finalize everything?" Tony grinned, "I'd like to have everything finished by Friday, so we can make a statement to the press and we can bring Cole Industries new staff together and explain the operation and their part in it." Derek smiled, "I'll do what I can. I've got everything taken care of on the West Coast, but I'll have to spend a couple of days in Houston. Oh, hell, I forgot to tell you; the new plane will be delivered Wednesday. I told them to land at Midway, Theresa is making storage arrangements there. Is that okay?" Tony clapped, "Hey, that's terrific. Why don't you start the procedure with Krug and Emerson tomorrow and Wednesday? Then we'll take the new plane to Houston on Thursday." Derek let out a laugh, "That's fine, but who's going to fly the damn thing?" "Christ, I never thought about that," Tony was confused. "Hell, we've got to hire a pilot, quick. Know one?" Derek shook his head, "Hell no." "Theresa, come here!" Tony demanded. "Theresa, call Lear Western Aircraft and find out if they can recommend a pilot we can hire, quickly." "Derek, sit down," Tony pointed to the couch, "You know, I have a feeling Cole Industries is going to be moving like a gazelle. With the addition of Krug and Emerson, it really opens up many other things. Listen to what I'm thinking. I'd like to get into the restaurant business and since we're going to own a shopping center and industrial park, why shouldn't we have one of our own restaurants there. Plus, I'd like to move into the retail business – say department stores. What do you think?" Excitedly, Derek began to walk around, "Terrific idea. Listen to this. If we entered the department store business, we could have our store as one of the anchors in the plaza. Oh, shit, you're right. There are no boundaries for Cole!" Tony reached for a cigarette, "But, it poses problems.

Derek, would you mind if I obtained another attorney?" "I don't want you handling legal affairs anymore." A hurt look came over Derek's face, "Why? Aren't you happy with the way I've handled things so far?" Tony stood and looked Derek directly in the eye, "Of course, but I need you more for something else. I want you to be the Executive Vice President of Cole Industries. I want you to be the coordinator between the different divisions." God damn, yes; I'd love it," Derek beamed! "Fine, your office will be the connecting one to mine. How's $250,000 a year to start sound for a salary?" Tony asked. Derek was in shock, "I need a drink. You know, you're the best friend anybody ever dreamed of having. I'll work my ass off, Tony." Tony poured drinks, "Then, you'd better hire a secretary and a personnel manager, too. We'll have to put together an employee benefit package and insurance program." "I'll get on it as soon as we've concluded what's started right now," Derek said. "Good, let's get that over with quick. Here's to a long and successful relationship," Tony toasted Derek.

Theresa came in, "Tony; Lear has four pilots to recommend. What do you want me to tell them?" Tony said, "Get their phone numbers, call each one personally and set up interviews for them here tomorrow afternoon. Then call the airlines and reserve them a first class flight." "Yes, sir. Boy, you don't waste any time, do you?" Theresa grinned. Tony returned the grin. "I'm going to go to work on the contracts in the works," Derek said and departed to another office. "Theresa, could you come in here?" Tony asked. She sat down in front of him, "Theresa, I don't like the décor of the offices. Would you contact a decorator to come in here and redo them immediately? I want them done by Friday," Tony requested. Theresa looked around, "God, I think they're gorgeous." "Yeh, this one is. But Jonathan wasn't one for style in offices. I want the Cole Industries headquarters to be the most impressive in Chicago. This office won't need any changes, but the connecting office should be just as nice as this and the rest of the offices on this floor should be done in very good taste. This floor will house the leaders of the company. I'll trust your judgment. Tell them they must have all offices completed by Thursday night. I don't care if they have to work 24 hours a day. We'll pay whatever it takes. Can you get it done?" Tony presented her with a big job. She rose to her feet, "It will be done. I only hope I get used to your quick way of doing things." "You're doing fine," he said as he left.

CHAPTER EIGHT

"Hello, the Weyland's residence," the voice on the other end answered. "May I speak to Peter, please?" Tony asked quickly. The woman replied, "I'm sorry, Mr. Weyland is out. May I ask who's calling?" "Yes, I'm Tony Cole, and…" the woman interrupted, "Oh, Mr. Weyland has just arrived. Please wait for a second." Peter took the phone, "Hello, Tony!" "Peter, I hope everything goes well out there. I would like for you to come to Chicago on Friday. In fact, I'd like for you to arrive Thursday night. I'm holding our first meeting, Friday." Tony asked more than ordered. "Of course, I'll be there," Peter replied. "Why don't you bring Maggie along? By the way, how did she take the news of moving to Chicago?" Tony was interested in how she reacted. "Maggie was pleased. She's from the Midwest, Cleveland. She'll enjoy it. We'll see you Friday," Peter seemed sure. "Good. Theresa will make all the reservations for you. You can pick up your tickets at the airport. See you then, Peter!" Tony didn't wait for a reply. He sat back in his chair, spun around and stared out at Chicago's skyline. He was anxious to see Maggie again. He visualized her dark hair blowing in the breeze. Her long legs as she glided in slow motion on the tennis court. Tony, Tony, get her out of your mind. He quickly spun back to his desk, picked up the phone, and dialed Claude Benaforte.

"Howdy, Tony. I've taken care of informing Sam about our deal. Just like you asked," Claude sounded like he was talking to his boss. "How did he react?" "Ya know, he acted like he was kicked in the ass by a mule. What the hell is it with you and Sam, anyway?" Claude replied with a giggle. Tony wasn't giggling, "Claude, I want you to put him on an airplane to Chicago. I'll explain later. Just tell him I want to discuss some things with him. I want him here tomorrow. Okay?" Claude didn't understand, but he would do as Tony asked, "Shore 'nuff, Tony. He'll be there. Be a talkin' to ya!" The phone went dead.

"Maggie." Peter went into the kitchen to talk to her. She called, "Peter, I'm in the dining room." He entered the dining room and kissed her cheek, "Hi, honey. I have to talk to you." "Sure, I'm just having a cup of coffee. Want some?" "No. Uh, uh," he sat down, "I just talked to Tony Cole. He wants us to come to Chicago on Thursday." Maggie's first thought was of Tony's smiling face, "So, this will really start it. You know, I've been thinking; I think I'll enjoy going back. Especially, if you'll be happier. What do we have to go back for?" "I'm not real sure, he said we were going to have a meeting on Friday and our airline tickets would be at the airport. That was it. Oh, he asked about your reaction to moving," he replied. He thought about my reaction. He cares about what I think. He cares about…Maggie's thoughts made her feel good. "Fine, I'll get everything ready. How long are we going to stay?" she questioned. Puzzled, he said, "He didn't say. Let's stay the weekend and look over the great city of Chicago." She walked over to him, "Good. That will be good for us; we haven't been away for a long time. I'm looking forward to it. Would it be alright if I bought some new clothes, my winter wardrobe isn't exactly the greatest for February in Chicago?" He shook his head, "Of course, since when do you have to ask to buy clothes?" She kissed him and began to leave, "I'm going to call Angela and go right now. See you later."

Maggie was looking in the mirror at the new dress, "I wonder if Mr. Tony Cole would like this dress? Who cares? You do, fool, he's the reason you're buying it! Wrong! I don't care what he thinks! Oh God, but I do. Just as I stop thinking about him – he moves right back into my mind. This is so foolish. Maggie Weyland, remember that name Weyland. It belongs to your husband – Peter. I know that. I've never been unfaithful or ever thought about it……yeh, I wonder what it's like to be in bed with Tony! That's it, Maggie. Don't you even consider thinking about that. Oh, God…….!" "Maggie, what are you doing?" Angela's voice stopped her thinking. Maggie was flushed, "Uh, uh, just looking at the dress. I think I'll take it."

Tony and Theresa picked up a pizza at Gino's on the way to the mansion. "Now, tell me," Tony asked as she was devouring her second piece, "Have you ever tasted pizza like that before?" With cheese dripping from her lip, she said, "No, my God, this is great. Chicago is great. Alfred came in, "There is a Mr. Carmen Lombardi to see you, Tony." Tony stood, "Show him into the library. Offer him a glass of wine or drink, Alfred. Thank you. I'll be right there." He took Theresa's hand, "Come on, I want you to meet an old friend that is about to become another member of the Cole Industries family." She stuffed in the last bite, "You've never mentioned him before. Who is he?" "You'll see," he said.

Carmen was sitting in a chair facing the huge walnut desk. He was awed at the elaborate room. He jumped to his feet the second they entered. "Sit down, Carmen, be comfortable. Theresa Williams, it is my pleasure to introduce Carmen Lombardi, a very good friend of mine," Tony was very gracious. Theresa couldn't help but notice the look on Carmen's face. He was proud that Tony considered him a good friend. He spoke first. "Miss a-Williams, I'm a-pleased to meet you. You're very a...pretty lady." She liked him immediately, "It's my pleasure Mr. Lombardi." Tony and Theresa sat in chairs facing Carmen's.

"Carmen, I know you want to get home to your family so I'll get right to the point of why I requested you to visit me here tonight." Carmen shook his head, "No hurry, my wife, she knows where I am. What can I do for you, Tony?" Alfred poured drinks for Tony and Theresa then re-filled Carmen's wine glass as Tony began to speak, "How long have you been the Maitre' di at my favorite place?" "Twenty-two years!" "Carmen, you once told me that you'd like to own your own restaurant, right?" Tony was allowing him to express himself. "Oh, yes. I worked very hard but can't save da money. So, I will stay to be Maitre' di," Carmen answered. "Carmen, I'm going to offer you something, not your <u>own</u> restaurant but very close; in fact even better. I'm going to build at least three restaurants but I don't know a damn thing about the business. I want you, Carmen, to become my Vice President in charge of restaurants. What do you think? Oh, before you answer, let me explain what the Vice President will have to do. 1) You'll have an office on the Executive floor of the Stuyvesant Building; 2) You'll answer only to me; 3) The food preparation and daily operations of the restaurants will be totally in your hands; 4) The first three restaurants will be in three different cities: Chicago, Houston, and Los Angeles; 5) The Vice President will have his own secretary and he will be paid $95,000 per year...Now, what do you think?" Carmen started to speak, but he was choked up and the words wouldn't come out. He tried again, but he began to cry, the tears ran down his face. He wiped away the tears and finally the words came out, "All the time, I spend in this life, nobody give Carmen Lombardi nothing'. I work hard and have nothin'. Why now? Why you offer, me, just a Maitre' di. Why you make such a nice offer to me?" Tony walked over to the humble man, he put his hand on his shoulder, "Carmen, for two reasons, one because I think you know more about the restaurant business than anyone I know, secondly, and this is the main reason…you're my friend, Carmen. Carmen began to cry again. So did Theresa. "I'm a-sorry. I make a fool of myself. But you make Carmen Lombardi happiest man in the whole world," he stood up, "Tony, I accept. You never be sorry. Never. I make you lotsa money." He pressed his hands on Tony's shoulders and kissed him on each cheek, "You make me very happy. Graci. Graci. Paison…my friend, my good friend." Tony said he would call him as he disappeared from the library. Theresa leaned up and kissed Tony with tears streaming down her face as she turned away from him, she said, "You're the most wonderful person I've ever met. That poor little man would give you anything he has now. Thank you Tony for being…uh, so wonderful." He smiled at her, "No, I'm not wonderful. I offered Carmen the position only because he's the best man for the job." She looked at him, wiping away the tears, "You know better and so do I. But I won't ever tell anybody." He started towards the door, "Hey, we have to finish our pizza." "Tony," she stopped him, "Tony, uh, uh, Tony would you do something for me?" He looked toward him, "Tony, would you make love to me?" He didn't even look shocked or surprised. He took her hand in his and said softly, "Theresa, I have thought about making love to you many, many times. I look at your lovely face, your cute little shape and it excites me. It is something I would enjoy very much; but I couldn't make love to you and work with you. So let's both control our urges so that we can continue to work together. You're the best damned secretary a man ever had. Come on, let's have a drink." Se pulled him to her, kissed his cheek and said, "Thank you for telling me you've thought about me sexually." She smiled and said, "Now, I have to go upstairs and change my clothes. I've gotten these soaking wet, all because of you." They both laughed, as Theresa went upstairs and Tony fixed himself a stiff Jack Daniels. She knew that she could never have him, but she was sure she'd always love him, as well.

When Tony arrived at the office Tuesday morning, Derek was already there. In fact, he'd spent the night there. Tony looked at him and laughed, "I wish some of your cute little bed time buddies could see you now." Derek gave him the finger as he grumbled, "Fuck you, this is all your doing. If you'd quit making deals like other people eat their meals, I wouldn't have to work so God-damned hard but…for Christ's sake, don't stop. "Why don't you go home and get some rest?" Tony said. "Oh, I slept a couple of hours on the couch, but I am going home to take a shower and change clothes. I'll be back in a couple of hours." Derek waved as he exited.

Theresa stuck her head in his office, "Good morning!" She felt stupid after last night. But as usual, Tony put her at ease, "Good morning, Theresa. You look lovely this morning, in fact, ravishing." She grinned, "Thanks. Do you need anything right away?" "Yes, would you call Claude Benaforte and find out what time Sam Parkinson will arrive?" She turned to leave, "Right away." Tony began pouring over the Five Star books covering his desk. Theresa was back in just a few minutes, "Mr. Parkinson is arriving at 8:30 on the Five Star jet." "Good," Tony stood up, "I want you and Rodney to meet him and give him the red carpet treatment. Make him feel very important and bring him directly here." She looked at him strangely, "I've never seen you act this way before!" He flashed that fantastic smile, "This is going to be very interesting. Mr. Parkinson must be highly impressed, okay?" "I'll give him the royal treatment. Oh shit; the decorator people will be here any minute." She waited for a response. Tony said, "I'll show them the offices that need reworked and hold them here until you return. You won't be gone that long." She replied with a wave of her hand, "Good enough."

The ringing of the phone surprised Tony as he was engrossed in the papers. "Hello, uh, Cole Indus…uh, this is Tony Cole." Her voice was laughing and scratchy "Since when do multi-millionaires answer their own phone. This is Roni, Roni Scott in case you've forgotten. Hi ya, lover!" He was pleased to hear her voice, "Roni. Damn, it's great to hear your voice. Where the hell are you?" The connection was cutting away occasionally, and it irritated Roni, "I'm somewhere in the…damn jungle…this phone connection is just like everything else down here…Hey, I miss you. We're not going to be here very long; we can't work with anything here. It's awful. Tony, can I see you when I come back?" He was picturing her in his mind…she really is a beautiful woman, "Well, that is the dumbest question I've ever heard. You just let me know when you are coming home and I'll meet you right away." She sounded happy, "Oh, Tony, I can't wait. I'll call before we leave here. I've got to go, they're screaming for me on the set. Bye-bye, and I think I love you!" The phone clicked in his ear. He smiled as he hung up the receiver. He really liked her.

The decorators arrived about ten minutes after Theresa left. Tony led them to each office and told them Theresa would return shortly to inform them of what she wanted. He then returned to his books.

Tony and Derek were discussing the Five Star situation when Theresa stepped in, "Mr. Parkinson is here and he seems excited, but he doesn't understand why he's here. Shall I show him in?" Tony waved his hand and said, "By all means, show him in." Derek moved to a chair next to Tony's desk, "Do you think, he'll go for it?" Tony just smiled.

Theresa opened the door and Sam Parkinson practically rushed through the door. Tony moved around the desk and approached him with his hand extended, "Sam, I'm Tony Cole. I'm glad you're here. Let me introduce Derek Hill." Derek was as gracious as Tony. "Mr. Parkinson, a pleasure to meet you." Sam shook their hands and agreed that it was a pleasure to meet each of them. They sat down, discussed his flight and Tony apologized for not meeting him on his trip to Houston. Tony noticed that Sam was uneasy and anxious to find out why he was there.

"Well," Tony was going to get to the point, "I assume you're wondering why I asked for you to fly up here?" He squirmed in his seat, "Uh, well, uh, yes as a matter-of-fact." Tony looked at Derek, then at him, "Sam, what do you think about my participation at Five Star?" This was the main question Tony wanted to ask. He watched Sam very closely. "Well, to be honest," he was choosing every word carefully, "I was quite surprised. It was no secret that Five Star has been slipping financially for some time; I, well, most people in the industry thought a merger was being staged." That was the statement Tony was waiting for, "A merger. I wasn't informed of any discussion of that. Could you expound on those discussions?" Sam frowned, "Uh, well, I don't know exactly how far the discussions went. Claude and I met frequently on the subject. Colonial Oil was very interested. But Claude and yourself came to terms." Tony now knew; it wasn't only the cash he had been taking from Colonial but he was in for bigger things if the merger had taken place. "I presume that you were in favor of the merger?" He shook his head, "Yes. Five Star could have been put into a blue chipper immediately." "Weren't you worried about your position if they would have merged?" Tony questioned trying not to sound like an interrogator. "I just wanted the best for Five Star. I felt that my performance as Vice President would keep my position intact." Tony leaned forward, "Sam. Are you worried about your position, now that I'm in the picture?" He was being very careful, "Uh, I have some concern; yes. Claude says that you'll be handling the financial arm of the company. I really don't know where that leaves me." "Sam, you have no worries," Tony wanted to put him at ease, "We need your help. Cole Industries is becoming involved in many other areas than oil. We need the sharpest finance man around and from what Claude tells me, you're one of the best." He could see the relief in Parkinson's face as he moved forward in his char. "Mr. Cole, what do you mean?" Tony rose from his chair and walked around the room, "Sam, first of all – I'm Tony, not Mr. Cole. As I said, we're moving into many things very quickly and we need help. Let me give you a very quick rundown. Within the last eight days, Cole Industries has acquired many acres of prime Southern California land of which we intend to build a shopping plaza and industrial park. Of course, you know about the Five Star acquisition." Sam was listening intently. Tony continued, "We acquired one of the largest construction companies in Illinois plus our own architectural firm. Besides building the shopping plaza, Cole will build restaurants, department stores, and who knows what else." He looked at Derek, "Now, Sam, maybe you can understand why we need a financial expert and quick." Parkinson was sold 100%. Tony painted a beautiful picture. Sam was intrigued, "That is amazing. It sounds like you want to meet your challenge immediately. What can I do to help?" I want you to become Vice President of Finance for Cole Industries. Which means you'll retain the control of Five Star Oil's finances as well as the rest of Cole's interests. Your salary at Five Star is $75,000. Right?" Sam nodded in agreement. Tony went on, "We will double that salary if you'll accept?" He didn't have to wait for a response. Parkinson nearly leaped from his chair, "Accept! Hell, yes. I'd love it. You're giving me the chance of a lifetime. When do I start working for Cole Industries?" Tony put a hand on Sam's shoulder, "As soon as possible; but I want you to take care of some matters at Five Star before you take control of Cole Industries." Tony moved to his desk and picked up a handful of papers, "Derek and I have been going over the Five Star books..." he noticed that Sam's excited look switched to fright... "And we couldn't help but notice a few problem areas." He directed Sam to the investments that cost Five Star millions, "The investments shown here, have to be dissolved...sold somehow immediately. Can you get rid of them?" The face of fright switched back to anxiety as

Sam answered, "Well, it won't be easy, but I'll try. I don't understand why they didn't payoff." Tony looked directly at him and said sternly, "At Cole Industries, we don't try. We do! Do you feel you can fit into that way of doing business?" With a wide grin, Sam said, "Tony, don't worry about a thing. I'll recover the largest part of those losses quickly." "How quickly?" Sam was confused, "Uh, a month, maybe two." Tony once again said sternly, "No, Sam, not a month or two; a week should be enough time. Don't you think?" He rubbed his hands together and licked his lips, "Yeh, of course, uh, one week. I'll do it." Tony put out his hand and smiled, "Sam. I can't tell you how pleased I am that you're joining Cole Industries." He shook Tony and Derek's hand vigorously, "I can't tell you, how much I appreciate the opportunity you're giving me. I'd like to return to Houston right away so I can start moving on the problem areas." Tony nodded in agreement, "I think that's a great idea. I'll be in Houston Thursday, we can talk more then. Rodney will drive you to the airport, and Sam, I'm truly pleased that we'll be working together. Have a good flight, and give my best to Claude." Sam Parkinson left a very happy man.

Derek extended his hand to Tony, "Beautiful, he sucked it up as fast as you could spit it out. Tony, you know, I never realized that you were so damn shrewd. Did you learn that from Jonathan?" Tony shook his head, "No, <u>that</u> Jonathan didn't teach me...Sister Carolyn did." He thought for a moment about the Sister he cared for so much.

Derek was going to interview the four pilots, Theresa was pouring over swatches of wall paper and carpet...she was having a ball. Tony left to have lunch with Henri Vachon, an old friend.

As Tony entered the restaurant, Café Louis, a quaint French eatery visited only by the well-to-do; the talk and looks were switched immediately to him. The Maitre' di quickly approached him, "Good afternoon, Mr. Cole. It is such a pleasure for Café Louis to serve you today. Would you please follow me?" He was seated at a corner table, fairly secluded by plants. "I hope this will be to your satisfaction, Mr. Cole," the Maitre' di was good. "This is perfect. I'm meeting a Mr. Vachon, Henri Vachon." The Maitre' di grinned from ear-to-ear, "Yes sir, I'll bring a bottle of our best wine, also." Tony smiled, "That will be fine, but I'd like a Jack Daniels on the rocks, too." "Right away, Mr. Cole." The Maitre' di left. It was a standing rule that he was always early for a lunch, or whatever type of meeting he may be having. Tony felt that being early showed interest in the meeting. He was half an hour early for lunch today.

A large, impeccably neat gentleman, dressed in a grey pinstripe suit made his way to Tony's table, "Tony, how are you?" he said putting out his hand. Tony rose and with his gracious grin said, "Bob, hello! I'm doing fine, and you? Join me for a drink?" "Yes, I'd love to," the large man said as he sat heavily, "I'm doing real good." Tony motioned for the waiter to get a drink for him. Bob Underwood, President of American National bank had been a long time friend and business associate of Jonathan Stuyvesant. Tony deposited his inheritance in Bob's bank.

Bob asked, "So, what's going on with you, Tony?" Tony lit a cigarette and said, "I'm making some investments and acquisitions. In fact, I'm forming a company. Right now it is in the speculation stage, but should take form shortly. In fact, I'm glad I ran into you. I'd like to discuss some things with you, soon." Bob agreed to a meeting, "Tony, anytime you want, I'll be available." He finished his drink in one swallow and stood up, "Give me a call, Tony, soon. Thank you for the drink." Tony stood to shake his hand, "Do you think we could have that meeting later today?" Bob shook his head, "Of course; how's three o'clock in my office?" Tony agreed and Bob Underwood returned to his table.

Henri arrived at exactly twelve-thirty, the time set for the lunch. He wasn't exactly a handsome man, but he was considered very attractive by most women…of which he had many. He's short, five-nine, and slim at 165 lbs. Henri is only 32 but looks five years older (he wants it that way). He's always perfectly dressed nothing out of place, and always wearing the correct clothes. He and Tony had been friends in college. Henri was studying to be a doctor, as his father had been, but he had more interest in women and fashion than stethoscopes so he graduated with a degree in Marketing. It has been said that Henri's IQ is close to 150. He was valedictorian of his high school class in the rich Detroit suburb of Bloomfield Hills. He owns three successful stores of men's and women's apparel all located in the better Chicago suburban areas. Henri's was one the first stores in Chicago to energetically introduce designer clothing to men. He traveled to Europe (never the Orient, God forbid) three times a year to stay on top of that market. He and Tony haven't seen each other in about a year.

After the hello's and good-to-see you's, and ordering of more drinks, Henri said, "Who the hell would have ever thought seven years ago, that we'd ever be sitting here like this? Hell, look at you; a fucking multi-millionaire at twenty-eight, and a celebrity, too. Shit, there isn't a magazine or a newspaper without an article about Tony Cole. Congratulations, old friend." Tony thanked him, "Thanks, but I wouldn't say you've done all that bad. How is business anyway?" The waiter came to take their order. After ordering, Henri answered, "Well, I wish I could say it's booming, but with this damn economy…it's hard." Tony didn't wait for further discussion, "How would you like to become a Vice President of my new company… Cole Industries?" Henri was shocked, "What? Explain further!" Tony went on, "We are involved in oil, real estate/land development, shopping centers, building/construction, architecture, and restaurants right now. I want to enter the department store business, too. I need someone who's knowledgeable in the retail field that I can trust. That's where you come in. You would be a Vice President of Retail Operations at Cole Industries and you would also carry the title President of Cole Department Stores. How's it sound so far?" He sat disbelieving, "Tony, this is amazing. It sounds great so far; but what do I do with my present business?" Tony waited for the waiter to serve their meal, then replied, "I have a proposal for you on that. How much are your stores worth?" Henri answered quickly, "Well, my best store does a little better than 2 million, next best does right at two, and the third is at about one and a half million. If I were to sell, I'd have to have ten million so I'd make some money after all my liabilities were taken care of." Tony leaned on one elbow, "Why don't you sign everything over to me – liabilities included – and I'll give you a check for one million dollars to you personally. You then accept the position I mentioned – what's your yearly salary now?" "Sixty to seventy grand!" Tony added, "Okay, you accept my proposed position at $125,000 a year. Now, how does it sound?" Henri put his hand out, "There's no decision; I think it's a helluva deal for both of us. When shall we finalize this deal?" Tony was pleased, "How about immediately. By the way, Derek Hill is the Executive Vice President of Cole Industries." Henri shook his head in satisfaction, "Terrific, I always liked Derek …he can really round up the ladies. I thought he was a lawyer?" Tony nodded, "He was." "Hey, what the hell is your real name, I forgot I've been calling you Henri for so long." Henri looked around so that no one could hear him, "Oliver Vincent Jr.; but nobody else needs to know!" Tony laughed. They finished their lunch with Tony explaining the other divisions of Cole Industries.

As they were leaving, Tony put his hand on his shoulder, "I didn't say this before, but you'll have an office in the Stuyvesant Building. I'd like you to come over for our first company meeting Friday and a cocktail party Friday night at the mansion. Okay?" Henri looked at Tony, "Sure. I'll be ready for both. Should I bring a date to the party?" "Of course," Tony said, "I want to see if you've still got good taste." They both laughed as they left the restaurant.

While driving to meet Bob Underwood, Tony phoned Alfred at the mansion. "Alfred, I want you to prepare for a cocktail party Friday night. There will be at least fourteen guests, but plan for eighteen to be safe." Alfred replied, "I'll get started on it right away, Tony.

His thoughts turned to how he had changed so many lives in such a short period; Derek, his dearest friend; Theresa, cute little Theresa; Claude Benaforte, knows the oil business but doesn't know how to handle finances; Carmen, he never asked for anything; Mike Emerson, he just wants to design the ultimate structure; Henri, huh, Oliver Vincent Jr.; Paul Krug, strong – the man sure knows building – Georgina's father; Sam Parkinson, oh, am I going to change his life; Peter Weyland, I'm still not sure about him; Maggie, lovely Maggie, it will be good to see her again…it seems like its been months…he began to picture her on the tennis court, then walking away from him and turning to look at him, then her wondrous beauty in the black evening gown. He wasn't aware that the car had stopped, "Tony, we're here," Rodney exclaimed.

Bob Underwood was in the lobby of the bank when he entered, "Tony, right on time…just like Jonathan; he was never late…you remind me of him." "Thank you, Bob, I take that as a compliment," Tony replied. "You should, it was meant to be." Bob said as he led Tony to the elevator that would take them to his office.

After they sat down, Bob asked, "How 'bout a drink…Jack Daniels, right?" Tony nodded, "Yes, I'd like one, thank you." As Bob poured the drinks, Tony said, "Bob. I'd like your help. I want to be introduced to a bank in Houston and Los Angeles. I'll deposit ten million in each if they'll guarantee me unlimited credit." "Is that all? Tony, that's a very simple request. All I have to do is make two phone calls." Bob was pleased that the request was small, and he could be of help to Tony. "Fine. Please transfer the funds as soon as possible. Bob, I would like you to recommend somebody who could handle personnel matters for the company I'm forming. I'll need someone who can put together a good benefit package, insurance program, etc., etc., you know what I need. Could you help me?" Bob rubbed his chin, "Would you mind telling me what type of company you're forming?" "No, not at all," Tony asked for a drink refill," "The name will be Cole Industries with interests in oil, land, real estate, retail stores, construction, restaurants, and nobody knows what else." "Sounds exciting. Starting from the ground up. How much are you planning on paying for this position?" He was interested in the new company. "That depends on the person, but it will be attractive." Tony replied. Bob moved around his desk, "Tony, why don't I take the position?" Tony looked at him for along moment then said, "Why?" Bob walked around the room, "Look, Tony, I'm forty-five years old, at my age, I'm probably the youngest President of a bank this size in the country. Tony, I'm bored, what you're doing excites the hell out of me. I could be an asset in financial matters and investors if needed. What do you say?" Tony stood and looked at Bob, "I think that's a great idea, you'll be the new Vice President of Personnel for Cole Industries. When can you start?" They shook hands. Bob Underwood was elated, "I'll start immediately. I can't just walk out of the bank, but I can start working on the things you need while I'm closing out my duties here. Okay?" Tony had no idea, when he came to see him that he was going to land such a plum, "Bob, that's perfect. I'd like you to attend a meeting Friday morning in the Stuyvesant Building...which is where your new office will be...and we'll have a cocktail party Friday night for the entire staff and their wives to get to know each other. Oh, by the way, what's your salary now?" Bob laughed, "Salary doesn't really matter, Tony, I'm quite comfortable from my investments. But to answer your question, my salary is $125,000 plus incentives." "Will it be sufficient if we leave it at that for now?" "Very sufficient!" Bob smiled. "My secretary will inform you of the time on Friday, I'll be in Houston the next two days. Don't forget about the banks I first asked you about. I'll see you Friday." He left as Bob said, "Thanks, Tony. We're going to make one helluva team. The banks will be set up by tomorrow afternoon."

Tony and Derek spent the evening in the office discussing how Cole Industries stood. Derek had been working night and day preparing contracts to be ready. He hired a young lawyer to assist him, but he got all contracts prepared, besides hiring a secretary and a pilot. Theresa was acting like a foreman, ordering the decorators around as they painted, hammered, carpeted, moved furniture, and took very few breaks. Theresa had them working continually. She was determined to have every office completed by Friday morning, and she was going to be proud of the Cole Industries Offices.

The bright orange and blue Lear jet was delivered at Midway airport early Wednesday morning by the new Cole pilot, Chris Pike. Tony and Derek were there when the jet landed. They immediately took off for Houston. Tony, Derek, and Claude Benaforte spent the entire day going over Five Star's books; Tony pointing out areas where he felt changes should be made. He told Claude about Sam Parkinson. When Claude was convinced of Sam's plot, he was enraged, "I'll kill that little son-of-a-bitch!" Tony informed Claude of his own plot against Sam. "You smart, mother-fucker. I mean to tell you, I'm one happy Texan that you're workin' with me and Five Star. Do you think it'll work?" "Well," Tony smiled, "If it doesn't both Five Star and Cole Industries are in trouble, but don't worry; I have a feeling that Mr. Parkinson will find a way to dump those bankrupt companies." They drank a toast to Sam Parkinson.

Tony sat down, "Claude, I want Five Star to open a West Coast headquarters. What do you think?" Claude choked on his drink, "My God, boy, how ta hell do you suppose we do that. Have you plum forgot that you just laid out millions to bail us out of trouble?" "Claude, the majority of Five Stars drilling fields and exploration interests are located in Southern California. It only makes sense to have some kind of headquarters created there. We'll have the funds soon. The money Parkinson receives from the sale of those companies will give us what we need to start construction the rest will come from bank loans. We'll construct a large office building, Five Star will occupy whatever space needed, and the rest of the building is leased out; that way the lessees will pay for the building." Claude sat dumbfounded, "Ya know, I think I've learned more about business in the last fifteen minutes than I have in the last twenty years. I jus can't get over it...one smart fucker. Hell, let's do it. Let's build us a Texas style office building in oil rich California."

Claude sprung for an entire night out; dinner and a lot of heavy drinking. The formal signing of the transaction was set for noon the next day. Claude had arranged for a press conference at the signing.

The press conference was filled with questions about what else Tony was planning. The press was told only that <u>he</u> personally was investing into

Five Star. They know nothing about Cole Industries. That surprise will have to wait another day…in Chicago. When they returned to the office, Sam Parkinson came in, "Gentlemen, what a great day this is. Not only have you just agreed to supply some cash to Five Star, but we just sold the companies we owned that was draining us dry. Five Star Oil is now extremely solvent. Was that fast enough for you Mr. Cole?" Claude started to stand, but Tony stopped him, "That's great, Sam, are the transactions complete?" He was grinning from ear to ear, "They were completed early this morning, but I wanted to wait until after the press conference to tell you. We are completely rid of those liabilities. Here are the signed papers." Tony handed them to Derek, "They're all in order, Tony," he said after examining them. Sam, still smiling, "Can we tell Claude now, Mr. Cole?" Tony lit a cigarette slowly, "He already knows, Sam." Parkinson now looked puzzled. Tony continued, "Claude knows everything. I told him yesterday. Now, I'll tell you what we've decided…Sam, we feel that you should see how fast you can get your traitorous, Ivy League, cheating ass back to Colonial Oil, that is if they'll have you." Sam stood stunned, speechless. Claude rose to his feet, "Sam, I'm a very angry Texan right now, and I'd do as Tony says before I kick the hell outa you." He realized that Tony had known about his dual role all along, he began to back out of the room, "Congratulations, Mr. Cole, you're as good as I've heard. I'm sorry Claude." He shut the door as he left. Claude was jumping up and down, "Sonufabitch, you were right. You pegged him all the way. We can build us another headquarters. Tony, I don't know how to thank you!" Tony put his hand on Claude's shoulder, "Just bring in a lot of oil… pahdna!" They laughed aloud.

CHAPTER NINE

It was late when Tony and Derek arrived in Chicago, but Tony had to see how the offices were coming along. He wanted everything ready when his staff met there for the first time. Theresa called him in Houston and said they may have to work all night to finish. She had been at the office continually since the decorators had begun working. Tony was really proud of her. Theresa was talking to the decorator as they stepped from the elevator. She smiled and ran toward them, "Oh, I'm so glad you're here. They're almost finished; let me show you around." She led them to Tony's office, "We'll start here, as you can see, we've done nothing, but Mr. Hill, Executive Vice President of Cole Industries, take a look at where you'll be spending sixteen hours a day for the rest of your life." She opened the door adjoining Tony's office. Derek exclaimed, "Beautiful, God damn, this is fantastic. I love it!" She pulled his face down and kissed him, "I'm so glad you like it." The office was totally masculine, a large mahogany desk with a dark brown tufted leather chair. There was a couch and three chairs to match his chair. The pictures were all Nieman sports prints. Theresa could not have done a better job of designing Derek's office. Derek picked her up by the waist, "I'm going to take you to dinner to show my appreciation for a job perfectly done. Exactly the way I wanted it." Tony agreed on the excellence of the office. "Come on, I want you to see the rest. They're almost done, another hour and every office will be ready for it occupant." The conference room was directly across the hall from Derek's office with an adjoining door to Tony's office, which was located at the very end of the hall, they stopped there first. As she led them down the hall, she opened each door and went into a dissertation about each. The closest office to

Tony and Derek's was Bob Underwood's, right next to Derek's. Across the hall was the office of Peter Weyland, Paul Krug's office was next to Peter's, Mike Emerson is next to Bob's, Carmen Lombardi's and Henri Vachon's were the next two directly across from each other. Then came the general office area on each side of the hall. When the tour ended, Theresa waited for their response. Tony looked at Derek, Derek looked at Tony, Tony spoke first, "Ah, I guess it'll do." Derek shrugged his shoulders, "Yeh, but that's about all." They looked at Theresa, and she said, "Ohhh, you two, you really like it. I'm so happy you like it, don't you?" "We love it!" They said in unison. She hugged both of them. Tony said, "Theresa, you've been working very hard and you look tired, but I'm up for buying a round of drinks. Are you two interested?" Derek took one of Theresa's arms and Tony took the other and they headed toward the nearest bar. As they entered the elevator, Derek said aloud, "Cole Industries comes alive tomorrow with a beautiful new home."

The first meeting of the Cole Industries Executive staff was to begin at nine a.m. and a press conference was to be held at two p.m. Tony arrived at six-thirty, Derek around seven. Theresa came in about seven-thirty. She had stopped to pick up cigars, cigarettes, and coffee. The three of them were excited. They were guessing on who would be the first to arrive. Derek said, "My guess is Henri, he's really ambitious, hell he was ambitious in college." Theresa shook her head, "No, it will be Carmen Lombardi, because he's so thankful to Tony." "You're both wrong," commented Tony," Peter Weyland will be first." "Why do you say Peter?" Derek asked. "Because he's the best businessman of the bunch," Tony replied. No sooner had the words left his mouth when there was a knock at the door. Theresa went to see who it was. She returned in just a few seconds, "I get so tired of you being right." She looked at Tony, "Peter Weyland is in my office."

Tony took Peter to his office, discussed his flight and hotel accommodations, and inquired about Maggie. The others began arriving in the order of Henri, Paul Krug, Mike Emerson, Carmen, and finally Bob Underwood. Theresa assembled them in the conference room. Tony wanted Derek to be seated at his right and Bob Underwood to his left. He didn't care where the others sat.

They were all seated, not saying a word when Tony entered. It was interesting to see the arrangement of such different personalities. The right side of the table had Derek, Peter, Mike, and Carmen. The left side was Bob, Henri, and Paul.

"Good morning gentlemen. Welcome to Cole Industries. Let me introduce you to each other. I must say, we have assembled many different personalities, but we have assembled the best in each field of endeavor. Let me start with Derek Hill. Derek will be our Executive Vice President and my right hand man. You all can turn to Derek as well as me. He'll be working very close with all of you." Looking at Bob, "Bob Underwood is our Vice President of personnel. Bob will be putting together our benefit and insurance programs. I would appreciate it if you would give him the details on the programs you have had in your respective businesses. Since Cole Industries will have its own benefit and insurance programs your present employees will be covered under our new plan. You can assure your employees they will be better off with the new plan. I'd like for each of you to sit down with Bob as soon as possible. Bob has been the president of American National Bank here in Chicago for the past five years. He has a vast knowledge of finance and personnel. Please listen to him." Tony pointed to Henri, "Henri Vachon will be our Vice President of retail operations. I have known him since our college days at Northwestern. I must say this, Henri; he is the black sheep of his family because he's not a doctor, as his father in Michigan. But, he's certainly not a black sheep to the retail industry in Chicago. In six short years, he has built one of the finest men's and women's clothing store chains in the state. Some of you may have purchased something from Henri's before. Cole Industries will take over his operation immediately. Henri will begin working out a plan to complete department stores to rival the major stores in each area of operation. We'll need a lot of information and suggestions from all of you in this area. Welcome Henri."

Tony next looked at Paul Krug, "Our next Vice President is a man I have admired since my high school days. Paul Krug and I had something in common then, we both thought very much of the same girl, Georgina Krug, his daughter." Paul smiled, as did the others. Tony continued, "Paul is a self-made man. I want you all to know, he's tough. Paul Krug is the Krug in Krug construction; the largest construction firm in Chicago. I should state the best also! Paul will be Vice President of building and construction. He's going to be very busy. It's a true pleasure to join forces with Paul Krug. Welcome Paul."

Tony's eyes moved to the other side of the table and stopped at Carmen, "It is such a pleasure to introduce Carmen Lombardi. He has been a dear friend of mine for the past several years. Carmen has agreed to become our Vice President of food service, restaurants actually. We are going to build the best restaurants on this continent. That is an easy statement for me to make because of Carmen Lombardi. He has been a Maitre' di for over 20 years at a famous Chicago restaurant. If we, Cole Industries, are going to build great restaurants, he'll do it. Thank you, Carmen, for joining our company."

"Mike Emerson," Tony turned his eyes to Mike, "is going to be extremely busy for the next many months. Mike is our Vice President of architecture and design. He has owned his own architectural firm for almost ten years. Yes, Mike is a friend, too. Ever since I've known him, Mike Emerson has wanted to design, what he calls, the ultimate structure. Well, we're going to give him the chance to design, not only one ultimate structure, but many. Mike, you and Paul will have a chance to go down in building history, because I want every building bearing the Cole name to be unique. Welcome to Cole, Mike."

Tony shifted his look to Peter, "We come to our final new member, although Peter Weyland is the last to be introduced, he was the fourth member of Cole Industries behind myself, Theresa, and Derek. In fact, it was Peter who gave me the idea of what I was going to do. If it weren't for him, none of you would be here today. Three years ago, Peter was an aspiring lawyer in Los Angeles. He dabbled in real estate and found that there was money to be made. Well, he made some, quite a bit to be exact. So for the past three years, he has been wheeling and dealing in one of the toughest, but lucrative, fields possible. Most of you, well all of you, I have known for quite a while. I've known Peter Weyland for a little more than a week, but I have some close friends that have assured me that I won't go wrong with him because he's one of the brightest real estate developers around. Peter is our Vice President of real estate and land development. I hope you'll make Peter and his lovely wife, Maggie, feel at home in their move to Chicago. Welcome to Cole and Chicago, Peter."

Tony rose from his chair, "So, now that we've all been introduced, let's have some coffee and start talking business." Theresa wheeled in a tray of coffee and pastries. Tony declined both, "I'd like to start from the beginning of where we want Cole Industries to start. I have already done some investing.

As most of you have read, Cole Industries owns 51% of Five Star Oil in Houston, Texas. For those of you, who might not know of Five Star Oil, it is a small oil company. Claude Benaforte started the company back in the wildcatting days. He owned all of the stock except for a very small part owned by each of his two brothers. We intend to make Five Star a much larger company. Claude will run the daily operation of the oil company and will have no say at Cole Industries, but Cole will operate the financial and personnel end of the business. We are going to build a west coast headquarters as soon as possible. I'll come back to that later in the discussion. Any questions about Five Star Oil?" Paul Krug had a question, "I have one, Tony. Will the profits from the oil company be seen anywhere in Cole Industries?" "Yes," Tony replied, "the 51% ownership is owned by Cole Industries, not Tony Cole. So Cole will receive their share, but most of the oil profits will be put into investments in an attempt to enlarge the company. Any other questions?" He looked at Peter, "Yes Peter." "Are there plans, at this time, of what investments will be made?" Tony shook his head, "no." Tony looked at each man, "Anybody else?" There were no other questions about Five Star.

Lighting a cigarette, he went on to other business. "Okay, I'd like to discuss our first endeavor. Peter and I closed a deal on some prime commercial land in southern California. We are going to build a shopping plaza on part of the land. Derek, Peter, and I will be contacting some of the better retail operators in the country in an attempt to convince them to open an outlet in our plaza. The first Cole department store will be one anchor in the plaza. Mike's department will design the plaza and the store. Paul, you'll build both. Henri will put together the store products, fixtures, and personnel. Peter's area will handle the leasing in the plaza. Located on the same grounds as the plaza, but not attached, we'll build a restaurant, a very interesting, unique restaurant. Again, Mike will design, Paul will build, and Carmen will take care of the restaurant itself. Any questions?" Mike raised his hand, "Tony, you've definitely got my mind running rampant, but I have one major question. How am I going to design a shopping center, a department store, and a restaurant in a short period of time, which I presume you want?" A wide smile crossed Tony's face, "Mike, as I told you the other day, I want you to design. You'll have to hire some people. Hire people you can be sure of. There is no way that you can do it yourself. Just be sure, everything goes through you. I'm sure you'll be pulling your hair out before this day is over." Paul chimed in, "I must admit, Tony, I'm damned excited, but I feel I'm in the same boat as Mike. I can't see how I can put together a work force that I'm confident in, on a short notice. Exactly how soon do you want to start this venture?" Tony turned to Derek, "You answer that Derek." "Paul," Derek approached his question, "Everything is set to start tomorrow, if we could. We'll begin as soon as Mike completes the rendering. Obviously, we want to start right away. This shopping plaza is our top priority." Paul Krug smiled," I like it. This'll put some excitement back in my life." "Same here, this is really exciting!" exclaimed Mike. "Carmen, do you have any questions?" Tony pointed to him. "Uh, yesa, Tony, I most excited too. Uh, Tony, whata kinda restaurant you want?" Tony put both hands on the table and leaned towards Carmen, "That is why you are the Vice President of food services for Cole Industries. What do you suggest?" Carmen with a broad smile, "Ya mean, you wan me ta tell you? Yeh, okay, I tell you. I think very important thing is what it's a gonna look like an da menu, the most. No mattuh where a ya go, Cheecago, New Yorka, or Caleefornia you serva da great steak, prima rib and a fancy quality dessert an a you gotta 'em." Carmen leaned back in his chair and sighed. "Carmen, that's your department, if you think that's the way to go, then that's the way it will be. Any objections?" Tony was attempting to involve everybody in all aspects. There was nothing but agreement. "Fine, we'll be a prime steak house. Thank you, Carmen. Let's move on," Tony insisted.

The restaurant and department store I would like to see duplicated in other cities, but California will be our top priority, as Derek explained. Finding property in Houston and here, in Chicago, will be up to Peter," Tony added. Paul raised a question, "Tony, how soon could I get out to California to view the property?" Mike Emerson added, "The same goes for me, when can we go out?" Tony lit another cigarette. He was pleased to see the enthusiasm, especially from Mike and Paul, "When do you want to go?" "I'd like to go tomorrow," was Mike's answer. "Me too," Paul said. Tony looked at Peter, who had excitement written all over his face, Peter said, "Tony, I'd be glad to go along and show the sight, we could get the first flight out tomorrow." Bob Underwood jumped in, "I'd like to see it, too!" Tony was beaming, he looked at Derek, who was smiling at him, "Why don't you all go tomorrow, take the weekend. Leave in the morning; spend the night in L.A. and fly back Sunday. Oh, I didn't even tell you, Cole Industries has its own Lear jet and pilot. You can take it. Henri, Carmen could you go out tomorrow?" Both men eagerly agreed. Tony said,

"Good, it's settled." He turned to Theresa. She said, "I'll inform Chris to get the plane ready. What time?" Tony looked at Derek, "Six o'clock okay?" All agreed on the time.

"Gentlemen," Tony said with a broad grin, "it truly pleases me to see your enthusiasm for our initial project. Peter, while you're at the plaza sight, show them the rest of the land. That is where we're going to build an industrial park. In fact, the new Five Star Oil west coast headquarters will be the first tenant. So, Mike, Paul, and Peter there is more work for you. We'll design, build, and lease the property. "Fantastic!" Mike exclaimed. Paul Krug smiled and held up his coffee cup in a toast of agreement. Peter smiled and shook his head. Bob Underwood stood up, "Tony, would you mind if I say something?" Tony gave him the floor. "Gentlemen, I've been in business for many years. I've done business with some of the great financial minds, great builders, people with high initiative, and people with great intuitiveness. The one person, who came close to possessing all of these qualities, was Jonathan Stuyvesant. I can now say that I've met someone who doesn't come close, but does possess all of these qualities. I for one, would like to say that I'm damned excited and proud to be associated with Tony Cole." Everybody applauded, even Theresa. Tony waited for a moment, "Well, thank you, Bob, but the credit must be shared with Derek and Theresa. Believe me, we wouldn't be this far without them. Now, none of you has seen your new offices. Why don't we take a break and allow Theresa to give you a tour of your new home. The press conference is going to be a two p.m. Let's meet here at eight o'clock Monday morning to discuss your feelings about what you've seen in California." They all stood up and Tony went to each one and shook their hands, then they all shook each other's hands. Theresa led them into the hallway toward their new offices. Derek looked at Tony, "Tony, I want to thank you for including me in this. With the people you have persuaded to come with us, we can't miss." Tony put his hand on Derek's shoulder, "Listen, buddy, I want to thank you. You're right, we can't miss."

The press contingent was all arranged. The entire Cole Industries staff was seated in the front row. Tony stepped to the podium, "Ladies and gentlemen, I thank you for coming. The past two weeks have been very interesting, to say the least. You fine people of the press, have been much more interested in me and my new wealth than I ever expected. I have had very little time to be by myself. Your counterparts met my plane in Los Angeles, they met me in my hotel in Houston, and again here, in Chicago, at the airport. I'm continually getting phone calls asking for interviews. This has been a totally new experience for me, but I must be honest with you, I've enjoyed it. Jonathan Stuyvesant left me a lot of money, a fortune, and something that meant much more to me than the money. He left me with a challenge. This challenge has caused quite a stir within the media; you've had a field day with it. The one question everybody asks is how am I going to meet the challenge? I wasn't able to answer that, because I didn't know. Well, I know now, and that is why you were invited here today. Ladies and gentlemen, you are here to see a corporation take its first step. You are here to witness the birth of Cole Industries, Inc. You're going to see it grow into a large, profitable, multi-national company. What is Cole Industries all about? Let me introduce the people that have decided to be a part of this birth. When you see who they are and what capacity they'll be in, then you'll know where we're headed. The first member I'd like to introduce is my personal secretary, Theresa Williams; he motioned for her to stand up. This lovely young lady was one of you until we met. Theresa was a very eager staff reporter for the L.A. Times, who persuaded me to give an interview. She was so good, that I then persuaded her to work with me. Theresa was the first member of the Cole Industries team. She is the person for you to contact if you want an interview from me. I'm very proud to have Theresa with us. The next member is my very best friend, in fact, he's always been by best friend. Until joining forces with me, he was a struggling attorney here in Chicago. He is coming to Cole in the capacity of Executive Vice President, my right arm. Ladies and gentlemen, Mr. Derek Hill. By the way ladies, he's not married." Laughter filled the room as Derek stepped next to Tony.

"It gives me great pleasure to present a man with awesome credentials. For the past five years, he has been the president of American national bank in Chicago. He is on the board of directors of that bank and two other corporations. He has joined Cole Industries as our new Vice President of Personnel, and I'm adding Finance to that title, Mr. Bob Underwood." He shook Tony's hand then took his spot next to Derek. The media looked surprised.

"Going on with the introductions, Cole Industries will be heavily involved in the building and construction industry and the man who'll head up that department as Vice President of Building and Construction is Mr. Paul Krug. Paul is the owner of Krug Construction, one of the largest construction firms in Chicago." Paul moved in next to Theresa.

"Since we're going to build things, somebody must design them. Cole Industries will be a very unique company, and the uniqueness will begin with the architecture of our buildings. We want to hear people say, "Hey, that's a Cole building." For us to achieve that, Cole Industries will have a very smart, artistically aggressive man in charge of our architecture. Our Vice President of Architecture and Design is Mike Emerson, graduate of Purdue University. Ladies and gentlemen, Mr. Mike Emerson." Mike stepped next to Paul.

Tony continued, "The reason I'm introducing each member separately is two-fold. One, is so that you can see the quality of Executives Cole Industries will have running the company. Two, I want you to get it all straight right here. Okay, you now know that we're going to design and build some buildings, correct? Well, that means that we'll have to buy some land so we'll have a place to put our new buildings. We've taken care of that by having a real estate and land development division. We've gone after another lawyer to take over this area. We went all the way to California to get him. It's a pleasure to introduce the Vice President of Real Estate and Land Development, Mr. Peter Weyland." Peter took his place next to Bob.

Tony flashed a grin, "You know, this reminds me of when I introduced our high school basketball team." Everybody laughed. "Now then, we're architects, builders, and land developers. So, I suppose you want to know what kind of buildings. Alright, how about a shopping plaza with one of its anchors a Cole department store. We have the land to begin building this shopping plaza immediately. We'll break ground shortly in southern California, with intentions of building two more, one in Houston and one right here in good old Chicago. That means that we'll need someone to be in charge of our retail operations. Have any of you ever purchased any clothing from Henri's? If so, you purchased that from our new Vice President of Retail Operations, Mr. Henri Vachon." Henri had a broad smile as he moved in next to Peter.

Tony motioned for Carmen to come up with him, "The next person I'd like to introduce many of you may recognize and then maybe you won't recognize him at all." Tony had his arm around Carmen's shoulder. "You see, this gentleman, right here, has been a Maitre' di at one of Chicago's finer restaurants for over 20 years. He knows more about food and the presentation of food than anyone in Chicago, that's my opinion. He's going to be our Vice President of Food Services. We are going to build three restaurants, one in each of the three cities I've previously mentioned. Ladies and gentlemen, my friend, Mr. Carmen Lombardi." Carmen hugged Tony around the waist.

Tony began his summation as Carmen moved beside Mike, "I thank each one of you for coming. I have given you an overview of what Cole Industries will be all about. So when you see this trademark," Derek held up a large bright orange sign with bright blue "Cii" on it, "You'll know that it's a company on the move. Now, I'd like to have you circulate and ask any questions of any of us. Thank you, again."

Maggie Weyland was in the audience, and was amazed at this man, Tony Cole. She wondered, "How can a man who has all that money, and be that good looking, be so nice?" He had introduced each person with patience, making sure that each one had his moment. He didn't have to.

"Mr. Cole, you didn't mention anything about your interests in Five Star Oil. Why? One of many questions being thrown at him by the reporters. He smiled, "First of all, the interest in Five Star Oil is by Cole Industries, not Tony Cole. I just figured that was old news." The entire group answered questions for a quarter of an hour, or so, before the conference finally broke up. Tony said to all the staff members, "Well, we'll all be known tomorrow. Why don't we get ready for a little party tonight? Thanks again, to all of you."

During their ride to the hotel, Peter talked incessantly, to Maggie, about Cole Industries and Tony Cole. When she finally got in a word, she said, "Peter, I've never seen you this way. You really are excited, aren't you?" He replied, "Maggie, this is going to be the most exciting venture of the century! Tony Cole Is a genius! He'll build one of the largest conglomerates this country has ever seen! Oh, I've got to return to California tomorrow. We're all going out on the corporate jet to view our property." "What am I supposed to do? I thought we were going to see Chicago this weekend?" Maggie asked. "I know, but we'll have plenty of time to see Chicago after we move here," Peter reminded. Maggie responded, "I wonder if Tony could arrange for somebody to show me around, maybe I'll look at some houses. What do you think?" Peter answered, "Terrific, I'll call him as soon as we get to the hotel and see if he can arrange it." Peter did call, and Tony said he would arrange it for Maggie.

CHAPTER TEN

She was putting on her earrings, when the thought entered her mind, "I wonder if Tony will like this dress?" Her face flushed. Maggie could not understand what had come over her. When she first saw him, today, she felt her breathing change and her palms began to sweat. Now, she's wondering if he'll like her dress. She sat down and stared into the mirror. Maybe I could pretend being sick, and not attend the party. No, can't do that. Why are you acting like this? You love Peter, your marriage is okay. I'm really being silly; so what if he's the one man in the world that made Roni Scott chase him to Texas. Yeh, so what, she's damned in love with him. She said he's wonderful – in all ways – that's it." She got up, "Peter, come on, let's go, I'm ready." He looked at her admiringly, "Damn, I don't think I've ever seen you look quite so lovely." She thanked him as she kissed his cheek, then bit her lip as she thought, "Oh, I hope Tony thinks so."

The guests were in the large parlor that Jonathan built especially for cocktail parties. Alfred had everything in its proper place, as usual. Tony wondered what he was going to do when Alfred retired to Florida. Alfred entered the parlor, "Mr. And Mrs. Weyland, Mr. Cole." As Tony walked toward them, he couldn't believe the way she looked. Her gown was light beige that covered only one shoulder, it accentuated her dark tan. Cold black hair shining, a gold choker and gold bracelets gave her the look of a Goddess. He thought, "She could pass for Cleopatra!" He shook Peter's hand, then took her hand in his, "I must admit, I can't remember seeing a more lovely lady, and to think you win at tennis, too." Maggie kissed his cheek; her heart was beating like a drum. Tony looked at her with a smile that melted most women, and Maggie was no exception, "Come on, we'll introduce you to the others." She couldn't wait to get away from him; he was scaring her to death. She was beginning to find it hard to control her emotions.

He introduced Maggie to the Lombardi's, the Krug's, Derek's date, Henri and his date, and the Underwood 's. "Tony, Tony my friend. My most handsome friend!" Stephanie Emerson squealed as she and Mike entered before Alfred could present them. Tony turned around just as Stephanie threw her arms around his neck and kissed him hard on the mouth. He pulled away, but kept his arms around her waist, "Stephanie, you look lovely. You know, every time I see you, I get more envious of Mike." She kissed him again then said quietly, "It's your fault, that you're envious. I was yours for the asking." Stephanie Emerson is the former Stephanie Alcott. Her father and Jonathan were close friends and she always had a crush on Tony. She was a year younger than he. Once, while they were both at college, they attended the same party and ended up sleeping together. Stephanie didn't have a crush on him anymore; she was in love with him and still is, even though she's happy with Mike and her two boys. Tony introduced Stephanie to Maggie and stated, "Stephanie is going to show you our fine city tomorrow. She's looking for a house, too." He left with the two of them talking.

Everybody talked and laughed throughout the evening. Tony was pleased that even though, there were so many different personalities; they were hitting it off beautifully. Late in the evening, Stephanie came up to Tony, "You know something? I want to thank you. For what you've done for Mike. He's so happy. He came home this afternoon and started drawing buildings. You won't let me forget you, will you?" Tony kissed her cheek, "No, because I want you to always care as much for me as I do you. You're one of my favorite people. I'm glad Mike is happy." Derek interrupted them, he was aware of Stephanie's feelings for Tony, and he didn't want her starting problems now. The Emerson's were the first to leave, one of their boys wasn't feeling well and they didn't want to leave him with a babysitter very long. Stephanie and Maggie got along fine and Stephanie told her, as she was leaving, that she'd pick her up around nine in the morning. The rest began to leave shortly after midnight. The men were excited about their trip to California. The party had been successful, the men got to know each other some, and so did the women.

When they were all gone, Tony asked Theresa if she'd like to join him for one more drink, but she said, "Thanks, but I'm really bushed. This has been a very exhausting day. Aren't you pooped?" "Not really, it has been the most fun day of my life. Good night." He then sat down with a drink and stared into the fire. Theresa looked back at him for a moment before retiring. She wondered what his thoughts were.

He was reading the morning paper; it was filled with articles about Cole Industries, all favorable. Alfred came in, "Tony, Mrs. Emerson is on the phone and would like to speak to you." Tony looked at his watch, eight o'clock. "Good morning, Stephanie. What do I owe this pleasure?" She said, "Tony, my son, Danny, is really sick. I have to take him to the doctor. I'm afraid I'll have to renege on showing Maggie around. Will you call her for me? I feel terrible." Tony thought, then answered, "Of course, is there anything I can do. Did Mike go to California?" She sighed, "Yes, I told Mike to go ahead and go, no, there's nothing you can do, it's just a fever and a cough, but I want him to see a doctor. You understand, don't you?" He sat for a moment and thought, "I'll ask Theresa to take her, hell she doesn't know Chicago. I could but, what the shit, I might as well do it. He called the hotel, "Peter Weyland's room please." She looked at her watch as she heard the phone ring, "God, that can't be Stephanie yet." She picked up the receiver, "Hello, this is Maggie Weyland." That same funny feeling struck the instant he heard her voice, "Good morning, Maggie, this is Tony Cole." She almost dropped the phone. She had dreamed about him all night, and now, with Peter out-of-town, he's on the phone, "Uh, uh, I thought you were on your way to California?" "No, I wanted the guys to go alone, they'll be more themselves without me there," he said. She didn't know what to say, "Uh, well, okay." He interrupted, "Stephanie Emerson just phoned me, her son is pretty sick and she's taking him to the doctor. I'm afraid she won't be able to go today, but, uh, if you'd accept me as a substitute, I'd be glad to show you around?" She was flushed all over, this is what she dreamed about during the night, "Well, uh, yes, of course, that will be fine, but I don't want to put you out." He grinned, "Hey, this is my city; I'd love to show it to you. I'll pick you up in about an hour, and dress casual." She said, "Okay." The phone clicked. Maggie sat stunned. She's going to spend the day with the man she had dreams about. "Oh, my God," she said aloud. "I hope the real thing doesn't end like the dream!" She was flustered, "What am I going to wear, casual, what does he consider casual, jeans, no stupid, what if he's feeling the same feelings, now you are stupid, oh, what am I going to do , I mean wear. She began to cry, tears of fear.

He pulled the Mercedes in front of the hotel, went in and dialed her room. She answered, "Hello." He replied, "I'm in the lobby, whenever you're ready." She had been ready for ten minutes, "I'll be right down, I'm ready." He stood in front of the elevators to greet her.

The elevator door opened and she saw him immediately, her heart began to pound, she said to herself, "Don't act like such a schoolgirl, you're married and happy." He was smiling, in that fantastic way of his, as she emerged from the elevator, "Every time I see you, I'm more amazed. I think you get more beautiful each time!" Her knees weakened. She somehow got control of herself, "I could say the same thing, you know!" He took her arm and led her to the car, "by the time this day is over, you're never going to want to return to California." If he only knew, I might not want to already," she thought. "Oh, yeah, I love the sunshine," she said as she slid into the car.

As Tony drove away from the hotel, he said, "First, we'll go to the northern suburbs, I think you'd enjoy that area. Evanston is a great place. Do you like a college environment?" She shrugged, "I don't know, I've never lived in that type of atmosphere; if nothing else I'd be around some young people. Palm Springs is loaded with a lot of old fogies." They engaged in small talk about Chicago, with Tony pointing out certain spots along the route to Evanston, and Maggie remarking about California. Once they arrived in Evanston, Tony drove through the campus of Northwestern University and he told her some old college stories, then she would tell him a similar story she had at UCLA. After one of Tony's stories, Maggie laughed till she cried and her eye makeup ran down her face. "Oh no," she said as she rummaged through her purse, "I don't have a handkerchief or a Kleenex." Tony handed her his handkerchief. "Thank you," she laughed. When she touched the handkerchief to her face, she noticed that it smelled just like Tony, a soft fragrance that seemed to be always around him. Maggie's laughter faded as she turned to look at him. Here's a man she hardly knows but she's been having dreams about, she's having a great time with, why? "Tony," she said softly, "Would you show me where you grew up?" He looked at her, "Would you believe that you're the first person to ever ask me that?" He was touched and happy that someone, especially Maggie, would want to see where he lived as a kid. "Yes, I'll show, but first I want to show you where I'm going to live." "What do you mean, going to live?" As he swung the car towards the lake highway he said, "I'll show you. They had driven about five miles when he drove into an open lot sitting directly on the lake. "Come on!" He got out, went around to let her out. Maggie had no idea what he was doing. The air was cold as the wind blew along the lake. They were standing on the edge of a cliff when Tony turned his back to the lake and said, "This is it. This is where I'm going to build my house!" She looked at him and pulled her collar around her neck, "Why since you've got that gorgeous mansion?" He laughed, "Jonathan left the mansion to the state. We're just staying there until we find another house. The state will take it over one year after Jonathan's death. Let's go, your freezing." He started towards the car, but she stayed, "Tony, I think it's a beautiful place for a house!" He looked at her and thought, "How beautiful she is with the wind blowing her hair and making her cheeks rosy." Finally, he said, "Maggie, thank you, it was very important that you liked it. You're the only person that's ever seen it; in fact, you're the only one that knows I own it. It was the first thing I ever purchased. I had a ten year loan on it, but I paid it off a few days ago. The first time I laid eyes on it, I knew I wanted to build a house here. I love it." "You really know what you want, don't you?" Maggie moved next to him. His heart began to pound as he faced her, "Yes, I know what I want, but I also realize I can't have everything I want. There are some things money can't buy, trouble is, and they're the most important." She didn't have to ask for an explanation, his eyes told her exactly what he meant. As they stared into each others eyes, for what seemed hours, Maggie thought, "Please, Tony, please hold me. I want you!" He took her arm, "Let's go, I don't want you freezing to death." She wasn't sure if she could move, but she knew that he was having the same feelings as she.

"I'll bet you're starved," Tony remarked as they headed toward downtown Chicago. "Do you like pizza?" She heard him, but didn't answer immediately, because she was thinking about what was happening between them. "Pizza, yes, I love it. Are we going to have some?" He smiled at her, "I'm gong to get you the best pizza in the entire world, guaranteed." They talked about the differences of California and Chicago, baseball, tennis, and whatever else changed the subject of the electricity between them. Tony couldn't remember when he had so much fun. She was so enjoyable to be with, even more than he had dreamed. Maggie couldn't remember ever meeting anyone like him, "He's everything a woman would ever want. I understand why Roni said she fell in love with him so quickly. "God, it would be so easy to love this gentleman," she thought to herself.

Before they entered the restaurant, Tony spun her around to look towards the street, and said, "Look, just look at this city. This is my city, and I love it. This is the Rush Street area, nightlife at its finest, and lovely lady," he turned her towards the entrance to the restaurant; "This is Gino's, home of the world's greatest pizza. Are you ready?" She was laughing, "God yes, I've got to try something that terrific, besides I'm starving and cold."

"You're right," she remarked as she finished a bite, "This is fantastic." Tony was watching her, she sometimes reminded him of a small girl. "She's so full of life," he thought. They drank two pitchers of beer with their pizza. They, once again, shared happy moments from their pasts, they laughed a lot. As she finished the last swallow of her beer she asked, "Are you going to show me your old neighborhood, now?" He stood up, laid a twenty dollar bill on the table, reached for her hand and said, "Come, I'll lead you to my past, my glorious past, where I fought off dragons to save my princess." She shook her head, "I'm not sure I want to go if there are dragons." They both laughed. He held her hand until they were halfway to the car then he dropped her hand and stuck his hand in his pocket, "Boy, I'm cold." He really wasn't.

As they drove through the Southside of Chicago, Tony pointed out homes of his old friends and told her what most of them were doing now, which a good many were in jail. He stopped the car in front of a boarded up building that looked like a school. He said, "Let's get out." She was out of the car before he could get around. Tony pointed at the decayed structure, "This is my heritage. I lived here, went to school here, went to church here, I did everything here. This was St. Michaels' orphanage. It was home for about 120 kids." Maggie couldn't help but feel pity for him, but she also felt he missed it, "Tony, it seems like I should be saying I'm sorry, but I think you, uh, did you enjoy it here?" He sighed heavily, "Oh, yes, I loved it here. Here with Sister Carolyn. This was my home, and Sister was the only mother I ever knew. How many people do you know that has 120 brothers and sisters?" Maggie was staring at him as he talked about "his family." Tears were running down her face. He turned and saw her crying, "Hey, what's wrong?" Maggie touched his face as she spoke through her tears, "You're the most amazing person I'll ever meet. You spent all of your growing years in an orphanage, not knowing your parents, undoubtedly you were poor, and yet with all that adversity, you have all that love. You are very special, Tony, very special." She cried harder and returned to the car. While wiping her face she prayed, "Oh, please God, help me. I think I'm surely falling in love with this man, this wonderful man." "I'm sorry; I didn't mean to make you cry. I…" she interrupted him, "I know you didn't, I'm very sentimental and, I've never met anyone like you." She turned her face to the window and started to cry again. He started the engine and said, "I'll take you back to the hotel." "No!" She said quickly. "Let's go have a drink."

He took her to his favorite bar. They were seated in the back, where he always sat. There were very few people there. "What would you like to drink?" "Scotch and soda," she replied. He held out his cigarettes to her, "Have one?" "No, I'll have one of my feminist cigarettes, Virginia Slims, because I've come a long way baby," she kidded. He ordered her scotch and a Jack Daniels for himself. Maggie questioned, "Tony, what are your plans. What are you going to do with yourself?" He was puzzled by her question, "That's quite obvious; I'm going to build an empire." She shook her head, "No, I know that. I mean what are you going to do. Like with your personal life?" "Live it like I always have. My interests are in business. My hobbies or leisure time I spend playing tennis, golf, or going to ballgames. I really enjoy my life, Maggie." She puffed on her cigarette, "What are you going to do about Roni?" He smiled, "I really like her, she's a lot of fun, she's beautiful, she's exciting, a celebrity, she's great, but she has her career and I have mine. We're a million light years apart. I'm sure we'll see each other from time to time." Maggie dropped the subject. She wasn't sure why she had asked the question, but down deep she was sure she wanted to know if he loved her. He didn't! Tony sat his drink down, "So, what do you think of Chicago?" She finished a sip of her scotch and answered, "Well, let me put it this way; it's cold, windy, big, dirty, old, congested, exciting, and beautiful. I love it, especially the pizza!" They laughed again. She asked, "What kind of a house do you want? Big, small, what?" He leaned up in his chair, grabbed a napkin and started to draw, "I'll show you," he was excited about it, "I want a big house, one people will marvel at. Here, on the north side will be a large party room with bedrooms above, on the right side downstairs will be the living room and directly behind will be my study, above that will be more bedrooms. As you enter, the foyer will be large and there's a stairway that starts out narrow and widens as it gets to the top. Each bedroom will have its own balcony. A stairway will lead from the upstairs to the pool in the back. Attached to the back of the party room will be a game room, equipped with a pool table. The kitchen and dining area will be in the middle of the house in the back. That's my idea, it's sketchy now. I'll have Mike Emerson draw up a plan for me. What ya think?" Maggie had watched him while he talked about "his" house. She thought, "He'll build this beautiful house and live in it alone. He's actually a lonely person." She picked up the napkin and looked at it admiringly, "I think it will be beautiful, something to marvel at!" Tony ordered more drinks as they changed the subject to her house in Palm Springs, and then her life there. She was happy there. She enjoyed her friends and the climate. More drinks.

"Why haven't you had any children?" Tony asked, surprising Maggie. She waved her hand, "I can't, and I can't have any; some kind of birth defect. Why do you ask?" He was sorry he had asked, "Uh, I'm sorry, I, uh thought there may have been other reasons. I shouldn't have asked. I was getting too personal." She put her hand on his without thinking, until they touched, then drew it back quickly, "Tony, it's quite alright. It doesn't bother me much anymore. Please don't feel bad because you asked. Okay?" He didn't answer. He was thinking about her touch, how she did it, but then realized she had. He wondered, "How am I going to control my emotions when I'm around her? Right this minute, I'd give anything to make love to her, hold her, squeeze her, kiss her all over, touch her, just look at her, she's so beautiful." "Tony, oh Tony!" She was trying to break his concentration. He was embarrassed, "Christ, I'm sorry, I was thinking about something very beaut…uh, never mind." He had confused her. He clapped his hands together, "When was the last time you went to a museum?" "A museum, God, I don't know," she answered. "Finish your drink," he said as he stood up, "I'm going to take you to the Field Museum of Natural History. It's amazing. You'll love it." Maggie jumped up, "Whatever you say, you're the tour guide today."

They walked through the museum looking at bones of dinosaurs, elephants, humans, a mummy, pre-historic pottery and weapons. They examined everything they could until the museum closed and they were forced to leave. While walking to the car, Maggie commented, "If you don't make a go of it in the empire building business, you'd make one helluva tour guide." Once again they laughed. Tony opening the door, "I don't remember ever laughing as much as I have today. Thank you." They were standing face to face. They looked at each other for a moment, both realizing what was happening between them, and Tony said softly, "Better get in before you freeze." She didn't move and uttered, "Yeh, you're right." Before Tony started the car she asked, "What now, Mr. Cole?" "I've got it. We have to eat, right? Sure we do. The Midtown Dinner Theatre is playing "Come Blow Your Horn" and their food is terrific. How's that sound?"

"Okay, Mr. Tour Guide, but won't we have to change?" He turned onto Lake Shore Drive, "Naw, not at the Midtown. We can go as we are."

They had prime rib, baked potato, salad, and a nice valpolicella wine at dinner. Their seats were the best in the house, because the Maitre' di was a friend of Tony's. They had enjoyed the play immensely. It was shortly after midnight when the play was over. Maggie was exhausted, besides beginning to feel slightly tipsy. As they stood up, Tony said, "I think it's time I took you to the hotel. We've had a long day." She agreed, "Yes, a long day, and a beautiful day."

The Mercedes rolled to a stop in front of the hotel, Tony got out as the doorman helped Maggie from the car. They entered the lobby and Tony said, "I'll see you to your room." Maggie nodded in agreement. They didn't speak during the elevator ride, but they thought. Maggie was nervous, she wondered, "What am I going to say if he asks to come in, should I ask him in, of course you have to be polite, oh God, I want to sleep with him, stop." Tony was thinking, "I've had a great day with a great lady, a married lady, you don't do anything with married ladies, maybe I can change, I want to, I want her, I want her." Ding, the elevator bell brought them both back to reality. They walked to the door of her suite, she handed him the key and said, "Would you like a night cap?" Her voice was nervous. As they stood face to face the electricity between them could light up all of Chicago. Maggie was trembling; she knew that she wasn't going to say no to anything. Tony touched her face, "Maggie, I'm glad Stephanie couldn't make it. I've never enjoyed myself more. You're the most beautiful, most fun-to-be-with woman I've ever met. Thank you for sharing this time with me. Good night." He turned and headed for the elevator. Maggie nervously called to him, "Tony!" He turned to look at her and smiled. "Thank you, Tony. I'll never forget this day. Never!" She disappeared as the door shut behind her. She stood at the door; the tears were flowing down her cheeks. She cried, "I'm in love with him. Oh God, I'm in love with him. Tony, Tony, I love you," she fell on the sofa sobbing.

Tony sat behind the wheel of the Mercedes, trying to get his mind back to normal, "What am I going to do? I definitely love her. So you love her, yeh, so what, you can't and won't do anything about it." He headed for Rush Street. He owes himself a good drink.

CHAPTER ELEVEN

He parked the Mercedes on a side street and walked around the corner to Mario's. He found a seat at the bar and ordered a double Jack Daniels. Six doubles later, he looked at his watch; it was after three. He put down a handful of bills and staggered out. He was, undoubtedly, intoxicated. He was fumbling in his pocket for his keys when a voice said, "Hey, muthuh fuckuh, you got any money?" As Tony turned around, a sharp pain went through his stomach. Instinctively, he swung his left leg up and caught one assailant in the groin, but there was another voice, "Oh, the rich fuckuh wants ta fight." Tony swung around, just in time to feel another pain on his face. Quickly he struck out, his right fist meeting its mark. The target fell with a thud and gasp. Tony's fist had struck the would-be robber directly in the throat. He turned again, and this time he was staring into the barrel of a gun, "You kilt him, fuckuh, you kilt him, now you gonna die." The pain was horrible, as he fell onto the hood of his car, his chest was burning up, and everything went dark as his limp body slid to the ground. Blood was running down the fender of the Mercedes.

The siren made a shrieking sound as the ambulance sped through the quiet city in the early morning hours. "Christ, the bleeding won't stop; he's got a severed artery. Hurry this son-of-a-bitch up Ralph, or he'll never make it to the hospital!" The paramedic was working feverishly over Tony. Two doctors and four nurses met the ambulance at the emergency entrance to the hospital. The paramedic shouted at the doctor, "You better hurry, doc, he's almost gone, in fact, he might be!" Wheeling Tony into the emergency room, the doctor asked, "Do you have any idea what hit him?" The paramedic replied, "A small caliber pistol at point blank range, I think. He took one with him, though. Crushed esophagus. Must've hit him a ton." Nurses and orderlies were running all over at the command of the doctors. A nurse asked the paramedic, "Do you know who he is? Did you check for any identification?" The paramedic shrugged, "No, they took his wallet. The police are coming in now; maybe they got something from the car." A nurse with a clipboard asked the policeman, "Do you know his name, or do we list him as a John Doe?" "No," the officer said, "There wasn't anything in the car; I guess you'll have to list him as John Doe for now. We'll have a make on the car, shortly. The gurney carrying Tony came through the door heading for surgery, and a police reporter look down at him, "Jesus Christ, that's Tony Cole, the millionaire!" The reporter then called to the police officer, "Hey, Brodsky, he's been the hottest news since Elvis, lately." Brodsky, the police officer, "Do you know where he lives, or anything else?" "Yeh, he lives at the Stuyvesant Mansion." Brodsky asked the nurse with the clipboard, "I think we know who he is, one Tony Cole. Do you think he'll make it?" The nurse sighed, "No, it looks real bad. Are you going to contact the family?" Before he could reply, the phone rang and the nurse answered. "Officer Brodsky, the phone is for you," she handed the phone to him. "Brodsky, here." "Okay, thanks." He said to the reporter, "Well, bloodhound, you were right; the car's registered to Jonathan Stuyvesant." He then told the nurse, "I'll get somebody out there, right away." The reporter was on the phone within seconds.

"Man, I hate this duty," one of the policemen said as he rang the bell at the mansion. A sleepy-eyed man opened the door, "Yes, officers, what may I do for you?" "Who is it, Alfred?" Theresa was standing on the stairway. The policemen asked if they could step in and then asked, "Is this the home of Tony Cole?" Alfred looked at Theresa, "Yes, Mr. Cole resides here." The policeman reluctantly said, "Mr. Cole has had an accident…" Theresa screamed. The policeman continued, "Mr. Cole has been shot and is at Memorial Hospital." Theresa ran to Alfred, crying, "Shot! Is he okay! Will he be okay?" The second policeman answered, "We don't know. We weren't informed of his condition, we were just told to inform you of the accident. We don't know how or where the shooting took place. I'm really sorry. We'll be going, now." Theresa was sobbing, "How, why, who, where? Alfred, I've got to go to the hospital. Oh God, what if he's…" she sobbed harder. "I'll go with you, Miss Williams. Now, go get dressed," Alfred said as he led her up the stairs.

"Yes, hello," Derek said with a sleepy voice, but all he heard was a woman crying. "Who is this, what the hell do you want?" Through the crying she managed to speak, "Der, Derek, this is Ther, uh, Theresa. Oh Derek, Tony's been shot!" He jumped up, "Theresa, what did you say. Tony's been shot?" "Yes!" Derek was screaming into the phone, "Where is he, how is he, what happened. Stop crying and tell me!" She was trying to gain her composure, "I, I, uh, don't know, any, anything. Alfred and I are leaving for the hospital right now. He's at Memorial. Oh Derek, I'm so scared, please come back, he'll need you, I need you, please come back!" "We'll leave right away. I'll meet you at the hospital, shit, it'll take at least five hours before I can get there. You hang on honey. Now go to Tony." After hanging up with Theresa, he called Chris Pike, "Chris, get up now, we're leaving right now. I'll explain later!" He then called the other Executives of Cole Industries. They all met in Derek's room within twenty minutes. Mike Emerson was the first to speak, "What the hell is going on, Derek?" Derek answered sternly, "Tony's in the hospital, he's been shot. That's all I know. Let's get going!"

The hospital was quiet as Theresa and Alfred approached the emergency room desk, "We're here about Tony Cole. How is he?" Theresa questioned. The nurse replied, "Just a moment, please." She walked down the hall, and in seconds she returned with a large policeman. He looked at Theresa and Alfred, "Are you related to Mr. Cole?" Theresa said, "No I'm his secretary and this is his, uh, friend. How is he? Please tell us!" The policeman ignored Theresa's questions, "When will his family arrive?" Alfred, always the gentleman, answered, "We're the only family he has sir. I'm his butler. Could you please give us some information?" The policeman now seemed more congenial, "I can't tell you anything about his physical condition, the doctors will have to do that." Theresa was losing control again, "Can't you, at least, tell us what happened?" The nurse suggested, "Why don't you sit down." "Yes, please sit down," the policeman pleaded, "I'll give you the facts we have." Theresa and Alfred did as requested and sat down. "Is he alive?" Theresa begged. The nurse glanced at the policeman, then answered, "Yes, he's alive. He's in the operating room. They'll do everything they can for him." Theresa broke down again. They waited for her to calm down. Finally, she stopped sobbing, "I'm sorry, please tell us what happened." "Well, Miss," the officer began, "It looks like Mr. Cole was a robbery victim. We arrived at the scene, near Rush Street, at about three-forty. Mr. Cole was lying on the curb and another man was lying next to him. The other man was dead, a crushed esophagus. Mr. Cole had been shot twice in the chest." Theresa gasped, "Oh God!" The policeman continued, "Since we found no weapon, we figure that Mr. Cole was jumped by at least two assailants. He put up a pretty good fight but the attackers brought out the heat, gunned him down and took his wallet. That's about all we have until we can talk to Mr. Cole." The nurse got up to meet a doctor, who entered the room. They talked for a moment, then the doctor approached Theresa, Alfred, and the policeman, "May I have a word with you folks, please?" Theresa quickly asked, "Can you give us any word on Tony's condition?" The doctor stated, "He's in the operating room, and will be in there for some time yet. I must tell you, Mr. Cole is wounded critically. He was struck twice in the chest, but not in the heart luckily. Both bullets entered the upper chest just above the heart and below the neck. He has lost a lot of blood. That is our main concern now. If he makes it through surgery, he stands a good chance of a full recovery. For now, we'll have to wait and pray."

Reporters were swarming all over the hospital. Theresa and Alfred had been taken to the waiting room outside the operating room so that they could avoid the reporters. The large policeman sat with them. Theresa looked at Alfred, "What was he doing there, at that time, alone?" The policeman answered instead of Alfred, "He had been in Mario's Bar, around the corner, for a couple of hours. The bartender said he'd been drinking quite heavily. Does he do that frequently?" Theresa looked at Alfred for an answer and he replied, "No, not really, Tony drinks, but very seldom in local bars. Do you know who he is?" The policeman nodded, "The reporters told me." "What time is it?" Theresa asked. "Seven-thirty," answered the policeman.

She flipped on the TV. There was nothing on, so she switched on the radio, and twisted the dial until she could find something other than gospel music. "Christ, seven-forty, Sunday. What am I doing out of bed." She sighed, opened the drapes to allow the light to enter. She was pouring herself a glass of orange juice when she heard his name mentioned on the radio, "Tony Cole, local heir to a large piece of Jonathan Stuyvesant's billions was shot early this morning, near Rush Street!" Maggie dropped her glass, "No, no!" The newscaster continued, "Mr. Cole was found lying in the street at about three-thirty. He had been shot twice in the chest. It was an apparent robbery, according to the police. An unidentified man was found dead next to Cole. The police said Cole must have put up a fight before he was shot. Mr. Cole was taken to Memorial Hospital where we understand is still in surgery. We'll have more later. Maggie grabbed the phone, the front desk clerk answered and she requested a cab to take her to memorial hospital.

Maggie arrived at the emergency room desk at about eight-thirty, "Could you tell me the condition of Tony Cole, please?" The nurse replied, "I'm sorry, I can't give you any information about Mr. Cole. Are you a friend?" Maggie thought, "No, damnit, I'm in love with him!" "Yes, a very close friend," she said. "Come with me, "The nurse led her to an elevator, "Go to the fourth floor, there are two other people waiting there." Theresa and Alfred were sitting with a policeman when she entered the waiting room. Theresa looked up and ran to her, "Oh, Mrs. Weyland!" Both women stood crying in each other's arms. "Do you know anything yet?" Maggie managed to ask. Theresa shook her head, "No, he's still in surgery. He's been in there for over four hours. We haven't heard anything." Alfred pleaded, "Come on now, why don't you both sit down. I'm sure we'll hear something soon." "What have they told you?" Maggie looked at Alfred. "All we know is that if he makes it through surgery, he'll stand a chance of pulling through. We can only wait." They all sat silently for a moment. "I heard it on the radio, I came here immediately," Maggie said as she lit a cigarette. Theresa pointed at the policeman, "This is Officer Brodsky. He's been very nice. He was at the scene." Maggie took a long draw on her cigarette, "What do you think, Officer Brodsky, is he going to make it?" Brodsky smiled, "Sure." "I called Derek; they were going to leave right away. I guess we should inform the hospital that they'll be arriving. I know Derek will want to be with him," Theresa sniffled. Alfred got to his feet, "You're right, I'll go tell them. Will you be alright?" He touched Theresa's shoulder. She nodded as he left. The two women sat silently.

Maggie's thoughts turned to the beautiful day she had spent with Tony. "He was so much alive, he seemed so happy, he made me feel so good, and we had such a good time." The tears trickled down her cheeks as she continued to think about yesterday. "If I would've asked him in, this wouldn't have happened, I could have held him in my arms, loved him, God, please let him live, why didn't he go home, I love him, yes, yes God I love him…" she cried much harder. Theresa squeezed Maggie's hand.

Another forty-five minutes passed, it was now nine-fifteen. Tony had been in surgery for over five hours. The sound of automatic doors made them look up. A doctor stood looking at the three of them—Maggie, Theresa, and Alfred—fear was written all over their faces. They knew the time had come to see if their prayers and hopes have been answered. The doctor approached them, looking totally exhausted, "Hello, I'm Dr. Reardon." They didn't say anything, they watched his face. "He's alive." Maggie and Theresa hugged each other and sobbed. Alfred wiped away a tear. The doctor continued, "Yes, he's alive, but he is still in a lot of danger. He's lost so much blood; in fact, he shouldn't be alive because of the amount of blood he's lost. Mr. Cole had to be in top physical condition. He is in our Intensive Care Unit where he'll be watched continually." Dr. Reardon sighed heavily, "I wish I could say your waiting and praying was over, but he's really not out of the woods yet. Only God knows. I'll let you know as soon there's a change." The doctor departed. The three of them stood speechless. Alfred was the first to speak, "Why don't the two of you go get something to eat, and I'll wait her?" They both said no, they'd wait. Then Theresa said, "Alfred, there really is no reason for all of us to sit here and Rodney to sit in the car. I'm sure the phone, at the mansion, is ringing off the wall, why don't you go. I'll call you the minute there's any news." He agreed and hugged Theresa warmly.

Theresa looked at Maggie, who was staring out the window. She wondered about her, she liked her, "Maggie, are you scared?" She turned to Theresa, "Oh shit, I've never been so scared. I've never known anybody that's gone through something like this. Why does it always happen to the best ones!" Theresa looked hard at Maggie, "You think the same as I do, and Tony is definitely the best." She put her face in her hands and started to sob again. Maggie put her arm around her and offered her a cigarette, then asked, "How long have you been in love with Tony?" Theresa wiping her nose, "How did you know? Oh hell, it doesn't matter. I think I fell in love with him the first time I spoke to him." She then told Maggie of the interview with Tony. She told her about asking Tony to sleep with her and his decline. Maggie thought about the first time she met him. It was the same day as Theresa. He turned Theresa down, why? He really doesn't waver from his principles. He just may be the nicest person in the world. Please God, make him well!" Maggie checked her watch, it was nine-fifty.

As the elevator doors opened, both women looked; Theresa ran to him, "Derek, oh, thank God you're here!" He held her in his arms, "Come on sit down and tell me what's happening. I read about the shooting in the paper. Is there any word yet?" He said hello to Maggie as they all sat down. Theresa couldn't talk about it. So Maggie explained what the doctor had told them. The doctor entered the waiting room, "I just wanted to tell you, there's no change. He's still unconscious, but his vital signs are okay. We should know something in the next few hours. Maggie introduced Derek to the doctor. Dr. Reardon said, "Since he has no family, I guess you would be the most probable person to handle his affairs. Correct?" Derek agreed. "Would you come with me a moment?" asked Dr. Reardon. Derek turned to Maggie and Theresa, "I'll be right back." As the two men walked through the automatic doors, Dr. Reardon said, "Mr. Hill, I'm glad you've arrived. I couldn't say anything to the women, but Mr. Cole has been calling for a woman, and I wasn't sure of the consequences it may cause if he was asking for the wrong one. He was asking for Maggie." Derek was startled, "Maggie? Are you sure?" The doctor nodded, "Oh yes, it was very clear. Would you like to see Mr. Cole?" "Of course." Tony lay motionless. There were IV's in his wrist, and arm, there were tubes in his nose. He was very pale. "He looks dead," was Derek's first thought. He felt as though he'd be sick. Derek asked the doctor, "Tell me the truth, do you think he'll make it?" Dr. Reardon looked at the nurse seated beside Tony, then looked at Derek, "Mr. Hill, that is a question only God can answer." Derek sighed, "That's a cop-out, doc, I'm his best friend, the closest thing to family he has, what is your opinion, please?" The doctor walked from the room, Derek right behind him, "My opinion, well, Mr. Hill, I would give him less than a 20 percent chance of ever waking up, he just lost too much blood. I'm sorry, but you asked." The tears swelled in Derek's eyes, "Thank you Dr. Reardon. I appreciate your concern about the women. I'd also appreciate it if you didn't mention it to anybody else." The doctor assured him that he would forget it, and Derek left. He stopped before he faced Theresa and Maggie, he had to compose himself. He attempted a smile, as the two women waited anxiously for answers. "The doctor," Derek began, "Allowed me to see him for a second. He's resting quietly. There's a nurse sitting right at his bedside." He couldn't mention how bad Tony looked. He lit a cigarette and looked at Maggie. He thought, "Why would Tony be asking for her? Then he remembered how Tony had looked at her. Did they have a thing going? That's against Tony's morals! Oh, hell, who knows?" He took Theresa's hand, "I know you've been here a long time, I want you to go downstairs and get some coffee. Maggie and I will wait." She shook her head, but Derek insisted, "No, go on, if for no other reason, you can get me some coffee." Reluctantly she agreed and started for the elevator, "I'll bring back a lot." As soon as the elevator doors shut, Derek walked to the window and said to Maggie, "This is hard for me to ask, but I must.

Are you and Tony having an affair?" Maggie was shocked, "No, why did you ask that?" He offered her a smoke, "Dr. Reardon told me that Tony had asked for you, he called your name very clearly, (Maggie). Why would he do that?" She sat down, once again, the tears began to roll down her cheeks, "I don't know, unless my name was fresh in his mind. He took me around Chicago yesterday. He took me to Evanston to look for a house," she sniffed, "He took me to where he wants to build a house, he showed me where he grew up, and talked about his family, the 120 brothers and sisters, and Sister Carolyn." Maggie broke up, sobbing uncontrollably. Derek pulled her close to him as she sobbed. "I'm sorry, Derek, it's just," Derek interrupted, "It's just that you're in love with him!" Maggie bit her lip, "I don't know. I'm so confused. I've never had as much fun as yesterday. I do know that I wanted him to make love to me last night. I know that I couldn't sleep from thinking about him, and I don't want to face Peter anymore. You tell me, Derek, am I in love with him? Before you answer, no, we didn't sleep together; he just said goodnight and walked away. So tell me!" Derek smiled at her, "I'm afraid you are." The sobbing began again.

Theresa brought back coffee along with Mike and Stephanie Emerson and Paul and Hilda Krug. They were discussing the accident when Officer Brodsky asked for the attention, "Excuse me, but is there any of you here might be able to answer some questions for me?" Derek stood, "I can. Brodsky, "Do you know if Mr. Cole was into martial arts? Derek nodded, "Yes, he holds a black belt in karate". Brodsky grinned, "Well, he sure used it to perfection on the one assailant. He literally crushed the guy's esophagus. The coroner said he died instantly." He asked Derek a few more questions then excused himself.

Theresa, now very composed, said, "I never knew he knew karate'. Derek replied, "Yeh, he's been studying it for years. Maybe it paid off for him." The automatic doors opened. All eyes were fixed on Dr. Reardon as he approached them. Maggie clutched one of Derek's hands and Theresa the other. "Well," the doctor said, "He regained conscious. I'd say he's out of real trouble!" They all cheered. The men shook hands and kissed the doctor through their tears of joy. Derek walked to the window; he was wiping away tears as Theresa put her arms around him from the back and cried. "You know, Theresa, I really love that guy!" She squeezed harder and said, "So do I." Dr. Reardon was all smiles as he shook off any compliments and said, "Mr. Cole must be quite a guy. All of you folks and God on his side, too. Mr. Hill, would you like to see him?" Derek smiled, "Oh yeah!" The others wanted to see him, too, but the doctor informed them that only one at a time and no more than three minutes. It was agreed that Theresa would be after Derek and then Maggie, since they had been there the longest.

Derek stood in the doorway, to catch his breath, then smiled as he walked up to the bed. Tony could hardly turn his head, but managed a slight smile. Derek touched his hand, "You gave us quite a scare, old buddy. Why the hell didn't you take out both thugs?" Tony tried to grin, he was breathing heavily. Derek ordered, "Don't try to speak! Everybody is here. We're all happy you're alive. Don't worry. We'll take care of business. Theresa wants to see you for a minute and Maggie too." Derek noticed Tony's eyes light up, "I'll see you later." He left without saying anything else. As Derek entered the waiting room, he said, "Listen, I don't want either of you to be surprised. Tony looks like hell, and he can't speak. Try not to let him see any shock on your face." Theresa and Maggie agreed and Theresa went in. Taking a deep breath, "Hi ya boss, feeling a little lousy?" Tony attempted to smile. She was trying hard to keep smiling so she wouldn't cry. "Lord, he looks terrible," she thought. Theresa leaned down and kissed him on the cheek, "You hurry and get well. There are a lot of people who need you and love you. I've got to go now, but I'll see you tomorrow." She kissed his cheek and her tears dripped onto his face. She walked out of the room. As the door shut to his room, Theresa leaned against the wall and breathed heavily. Finally, she walked through the automatic doors; the tears were streaming down her face. And Derek put his arm around her. Maggie didn't hesitate; she went straight to Tony's room. She stood and looked at the figure of a man lying so still. The tears flowed from her eyes uncontrollably as she thought, "Here is this great person, so helpless, with so many people caring about him, but nobody to really be with him, to love him." She walked slowly to him. He was motionless. She touched his forehead. He didn't move. She began to worry. "Tony, Tony please look at me, say something to me Tony!" His eyes opened almost in slow motion. Maggie put her hand to her mouth and sighed, "Oh Tony, I've been so worried about you." Her heart sounded like a drum. Tony managed a smile as she ran her hand through his hair. "I, I know.," he uttered barely loud enough for her to hear. She kissed his forehead, "You rest. We'll talk later. There are a lot of people who love you, and I'm one of them." Tony weakly raised his hand. Maggie took his hand in hers and squeezed it lightly. She kissed him on the forehead again and said, "Goodbye." She left as his eyes closed. While walking toward the waiting room she wondered, "What am

I going to do now? My whole life is turned around. How am I going to feel about Peter?" She stopped, and put her hands to her face and said aloud, "Thank you, God. Thank you for keeping him with us."

Derek, Theresa, and Maggie took a cab to Maggie's hotel. They decided to have something to eat. The morning seemed like it was three days long. "Derek," Maggie asked, "Do you know when Peter is arriving?" Derek looked at his watch, "Yes, he should be here in about two hours." She finished the last of a Martini she ordered, "I hope you'll excuse me. I've just got to take a shower. I can't remember feeling as rotten as I do now. Will we see you later?" Derek said, "Why don't you and Peter have dinner with Theresa and me tonight? We'll meet you here?" Maggie squeezed his hand as she agreed to the dinner and then kissed his cheek, "Thank you, Derek, you're quite a guy, too." She leaned down and touched her cheek to Theresa's, "Keep smiling." They watched until she had left the room. "I really like her!" Theresa exclaimed. Taking a large swallow of his drink, Derek agreed, "Yeh, so do I. She's quite a woman." "You must be exhausted, why don't you go home and get some sleep?" Theresa requested. "I would, except I want to go to the Mansion. I'm sure there have been a zillion phone calls. I want to answer the important ones. Come on let's go."

Alfred opened the door and Theresa hugged him tightly. Alfred asked Derek "Is Tony going to be okay?" "Yes, it looks like it, for now anyway." "Has the phone been ringing off the wall?" Derek mused. Alfred smiled, "Not over 200 times. I'll get the book I'm keeping for you." Derek sifted through notes and picked out the ones he felt were important enough to answer. Theresa went to her room to shower.

With a drink and a cigarette, Maggie sat in front of the window that gave her a great view of Chicago. Her mind began to wander, "This is my city, that's what he called it; his city. What will I say to him? What will I say to Peter? I'll spend as much time in California as I can. That's it, I'll avoid Tony. Poor Tony, he's so helpless now, so sick. Oh god, I wish I could hold him, he needs me, he needs me, I need him,"...she dropped off to sleep.

"Damn, I hurt all over," Tony thought as he lay perfectly still, staring at the ceiling of his hospital room. "Will the pain ever go away?" He closed his eyes and a vision of Maggie entered his mind, "She was here, here when I needed her. She's married, married....why" "Mr. Cole, Mr. Cole." The nurse was standing beside him as he opened his eyes, "Mr. Cole, I'm going to give you something for the pain." She lifted his arm, wiped it with alcohol, and stabbed him with the syringe. He didn't feel a thing. His chest hurt so bad. The nurse smiled at him, "There, now go back to sleep, I'll be right here." Instantly he was asleep.

"Maggie, Maggie," Peter was trying to wake her. "Oh, Peter, I'm so glad you're here!" She hugged him. "He had a rough time, huh?" Peter stated. "Yes, a very rough time. I'm sure that the doctor didn't expect him to live. Peter, he looks terrible, as though he's hanging on by a thread." Peter, fixing a drink, "I wish I could've been here. How long were you at the hospital? Want a drink?" She stretched, "No, no drink. I got there sometime after eight. Theresa and I waited until he was awake. That Theresa, she's quite a gal. I'm going to take a shower. Oh, we're having dinner with Derek and Theresa." He came into the bathroom and sat down while she was showering, "It's all over the news, this shooting of Tony. They say he killed one of the attackers. I can't imagine him killing anybody, or even hurting anyone." She spoke loudly from the shower, "Derek told the police that he was some kind of belt, in karate." Peter asked, "A black belt?" "Yes, that's it." Peter shook his head, "Damn, is there anything he can't do?" Maggie thought to herself, "Yes, he can't make love to his secretary or a married woman." Peter continued, "You know, Maggie, I really like Tony. He's just a super guy, and smart as hell. What do you think of him?" She gasped at the question, "Uh, uh, I agree with you, he's really a nice person." Peter went on, "I almost got sick when Derek called me this morning. I just couldn't believe it. Tony shot!" She couldn't hear him, she was allowing the water to hit her in the face but her mind kept running, "I wish Tony was in this shower with me, touching my breasts, my God, I want him." Her knees were getting weak as she rubbed her breasts and the soft parts of her femininity. She turned off the shower and pulled the curtain back. Instead of drying, she stood dripping wet and said to Peter, "Make love to me, Peter! Right here on the bathroom floor. Please!" He came to her, pulled her to him and kissed her hard. He quickly removed his clothes. They immersed in passionate love making right there. When they had finished, Maggie didn't move. She lay there crying, she couldn't stop the tears. She had just made love to Peter, her husband, and made believe it was Tony, the man she wanted so desperately. "What's wrong? I've never seen you so passionate, and now you're crying?" Peter was confused as he stepped into the shower. Maggie didn't answer, she couldn't because she was afraid of telling him the truth.

CHAPTER TWELVE

As Derek entered the Stuyvesant Building, a horde of reporters greeted him. They wanted a statement. "Please," Derek held up his hand asking to speak, "If you'll be patient and wait just a little longer, you can come up to our conference room and I'll answer all of your questions. Give me half-an-hour and then come up to the eighteenth floor." Theresa was on the phone, talking to Claude Benaforte, when Derek arrived. "Just a moment, Mr. Benaforte," she held out the phone to Derek, "He wants to talk to you." "Tell him I'll call him back in a little while. Then get ready to usher a God damned million reporters into the conference room. They'll be here shortly," Derek said.

Theresa greeted the reporters as they exited the elevator, "Follow me please, Mr. Hill will be with you in just a moment." She went into Derek's office, "Well, they're all in there. Christ, there must be a hundred of them. Did you see Tony this morning?" He stretched, "Yes, he's doing a little better this morning. He's still having problems talking. The doctor said it's because of the pain killers. Well, let me get this over with." He disappeared into the conference room.

Derek was surrounded by the reporters, "ladies and gentlemen, I'll answer all of your questions one at a time, please." The first question came from the back, "What is the condition of Mr. Cole today?" "He is resting comfortably but he's in a lot of pain."

Reporter: "We understand that one of the bullets struck him in the head. Will there be any continuing problems?"

Derek: "There were no head wounds. Let me clear this up, he was shot twice in the upper chest. Twice, not more, not less, twice and that is all, he received no wounds anywhere else. He should have no lingering problems."

Reporter: "Has Mr. Cole been any help to the police in finding the attackers?"

Derek: "No, he is under heavy sedation and cannot communicate very well at this time."

Reporter: "Is Mr. Cole aware that he killed one of his attackers?"

Derek: "No, at least I don't think so."

Reporter: "The police say that Mr. Cole has a black belt in karate. Is this true?"

Derek: "Yes, that is true."

Reporter: "How long will Mr. Cole be hospitalized?"

Derek: "It is uncertain right now. We hope he'll be allowed to leave within a couple of weeks."

Reporter: "Who will control Cole Industries during Mr. Cole's absence?"

Derek: "We have very qualified people that will control their own divisions, and I will be the coordinator."

Reporter: "There have been rumors linking Mr. Cole with movie queen Roni Scott. Has she been contacted and if so, will she come to visit him?"

Derek smiled, "Rumors are rumors, let them stay that way. Besides, Miss Scott is in Brazil filming a movie." Derek answered several more questions and then asked to be excused.

"Uh, yes Claude, I'll stay in touch. Thank you, I'll tell him. Goodbye," Derek hung up the phone and let out a big sigh. Theresa came in, "The board members are all present and accounted for. Whenever you're ready." Derek looked at her, "You know what I say, I say fuck. I'm confused; hell, we can't continue anything until Tony can be consulted. We have to sit here twiddling our thumbs." Theresa smiled, "Go in there and tell them that, and when you want to talk dirty, come see me!" They both laughed as he left the room.

She stood beside him, watching him sleep. She just wanted to be near him. Watching him sleep, she fantasized about the things they could do together. She also realized that she had never known what true love was, because of the way she felt about this man. She would never be happy again, until she could have him, forever. Maggie wanted him to wake up and tell her that as soon as he is well, the two of them will runaway and spend the rest of their lives together.

"Derek, there's a call from Brazil for you. I wonder who it might be!" Theresa said into the intercom. He grabbed the phone, "Hello, this is Derek Hill." "Hello Derek, this is Roni, Roni Scott. I just heard about Tony. Please tell me, is he, is he okay?" Derek was glad to hear her voice; he was hoping she would come to Chicago, if any woman in the world can make Tony forget about Maggie, it surely was Roni. "Yes, Roni, he's going to be fine." Roni said sharply, "I'm coming to Chicago. I'm leaving as soon as I can. I want to be with him. Could you arrange to pick me up at the airport? Somebody will let you know when I'll arrive." Derek was smiling from ear to ear, "Sure, just let me know." She blew a kiss into the phone, "Give that to him, from me. I'll try to hurry. Bye-bye." The phone clicked in his ear. He sat back and grinned. He said to himself, "One potential problem solved, hopefully." He called Alfred and asked if he could arrange a room for Roni. Alfred was delighted to do so.

Derek was pleased to see the mass of reporters at the airport. He had informed every source of the media that Roni Scott was arriving in Chicago to visit Tony Cole. He hoped that the media and Roni would be able to convince Tony of a strong romance between the two of them. She entered the terminal amidst flashbulbs, cameras, well-wishers, and screaming reporters. Derek pushed his way through the crowd in an effort to reach Roni. He gasped when he saw her, "She's gorgeous!" Roni waved and ran to him, they embraced for a moment and Roni smiled, "Did you tell him I was coming?" Derek answered, "No, I thought I'd let you surprise him." Miss Scott," a reporter stuck a microphone in her face, "Is it true that you abandoned your movie to come here and be with Tony Cole?" She smiled, "I did not abandon the movie; we were finished. But, yes I did come here to be with Tony Cole." "Rumors have it that you and he are romantically involved. Is Tony Cole the new man in your life?" She graciously replied, "Tony Cole and I are very close friends and he has been hurt. I'm going to see him just as I would if it were another close friend." The reporter added, "But, is Tony Cole the new man in your life?" She smiled again, "You figure it out. Now, please let me go see my friend." Roni and Derek slipped through the throng of people and headed toward the car. Fans kept running up to her, asking for autographs as the walked, she didn't refuse a one, she signed them as they walked.

Once they were in the car, Roni looked at Derek, "Okay, now that the side show is over, how is Tony?" Derek leaned his head back, "Roni, he's damn lucky to be alive. A weaker man would have died. When you see him, try not to act alarmed, because he looks real bad. He lost an awful lot of blood. They've got tubes in him everywhere. I don't mean to scare you; I just want you to be prepared." She lit a cigarette, "Is there anything to drink in here?" Derek opened the liquor compartment, "What's you pleasure?" "Scotch." "Were you really finished shooting?" Derek asked as he poured the drinks. "Yes, we would've finished three days earlier if I hadn't been such a bitch. Derek, I haven't been the same since I met Tony. I'm going to ask him to marry me!" Derek choked on his drink, "What, marry you?" She removed her sunglasses and tears filled her eyes, "Yes, I love him so much; I mean it's like I'm a teenager again. I can't eat, I can't sleep, I drink to much, I smoke too much, I'm a total bitch, and all I think about his him. I was so worried about him. The news papers were so graphic. I was so scared. Oh, Derek, I want him to love me, too!" She put her head on his shoulder and sobbed. Derek thought to himself, "Tony, you're a damned fool if you don't marry this woman."

The scene at the hospital was the same as the airport and Roni showed why she's the best actress in Hollywood. The director of the hospital met them and led them straight to Tony's room. Roni went in alone. She put her hand to her mouth as she fought back the tears, then proceeded to his bedside. Tony rolled his head to see who came in, and smiled at her. She ran to him, she didn't know where to touch him, so she kissed his cheek and said, "Hi ya, Mr. Cole. I missed ya." Tony, still having problems speaking, said, "Thank you, thank you for missing me, uh, and thank you for coming here." She laid her hand on his forehead and whispered in his ear, "I came for two reasons. One, to make sure you're okay and two, to tell you I love you!" She kissed his cheek and said, before he could respond, "That's all I have to say now. The doctor is only allowing me to stay for one minute. I'll see you tomorrow, and the next day, and the next. I'm staying in Chicago until you get well. Bye, bye, my love."

"I'm going to watch the news, what about you?" Peter asked Maggie. "No, I'm going to bed." Maggie went directly to the bedroom as the television blared. She was undressing as the newscaster said, "Chicago has a very special visitor today, one that might stay awhile. Roni Scott, the beautiful number one box office attraction in Hollywood, arrived here today. She has come to visit a friend, a sick friend. That friend just happens to be Mr. Tony Cole, the multi-millionaire who was gunned down in the street last Sunday. Boy, a multi-millionaire and Roni Scott too. That's living!" Maggie sat motionless. For the past few days, she had spent as much time with Tony as the doctors would allow. He slept most of the time, but she would sit and watch him. She adored him. She had forgotten about Roni. Now, she felt hurt, that Roni has re-entered Tony's life, her world. She thought, "It's over, and I don't even know if he realized I was there. I've got to get away from him, I've got to get my life back together, Peter, poor Peter, Tony, Peter…" her head was spinning. She jumped up, ran into the living room, filled a glass half full of scotch and gulped it down, and poured another. Peter turned to her; he hadn't witnessed her actions, "Hey, guess who's in town? Roni, Roni Scott. She flew in from Brazil to see Tony." Maggie didn't acknowledge him. Peter continued, "I've got to hand it to Tony, he can handle anything. Looks like he did alright with Roni!" Maggie trying desperately not to scream, said, "Yes, I guess you're right." She went into the bedroom, and then returned, "Peter, I want to go home, tomorrow." He looked at her, puzzled; he didn't understand her actions of late, "What is it with you, lately? You've been acting differently, like someone else." She stared at him, "I don't know what's wrong, I guess to much has happened too quickly. I just want to go home." She returned to the bedroom. Peter was totally confused. He decided to leave it until tomorrow.

CHAPTER THIRTEEN

During the next several days, Tony began his road to recovery, his speech was getting normal, and he was walking and getting anxious to go home. The Weyland's returned to California, where Peter was checking into new ventures for Cole Industries. Maggie played a lot of tennis, but she drank more than anything else. Paul and Hilda Krug went on a week long cruise. Mike and Stephanie Emerson looked for a new house. Henri Vachon took a trip to Europe for ideas of what they would be selling in the Cole Department Stores. Carmen Lombardi worked night and day drawing different menus, color combinations, seating arrangements, etc. Bob Underwood and his wife went to Acapulco for a few days. Only Derek and Theresa stayed with Tony, of course Roni, too.

Maggie sat by the pool, having her normal morning scotch, when her thoughts turned to the night before she left Chicago, "Let's see, it was about three a.m., yes, that's it, I slowly dressed and snuck out of the room, took a taxi to the hospital. There he was, lying so peaceful, fast asleep. I just watched him sleep, and then he looked at me and smiled. I began to cry, he reached for my hand, and he held it for a long time. We didn't say anything, we didn't have to. I finally told him that I was returning to California that day. He squeezed my hand and softly said he'd miss me. I kissed his forehead and ran out the door." Maggie dropped her glass and sobbed into her hands. What she doesn't know is that Tony watched her leave and the tears trickled down his face.

"Well, buddy," Derek exclaimed, "I'll bet you're ready to get out of this place!" Tony looked around the room, "How the hell long have I been here, anyway?" "Let's see, twelve days, yeh, twelve," Derek answered as he counted on his fingers. "Christ, it seems like forever," Tony murmured. Derek helped him on with his trench coat, and said, "Tony, Roni has been super. She's acting like she's bringing home a new baby. She's got Alfred, Rodney, and all the servants in the palm of her hand. Damn, she's remarkable, and I don't have to tell you, she loves the hell out of you, buddy!" Tony didn't look at Derek, but asked, "Tell me, Derek, why are you trying to shove Roni down my throat?" "Shit," Derek realized he had been to pushy, "Well, uh, I, uh, oh hell, only because I thought Roni was the one woman that could make you forget about Maggie Weyland!" "Forget Maggie Weyland? What the hell are you talking about?" Tony shot at him. "Look, I don't know what you two have going, I just didn't want you to get involved with her and everything at Cole Industries to get sticky. I'm sorry." Derek was always honest, especially with Tony. "What makes you think Maggie and I are doing anything?" Tony questioned. "When you were brought into the hospital, you were barely conscious and you began asking for Maggie," Derek explained. "Who else knows that?" Tony asked as he sat down next to Derek on the hospital bed. Derek looked at him, "Only me, you, Dr. Reardon, and Maggie." Tony sat silent for a moment then looked at Derek, "Question, then we'll drop the subject, what did Maggie say?" Derek half chuckled, "She loves ya, buddy, just like all the rest!" They headed for the door when Tony stopped, "Derek, I'll tell you, and only you, you're right, I am in love with Maggie, but I know I can never have her. So don't worry about emotions getting in the way of Cole Industries success. You're right about something else; Roni is the only woman that might turn me around."

Roni had decided to wait at the Mansion, instead of going to the hospital, because she was afraid there would be another media episode. Besides, she and Alfred had made everything perfect for his arrival. They had champagne and cake, a cake that Roni made herself. She was so excited about Tony coming home and the preparations that she hadn't called Maggie. She can talk to Maggie anytime, today is Tony's day.

During the ride home, Derek explained to Tony of the whereabouts of his staff and the limited work accomplished during his absence. "We've got to make some changes, immediately," Tony said, "I want it known that you have full authority over Cole Industries and what takes place if something like this was to ever happen again. Have you hired another lawyer yet?" "Yes, Larry Shapiro, I went through law school with him. He's been with the Caldwell & Maine firm. He's smart as a whip. He's very anxious to meet you." Derek was proud that Tony had allowed him to hire a lawyer on his own. "That's good; have him come to the Mansion tonight. In fact, contact everybody, wherever they are, and have them here for a meeting Monday. We'll hold it at the Mansion." Derek was dumbfounded, "You don't mean to tell me, you're going to start working right away, are you?" Tony grinned, "Twelve days is long enough. Cole Industries will start moving again." Derek shook his head in disbelief.

Once they arrived at the mansion and had a glass of champagne, Roni insisted that Tony rest. He went upstairs, with Roni's help. He slowly crawled onto the large bed and cringed in pain, "Son-of-a-bitch, it hurts every time I move, cough, laugh, or any damn thing!" Roni sat down on the bed beside him and kissed his cheek, "I know, if there's anything I can do, please tell me." Even through the pain, he managed a grin, "Thank you, but I don't think I could handle what I'd like you to do for me." She laughed and laid her hand on his penis, "Thank God, they didn't shoot that." They both laughed, then she kissed him. Roni stood up quickly, shook her head, and said, "Damn, I've never had a man affect me like you. Even half alive, you're still more of a man than any I've ever encountered. Now go to sleep for awhile." He was asleep before she was out of the room.

Derek spent the afternoon locating the staff members. Roni spent a lot of time on the phone with her agent, studio executives, director, producer, and half of Hollywood. They were pressing her to return to California to complete the shooting of the film. She told them to shoot all the scenes she wasn't in and she would return when she just had to be there. Tony joined them in the dining room, "Good afternoon." Roni ran to him, "What are you doing, coming down those stairs alone, you're still awfully weak." "Could I have a cup of coffee?" He asked as he sat down slowly and winced. Once he was finally at ease, Tony asked Derek, "So what's new in the business world?" Derek replied, "I was thinking, we're building new businesses and spending a lot of cash and I'm not sure if we're going to come out in a healthy situation when it come to taxes. I think we should buy out a bankrupt company or one that is losing money and is on the verge of bankruptcy. What do you think?" Tony took a sip of his coffee, "I thought about that a while ago. I think you're right. Why don't you see if there's a company like that around, one that doesn't take a lot of capital to purchase?" Derek grinned, "Funny you should say that, it just so happens,

I know of one." Tony smiled as Derek continued, "While sitting in that damn hospital, waiting to see if you were going to live or die, I read an ad in the journal about a solely-owned cosmetic company in California that was looking for investors to keep them afloat. I took the liberty to contact the owner." Tony nodded, "Go on." Derek poured himself a cup of coffee, "The guys name is Irving Epps, the name of the company is Miss Diane Cosmetics. Irving owns the company lock, stock, and barrel. Roni, have you ever heard of Miss Diane Cosmetics?" She shook her head, "No, I don't think, hey wait, yeh, I heard of them when I was a kid, real cheap I think." Derek, "You're right, real cheap. They flourished back in the late 50's and early 60's but sales have dropped gradually every year for the past twelve. They have finally reached bottom, Irving says he can't continue without some financial help. I think we could get it for a song." Tony looked at Roni, "This boy's going to do quite well in this business." He turned to Derek, "Go for it. Set up a meeting with Mr. Epps. We'll talk deal with him."

Tony did as every one suggested, he laid around and just plain rested for the next few days. He couldn't wait until Monday, he was anxious to start working again, even though everybody begged him to take it easy. Roni couldn't put off returning to California, she agreed to be on the set Monday. She assured him she would return to Chicago as soon as the shooting was finished. Tony had met the new lawyer, Larry Shapiro, and was pleased with Derek's decision.

"Are you sure you won't change your mind and go with me to Chicago?" Peter begged. Maggie answered, "No, I'd rather stay here. I can use the time to get things prepared for the move." Peter put his hands on her shoulders, "Honey, you really don't want to move to Chicago, do you?" She turned away from him, "Uh, sure, oh I don't know. Peter, why can't we stay here? You could commute. You'll be spending most of your time out here anyway, that means I'd be stuck there all alone." He had been confused about her actions and attitude ever since they returned to California, it was no different now, "I really don't understand you anymore. Ever since we got back you've been moody, grouchy, tired, you drink too much and, our sex life has been non-existent. Are you mad at me? Please tell me what the hell is wrong!" Maggie folded her arms, threw back her head, and sighed, "Just go to Chicago and I'll be alright when you get back, really I will." He just looked at her, "Whatever you say. I'll be back on Tuesday, I think." Peter left as Maggie broke down and sobbed uncontrollably, "Tony, oh Tony, I hate you, I hate you. Oh, God, no, I love you. I hate you! Why did you have to come into my life? What am I going to do?"

"Are you sure you feel up to holding a meeting? You're still damn weak," Derek was worried about Tony. "I feel fine, well maybe not fine," Tony replied. Everybody arrived and they all wished Tony well. "I'm sorry to drag you all away from your vacation, but I thought we should get on with business. Because of my not-so-up-to-par physical condition, Derek will do most of the talking. Thank you for coming." Tony sat down, very slowly. He was still in great pain. Derek began, "I, too, would like to thank you for coming. I'd like to start by introducing the newest member of Cole Industries; Larry Shapiro is now in full charge of legal matters at Cole. Now, I'd like to ask each of you to explain where your department stands presently. Would you begin Paul?" Paul Krug stood, "Welcome aboard Larry. As far as I'm concerned, I'm ready to start construction in California. My foreman and I have been out there arranging what we need, equipment, personnel, etc. I'm ready." Derek asked Mike Emerson to speak next. Mike also stood and acknowledged Larry then said, "Well, I'm not as far along as Paul. All of my people plus myself are working as fast as we can to get some specs together on the shopping plaza. I should have a rendering finished by the end of the week. I'll give each of you a copy so that you can examine it and make any suggestions you may have. That's all I have." Peter was next in line, "I have some great news. Nieman Marcus is on the verge of agreeing to occupancy and I. Magnin of California has agreed. That will give us two extraordinary retailers as anchors to compliment the Cole store. Nieman may want to see the plans and meet you Tony, personally. All zoning regulations and building permits will be ready in just a few days. I have been getting many inquiries from retailers all over the country, the interest in our plaza is extremely high," Peter was finished." Tony leaned on the table and said, "Peter, if meeting me is all that holds up Nieman Marcus, then set up a meeting. That's no problem, if we could get a quality anchor like that." Peter acknowledged, "I'll take care of it." Derek turned to Carmen Lombardi, "Carmen, how are you doing?" Carmen was excited, "The menu is-a finish. I'm-a gonna go to Caleefornia tonight, spend a fewa days, visit some-a restaurants, just ta know the area. If-a tha-tsa okay?" Tony smiled at Carmen, "Of course, you go and do whatever you think is necessary." Derek rose, "Since Henri couldn't leave Europe immediately, we'll have to wait for his comments. So I'd like to open some new business. I'll start then anything new from you, please insert it." He looked at Tony, "We are spending a lot of money which will help our tax situation, but with the acquisition of the three companies, Paul, Mike, and Henri, we could still be in a fix come tax time. Tony and I have discussed this and we feel that we should attempt to purchase a company that is either losing money or is in bankruptcy. I have found just such a company, Miss Diane Cosmetics in Los Angeles. The owner is in bad trouble, and I think we could buy him out with less than half-a-million and take over his liabilities, which only total $300 thousand. That means with a small investment we could enhance our tax situation considerably." Bob Underwood asked, "What do you propose to do with the company once it's purchased?" "Let it operate at a loss," Derek replied, then gave the floor to Paul who asked, "Who is going to run the operation while it's losing money?" "The man who owns the company now, Mr. Irving Epps," Derek answered. "No more questions?" He looked at each one and there were no further questions. "Fine, nobody is in disagreement. We'll pursue the acquisition. Any other new business?" "I would like to bring something up," Mike Emerson stated, "Has anybody given a thought to a hotel near the plaza?" They all looked at each other and shook their heads, except Tony. He reached in his pocket and removed a crumpled napkin; he threw it to Mike and said, "I wrote that down one night in the hospital, I'm glad to see the subject brought up." Mike opened the napkin, it said only "Hotel?" Mike grinned at Tony. Peter slapped his hand on the table, "Yes, perfect. We have plenty of land for it. We could locate between the plaza and the industrial park!" Carmen clapped his hands, "Our restaurant could-a be on-a da top of the hotel and could be a revolver!" They all laughed at the play on words. Bob Underwood added, "We could build it to house conventions. In fact, it could be made into a real showplace, tennis courts, indoor racquetball, etc." Derek and Tony looked at each other with broad smiles. Tony strained to stand. All went quiet and Tony smiled, "Well, it sounds like you guys think we should go into the hotel business!" Everybody answered in unison, "Yes!" "How long will it take you to design the most fabulous hotel of all time?" Tony asked Mike. Mike was beaming, "Hell, I've already got the idea; I'll have a sketch done for you real soon!" Tony said, "Fine, but if we're going to build one in California, why don't we build one in Houston and here in Chicago as well?" He turned to Bob Underwood, "Bob, contact our banks in each city, explain what we want to do. I'm sure they'll do the financing. Peter, find us some land. Let's get moving on it, in fact, let's drink on it." The meeting ended with everybody excited, especially Tony. He was glad to be working again, even for a short time. As everybody left, Derek and Theresa stood beside Tony and Derek said, "That took a lot out of you, right?" Tony sighed heavily, "Yeh, a lot. I think I'll lay down." After Tony went upstairs, Derek and Theresa went downtown to the office.

He lay there, thinking, "Why didn't she come back with Peter? Why did she return so quickly?" He looked at the phone. Tony couldn't get his mind off of Maggie. It was even hard to think about business. He had really tried to make Roni take her place in his mind; but even as beautiful, caring, and loving as she is…Maggie is the woman in his heart and mind. He looked at the phone again; he reached for it—then stopped. "What would I say to her, if I did call? He wondered. "Oh, shit, I'll think of something," he said to himself as he dialed her number.

Maggie had given the maid the day off – she wanted to be alone. The sun was hot as she lay by the pool, as always thinking about Tony. The ringing of the phone frightened her; she jumped up and ran to the bar where the phone was ringing. "It's probably another club wanting my time," she thought as she grabbed the receiver. "Hello, Weyland's residence." She answered as if she were the maid so she could say Mrs. Weyland wasn't in. She gasped when she heard his voice. "May I please speak to the lovely Mrs. Weyland?" Her heart began to pound, she thought it may jump out of her chest, the palms of her hands were instantly sweating, she sat on, rather fell onto a bar stool. "Hello, Maggie, are you there?" He asked when she didn't answer. She took a deep breath, and said, "Uh, I mean, uh, hi." She was completely flustered. Tony added a smile to his voice, "Everything thing is fine, well one thing is wrong." She bit her lip in anticipation of bad news. "I was disappointed that you didn't come back with Peter." "What am I going to say to him," she thought. Then she answered, "Oh, uh, I just decided I could use the time alone, uh, to get things ready to move." She didn't feel that she was disguising her feelings very well. Tony spoke, "When are you planning to move?" She ran her hand through her hair and bit her lip again, "Uh, I'm not sure. I never did find a place. I, uh, I was thinking that….." Tony interrupted, "I miss you! I missed you my last few days in the hospital, and everyday since. I want you to come back, Maggie!" The tears burst from her eyes, she couldn't stop them, she cried, "Oh, Tony! Oh, Tony, why did you say that?" He knew she was crying, so he tried to make her laugh, "Because I need somebody to eat pizza with!" The tears were pouring now as she tried to speak but could only cry. He spoke softly again, "I want you to get on the next plane to Chicago. I think we should have a talk." Maggie knew she had to go, no matter what circumstances became of it, "Okay, uh, but I'll have to let Peter know. I'll get the first flight I can. Where is Peter now?" "He's on his way to Houston. He'll probably be there a couple of days. He was going to call you when he arrived. I'll make sure he gets a message telling him you're here." Tony, too, was excited. He couldn't wait to see her. She regained her composure, "Fine, I'll be there as soon as I can. Will somebody meet me?" He grinned, "Yeh, me!" She asked puzzled, "But how, you can't move around, you..." once again, he interrupted, "Don't worry about that. Just look for me when you get off the plane. Which airline will you take?" "Uh, uh, oh, hell, United. I'll fly United." She couldn't think straight. "I'll see you in a few hours. Goodbye," he said as he hung up. She put the receiver down slowly and thought, "This is it; this is the beginning of our affair, the end of my life with Peter. She then dialed United Airlines.

Tony called Theresa, to find out where Peter was staying and to tell her that he was going to take a pain pill and sleep the rest of the day and night. It was the first time he had lied to her, in fact Tony never lied. He thought for a long while about what he was going to say to Maggie. Finally, after a few hours, he called United Airlines and found out that Maggie would be arriving in Chicago at eleven-thirty. Around nine o'clock he managed to take a shower. Since Rodney was chauffeuring Derek, Alfred would be the only one who would know that he took the Mercedes. He instructed Alfred to keep it quiet. Alfred begged him to stay home, that he wasn't well enough to be driving. But after realizing it was futile, he agreed to keep quiet.

He was in pain, but it was bearable, as he drove to the airport. He parked the car in front, handed a police officer a fifty dollar bill, and asked him to watch it for him. The officer was pleased to do so. Tony hoped he wouldn't be recognized, he wore slacks, sweater, and a leather jacket to hopefully fit in with the crowd. He walked slowly as each step caused more pain in his chest. He could feel the adrenalin begin to pump through his body, he was so anxious to see her.

CHAPTER FOURTEEN

He watched as the plane taxied its way to the terminal. Part of the crew was first off, then came Maggie, she was the first passenger to disembark. They saw each other immediately. Maggie wanted to run, but she wasn't sure if her legs would allow it. Her heart beat faster the closer she got to him. Finally, they were face to face, both of them wanting to grab the other, but, instead, Tony squeezed her hand. She leaned up and kissed his cheek and said, "You look good, a little thin, but well." He looked into her eyes, "You get lovelier every time I see you. I'm glad you came." As they walked to the car, they discussed Tony's physical condition and her flight. Maggie insisted on driving so he could rest. It was obvious, although he attempted to conceal it, that he was in a lot of pain. He instructed her to drive to the Hyatt Regency on Wacker Boulevard, where he had made her a reservation. They could have a drink at the bar. Their discussion was limited to the area they were driving through. They went directly to the lounge when they arrived at the hotel. Once they ordered drinks, Maggie lit a cigarette and asked, "Tony, what am I doing here?" He also lit a cigarette, "You know I almost gave these up. They tasted horrible in the hospital." Maggie asked again, "You didn't answer me, what am I doing here?" He looked at her for a moment and finally said, "Maggie, I want to be very honest with you. I haven't been able to think about anything but you, ever since that day we spent together, actually, even before that day. I laid in that hospital bed and thought about you, and more times than not, when I looked up there you were, either standing or sitting, you were there. Then one day, you were gone. I've missed you terribly. I have never missed anybody in my life; I'm not sure what's happening to my emotions. I have ideas, but I'm not sure. I just want you to know what's going on inside me."

She knew, very well, what was going on inside him, the same things were happening to her. She put her hand on his as she began to speak, "Tony, all the way out here, I wondered what I was going to say to you, about my feelings. Tony, I too, spend all of my time thinking about you. That day we spent together was beautiful, and when I heard that you had been shot, I, uh, I was mortified, I was so afraid you would die and I'd never be able to tell you how I felt. Tony, my emotions are doing the same as yours." She squeezed his hand. "I love you, Maggie!" He blurted out before he could stop it. She drew her hand back, and grabbed a handkerchief to wipe away the tears, that seemed to always be present; she sniffed and said, "Oh, Tony, I love you too!" She cried harder. Tony stood up, took her hand and said, "come on, we can't talk here." They registered Maggie at the front desk, and then went up to her suite. Tony was in pain as he sat slowly. Maggie sat next to him, "Is there anything I can do for you? You look as though you're ready to faint." He smiled, "No, I'm okay. Really, I am." Maggie went to fix drinks. Tony questioned, "Why did you leave in such a hurry, and not come back with Peter?" She didn't turn around but said, "Because Roni was coming, and I was jealous. I knew that I wanted to take care of you and be with you, and that it was impossible. So I left. I've been an absolute bitch ever since. I drink too much, my tennis game has gone to hell, I treat Peter like shit, I cry all the time, and all of that is happening because I realized that I'm in love with you and there is nothing I can do about it, except feel guilty every time I look at Peter." The tears came again, "And, uh, sniff, I don't, sniff, I don't want to love you!" She ran across the room, sat on her knees, and laid her head on his lap and sobbed, "What are we going to do Tony?" With tears swelling in his eyes, he lifted her face up, and said, "We'll have to try to live with it. Too many people will get hurt if we pursue our love. God will bring us together, somehow, if it's to be that way." She begged him, "What do you mean? Please explain what you just said." "Maggie, I would love to lay you on that bed and make love to you, like I've never loved a woman before. I dream about that, but if we did I'd never be able to leave you alone or be able to look at myself in the mirror again. I don't know if I'm old fashioned, high moraled, or what, but I do know that I couldn't live with myself if I were to sleep with a married woman. Falling in love, one cannot help, but I can't do anything more. We'll just have to live with our emotions. Do you understand?" Maggie touched his face, "Of course, I understand. Your feelings and good heart are part of the reasons I've fallen in love with you, and I also have morals, but I couldn't say no to you, I wouldn't want to. I just don't know how I'll act when I'm around you, or how I'll be with Peter." Tony replied, "We're both adults, I'm sure we'll be able to cope with our emotions. How we'll do it, I don't know, but I know that I want you to move here so I can be near you." She stood up, "Yes, I'll move here, and we'll control ourselves, but I'll not let you leave tonight until you, at least, kiss me even it's the first and last time." Tony stood, they faced each other. Maggie snuggled up to him, slid her arms around his waist, and lifted her face to his. For a long moment the stared into each others eyes, then Tony kissed her forehead, her nose, her cheeks, and finally their anxious mouths met. They were devouring each other, reaching emotional peaks neither had ever reached before. They were totally entwined in each other. Finally, after many minutes they separated, "I don't want you to leave, ever! Tony, I love you so deeply!" She spoke into his ear. He pulled away from her, "I've got to leave, or I never will." With her arms still around his neck, Maggie asked the one question she had to know, "One question, I have to ask, what about you and Roni? She loves you, too, you know." Tony sat down again, "That is a very good question. Roni is terrific. I've been nothing but honest with her. She realizes that I'm committed to building an empire. I do enjoy her company, but I could never be "in love" with her. I will continue to see her, if I don't, I'll go absolutely insane thinking about you. I'll never mislead her though." Maggie was staring at him with loving eyes, "That's what I thought you were going to say. I can't blame you, I agree in as much as she's terrific. She doesn't deserve to be hurt, any more than Peter. Will you marry her?" Tony didn't hesitate, "No! I promise you, I'll never marry her. How could I marry Roni, or anybody, when I love you so much?" Maggie, "I'm going to cause you nothing but unhappiness. I'll be married and you may never have that, even though I'll never enjoy it again. What have we done Tony?" He stood, "Kiss me, once more, and I'll get out of here." They spent the next several moments in delirious passion, enjoying this short time together, which may be their last. Tony left, and Maggie cried herself to sleep.

Maggie called Peter early the next morning. She informed him that she was in Chicago that she had changed her mind, and would find them a place to live within the next few days. If all she could have was being close to Tony, then that's what she'd take. By the end of the second day, she leased a luxury apartment in downtown Chicago. They would move within the next two weeks.

Tony spent most of the next few days submerged in the business of building his empire. He talked on the phone continually. He was getting stronger everyday. Roni called him each night, without fail. She had about two more weeks of shooting, and then she would return to Chicago.

CHAPTER FIFTEEN

"Hello Mike, come in. Will you have a drink?" Tony ushered Mike into the study. Mike was carrying a rolled up sheet of paper. He was all smiles as Tony handed him his drink. Tony held up his glass as a toast, "You look like the cat that ate the canary." Mike laughed as he unrolled the paper and laid it across Tony's desk, "Tony, I haven't been this excited since my first sexual encounter. I've finished a rough sketch of a hotel. I've implemented every idea the others mentioned plus some of my own. "This is a showplace! I wanted to show it to you right away. If you like it, I'll begin the actual drawings tomorrow." Tony inspected the sketch thoroughly, "It looks beautiful, explain what everything is." Mike leaned over the sketch, "Let's start with the exterior. I figured twelve stories, that way we do away with the thirteenth floor superstition. We'll use bronze colored glass; you can see it from anywhere. The entrance will be graced with large pillars, giving it a rich gothic presence. Right here, these are two elevators that go up the side of the building, bronze glass of course, the guests can get a view of the area as they ride to their rooms. The two cylinders are on each side of the main building, which will have a roof that resembles a cathedral, slanting to the back. I did some thinking and disagreed with a revolving restaurant on top. I felt the restaurant would draw more people if it were on the ground floor. Right here, the restaurant will be a separate building on the left. It, too, will have the cathedral roof. As you enter from either the main lobby or the restaurant door, you'll descend three steps to the left and ascend three steps to the right. That gives three levels; there'll be a special stairway at each end of the restaurant which takes you to an overhanging balcony." He looked at Tony, who said, "Go on." Mike continued, "On the right side, there is another building. This will house the pool, which is indoor/outdoor, a health club with saunas, a running track, and two racquetball courts. The second floor would be nothing but conference rooms. Guest rooms start on the third floor. The main hotel's first floor will house a coffee shop, lounge, and billiard room. As you enter the lobby three steps will descend into a circular area with couches, chairs, and tables. Pillars will be in the main lobby, also. Well, it's basic but it's a start. What do you think?" Tony extended his hand, "Draw up the plans, I love it. Call Paul Krug, show this to him immediately so he can give you an approximate cost and suggestions." Mike was overjoyed, "Tony thank you! Thank you so much for this opportunity. Saying thank you, isn't enough, what can I do?" Tony smiled, "You're doing it, helping me build my empire." They drank to each other. "Oh, Mike, there is something I'd like. Do you think you could design a house for me, I mean me personally?" "I'd be honored and flattered. I'd love to. Do you have any idea of what you want or where?" Tony thought of Maggie for a fleeting second, she was the only other person who even knew about his land, he said, "If you'll drive north on Lake Shore Drive about five or six miles from here, you'll see a strip of land that broadens out for about three quarters of a mile then narrows again. It must be half-a-mile deep from the road. It drops off into the lake. That land is mine; I've owned it for a few years now. Why don't you take a look at it and decide what type of house would be right for me and the land." "I know exactly where that is, I've been passed it a thousand times. What a place for the Cole Mansion. Tony, I'll get to it as soon as I can," Mike was a changed person. He was finally happy after 32 years of life, and he realized he owed it all to Tony Cole.

CHAPTER SIXTEEN

"Well, Tony, I'd say you're as good as new. You've done fantastic. If you haven't already, you can resume all normal activities," Dr. Ballinger said as he completed Tony's chart. "Thanks, Fred, I'm glad this over with. It seems like five years instead of five months since that damn shooting, but I really feel good, maybe I'm just glad to be alive," Tony remarked. Dr. Ballinger asked, "Do you think they'll ever catch the guy that shot you?" Tony answered as he was buttoning his shirt, "Hell, I don't think so. He was just a street punk that faded into the ghetto. I just hope he doesn't hurt too many people before he gets his." You would've thought he could've been linked to the one that was with him, the guy you ki..." he stopped before he completed the sentence, but Tony knew what he was about to say, "The guy I killed Fred." "Well, I didn't mean it the way it was said, Tony; I guess that's been pretty hard to handle?" Tony looked at Fred, "Not at all, Fred. It was me or him, out in the street. When you go out in the street, it's a war zone that guy lost, simple way of life and death." I don't think I've ever heard you talk so cold. In fact, I didn't think you were capable of ill feelings against anybody," said a shocked Dr. Ballinger. Tony put his hand on the door to leave, "Fred, don't forget, I grew up in that street. Goodbye."

Tony went to the pool, where Roni was basking in the warm Chicago sunshine. She saw him and jumped out of the chaise to greet him, "Hi, a-okay, I presume?" She kissed him and waited for an answer. Tony grinned and said, "Good as new." She was so happy, she kissed him again and then said, "I heard from the studio today. They're finally going to release the movie. The premiere is set for September 15th in New York. Can you make it?" He looked at her and said, "Well, I'm not sure. We have a lot going on, but I would believe that I'll be able to go, in fact, I wouldn't miss it." She kissed him again. Roni had never been so happy. Tony became her whole life. He sat down, "Why don't we take a combination work/play trip. We've got a month before the premiere, and I've got to go to California and Texas. We'll just get in the plane and go. We'll stop over in Vegas and maybe Acapulco for a couple of days then go on to New York." "Oh Tony, I love you so much. I'd love it. When can we leave?" Roni was exuberant. He shrugged his shoulders, "Oh, I don't know, how about tonight?" She shrieked. Tony explained, "We'll go to Vegas tonight, spend the week-end then go on to California for work." Roni jumped up, "I'll call Maggie; she and Peter are still in California. Maybe they could meet us in Vegas. We could have a ball." As Roni went into the house to call Maggie and prepare for the trip, Tony thought, "Yes, call Maggie, we haven't been alone together since that night, Christ I've only seen her a few times, yes call Maggie." Derek interrupted Tony's thoughts, "Hey, I understand you got a clean bill of health, buddy." Tony nodded, "Hi Derek." They exchanged their joy for the good weather and their disgust for the dismal play for the White Sox Baseball Team before they began any business talk. Tony asked, "Have you talked to Irving Epps lately?" "Yes, I talked to him last Friday. Why?" Tony requested Alfred to bring more drinks, then said, "I'm going to take a trip to California and I thought I'd pay him a visit and see how our losing investment is doing." Derek laughed, "Irving will have kittens. Just the thought of you scares the hell out of him. He's really a nice little guy though. Do you want me to let him know your coming?" Tony smirked, "Yes, tell him I'll be there Tuesday. I'd like a tour of the facilities. Nothing I'd rather do than visit a place losing our money." "Derek, when did you get here?" Roni said coming out of the house, still in her bathing suit. "What big deals are you two discussing now?" Derek hugged her, "I just arrived, we were just talking." "Yeh, just talking about our non-profit cosm…." Tony stared at Roni, "Our cosmetic company." Tony leaped from his chair, put his hands on Roni's face and excitedly said to Derek, "How many women would like to look like this?" Derek smiled, "All of them, why?" Tony was now overly enthusiastic, "We're sitting on a possible gold mine and letting it lose money. That grinds me. I've got an idea!" Derek and Roni looked puzzled. Tony gulped at his drink and lit a cigarette, "Roni, how would you like to venture into the cosmetic business and make some money with no investment?" Smiling, she replied, "Well, I've never thought about going into business, but I like the thought of making money without an investment. What are you talking about?" Derek was beginning to follow Tony's thoughts, "I think I know what you're driving at, but tell me." "Okay. Sit down Roni," he was genuinely excited, "Roni just happens to be the most popular female personality in the world, she's noted to be one of the most, if not, the most beautiful woman. She has the name, the face, and the popularity and Cole Industries has a losing cosmetic manufacturer. If we would combine the two, use Roni's name and face, and market it correctly, we could make millions. We could create a complete line of cosmetics called "Roni." The investment from you, Roni, would be the use of your name and your time to market it. Hell, we could do it immediately. All we have to do is change the name on our packaging and start advertising. What do you think?" "God damned," Derek clapped, "One helluva an idea. We could design special packaging, maybe even subcontract a perfume company to make a perfume for us. Roni could appear on TV, radio, newspapers, hell yes, I love it!" Roni was grinning from ear to ear, "Me too. It sounds really exciting. I'll call my agent, he can tell me if I'm prohibited from doing anything like this, but I'm sure I'm not." Tony, still excited, "Tell your agent you'll receive ten percent of the gross, which will make him a richer man in the future. Derek, call Henri and have him contact a designer for the packaging, see if he can set up a meeting quickly, then call an advertising agency for a meeting. I'll inform Irving of the upcoming change so he can gear up the factory. Miss Diane Cosmetics will no longer be losing money. We'll change the name to "Faces of Roni." Derek exclaimed, "I'll call Henri right now. Damn, this is exciting!" Roni looked at Tony, "You never quit thinking of ways to make money, do you?" He laughed, "I have a challenge to meet, remember!" Tony stood, "Now, let's get ready to go, we'll need a week-end now, because I want to get this thing going. Can you take some time off to do the advertisements?" Roni answered, "Of course, I'm not scheduled for another picture until January or February."

CHAPTER SEVENTEEN

"Peter and Maggie will be here any time. Are you ready?" Tony asked. "Yes," she came into the living room of the suite, she looked like a goddess, "But we have to wait for Milton, agents are always late." Tony stared at her for a moment and thought, "She's beautiful, no, gorgeous, why then do I still think of Maggie?" "That's Peter and Maggie," she said as she heard a knock on the door. As they entered, Peter kissed Roni then hurried to Tony. Maggie and Roni hugged one another and traded compliments. Tony had been nervous all day, anticipating seeing Maggie. She had been the same. Their eyes met and Tony released Peter's hand. Maggie kissed his cheek and squeezed his hand, "It's great to see you again, Tony." Her knees were trembling. She thought she was doing better, being away from him for awhile, but now, just seeing his face, touching him, she knew that her love for him had grown even stronger. Tony looked at her, "You look magnificent, Maggie, just magnificent!" Even though Roni treated him like a king, it will always be Maggie, "Nobody will ever make me feel this way but her," he thought. "So, what do we owe this occasion? You two going to tie the knot?" Peter asked. Maggie's eyes darted at Tony. "He said he'd never marry her," she instantly remembered. "We haven't discussed it, but I think that's a splendid idea!" Roni remarked as she put her arm around Tony. Tony looked at Maggie, "I'm not ready for that and neither is she, really." Roni shrugged, "Oh well, it was a good thought. Maybe some other time, right honey?" Maggie's eyes were fixed on Tony. He answered, "One never knows, does one!" Maggie sighed; she knew that was Tony's way of saying no graciously.

"Ah," Roni went to the door, "This will be Milton." "Milton, my dear," she hugged him, "come in. Milton this is Tony Cole." Tony extended his hand to Milton, who anxiously accepted, "Mr. Schraff, it's a pleasure to meet you. Roni has told me a lot about you." Milton remarked, "I must say it is truly my pleasure to meet the man that's made Roni so happy." He then shook hands with Peter and hugged Maggie. He had always been fond of Maggie. He attempted to get her in the movie business but she wasn't interested. "What's everybody drinking?" Tony questioned. "I'll have a scotch and soda," said Maggie. Roni agreed, "I'll have the same." Peter asked for a whiskey on the rocks and Milton preferred a martini. Tony had his usual Jack Daniels on ice. They sat down to small talk while Tony fixed the drinks. While serving them he said, "Milton, I've offered Roni an interest in a business venture. She seems to like the idea, so we'd like to discuss it with you." Peter, realizing he wasn't aware of this asked, "Tony is this going to be a Tony Cole/Roni Scott venture or a Cole Industries/ Roni Scott venture?" "It will be a Cole Industries investment with Roni getting part of the action," Tony replied. Maggie couldn't take her eyes from him, "He's so powerful!" "Milton," Tony continued, "Roni is the best known female in the country and I think we could both benefit from her popularity. Cole Industries presently owns a cosmetic firm that is close to bankruptcy. In my opinion, we could change the name and packaging to include Roni's name and grab a share of the cosmetic market. Cole will put up the money to change the company around. What we'll need from Roni is the use of her name, and her time to do advertising. For that, Roni will receive ten percent of the gross, which means you'll also receive a piece." He waited for Milton's response. "I've been trying to get Roni to do commercials for two years. She has always been against it. So what do you say Roni?" Roni was all smiles, "Milty, I'm excited as hell about it. I think Tony's right; it could take the cosmetic industry by storm." "What a helluva an idea!" exclaimed Peter. Milton dug for a cigarette, "I agree, if you need my blessing, you've got it." "Good, we need one other thing. We want you to keep Roni from working until the first part of next year at least," Tony commanded. Milton, now with a broad grin, "She's not scheduled for anything until then anyway. However, from what I'm hearing, you may be nominated for best actress for the work you just finished. If so, you'll be even more in demand and you won't be able to get out of most of it." "Oh Roni, that's terrific! Congratulations, I hope!" said an excited Maggie. "Thanks, Mag, but it's awfully premature for congratulations, but if that were true, it would only enhance my position with the cosmetics. We'll work out the scheduling problems. Milton, we're going into this and, hopefully, it will be a lot of fun and make us all a lot of money." Roni could be very strong when she wanted. Tony shook Milton's hand and said, "Our lawyer will draw up a contract so we'll be nice and legal. Now, let's get something to eat. Oh, one more thing, I don't want this let out, we're going to surprise the competition with it. The cosmetic industry is full of spies; they'd steal an idea from their mothers company if they get the chance."

Peter was dancing wit Roni and Milton had retired for the evening. Tony and Maggie were left alone at their table. They sat in silence for a moment, just looking at each other. Tony finally spoke, "You look lovely. How have you been?" She spoke in a very soft voice, "I've been okay. Would you dance with me? Tony smiled, "I'd love to!" The music fit their mood perfectly; the singer was doing her rendition of the Carpenter's "For All We Know." Maggie snuggled her head on Tony's shoulder. He held her tight, enjoying the softness of her hair, the faint whiff ofJoy perfume, he remembered the fragrance always, he could feel the softness of her breasts against him. "I think of you always, I miss you terribly," he whispered in her ear. Without raising her head, she responded, "Please, don't make me cry, when you talk like that I can't control myself. Tony, it's hard to be adult, it's hard to control my emotions, I want to be with you; I miss you more everyday." He leaned back; she raised her head to look at him, he said, "I love you, Maggie." She licked her lips and breathed heavily, "Oh Tony, I love you too, I'm going to cry!" He pushed her head back on his shoulder, "No, you're not going to cry. We should be happy, after all, this is the only way we can be this close, let's enjoy it while we can." The music stopped and Maggie whispered, "Don't let the music or this moment stop, please Tony." They held hands all the way to the table. Roni and Peter were engulfed by Roni's fans. She was signing napkins, business cards, anything people could have autographed. As Tony and Maggie were seated, Tony remarked, "We may be here awhile. Roni truly enjoys signing autographs." Maggie watched the crowd surrounding Roni, "Yes, she's a perfect star. She really loves you Tony." Tony lit a cigarette, "Yes, it seems so. What do you think of our new cosmetic venture?" "You'll do exactly what you said, make a lot of money. I guess that will make you happy," Maggie replied. "Making money, or rather building Cole Industries is keeping my sanity. I spend most of my time thinking about you," Tony explained as he lit her cigarette. She started to say something when Peter arrived and said, "Boy,

I don't think I could handle being a super star, but Roni sure does well at it." Tony agreed, "Yes, she does."

Roni had finally signed her last autograph and the night was coming to an end. They all decided to turn in for the night. Roni had enjoyed one of her few nights out in public, Peter was overjoyed just being with Tony and Roni, and Tony and Maggie had seized their moment together. All in all, it was a good evening for everybody. The next morning, they would all depart for L.A. Peter and Maggie were driving while Tony and Roni would fly aboard the Cole orange and blue jet.

CHAPTER EIGHTEEN

Irving Epps scurried around the Miss Diane Cosmetics offices making sure everything were in the proper place. He was a nervous wreck, just thinking about meeting Tony Cole for the first time. He glanced at the clock on the wall, eight o'clock; he had an hour before he arrived. Irving wondered, "Why is he really coming? A man of his stature doesn't come to just look; I hope the place looks okay."

The rented limousine rolled up to the main entrance of the small factory and the driver said, "Here we are Mr. Cole." The driver opened his door and Tony stepped out and took a long look at the building. "It doesn't look like much, does it?" The driver was definitely right. Tony didn't like the looks of the building with broken windows, cracked entrance steps, handrail hanging loose, and the little sign by the entrance with two missing screws, and especially the trash along the building. "I'll probably be a few hours, so make yourself comfortable somehow," Tony told the driver. The lobby was small with a faded green tile that had pieces missing and a cracked dusty picture of Irving on the wall, two torn orange plastic chairs, and a sliding glass with a heavy set gum-chewing receptionist behind the glass. Tony stood at the glass for over five minutes before the girl realized he was there. He was disgusted by the whole scene. The girl slid the glass open, "Yeh, can I help you?" "Irving Epps, please." "Who can I say wants him?" The girl's unprofessional attitude was disturbing Tony a great deal. With no expression, Tony replied, "Tony Cole." The girl quickly put the gum in an ashtray, fluffed her hair, and said, "Oh, Mr. Cole, we've been expecting you. Come in. I'll get Irving, uh, Mr. Epps." Tony followed the girl through the door. "At least they cleaned the office!" He said to himself.

Irving almost ran out of his office, "Uh, hello, Mr. Cole. I'm so glad you, uh, I mean, uh, it's a pleasure to meet you. I'm Irving Epps." Tony shook his hand as he thought to himself, "You're going to have to change Irving." Tony didn't respond. Irving then said, "Come in, we can talk in my office. Carol, bring us some coffee." He ordered the receptionist who was all but pressing her large breasts against Tony. "Of course Mr. Epps, anything for Mr. Cole!" She then turned away swinging her rear end like a back porch swing. "No, I don't want coffee. Why don't we walk through the plant as we talk? You can show me how cosmetics are made," Tony insisted.

Tony and Irving spent the next hour touring the small plant. Irving was very proud of the operation. He had seen to it that the general working area was kept clean, in fact, it was spotless. He pointed out each phase of the operation. Tony was impressed with his knowledge and enthusiasm. Once in Irving's office Tony said, "I'll have that coffee now." Irving stepped out to inform Carol to bring in the coffee. He offered Tony his chair, but Tony instructed him to use his own chair. Finally, the coffee was served, Carol had rubbed her breasts across Tony's shoulder, and the door was closed. "Irving, what would you have to do to triple sales? I mean new equipment, personnel, etc.," Tony questioned. "Triple sales! Wow, I'm not sure!" Irving was flabbergasted by the question. Tony asked, "What if Roni Scott advertised our product?" Irving swallowed as though he were swallowing a golf ball, "Uh, Roni Scott, the movie star? Whew, that might do more than triple sales. We're set up now to do at least twice the business. I'd have to hire more people. Can you get her to do it?" Tony evaded answering him at that moment, but commanded, "Irving, I want you to hire enough people to accommodate sales tripling. I also want the offices enlarged and completely re-done, walls, floors, furniture, and everything, I want a high fence constructed around the building, the entire outside appearance of this building will be changed, put in grass, plants, flowers, trees, etc. Hire a maintenance department to take care of the building and grounds, and most of all, get rid of that offensive receptionist out there. Hire a professional; I'll expect her to be gone today!" Irving sat dumbfounded, "Mr. Cole, I don't mean any disrespect, after all, you are the owner, but all those things are meaningless. The finished product is what really matters. All the things you just mentioned cut into the profits that could be put into new products." Tony lit a cigarette, leaned back in his chair, then said sternly, "Irving, listen to me very carefully." He paused then continued, "This Company is now a division of Cole

Industries, and Cole will not, I repeat, will not have a pig sty as a part of its operation. This cosmetic company will take on a totally new image, starting immediately. Do you understand?" He understood perfectly, "Uh, yes, of course, whatever you say." Tony smiled, "Good. Here's what we're going to do. First, give all of your present employees a month off, with pay, but hire a new receptionist to start right away and go ahead and hire new help and have them start a month from today. When you inform your present employees that they have a month off with pay, also inform them that when they return they'll all receive a raise. Stop all production of Miss Diane Cosmetics. Second, the changes I mentioned earlier, they'll take place immediately. Irving, we're changing the name of the company. It will become Cole Cosmetics and Fragrances. All products will carry the label of "Faces of Roni". We'll have all new packaging. Roni Scott will be doing TV, radio, newspaper, magazines, and billboard advertising. I want to start production of the new product within 30 days. We'll use the same formula you use now. The product remains the same, the name, packaging, and image changes." Irving sat with his mouth open, he couldn't speak. Tony waited and finally Irving spoke, "I'm overwhelmed, Mr. Cole! I really don't know what to say!" Tony stood, "Derek Hill will be here tomorrow to direct reconstruction. I'm meeting with a designer tonight to come up with the new packaging. Irving, I'll be in touch. Thank you for the courtesy." He shook hands with Irving and left before he could respond. As Tony walked out, he told the receptionist that Mr. Epps wanted to see her.

Tony, Derek, and Henri sat on the balcony enjoying a drink, while they waited for Jacques DuPont, the well-known French designer of women's accessories. "Derek, I want you to be at that damn cosmetic factory first thing in the morning. I'm not sure Irving is capable of fitting into our type of operation. You stay out here until the job is finished. You make the decision of what you want it to look like," Tony commanded. Derek asked, "Sure, do you have any ideas?" Tony replied, "I want all windows covered, a circular receptionist area, and the color combination to be the Cole bright orange and blue. You do the rest."

Henri introduced Jacques to Tony and Derek. They began to discuss the future of their new venture. "Henri tells us that you're quite interested in doing the designs for our Roni line of cosmetics. Well, I must tell you, that we feel quite honored to have someone with your reputation and knowledge in our corner," Tony made sure Jacques knew that Cole Industries realized his importance in this field. Jacques DuPont was the epitamy of the romantic Frenchman, medium height, slender, in his forty's, graying temples, impeccably dressed, gracious, and extremely polite. He spoke excellent English although he had never spent much time in this country. Jacques was pleased that Tony acknowledged his reputation, "Thank you Mr. Cole. It is my pleasure to work with you. You may not realize it, but we know of you in Europe, too. Now what would you like to do? I am very excited to design something for Roni Scott; such a beautiful woman shall receive the most exquisite package of cosmetics this world will ever see." It was obvious that Jacques was one of the many millions that so adored Roni. "Jacques, you're exactly right," Tony exclaimed, "We want a design that will capture the eyes of the public, we want an extension of Roni!" "Have you ever met Roni?" Jacques smiled, "I have always had that desire, but I've never had the pleasure. Could you arrange it for me?" "That, Mr. DuPont, is no problem, you'll meet her tomorrow," Tony assured him. Jacques was surely pleased, "Mr. Cole, thank you! I will certainly look forward to that."

Jacques removed a scratch pad and a box of colored pencils from his briefcase, "I believe the packaging should be simple, but unique. It should look more expensive than it is, by doing that, the customer will think they are getting a bargain as well as quality. I think the color will be the most important ingredient in perfecting the package." He was drawing on the pad while he talked. His first drawing was done in a soft pink background with silver stars all over the box. He handed it to Tony, "Here is my first idea." Tony examined it, and then handed it to Henri; Derek moved to look at it with Henri. Tony waited until they had finished, "What are your thoughts?" Derek answered, "I don't know much about this, but I think it might be a bit gaudy." Henri was next, "I like the idea of stars, it is used to pronounce Roni's field of excellence, and I'm sure. I don't think I like the pink color." Tony simply said, "Let's try another." This process continued for over three hours. Jacques drew designs using nearly every color combination, shape, and idea he could come up with, and still they could not agree on a combination. Jacques put down his pad and said, "I've got to stop for a moment. Could I please have another drink?" He stood up, stretched, and lit a cigarette; he started to say something when he ran back to his seat, picked up his pad, took out another colored pencil, "I think I've got the right combination! Oh, yes, this is it. This one you'll like, no you'll love it!" When he had finished, he held it up, looked at it, and then with a large sigh he handed the paper to Tony, "<u>This</u> is it. Roni cosmetics come alive!" Tony looked at it with Henri and Derek over each shoulder, "Yes, I love it!" Henri exclaimed. "Me, too!" agreed Derek. Tony smiled, "Well, Jacques, I, too, agree. This is what we were looking for.

They agreed on a smokey grey package with a simple Roni spelled out in an ivory color; the only star left on the package was to dot the i in her name.

As the four of them sat discussing the last few hours, Jacques stated, "You should add a fragrance line – perfume – to complement the cosmetics. That would allow the consumer to purchase a full line of Roni female aids." "Yes, a terrific idea!" Tony acknowledged, "But I don't want to purchase a perfume company right now." "You don't have to. You could contract someone else to do it for you; I just happen to know a small French company that could do it," Jacques reported. "What do you think?" Tony asked Henri. "I trust Jacques. He knows this business. I'd say go for it." Derek stood and said, "Why don't we have different clothing outfits designed in the smokey and ivory colors for Roni to wear in the advertising?" "Very good! Very wise idea!" Jacques agreed. "That would exemplify the packaging. Hell, we could have her in evening gowns, career/women suits, riding outfits, bathing suits, casual slacks, blouses, and…oh, shit…the possibilities are endless. I think we should add it." Henri was very excited. Tony sat smiling. He sipped at his drink, and then said, "Okay, it looks like you guys think we should go the full route on this. I agree with you. Jacques, can you design clothing?" "Of course, I have already!" Tony continued, "Fine. If we're going to add the expense of designing clothing for advertisements, then let's reap benefits from it. We'll offer Roni clothing in the Cole Department Stores. In fact, we'll have a complete Roni Department in each store. But we'll market the entire line in other parts of the country such as the East Coast. By doing that, we'll monopolize the sales of the Roni collection in our own market areas but sell it to selected fine stores throughout the rest of the country." Henri was practically jumping up and down, "Damn, this is really exciting. I'll contact a clothing manufacturer in Italy…I know him well, and he's very reasonable. I can head for Europe tomorrow!" Jacques added. "I'll go with you. You can seal the deal on contracting the perfume company and the clothing company this week. I can have some designs finished very soon; at least enough to start advertising with." "Good. We have another challenge. Derek, you stay very close to Irving Epps. Get that damn eye-sore of his looking like something Cole Industries will be proud of. I'll not call it ours until it's changed."

It was after two a.m. before they finally stopped the discussion of the newest venture of Cole Industries. Henri, Jacques, and Derek had left Tony in his suite. He poured another drink, lit a cigarette and sat on the balcony enjoying the quiet, dark, warm, early morning hours. Roni had driven to Palm Springs; she wanted to open her house for a couple of days. Tony wanted to miss her, but he didn't…he adored her, as a person, but he couldn't love her. His thoughts turned to Maggie, "…I wonder if she's asleep…I'd love to call her…just hear her voice…shit, I should be happier than ever, and I'm the most unhappy…all because of a damned woman… oh, but what a wonderful woman…she's per…" he fell asleep thinking about her.

CHAPTER NINETEEN

Her soft hands felt good as they moved slowly over his chest. Her breasts were pressed against his back. She was doing a masterful job of exciting him. With her hand wrapped around his penis, she began kissing his back then slowly downward until she softly kissed his buttocks. He rolled onto his back, as she gently stroked his rock-hard penis. He sighed aloud when her mouth took all of his masculinity. He could hardly stand it, the sensation was beyond belief. She lifted her head and began moving up his body darting her tongue across his chest. When she reached his mouth, she pressed her lips hard against his, then brought her knees up until her vagina was just touching the head of his penis – then with a thrust of excitement, he pushed himself into her, and she moaned, Oh, Peter, you always make me feel so good, you make me feel like a cheap whore…ohh, God, don't stop; please don't stop!"

They lay there, motionless; both breathing as though they had ran a mile instead of enjoying intercourse. Peter reached for his cigarettes, "Want one?" "Yes." "How long are you going to be gone this time?" she asked with a hurt in her voice. "I don't know. Listen, Wanda – honey – I didn't take this position in Chicago because I wanted to get away from you. I had no choice. I still pay the rent, the car, give you spending money; what the hell else do you want from me?"

Wanda took a long pull on her cigarette. Her big blue eyes staring into his, "I want you! Why? I sure as hell don't know. You've been telling me for over two years that it wouldn't be long, and then we'd be together – all the time. I think you're a lying son-of-a-bitch. I think you're happy with this arrangement – you slip in here, fuck me for a couple of hours, whenever you feel like it – then you run home back to Maggie, dear, sweet, little Maggie. Fuck you, I want you now – damnit – I want you now!" She put her face into the pillow and sobbed. Peter got up and started toward the bathroom, "I'm going to take a shower; you coming with me?" He had gone through this scene before.

He had been in the shower only a few minutes when Wanda stepped in with him, "I'm sorry, Peter, I really am. It's just that – well, you're gone all the time now. I used to see you three or four times a week – now, I'm lucky if I see you once a month. I miss you. Our arrangement was fine before – but, Peter, I need more of your time. Don't you understand?" He pulled her to him, and kissed her letting the water from the shower spray on their faces, "Yes, of course, I understand. I just can't help it. I work for somebody else now. He tells me where to go and when. Hell, I had to drive up to Vegas to spend a night out with him. I would've much rather been here with you." He ran his hand between her legs, and she began to move up and down while he rubbed her vigorously. She reached for him, and began stroking him. She turned around quickly and bent over, her hands pressed against the wall, her buttocks upward. Peter maneuvered behind her, and she reached back until she found his stiffness, then she guided him into her. In just seconds, she screamed out loud, having a thunderous orgasm.

They had finished their shower, and Peter was dressing. Wanda was sitting on the bed, still nude, "Do you have a girl like me in Chicago?" He chuckled, "Hell no. I've told you, before; you are the only woman I want." She didn't smile, "That's why you're still married to Maggie. Right?" Peter acted angry, "Listen, damn it, I took you out of that fuckin' dingy restaurant, gave you a nice place to live, nice car to drive, nice clothes to wear, and the only thing I've ever asked from you is some of your ass whenever I can get here. So what's with all this bullshit?" She didn't cry this time. She just stared and said, "You're right. I should be thankful. Shit, I'm one of the purest whores in California – I only use it once every 30 to 40 days. Get the fuck out of here. I don't need you. Get out!" Peter leaned down, kissed her cheek and said, "I'll call you in a couple of days. Be good." She watched the door close, then picked up a perfume bottle and threw it at the door.

CHAPTER TWENTY

As Tony was dressing, he looked in the mirror and thought, "I can't remember the last time I wore a tux." He was just as ordinary as everybody else when it came to movies. He had met most of the Hollywood elite and was sleeping with the Goddess of Tinseltown, but he was still excited about attending his first premier.

The film had been acclaimed as the new "Gone with the Wind." It was a spectacular performance by Roni. She was practically assured of a best actress nomination...some critics were already calling her the winner.

Derek and Theresa came in. "Hey, Tony, are you ready?" Derek yelled from the living room of Tony's presidential suite in the Waldorf. Tony was putting on his jacket when he came from the bedroom, "I think this is the first time you've ever been early," Tony remarked. "Hi, Tony." Theresa gave him a kiss. Derek and Theresa were both smiling like two little kids keeping a secret. "Okay, you two, what's up?" Tony pressured. Theresa took Derek's arm as he said, "I've got a question to ask you, old buddy." He waited for Tony to look at him. "So, ask!" Derek looked at Theresa then smiled at Tony, "I'd like to know if you'll be best man at my wedding. We're getting married!" Tony grabbed his heart and leaned against the couch as though he was having a heart attack, "Oh God, this is too much!" He laughed. "We're not kidding. We're really getting married," Theresa said excitedly. Tony walked to them; he took Theresa in his arms and said, "I'm not sure I'll allow it. She's too damn good for you." He then pulled Derek over and hugged both of them,

"Of course, I'll be your best man. I'd have you shot if you'd have asked someone else. When did it all of this come about, anyway? Let's have a drink on it." "It started when you were in the hospital," Theresa said. "We spent a lot of time together, we got to know each other and the next thing you know, he had me in his bed." Derek patted her on the bottom, "That's all it took. I fell in love with her right then." Tony thought to himself, "Damn, maybe I was wrong to have passed her up. She must be quite a woman to snare Derek…hell; he's balled half the women in Chicago…"

They toasted their good news and Tony asked, "When is the wedding scheduled?" "We'd like to make it on Thanksgiving weekend," Theresa replied with a big smile. Tony grinned and said, "How would you like to have the reception in my new house? It will be my gift to you." They looked at each other and then Theresa hugged Tony, "That would be marvelous. Thank you!"

They were leaving the suite when Theresa said, "I'm going to ask Maggie Weyland to be my Maid of Honor. Do you think she'll accept?" Derek shot a quick look at Tony. Tony just grinned, "I'm sure she will. She'll be as excited as I am." Tony stopped in his tracks, "Hey, I'll bet this means I'll have to get a new secretary!" Derek slapped him on the shoulder, "Oh, no. I'm keeping her working. You don't think we're giving up her healthy salary, do you?" They all laughed as they entered the elevator. Roni was staying in a suite one floor up. Premiers made her very nervous and bitchy so she had decided to stay in her own room.

The limousine pulled to a stop in front of the Paramount Theatre. There must have been 20,000 people crowding around the entrance. They all wanted a glimpse of Roni. She had been popular before, but the critics and media had praised her so much that Roni's name was surely a household word.

When the door opened, the crowd began to shout. "Roni, Roni, Roni… we love you!" She was absolutely gorgeous, dressed in a white gown and white Ermin fur. Once she appeared from the car, the police could barely hold back the crowd. She smiled and waved to them. Tony emerged beside her and she took his arm. As they walked toward the entrance, she shook hands with every fan she could reach. Roni Scott would have made an excellent politician. Flashbulbs from cameras looked like fireworks. The

TV commentator stuck a microphone in her face, "Can you say something to your fans that aren't here, Roni?" She smiled into the camera, "I wish each and everyone of you could be here tonight. But, all of my love goes out to all. Thanks to everybody. Please, go see the movie, you'll love it. Bye, bye!" They disappeared into the theatre where they were seated with Derek, Theresa, Milton Schraff, and his wife.

The picture was, indeed, all that the critics claimed it to be, there was a fifteen minute standing ovation when it ended. Roni was besieged by the fans in the theatre. Police had to fight off some very aggressive fans as they left. Roni wanted to sign autographs but the crowd was to unruly. The police escorted she and Tony to their limousine. Leonard Foulkrod, her producer, had acquired the entire "Tavern on the Green" for a party.

While enroute to the party, Roni asked Tony, "Well, what did you think?" He flashed his famous grin, "Magnifico, my darling!" She threw her arms around him and kissed him passionately, "Tony, this is the happiest day of my life. I can't believe how the picture turned out. I was such a bitch during the shooting. I'm so glad you liked it."

The party was noisy. The majority of the cast was there, along with many of the behind the scenes personnel. Besides the movie people attending the party were celebrities who lived in New York including the mayor of the city. It was a large affair, even for New York. Roni wasn't alone all evening. Tony hadn't been near her since they arrived. Derek and Theresa were engaged in a lengthy discussion with Clifton Peay, the renowned author. People kept coming up to Tony to start a conversation, but somebody would pull him away. He decided to take a stroll outside. The September air was cool in New York. It felt good. Stars were shining brightly along with a full moon. The night was beautiful. Tony had just lit a cigarette when he heard someone behind him. He turned, and there she was, more beautiful than the night. "Can't you say hello?" Maggie asked with a smile. He was speechless for a moment, then said, "My god, you're beautiful. I didn't think you were coming, Peter said he wanted to stay close to the building sight." She walked toward him, "Peter did, but I didn't. I came without him." They were face to face, Maggie touched his cheek then Tony put his arm around her waist, pulled her to him, and kissed her. Derek stepped into the parking lot and started to take a sip of his drink when he saw them. He watched them embrace, then returned to the party. Tony asked, "When did you arrive in New York?" "About two hours ago, I came straight here," she said as she lit a cigarette. They said nothing, just looked at each other. Finally, Maggie said, "Tony, I'm not doing well, I love you, I love you so much!" He sighed, "I know the feeling, I'm not doing well either, every time I see Peter or talk to him I think of you, when I'm with Roni I think of you. Everything and everybody makes me think of you." She reached for his hand; he took it and smiled, "Let's join the party."

Roni hugged her, "Maggie, when did you get here?" "Just now, how did it go?" Roni beamed, "Perfect, everything is perfect." She nudged close to Tony, "Doesn't he look absolutely gorgeous in a tuxedo?" Maggie attempted to smile but couldn't, "Yes, I've noticed." Roni took Maggie's hand, kissed Tony on the cheek, and said, "Excuse us, darling, I want Maggie to meet Leonard." He watched them as they made their way through the throng of people, then turned to the bartender, "Give me a full glass of Jack Daniels, no ice." Derek had been watching from the end of the bar. He moved over next to Tony, "Drinking pretty heavily, aren't you?" Tony didn't answer; he finished the drink and ordered another. Derek was quiet for a moment, then said, "Would you like to talk about it?" Tony took a long drink, "Nothing to talk about, nothing can be done, forget it, okay!" Derek persisted, "Listen, you're my best friend and I think I'm yours. I know what you're going through. Maybe there's something I can do." Tony was almost belligerent, "There is nothing! I appreciate your concern, but you should know me well enough by now that I'll be just fine! Where's your beautiful fiancee?" Derek touched Tony's shoulder, "I saw you and Maggie outside together. Why don't you tell Roni and Peter? Hell, go after her, take her away, if you want her that bad." "No!" Tony exclaimed, then smiled at Derek, "Come on, let's find Theresa."

They found Theresa with Maggie sitting at a table next to the window. Theresa noticed them first, "Oh, Derek, Tony, come here. I'm just about to give Maggie the news." "Why don't you wait until later?" Derek requested. He thought he might change Theresa's mind and have her select another maid of honor, for Tony's sake. "I can't! I've got to tell her now!" Theresa was very excited. She and Maggie had become close since she had leased an apartment in the same building as the Weyland's. "Yes, you must tell me now, you've got my curiosity," Maggie insisted. Theresa smiled, "Derek and I are getting married!" Maggie hugged Theresa, "That's great. I couldn't be more happy for you both. Derek, you're getting a wonderful girl and Theresa, you're getting a great guy. When?" "Thanksgiving weekend," Theresa couldn't stop smiling, "Maggie, we want you to be the maid-of-honor. Will you, please?" The thought hit Maggie instantly, "I know Tony will be the best man, that means we'll be standing up together, watching another couple be married, I don't know if I can do it." She began to cry, "Yes, I'd be thrilled, I'm so happy for you." She hugged Theresa again, then hugged Derek. The party lasted well into the night with most everybody drinking excessively, especially Tony.

CHAPTER TWENTY-ONE

The next two months were hectic. Tony spent the majority of his time in the air between Chicago, Los Angeles, Houston, and Europe. Paul Krug and Mike Emerson and their crews were working, practically around the clock. The shopping plaza was two-thirds finished, the hotel was nearly finished in Los Angeles and about half finished in both Houston and Chicago. The cosmetic company had a new building and was now producing "Faces of Roni" cosmetics. "Faces of Roni" perfume and fashions were in production in Europe. They were going to introduce the complete line of cosmetics, perfume, and fashions the week following thanksgiving. Roni had traveled to ten major cities filming TV ads, radio ads, and doing all types of media interviews. The TV and radio ads would break on thanksgiving weekend and she explained about the new "Faces of Roni" line during her interviews. The orders were coming in, even without seeing the product, three times as fast as anticipated. The Cole stores, formerly Henri's, had increased sales since he took them over. Five Star Oil's sales increased dramatically. At Tony's suggestion, they implemented full-service stations and stopped all self-service. A brilliant decision. Five Star was building stations in five states not previously serviced, of course, Cole/Krug construction was doing the building. Once the rendering of the new hotels were released to the press, Cole/Emerson architecture couldn't handle all of the inquiries. Tony's house was completed the first week of November, he moved in immediately. Alfred retired to Florida. Rodney sold the real estate Jonathan had left him to Tony and he retired to California. Tony hired a new butler, Frederick, a maid, a cook, and a new chauffer, Willie. Willie had been Tony's karate instructor, so he actually doubled as a bodyguard. All preparations for

Derek and Theresa's wedding were finished and as their wedding present, the ceremony and reception will be held at Tony's house. Tony, of course, is paying for the whole affair.

Gossip magazines, movie publications, regular newspapers, and every type of media ran what seemed to be continuous articles about the Roni Scott/ Tony Cole relationship. About Roni and her new movie, and about Tony Cole himself. Cole Industries became the talk of Wall Street, all big business eyes were focused on them. Cole Industries was rapidly becoming a leader in the world of big business. Tony had been referred to as "The messiah to the business world, a genius, and even though linked romantically with Roni Scott, still the most eligible bachelor in America."Tony was becoming as well known as Roni, well not quite. Roni's new picture was breaking all box-office records, and it seemed as though she was a shoe-in to receive the "best actress award" at the Oscars. Tony asked Maggie to do the furnishing of his new home, and she was so excited to do it and never put so much time as she did that project. It made her feel as though it was her new home, she made believe she was preparing the house for her and Tony.

It was cool, as the morning air blew in from Lake Michigan. Tony was on the balcony looking out over the lake. He glanced at his watch, four-thirty, he had only slept a couple of hours. He thought about the upcoming day, "Derek will be married, Maggie will look beautiful, the mayor will be present, my new home will be viewed for the first time, Roni will steal the attention, no fault of her own, life was changing. He decided to go downstairs and have a screwdriver. He looked at Roni, sleeping so peacefully. He slipped out quietly.

He was sitting in one of the large leather chairs in the library, when he heard someone coming down the stairs. He stepped out to see who it was. "Oh, Mr. Cole, I didn't know anybody else was awake. I…" Tony interrupted her, "It's quite alright, Mrs. Williams. Would you care to join me for a screwdriver or coffee?" She giggled, "Yes, I would like a screwdriver. I'm so nervous, I can't sleep. Why are you up, Mr. Cole?" Tony motioned for her to sit down while he fixed her drink, "First of all, Mrs. Williams, would you please call me Tony, nobody calls me Mr. Cole." She was embarrassed, "Uh, I'm sorry, of course, it's just that, well, uh, a man of your stature, uh, well, okay, Tony it is." Elizabeth Williams, Theresa's mother, was an extremely attractive woman of forty. There was a great resemblance of her and Theresa. He handed her the drink then sat in the chair facing her, "Would you like a cigarette?" "Yes, please." Tony lit hers, then his, and she said. "It's so very nice of you to put Stan and I up in your house. It's such a lovely home, rather mansion. I've never been in a house like this before. Theresa is very excited about getting married in your house. When she was telling me about the wedding, I had a hard time determining whether she was going to marry Derek or you. She thinks the world of you, too." "I think a lot of her, also, Mrs. Williams," he responded. "I've agreed to call you Tony; don't you think you could call me Liz? Mrs. Williams makes me feel, well, very old." "Excuse me, Liz, I didn't mean to. You're a lovely lady, I see where Theresa gets her good looks," Tony said in his most gracious manner. "Oh, thank you. You know, Tony, you are quite a well-known man, and, I must say this, you are quite handsome. It's easy to see why all the women fall in love with you. Oh yes, Theresa told me about her feelings for you," she said as she squirmed in her seat. "You're most flattering, but i'm sure it's my money that women are attracted to," Tony was embarrassed. Liz walked to the fireplace and said, "You're wrong, your money might be the reason for women who have never met you, but, believe me, for those who have met you, your money means nothing. Take me, for instance, I've been married for twenty-three years and I think you are the most interesting and attractive man I've ever met." Tony was stunned by the conversation, "Well, uh, I, uh...." She walked over until she stood directly in front of him, then released the tie on her robe, the robe fell open, exposing her perfectly shaped nude body, "I'm all yours if you want me, take me, Tony, please!" He had an erection in seconds, he didn't move, he was in shock. She bent down and kissed him, placing her hand between his legs. His principles were going to take a hike, no way he could say no this time.

The shower felt good. He had drank to much, had to little sleep, and to many extra-curricular activities. The guests would be getting up shortly, and he wanted to be downstairs when they came down. Frederick scheduled breakfast at eight. The wedding was at two-thirty. Roni was still sleeping when he finished showering. He watched her sleep for a moment, then dressed. Once he was dressed, he woke Roni. She went into the shower as he left the room.

Frederick had everything in order for breakfast. He had each seat reserved. He was double-checking to make sure they would sit where Tony wanted them. As he walked around the table, he said to himself, "Mr. and Mrs. Claude Benaforte, Mr. Williams, Theresa, Mrs. Williams. That's one side correct. Roni at the end, Mr. and Mrs.Robert Stoner, Mr. and Mrs. Samuel Ulrich, and Tony at the head, very good." "Well, is it right, Frederick?" Tony laughed. "Yes sir. Mr. Cole. I have the bankers from Los Angeles and Houston together and Mr. and Mrs. Benaforte on the same side as the Williams family." "Very good," Tony complimented him.

Tony was nervous about the reaction Liz was going to have, but she acted as though nothing had taken place. This pleased him, because he didn't want anything to spoil Theresa's day. The breakfast passed and the women sat over coffee while the men went into the library, to discuss business, what else.

Tony entered the room where Derek was dressing, "Are you making out okay?" Derek was tying his tie, "Yeh, but son-of-a-bitch, I'm nervous, I can't even tie this damn thing." Tony laughed, "Here, I'll tie it for you." Derek asked, "Are you nervous?" Tony smiled, "What the hell do I have to be nervous about? You're the one giving up his freedom, not me." Derek said, "Tony, I really appreciate everything your doing. You're truly a great friend. I don't know how to thank you." "I just want you and Theresa to be happy and enjoy your wedding day. I don't expect any thanks. Hell, this is my wedding gift, it makes me happy," Tony was very sincere. Derek asked, "When are you going to be happy?" "I am happy. Let's not discuss my situation. Let's just get you married off," Tony exclaimed. Derek had known Tony since they were kids, he had never seen him so troubled or so unhappy. He wished he could do something to help, but he realized that Maggie Weyland was the only person who could make him happy.

The music is starting," Tony reminded Derek, "You've only got a few minutes to change your mind." Derek took a deep breath, "Nope, I never met a better woman before, I'm sure as hell not going to let Theresa get away. Let's do it!" They took their positions beside the minister. The music, an entire orchestra hired by Tony, was playing louder. Mike Emerson led Derek's mother to her seat, his father following. Derek's brother, David, ushered Liz Williams to her seat. Tony couldn't help but think about the sex they had enjoyed just a few hours before. If Theresa was like her mom, in that way, Derek was going to be a lucky man in the bedroom. Liz gave a quick look in Tony's direction. Obviously she had been satisfied as well as him. The music volume increased. Tony couldn't believe his eyes. Maggie always looked beautiful to him, but there were no words to describe the way she looked as she glided slowly toward them. Her eyes never left Tony, and his never left hers. He felt a rush of excitement run through his body. It was as though she was coming to him, as if she was the bride and he the groom. He fantasized it was true. He loved her so much. "Why, God, why can't I be Tony's bride," Maggie thought as she got closer to him. She blocked out everything and evrybody except Tony, "He's so handsome in a tux." When she reached him, Tony took her by the hand to lead her to her position. They held hands for a second longer than normal, their eyes were fixed to each others, "I love you," Maggie whispered. Tony grinned in acknowledgement. Derek was the only one who could see that she had said something. He felt sorry for them. The orchestra played "Here comes the Bride" and the guests rose. Theresa was gorgeous in the ivory wedding gown. She held tightly to her father's arm. She was so happy. Tony glanced at Derek, he was all grins. "How lucky they are," Tony thought. He looked at Maggie and the ever present tears were trickling down her face. Tony, himself, choked back the tears.

After Derek kissed his bride, the orchestra played "We've Only Just Begun", then Bobby Russo, the number one Chicago night life personality, sang the song. Derek and Theresa both gave Tony a smile. Bobby Russo was another of Tony's surprises for their wedding. When Bobby completed the song, they started their walk together, as the orchestra played "Love Story". When Tony took Maggie's hand, her face was streaked from the tears, and he whispered,"Let's pretend it was our wedding." "That's what I've been doing," she whispered in reply.

The reception was in full swing, Derek and Theresa had departed for a week-long honeymoon in Bermuda, also paid for by Tony. Tony spent most of the evening talking with Claude Benaforte, the bankers, and the mayor. He excused himself from Sam Ulrich, snatched a drink, and then interrupted Maggie and another woman he didn't remember, "Could I have a word with you, Mrs. Weyland?" She followed him to the balcony. Tony grinned, "I just wanted to tell you something, I love you, I love you a helluva lot!" She looked around, not seeing anybody close; she kissed him, "You are such a dear. I love you, Tony!" He held her, not caring if they were seen. "Mr. Cole, excuse me," Frederick said. Maggie jumped back. "Yes, Frederick, what is it?" Tony was irritated. "The guests are beginning to leave; I thought you would want to know. I'm sorry to have bothered you." Tony apologized to him, and said, "You're right, I'll be right there." He sighed, "Oh well, I said what I wanted to say." She smiled at him, "Go, go do what you must do. We'll talk again."

Peter was with Claude Benaforte and his wife; they had their coats on and were waiting for Maggie. Tony was saying his Goodbye's to the remaining guests. Roni walked the Weyland's and Benaforte's to their awaiting cars. Finally, they were all gone, just Stan and Liz Williams remained; they of course were staying at Tony's house for the night. Tony, with a big sigh, said, "I could stand one more drink, would anybody care to join me?" Roni put her arms around his waist, startling him, "I would!" Both Stan and Liz agreed. "Frederick, we'll have drinks in my office, I think it's the only place that's clean." Once in his office, which rarely did Tony allow anyone there, Liz remarked, "Wow, is this where you make all those million-dollar deals?" "No, this is where I escape. This is where all those million-dollar deals are dreamed up," Tony explained. "Mr. Cole, I would like to thank you for everything you've done concerning Theresa's wedding, you did a tremendous job. Liz and I are extremely grateful." Stan Williams said sincerely. Tony liked Stan, he watched him as he spoke, he was much to gentle for Liz, he wondered how many other men she had seduced before him. "No need for the thanks, it was my pleasure to do it for them, I love them both." Liz asked Roni, "What do you do next, Miss Scott? I must say, it's been a real pleasure to meet you, a real movie star, you know." "Thank you, but I'm a real person, just like you. It's been real nice meeting you, too, Mrs. Williams. As for what I do now, well, I'm going to hit the road again and try to sell some of Roni's cosmetics. I suppose you're returning to California tomorrow?" Liz, who was feeling her liquor, said, "Oh yes, back to the land of sunshine and boredom. You two, you're the ones that keep on having fun, but us, well, hell, we just return to being Mr. and Mrs. Boring mediocrity." Tony changed the subject realizing that Liz wanted more out of life than Stan had given her, "I'm glad you both enjoyed yourselves during your stay. You're welcome anytime." If that's the case, I just might stay," Liz remarked as she gulped down the rest of her drink. Roni looked at Tony as Stan said, "I think it's time we turned in Elizabeth. I'm sure Miss Scott and Mr. Cole are quite tired." He stood, "Thanks again, Mr. Cole, and I'll always remember meeting you Miss Scott, you are the only true super star. Good night." Stan took Liz by the hand and led her from the room, but not before she said, "Mr. Cole doesn't sleep much, he spends a lot of time roaming around in the middle of the night, right Tony?" Yes, Mrs. Williams, you're right, good night."

"I believe she was getting quite snookered," Tony said as he poured another Jack Daniels, "Want one more?" Roni shook her head "No," then said,

"What was she talking about? How did she know that you don't sleep well?" He sat down next to her, "She couldn't sleep last night and she came downstairs while I was there. We had a talk." He didn't lie, but he did just tell part of the story. "You know, I think Theresa's mother…who is a lovely woman…has a slight crush on you," she said as she put her hand on his. He grinned, "Yeh, you're right!" Roni slapped his hand, "Come on, I have a crush on you, too. I want you to make love to me." He didn't hesitate, just followed her up the stairs.

CHAPTER TWENTY-TWO

The next few months passed quickly. December brought Christmas, which Tony and Roni spent alone in Chicago; they flew to California to attend a large Hollywood New Year's Eve party.

Roni had completed filming and taping the commercials, so she began preparing for her next movie. Tony was very involved in business... especially Five Star Oil, which was building more and more service stations and beginning to make lot of money. January and February turned out to be terrific months for Cole Industries. The Roni Collection was surpassing all expectations ten-fold. The shopping plaza and hotel in California would be completed in early March...two months ahead of schedule. The Five Star office building would be finished soon after. The Houston hotel would be completed sometime in April. Tony Cole and Cole Industries were way ahead of their predicted timetable.

March was going to be a very busy month. Not only were the California properties going to open but Roni had...as everybody predicted...been nominated for the "best actress award". So Tony would attend the awards with her. She invited Maggie, Peter, Derek, and Theresa.

Roni had been in California for the month of February filming her new flick. She and Tony had not seen each other during that period, but he was going to arrive today for the grand opening of the Cole Shopping Plaza. She couldn't wait to see him. They would open the doors at nine a.m. Saturday morning. Peter Weyland arranged a cocktail party on Friday evening that included all of the store owners, the mayor of Brea and many celebrities from the Hollywood scene…he had Roni to thank for that… Tony would be attending numerous activities throughout the weekend, and they would attend the Academy Awards on Monday, which Tony had reserved Rocco's entire restaurant for a party in Roni's honor. If that wasn't enough, the new Hotel Anthony was to open for the first time the following Friday.

"We'll be landing in about half an hour, Mr. Cole," Chris Pike, the Cole pilot, said. "You better fasten your seat belts." Tony looked through the window, "I always enjoy flying into L.A.; I just think it's a beautiful sight." Derek and Theresa agreed with him. "When are the Krug's, Emerson's, Underwood's, and Lombardi's arriving?" Theresa asked. "Well, let's see," Tony said as he fastened his belt. "Paul's family came out yesterday, and… well, I guess Stephanie Emerson and her kids came on the same plane. Paul and Mike have been out here for a while as you know. They're going to make a vacation out of it. As for Carmen and his family, I don't really know. I can't get Carmen to leave the damn hotel. He's really giving his blood to the place. You can be sure the food and service will be fantastic." "I'll just bet we'll have the number one eating establishment in all of California!" Derek remarked. "I love the names of the restaurant and bar. The King Cole…now that is appropriate…and TC's Saloon…I love it! Who came up with the names, anyway?" Theresa added. Derek said, "Carmen thought of the restaurant name…I think he liked it because he thinks Tony is a king; and Mike Emerson dreamed up the TC's handle." "How many tenants do you have for the office building?" Theresa inquired. "We're full; but Paul has the second and third buildings under construction. They'll both be full by the time they're completed," Derek answered. Tony then said, "Peter thinks we should build an identical complex around the hotel in Houston. What do you think, Derek?" "Shit, I think we should go a little conservative; at least until we see how this venture is going to go," Derek answered. "Think about it. I tend to agree with Peter," Tony said. There was a screech as the wheels of the bright orange and blue jet touched down.

The media photographers rushed to the silver Rolls, as it pulled up to the curb. The doorman at the hotel opened the door and Roni stepped onto the red carpet that led to the entrance of the mall. The reporters were more interested in what she thought about her chances of winning the Oscar than anything else. She answered only once, "I have no idea, right now I'm going to enjoy the opening of this beautiful mall with my friends, thank you." Tony met her before she could enter. She embraced him and the photographers snapped pictures of the embrace. One reporter yelled, "When are you two getting married?" Roni looked to Tony, "Yeh, when are we?" They entered the mall without answering...Tony didn't answer her either.

Tony and Roni were talking with Alex Chandler...her new leading man... when one of the mall office girls asked if she could interrupt Tony. "Mr. Cole, uh, please excuse me, but there is a phone call for you, it's a Mr. Young from Houston. He said it was important." Tony excused himself and went with the girl.

Tony told the girl to get Derek and Bob Underwood. "What's going on Tony?" Derek asked as he and Bob came in. Tony was finishing a call, "Yes, right away. Goodbye." He put the phone down, "I've got to go to Houston, now, Claude Benaforte just died. Derek, I want you and Larry Shapiro to go with me." "Christ, what happened?" Derek asked in a shocked voice. "Heart attack; I just talked to Young and Claude's wife. This means that we'll now have total control of Five Star Oil. Bob, I want you to arrange for the money to be paid immediately. I sure as hell don't want business to suffer from Claude's death. Bob Underwood looked confused, "Exactly what money, how much, and paid to whom?" Tony looked at Derek for the answer. "Shit, we never informed Bob of the deal you made with Claude!" Derek exclaimed. He went on, "When Tony and Claude agreed to terms, Tony insisted that he be allowed to purchase all of Claude's stock at the price he paid then...if Claude was to die. That insured Tony a good deal if the price of Five Star Oil went up, plus it insured him of total control if Claude passed on." "You smart son-of-a-bitch! That was one helluva deal. But why did Claude go for it?" Bob was amazed. Tony said, "Poor Claude thought he'd live forever." Derek headed toward the door, "I'll tell Theresa and get Larry. When do you want to leave?" "I'll go down with you. I'll tell Roni. I'd like to leave immediately. Bob, you make sure everything goes right at this end, also inform Peter, Paul, and Mike. We'll be back Monday afternoon." Tony talked as they returned to the party.

During the flight to Houston, Derek and Tony filled Larry in on the contract between Claude and Tony. Larry was just as amazed as Bob Underwood. They were sure there would be no legal problems. When Tony purchased the Five Star stock, Claude's remaining stock was worth approximately $145 million; if Claude would have sold his share on the day he died, he would have received at least $1 billion for it. Derek stared at Tony, "You know what I'm thinking?" "No." "I just realized how much you're worth now." Tony smiled, "Yeh, a couple of billion." Larry choked on his drink.

Claude was cremated Monday morning. The attorney for his widow and Larry spent all day Sunday pouring over the details of the agreement. When they had agreed, Larry called Bob Underwood and told him to send Mrs. Benaforte $152,000,000 which was about one-tenth of what it was worth.

By noon Monday, Tony and Derek were on their way back to California. Larry remained in Houston to keep an eye on business. Tony would return Tuesday.

CHAPTER TWENTY-THREE

The crowd was held back by barriers and police. Spotlights were shining skyward. Tinseltown was alive. This was the night for the film industry. The parade of limousines was astonishing. The whole world was watching. The characters involved were producers, directors, actors, actresses, cameramen, writers, and everybody who had a hand in making films. The Academy Awards, there would be happiness and sorrow. Careers would crumble and careers would skyrocket before this night would end. Exciting was the only word to describe the feelings.

Tony could see the photographers surrounded by the mass of people. He said to Roni…who was taking the last puff of a cigarette, "Well, your fans are waiting." She took a deep breath, "Oh, shit, I'm nervous. I hope I don't show it." The silver Rolls pulled up to let them out. The TV announcer bellowed, "Here she comes! Nominated for best actress…the most popular female personality in the world…the beautiful Roni Scott!" The police could hardly hold back the screaming fans. Tony was amazed; they were trying to break through the barriers. She took his arm, smiled, and waved at the wild melee of fans. She managed to say to Tony, "Please hold me tight; I'm not sure my legs are going to hold me up." The TV cameras and the announcer closed in on them, "Miss Scott, it seems as though you're the favorite. What do you think your chances are of winning?" She took her time to make sure the words came out clearly, "I've won already. These fans, these glorious fans presented me with the real Oscar. I hope I can now be lucky enough to be awarded the golden statue from my peers. Thanks to all!" The cheers turned to a chant, "We love you, Roni!" as Tony ushered her into the building. The Weyland's and Hill's were already seated when they came in. When they approached their seats, the entire crowd stood up and presented her with a loud standing ovation. Sincerely, she threw kisses to her peers.

The preliminary awards were given out, the best supporting actress and actor award were decided; the best actor award was given. So far, Roni's movie – The Hour of Judgement – had received six of the awards. The time had come to announce the recipient for Best Actress. Alan Alda and Sally Field were the presenters for this award. They alternately read the nominees, Glenda Jackson...Meryl Streep...Patty Duke-Astin... Jane Fonda..., and read the final nominees name, "For her astounding performance in the smash hit, The Hour of Judgement, Miss Roni Scott. There was silence as a clip of the movie was shown...then he asked for the envelope; he handed it to Miss Field, who opened it, smiled and said, "The winner is...are you ready? Okay, the winner is...Roni Scott!" Roni trembled all over as she hugged Tony, then Maggie, then Theresa. Alex Chandler hugged her as she got up. The applause was deafening. She attempted, several times, to speak but the applause became louder. The tears were streaming down her face; she asked for a handkerchief. Finally, she spoke, "This is the happiest moment of my life. Very few people ever experience what I am at this moment. I want to thank everybody; you all know who you are. Thank you all so very much." She clutched the statue and left the stage.

There was a special award given to some director who had died during the year. Then to end the evening, and to climax, a great night for Roni, The Hour of Judgement received the Best Picture Award, which made a total of eight Oscars for the picture.

The scene at Rocco's was the same as at the Convention Center; Roni's fans were 10/12 deep, screaming at her, each one wanted to touch her. She waved and smiled as they walked to the door of the restaurant. At that very moment, Roni Scott was the most popular figure in America, and she loved it.

The party was loud. It seemed as though everybody in the place was drunk – all but Tony. He spent most of the evening trying to stay by himself. Derek and Theresa were having the time of their lives...they were both star struck. Peter and Maggie spent most of the evening with Milton Schraff and some Hollywood actor Tony didn't recognize. He wanted to grab Maggie and run out, but as always, he didn't even approach her. She didn't go near him either, 'cause she had made up her mind not to take a chance on spoiling Roni's night. Roni was never left alone. She was the epitamy of a SUPER STAR.

The party finally broke up at about four a.m. Roni was feeling no pain. Tony had to keep her from falling twice before he got her in the car. Once they were in the car, Tony told the driver to drive to Roni's house in Palm Springs. "But, Mr. Cole, she has a room reserved at the Beverly Hills Hotel," the driver said. "I know, but I don't want any press people to see her like this. So, drive us to her house," Tony insisted.

Roni grabbed Tony and kissed him passionately, "I want you to fuck me… right now…right in this car," she kissed him again. He tried to push her away, "Roni, Roni, don't do this. You're drunk and the driver is right there!" "I don't give a damn! I said I want you to fuck me, now!" she said, almost yelling. She pulled away and layed down, throwing one leg on the back of the seat, and pulled up her gown, "Here it is, lover, it's all yours. I'm all yours. I want you. I have everything I want…except you. You won't marry me, the least you can do is fuck me!" Tony didn't move except to take out a cigarette. As he began to light it, she said, "So, you're going to turn it down. You're too God-damned good to fuck me in the back seat of a car…no, a Rolls Royce…you go to hell!" She curled up and immediately fell asleep. Tony stared at her, and thought to himself, "I'm sorry Roni. I'm sorry for not loving you!"

He carried her into the house, undressed her and put her to bed. He gave the driver two hundred dollars, and told him to get a hotel room. He then fixed himself a drink, found some note paper and wrote Roni a note.

> *My dear Super Star,*
>
> *In case, you don't remember, I've gone to Houston. I'm going to drive your car back. I'll leave it at the Beverly Hills Hotel. Call you tomorrow.*
>
> *Congratulations Star,*
> *Tony*

The early morning sun was breaking through as he maneuvered the red Ferrari onto Highway 10. He picked up the mobile phone and asked the operator to dial the Beverly Hills Hotel. The morning clerk answered, and Tony asked for Chris Pike's room. "Yeh, hello!" the sleepy voice of Chris yawned. "Chris, this is Tony. I want you to get ready to leave for Houston right away. Call the desk, have them pack my stuff. I'll meet you in front of the hotel in an hour." Chris wasn't sure he was awake, "Mr. Cole, where are you?" Tony laughed, "I'm in a red Ferrari somewhere between Palm Springs and Beverly Hills. See you in an hour." Chris held the phone for a minute, "Yes. Sir, Mr. Cole. Right away. Boy, he's weird sometimes."

CHAPTER TWENTY-FOUR

"Hello, Martin; it's really great to see you. You look terrific," Tony said as he shook his old friend's hand. "You, too, Tony. You look a little thin, but well. You've been making lots of news. Jonathan was right about you." Martin Gold was always pleasant, but Tony felt a strain between them, "Is something bothering you, Martin? The portly attorney removed his glasses, then said, "Like I say, you've been making news. Are you going to marry that movie queen?" Tony smiled, "My love life isn't important. She's really a great girl. What's on your mind?" "Tony, you're making news in other ways. Take the oil business. You've done wonders with that little Five Star outfit; in fact, you've begun to cut into the Oklatex sales. I want to know how far you intend to push. Will you tell me?" Martin was nervous in his approach. He remembered that Jonathan had told him of Tony's keen business mind. Tony lit a cigarette, "Is Oklatex hurting that bad?" Martin snapped back, "I didn't say we were in trouble. I'm just curious, that's all!" "Martin, we've known each other a long time. I think the world of you, but I'm no fool either. Martin, you're one helluva lawyer, but I wonder about your ability to run an oil company," Tony got right to the point. "Who the hell do you think you are, J. Paul Getty? You've been lucky...just lucky at Five Star. You were dealing with an imbecile in Benaforte. I don't appreciate your remarks," Martin nervously replied. Tony sighed and said, "Martin, I'm sorry. I had no right to say that. It's just that, well, I know what's happening with Oklatex. I know that you've contacted some of the big boys attempting to sell, but they weren't interested. You're losing your ass and you want out, right?" Martin pulled out a cigar, played with it nervously, "Tony, I apologize for snapping at you. Hell, you're right! I've done a miserable job of running Oklatex. I tried to foresee the future, I thought the economy was going to go to hell, so I played it conservatively, closed down some marginal stations, shit like that. I just haven't been aggressive. Now we're losing our ass, and I don't know how to turn it around. He shook his head. Tony felt sorry for him, "Is there anything I can do, Martin?" "Christ, I don't know if anybody can do anything. Why would you want to help me; we're competitors now." Martin didn't know how to approach Tony. "The hell with business, Martin; our friendship goes a lot further than any damn oil business. If I can help, please tell me." Tony reminded him of days gone by. "Yes, Tony, you're right," he paused for a moment, then continued, "Would Five Star be interested in buying out Oklatex?" This is what Martin had wanted all along, Tony had known it, but he wanted Martin to ask him…that would make the selling price lower. "Well, Martin, we've never thought about that at Five Star. It sounds like a proposition to consider. What price were you thinking of?" Tony knew the worth to be near a billion dollars. Nervously playing with the cigar, Martin said, "Well, I'm not sure what you consider a fair price?" Tony laughed to himself, "Ol' Martin is trying to gouge me." "I'd have to do some research, look at the corporate books, you know. Give me a price to consider, to work from. Then we'll research it and I'll get back to you." He threw it right back in Martin's lap. Once again, he fiddled with the cigar, he broke it in half, then threw it away, "Okay, I'll quote a price. If it were anybody but you, it would be a helluva lot higher; I want you to know that. You've got to understand now, I want to sell so I can make a little money, too. Tony, I would offer Oklatex to you for one and a quarter billion." Martin almost choked when he said the figure. Tony was surprised at his nervousness, "Let me have Derek look over the books and we'll give you an answer." Martin had wanted Tony to commit then, but reluctantly agreed, "Okay, when would you like to see our records?" "That's up to you," Tony didn't want to sound anxious. "Anytime is fine…tomorrow, if you can start that soon." Tomorrow… they're in worse trouble than I figured…" Tony thought to himself. "It's impossible to do it that quickly, we're having our grand opening of our new hotel in California tomorrow. But, he could get on it first thing Monday." Okay, Monday will be fine. I'll alert my people in Tulsa to give him the red carpet treatment; Tulsa is where our records are."

Tony stood up, "Very good, Martin. Derek and Bob Underwood will be there Monday morning. I would like to extend my personal invitation to you and Mrs. Gold to the hotel's grand opening tomorrow." Martin grabbed Tony's hand, "Thanks, my boy, but we really can't make it; this weekend is my grandson's bar-mitzvah…Tony, you're a good boy, my old friend Jonathan would be proud of you." "Thank you, Martin. I'll talk to you later." He left abruptly.

Chris Pike had been waiting at the airport. They had flown to Chicago for the meeting with Martin only, and Tony wanted to return to California immediately. From the airport, Tony called Alvin Young at Five Star, "I want you to gather all the information you can about the situation at Oklatex; liabilities, how many station closings in the past year, just get everything you can, and especially what their position is with the refineries. I'll give you a call Sunday night for the information. Alvin, if you want to be the President of Five Star Oil…you'll have that information Sunday." Young was speechless. "Talk to you Sunday, Alvin." Tony hung up.

CHAPTER TWENTY-FIVE

"The advertising paid off, Tony," Derek said smiling. "The hotel is booked full for the weekend." Tony smiled, "I guess the prices we're charging aren't that exorbitant after all." "Okay, what's this secret business about…where the hell did you disappear to, anyway," Derek asked curiously. "Where is Bob Underwood? I want him in here…oh, here is our illustrious financial wizard. Hi, ya, Bob." Underwood extended his hand, "Everybody seems to agree that the Hotel Anthony is remarkable…they're having the time of their lives. Where have you been, you disappeared on us?" "Sit down, that's what I want to talk to you two about," Tony gestured toward the couch, then sat down across from them. He took out his cigarettes, offered one to each…Derek took one…and asked, "Bob, could we get a billion dollars?" Bob looked slightly dumbfounded as he muttered, "Uh, oh, I, uh…shit…I'm not sure!" Tony checked Derek's reaction, which was one similar to Bob's, "What are you up to?" Tony smiled, "We might be on the threshold of becoming a very large corporation…a mega-corporation," he stopped long enough to look at their reactions, then continued, "We might be able to pull off a deal that could drive the worth of Five Star Oil through the ceiling!" Derek couldn't control his curiosity, "Where the hell have you been, and what have you been stirring up. I've got to know!" "Me, too!" Bob chimed in. "If I'm right," Tony said as he moved to the edge of his chair, "We're going to steal another oil company, but only if I'm right about their financial situation." "Who?" Bob blurted. Tony smiled at Derek, as though to ask if he knew. Derek took a long puff at his cigarette, then clapped his hands together, "Oklatex…you've been in Tulsa to see Martin Gold. They're in deep financial straits and he wants to sell out, to you!" "I was in Chicago, you two are going to Tulsa. You're right, Derek. Oklatex is having some difficulty. Martin can't raise anymore cash, and his stations aren't bringing it in quick enough," Tony confirmed.

"What do you want us to do in Tulsa," Bob asked. "To see of it's worth purchasing!" Tony exclaimed. "When do you want us in Tulsa?" questioned Derek. Tony sat back and smiled, "Enjoy your weekend, but be in Tulsa, first thing Monday morning; Martin will have the red carpet treatment for you. I want you to pour over his records until you know them as well as your own address. How long will it take?" Bob and Derek looked at each other, then shook their heads, they didn't know. "Well, get it done as fast as possible, because I'm sure Martin wants to make a deal quick," Tony insisted. "Sure enough, <u>Boss</u>!" Derek remarked as he stood up. "Let's go down and enjoy our grand opening," Tony said as he put his arms around their shoulders and led them to the door.

The hotel was absolutely gorgeous. The Cole Industries colors of bright orange and bright blue were evident throughout the entire structure. The sunken pillared lobby was the main topic of discussion among the guests; that was before they had dinner at the King Cole...Tony gave Carmen the opportunity, and from the seating arrangements, silverware, napkins, service procedures, and most of all each meal he created a masterpiece. One patron remarked, "I've eaten in the finest restaurants in California, but they are all second rate to this." The press covering the grand opening turned out to be the best advertisement money <u>couldn't</u> buy; they were all similar to the L.A. Times article: "...the Anthony Hotel located in Brea held a grand opening last night...grand openings are usually an attempt by the owners to impress the public...Cole Industries, who owns and operates the hotel, put on a lavish party, and invited all the leading celebrities; just as all owners due. There was something odd about this grand opening...Cole Industries, which is headed by Tony Cole, has given Southern California the most fascinating hotel this reporter has had the privilege to visit...the bronze glass structure with its two cylinder spires standing like statuesque bookends guarding the main building covered with a cathedral roof looms as though it grew out of the ground instead of being constructed; the restaurant named appropriately, the King Cole, is nothing more than eloquent, elegant, beautiful, and...just superb. Not being a culinary expert, but one who knows good food and service from bad, I can say the King Cole is on the top of my list for eating establishments. Cole didn't stop there; on the opposite end of the hotel is the lounge, TC's...the initial's of

Mr. Cole, I presume...and what a lounge. When you get the chance to spend an evening at TC's, you'll be genuinely entertained by two different groups...never the same style...you'll have a choice between being seated at the bar, which is 25 feet long, or at backgammon equipped with tables, and if neither of those please you, there are couches and high back chairs to enjoy the evening...this bright orange and blue color combination is enjoyable to the eye, it makes you happy...Mike Emerson, a near genius architect and Carmen Lombardi, an absolute master restauranteur, has given us a plush, beautiful, and very exciting and enjoyable place to spend an evening of eating and drinking or a night to rest your body...try it, you won't be disappointed. I loved it all!"

Tony sat down heavily, "Christ, I don't think I've ever been this tired." Roni sat across from him, instead of taking her customary seat next to him. She said nothing, just stared at him. As he ran his hand through his hair, he asked her, "Do you think they liked it...the hotel that is?" "Yes, of course," Roni said softly. "Well, it's a damn good thing...considering we have two more practically open." Tony said as he layed his head back. He raised his head, and looked at her. He realized she was staring at him, "Is something bothering you?" She nodded, but didn't say what. "Well, "what is it?" Roni leaned forward, put her hands together and said, "Tony, are we ever going to get married?" He waited a moment before answering, "What brings that up now...it's three in the morning." "I just want an answer...yes or no. He knew this time was bound to come, but he wasn't prepared for it now...he was much too tired, "Can we please discuss it after a few hours of sleep...I'm really bushed?" She lit a cigarette, "No, Tony. I want you to answer me now...please!" "Okay, but if we're going to stay up, I'm going to have a drink; want one?" "No," she said and waited for him to fix his drink. "Roni, what's wrong? I thought everything was fine between us. We've discussed this before." "That was before. You haven't acted the same since the Academy Awards. Please, just answer me. Are we or are we not going to get married?" He began to walk around the room, "Roni, I hated your actions in the limo after the award's party. I really detested that. Maybe I'm a prude, but it bothered me...a lot. I'll get over it, but I must admit, it was a side of you I had never seen and damn sure don't ever want to see again." "I understand, and I apologize about that...it was the combination of booze and grass...it always affected me that way. I'm really sorry," she said apologetically. "You know how I feel about drugs, including grass. Why did you have to smoke it anyway? For

Christ's sake, you should have been high enough from your Oscar," he was almost mad! "So, because I smoked a little dope and attempted to seduce you in the back seat of the limo…you're going to shit on me, right?" He looked at her sternly, "Wrong. I think the world of you…and always will. That one incident upset me…that's all. Now let's go to bed!" "No!" She shotback, "I want you to answer my question. Marriage…yes or no?" Tony sat down again…he must tell her the truth, now. "Roni, I would have to think that our careers are to far apart for marriage, at least for a few more years. If I have to say, I'll marry you within the next year, I'll say no but you already knew that. Why all of a sudden do you have to pressure me to get married?" She sighed and the tears began to roll down her beautiful face, "Oh, I don't know. It might be because I love you so damn much and you have never told me that you love me…as for our careers, I'll give up my fucking career…Tony, you're all I want…I'm sorry, but I don't want to be away from you all the time…I just want to be Mrs. Tony Cole…" she began to cry harder. He walked to her, "I'm sorry, Roni. I just can't commit to marriage…I just can't. She put her arms around his leg and sobbed, "Let's go to bed!"

Roni stood over him, watching him sleep. "I love you so much," she thought, "But I can't compete with your empire…oh, God, I'll miss you!" She laid the note beside his wallet, and ran out crying.

The light of the bright California sun peeked through the orange drapes. Tony rolled over to touch her, but she wasn't there. "Roni…Roni…" he said as he got up. He looked in the bathroom, then in the living area of the large suite. "Where the hell is she?" he said to himself, then returned to the bathroom. When he came out of the bathroom, he opened the drapes and went to the dresser to get a cigarette. The note was next to his cigarettes; he opened it and began to read:

> *"My Darling Tony,*
>
> *I have given our relationship more than a year. I have loved you more than I'll ever love any man. It is time for us to go our separate ways. You have your love…your empire, and I'll live with my career. You may not agree with my decision, but please just let it be. I have no regrets, our time together will always be my most prized memory.*

> *Our parting has nothing to do with our business arrangement; just send my 10% to Milton. I'm going to take a long vacation…alone. I wish you the best of everything. Goodbye, my love!"*
>
> *Roni*

He felt sick. He didn't want her to go away. In his own way, he loved her. He laid the note on the dresser and went to take a shower. Standing in the shower he thought, "She's right…it is better that we call it off…shit, I'll miss her…I guess I can see her in the movies…" his tears mixed with the water from the shower.

CHAPTER TWENTY-SIX

Hello Alvin. Did you have a good weekend? Tony asked as Alvin Young answered the phone, "Yes, Mr. Cole; very good in fact; and you, did you have a nice weekend?" Tony ignored the pleasantries. "Do you have anything for me?" "Yes, Mr. Cole, I do. Oklatex has seen better days…we are knocking their socks off. In the past year, they have closed 22 operating stations, which leaves them with only 97. The ones that are closed were in direct competition with Five Star. It's rumored that they plan to close five more in April; but listen to this. The refineries are going to hold up shipments to <u>all</u>, yes <u>all</u> of their units unless they pay their outstanding receivables by April 5th. They don't have the money; there is no way they can meet the deadline. Martin Gold is supposedly trying to borrow the money but is having trouble." Alvin was smiling…he knew he had handled Tony's request correctly. "How much do they owe the refineries?" Tony asked. "Somewhere around $200 million. That's all I could find out," Alvin replied. "Thank you, Alvin. "You've done a very good job. I want you to fly to Chicago on Wednesday, come to my office in the Stuyvesant Building. I'll see you then!" Tony hung up. When Alvin put the phone down, he screamed out with glee, "We did it, Doris. I'm going to Chicago Wednesday. Cole wants to see me!" Doris Young, Alvin's wife hugged her husband and said, I'm so proud of you Al." "Let's not get our hopes up yet, but I think he's going to ask me to be President of Five Star," warned Alvin. "Mr. Cole sounds like a very nice person. Does he really go with Roni Scott?" Doris asked. "Yes, he does. He could have just about any woman he wanted. They say all the women want him." "Well, when do I get to meet Mr. Wonderful?" she begged. "Never…I don't want to lose you, and you might just want him instead of me if you met him," Alvin teased as he held her tight. "You're silly, just silly, Alvin Young."

The house was quiet, only Frederick and the cook, Mamie, were there. He asked Frederick to bring any messages into his office. He was going to watch the White Sox exhibition game on TV. He was tired; the last week had been a merry-go-round. It felt good to be back in Chicago. Tony removed his shoes and tie, then poured some Jack Daniels over a glass of ice. "I wonder what Maggie's doing now," he thought to himself. His mind began to drift as he fell into the chair in front of the TV. "What would happen if we would tell Peter that we're in love…yeh, it would affect Cole Industries…do I really care…yes, damn it…I'm almost there…Jonathan would be proud of me…it's happening faster than ever expected…Maggie, oh, Maggie, I want you here…Roni's gone…only Peter is in our way… oh, Maggie, Mag…" "Mr. Cole, Mr. Cole," Frederick interrupted his thoughts. "Oh, yes, Frederick," he said realizing Frederick was there. "Are you alright, Mr. Cole?" "Yes, I'm just tired. Are these my messages?" Frederick nodded, "Yes, sir. May I get you anything else?" "No, thanks… oh, yeh, turn on the ballgame if you would please." Frederick switched on the TV and left Tony alone. The ballgame was in the third inning… Giants 2…White Sox 1.

The first message was from Paul Krug, "Please call, important!" He layed it aside and went to the next one, it was from Theresa. Call Derek, call Peter, Martin Gold called twice, call the mayor, call Paul Krug, it's important, call Irving Epps, and call Derek. There was an envelope, no return address and postmarked from California. He was surprised when he opened it; it was a short note that simply read, "I've thought about our night together many times. Please, call me when you're in L.A." it was signed Liz Williams. He tore it up and threw it on the table. He finished the pile of letters and "bullshit mail" and he was disappointed that there was nothing from Maggie or Roni.

He phoned Paul Krug in Houston. "Hello, this is Paul Krug." "Tony here, what's up Paul?" Paul sighed, "Boy, am I glad you called. We're going to have to delay the grand opening of the hotel. I got here yesterday to find out that the building inspectors haven't completed the inspection, and can't possibly finish until the latter part of next week. What the fuck are we supposed to do?" "Are you ready to open? I mean, are you convinced that the hotel will pass inspection?" Tony asked. "Hell yes," Paul was adamant,

"We could open this minute. Everything is ready, right to the last detail. Is there anything you can do?" Tony commanded, "Paul, you just make sure that it will pass and I'll have the inspectors there by Wednesday. Do you know if Carmen's ready?" "You never have to worry about Carmen; hell he left L.A. on a four a.m. flight Sunday morning. I don't think he's left the restaurant since he arrived. We're ready, Tony!" Tony grinned to himself, "Fine, Paul, be prepared to meet some pissed off inspectors either tomorrow or Wednesday. Keep in touch."

"Hello," Derek answered. "Hi ya, buddy, Tony here!" Derek laughed, "You have a lot of fuckin' nerve, calling me buddy after sending me down here to act like an accountant!" Tony laughed, "Why?" "Man, this crap is boring. I guess I'm getting used to the executive's lifestyle," Derek remarked. Tony got down to business, "So, tell me, what have you found?" "Just that Oklatex owes more per month than they bring in. Martin Gold has ran this company into the ground," Derek insisted. "What is the total in liabilities? How about the refineries?" Tony questioned. Derek stared into the receiver, then frowned, "Have you done it again? You bastard, you already know the answers, don't you?" Tony smiled, "I don't know, I have to hear your answers before I can be sure." "Okay," Derek was disgusted, "I'll go through the motions. Oklatex owes nearly $300 million dollars in numerous loans, but he owes the refineries $200 million dollars, and they are going backwards each month. They are practically out of business unless they get some quick financial help. Does that confirm what your snoops have already told you?" "Yes, it does," Tony agreed. Derek was nearly livid, "What the hell did you send us down here for? Was it your way of making a fuckin' joke?" Tony laughed aloud, "It sounds as though you're mad at your old friend!" "Friend, hell, you wouldn't do this to a friend, only an enemy," Derek exclaimed. Tony explained, "I wanted Martin to see that we were going to examine this thoroughly before giving him an answer. By sending you and Bob in, instead of our accountants, he'd be convinced that we were more than interested. I don't want him to sell to anybody else in a panic. The refineries have given him a deadline of April 5th or they're cutting him off. So, he must do something this week. Are you still mad?" Derek had mellowed, "Did you know this information prior to us coming down here?" Tony answered, "No. Well, I found out late Sunday night. Do you think we should buy him out?" Tony valued Derek's opinion. He replied, "I agree with you, I think we could get it fairly cheap. Hell, we could pay off the loans out of Five Star's profits and get a tax break at the same time. I say go for it." Tony agreed, "Fine. I'll set up a meeting with Martin tomorrow. Why don't you get back here right away. Where is Larry Shapiro?" "Larry is in Houston. Bob and I will catch the next flight out of Tulsa. We'll see you in Chicago in the morning…asshole!" Derek laughed as he hung up.

Irving Epps was sitting at his desk when his secretary informed him that Tony was on the line, "Hello, Mr. Cole. I'm glad you returned my call. I need to talk to you." "Yes Irving, I'm here so talk to me," Tony commanded! Irving fumbled with his cigar, "Mr. Cole, I know it's not my place to tell you what to do, but there is a problem here and it needs immediate attention!" Tony spoke softly, attempting to calm him down, "Irving if you don't tell me what you need out there, how am I supposed to know? You're my man. So, please, tell me what the problem is so that we can solve it together." Irving felt much better, Tony had made him feel equally as important as himself, "Yes sir, Mr. Cole. We are receiving orders faster than we can possibly produce. We can only produce about half of the orders right now, and we're being flooded with new orders everyday. We've got to stop selling, we're going to make a lot of money with the customers we presently have." Tony's voice became stern, "Irving, why can't we produce our products fast enough? Do you need more employees, a larger building, what?" Irving, once again became nervous, "Uh, yes, yes we need more people and a larger building." Tony questioned, "How many shifts are you operating?" "Well, uh, one. That's all I've ever had," Irving answered. Tony ran his hand through his hair, ""Just a minute Irving," he put the phone down and walked across the room. "Stupid shit," he said aloud as he poured himself a Jack Daniels. He returned to the phone, "Irving, I want you to begin operating three shifts, seven days a week. I expect every order to be shipped complete and on time. Start hiring more personnel immediately, work your present staff double shifts until you get enough help. As far as a larger building goes, you don't need it. Irving, I think you should have figured this out yourself!" Irving was nearly speechless from nerves, "I, uh, yes, uh, Mr. Cole, you, a, you're right, I should have. What you say will be done." "Good, I'll be talking to you, Irving," Tony hung up and sighed heavily.

It was now nine p.m. Tony decided the other calls could wait until morning. He was pleased to see that the White Sox had taken a 5 to 2 lead. He wondered what Maggie was doing, he felt that she was avoiding him in Los Angeles, but he had done the same. Roni would be back on the set in a couple of days…he missed her, but he realized that she had done the right thing…he simply didn't love her…she'll be better off with someone else.

The house seemed abnormally quiet. Tony walked into the kitchen; Frederick was having a cup of coffee and watching the ballgame on a small black and white TV. "Why don't you join me in the office and have a drink?" Tony requested. Frederick rose from his chair, "Oh, Mr. Cole, I didn't hear you come in! I, uh, yes, I'd enjoy that." The two of them returned to Tony's office. "What would you like to drink, Frederick?" "Uh, just a glass of white wine, Mr. Cole. Thank you," Frederick replied almost apologetically. Tony looked at him, "Sit down; make yourself comfortable." Frederick was raised to be a butler, or valet (whichever); he was unaccustomed to drinking with his employer, "Excuse me sir, but I have never imposed on my employer's privacy before. I'm afraid I'm a bit uncomfortable." Tony laughed, "Frederick, you should never feel that way with me. I can assure you that I enjoy your company. I've never asked you before, are you a baseball fan?" "Oh yes, it's really the only game I enjoy. You sir, do you like the game?" Tony smiled and said, "Frederick, baseball is the greatest tranquilizer around…when I watch a ballgame, I forget all about the pressures that fill each day…it takes me back to being a kid again." Frederick couldn't help but notice that Tony was depressed, "Please tell me, Mr. Cole, if I'm overstepping my bounds, but you look tired and act somewhat depressed. Is business okay?" "First of all," Tony said, "Would you please stop calling me Mr. Cole…from now on, it's Tony… and for business, it couldn't be any better. You're right though…I'm tired and depressed. Frederick, what man, in his right mind, would pass up the chance to marry Roni Scott…the most beautiful and well-known woman in probably the whole world…me! That' what I did…Roni and I have parted ways." Frederick shook his head, "I'm terribly sorry. You made a terrific couple; I truly liked her…maybe she'll return." Tony said, "No, Frederick, you don't understand; I don't love her…it's better for her that we called it quits between us. What the hell am I boring you with this for; let's watch the ball game."

They watched the rest of the ball game and Tony gave him statistics on nearly every player in the game. Frederick was amazed at the knowledge Tony revealed about the game of baseball. The White Sox won 7 to 4 and Frederick excused himself and retired for the night. Tony slept on the sofa.

CHAPTER TWENTY-SEVEN

"Good morning Theresa. Did your husband return yet? Tony said as he entered his office. Theresa smiled, "Good morning to you, Mr. Cole. Yes, Derek got home about two this morning. Did you get your messages at home?" "Yes, but I didn't answer them all. Would you try to get Quincy Roberts for me? He's the mayor of Houston. Oh, where the hell is Peter Weyland?" Tony asked as he poured a cup of coffee. Theresa also had some coffee, "Peter is still in California, but should be back today or tomorrow." "Would you get him after Roberts, oh no, get the Chicago Mayor next. We're really into mayors this morning, aren't we?" They both laughed.

The Mayor's secretary answered the phone, "Good morning, this is the office of the Mayor." Theresa was impressed, "Good morning. I am the secretary for Mr. Tony Cole in Chicago. Mr. Cole would appreciate a moment with Mayor Roberts." The secretary replied, "I'm sorry, but the Mayor cannot be disturbed at this time; let me connect you to the Deputy Mayor's office; I am sure that someone there can help you." Theresa wasn't to be denied, "Oh, maybe you misunderstood, Mr. Cole wants to speak directly to Mayor Roberts, that's Mr. Tony Cole of Cole Industries in Chicago; I'll hold." The secretary was slightly stunned by Theresa's persistence, "I'll tell the Mayor you're on, but he can't be disturbed." She walked into the Mayor's office, "Sir, I apologize for the intrusion, but there is a very persistent secretary on the telephone; her employer would like a moment to speak to you. It's Mr. Tony Cole from Chicago." Quincy Roberts grabbed the phone, "Of course, I'll talk to him! Don't you know who he is, Adelaide?" "Hello, this is Mayor Roberts. What can I do for you?" "One second, your honor. Mr. Cole will be right with you," Theresa replied then connected him to Tony. Tony put on his most gracious voice, "Good morning, your honor. I appreciate you taking time out of your busy schedule to speak to me." The Mayor was pleased that Tony acknowledged his position, "That's quite alright, Mr. Cole; what can I do for you?" "Well, Mr. Mayor, I have a slight problem, that I hope you can assist me with," Tony said. "Name it; I'll do what I can," Roberts was anxious to help. "As you know, we are to open our new hotel in Houston; in fact, you should have received your invitation to the grand opening on Friday." Roberts had received the invitation and was quite interested in attending, "Yes, of course. It will be a pleasant evening, I'm sure. Houston is proud to have a hotel of that quality; but what does that have to do with your problem?" Tony had succeeded in getting Roberts approval, "It seems as though the building inspectors can't get around to the final inspection until sometime next week. If we have to wait, it will cost Cole Industries and the City of Houston a bundle of money. I'd like to know what we can do to speed up the inspection." Mayor Roberts laughed, "Well, Tony, you don't have a problem anymore. I'll have the inspection conducted this afternoon. It is ready, isn't it?" Yes, it's ready, but tomorrow will be soon enough. I appreciate your help, your honor; I owe you one!" Tony replied. "Good enough. You have your people ready first thing tomorrow morning. Oh, please call me Quincy. I'm looking forward to your opening. Call anytime, Tony." Tony pushed the intercom switch, "Theresa, get Paul Krug and inform him the building inspectors will be there first thing tomorrow morning." He then dialed Martin Gold.

"Hello, Martin, Tony Cole here." Martin was excited, "Oh, good morning, Tony. It's good to hear from you." Tony spun around to look out of the window, "Martin, I'd like to meet with you, at your convenience." "Well, I can make it right now. Do you want me to come over?" Martin was over-anxious. "Why don't we meet for lunch, at Indigo's, noon, okay?" "Yes, I'll be there. Goodbye, and thanks, Tony!"

Tony spent the rest of the morning on the phone and in conference with Bob Underwood and Derek. Both Bob and Derek were convinced that the purchase of Oklatex was a smart business move. Tony told Bob to arrange for a billion dollar loan and Derek to contact the proper commissions for requirements of the purchase. He was sure he could get for the price he wanted to pay.

Tony was seated in a private booth at Indigo's. He ordered a Jack Daniels and lit a cigarette. Martin was ten minutes early and Martin was never early, "Hello, Tony, it'll be nice having lunch with you." The waiter brought their drinks, Martin ordered an "Old Fashioned" before he was seated. "Yes, Martin, it's nice to spend time with an old and dear friend; but I believe we have more to discuss than our friendship," Tony wanted to get right to the deal. Martin smiled, because he, too, was anxious to make a deal…he had only one more week to raise the money for the refineries… "Right! Have you made a decision; I presume you have or we wouldn't be having lunch, would we?" Tony smiled, "What's your price, Martin?" "I thought we had agreed on the price, 1 and ¼ billion!" Martin replied. The smile was gone from Tony's face. He was now ready to negotiate, "Oklatex is not worth that, and you know it. You'll have to come down my friend, before Cole Industries becomes interested." Martin's anxiety slowed him considerably, "I can't come down, with the liabilities I'm faced with; no, I must have that amount." Tony picked up the menu, "Then we might as well order lunch and discuss another subject…this discussion is over!" Martin was floored at Tony's coldness, "You mean, you won't even discuss it?" Tony looked him directly in the eye, "We have no intentions of paying that price. If you don't want to come down, then you should talk to someone else…it's that simple. Let's order," he looked back at the menu. Martin sat dumbfounded, speechless. "I think, I'll just have a Chef's salad, what about you?" Tony acted as though he had completely forgotten about Oklatex. Martin began to stumble for something to say, "Tony…I…uh…I don't…uh, maybe I can reduce the price some. What would you pay?" He took a sip of his drink, "Martin, it's not what we'll pay, but what will you take." Before Martin could speak, Tony added, "Have you forgotten that we inspected your books? I'm aware of the losses you've taken, the outstanding debts you have, and I'm aware of your situation with the refineries. I'll say it again, Oklatex is not worth 1 and ¼ billion dollars." "How did you know about the refineries?" Martin couldn't believe he knew that…the refineries had assured him they would keep it quiet. Tony leaned back, "It doesn't matter how I know. Martin, Oklatex is worth one billion maximum…you couldn't peddle it for any higher to Exxon. I'll make you an offer…we'll pay you 900 million and the outstanding debts will come out of that. If you accept, and you'll be a damn fool not to, you'll personally come out with around 20 million in your pocket. I hate to put it this way, Martin…but, take it or leave it!" Martin stared at him and fidgeted nervously in his chair, "You've got me over a barrel, Tony. You know I have to accept; and you also know that it's actually worth the 1 and ¼ billion." "No, Martin. It was worth more than two when you took it over from Jonathan, but it isn't now," Tony was adamant. "Okay, okay…I accept…you win!" Martin extended his hand to Tony, and Tony said, "Bob Underwood arranged for the money this morning, so we should be able to consummate the transaction quickly and smoothly."

Martin stared at Tony and said "Jonathan was the best financial man in the world. I was with him on many negotiations, and I was always amazed at his superior way of handling negotiation; but I'm glad he wasn't alive to see himself become second best. He taught you well, Tony…here's to you!" He held up his glass in a toast. Tony acknowledged the gesture then motioned for the waiter without saying another word about it.

Tony returned to the office and found that Bob and Derek had completed their part of the Oklatex deal and the formal transaction should be soon. They congratulated Tony on a fine acquisition. He remarked, "Let's not live on our laurels, I want to go after Panhandle next!!!" Derek and Bob looked at him in disbelief, and Derek said, "Do you mean, you want to purchase Panhandle?" Tony had a broad smile, "Gentlemen, look at what we have invested in the two oil companies we own. We have less than two billion dollars. Since we ventured into Five Star, we have grown from 90 stations in Texas to 220 stations in Texas, Oklahoma, and Louisiana. Panhandle operates around 200 stations in Arizona, New Mexico, and Nevada. They don't even know we're in the business. So why don't we show our face in their territory." Derek was still puzzled, "I still don't understand what that would accomplish. I don't know what you're after." "You don't? Well, let me explain in detail. If we move into Panhandle's territory, the industry will begin to watch us…up to now, Five Star has been looked upon as a small, but aggressive oil company. With the Oklatex acquisition, they'll view us as someone to watch…keep an eye on us, so that we don't get too large. Expanding into Panhandle's area, we'll show them that we intend to go as far as we can. Now, if…are you following me so far…if I'm right, we should be contacted by either Panhandle or one of the larger companies in an attempt to buy us out. If that come about, we could stand a chance to make a killing. Do you understand?" "Smart, you smart son-of-a-bitch!" Bob Underwood exclaimed. "Do you really think it will work out that way?" Bob added. Tony replied, "If nobody attempts to buy us we will still have increased our operations and should be making more profits." Derek walked around Tony's desk and looked out of the window, then said, "You're right, we have less than two billion invested in oil, but right now, with the acquisition of Oklatex, our oil interests should be worth nearly seven or eight billion if it were on the market. Shit, you are a fuckin' genius, Cole!" Tony said, "If we were to sell out and make that kind of profit, it would allow us to pay off all our outstanding loans. Cole Industries could be debt-free and profit rich." Bob asked, "Who is going to run the oil company division, now that Claude's dead?" "Alvin Young, he'll be here tomorrow, to be announced as the President of Five Star Oil Division of Cole Industries. He doesn't even know about Oklatex yet. Derek, I'd like you to give him the news and explanation of Oklatex and our plans to expand into Panhandle's territory. Don't tell him why we want to go after Panhandle. I'm going to Houston in the morning; I want to make sure that hotel opens Friday.

CHAPTER TWENTY-EIGHT

When Tony arrived at home, around nine o'clock, he decided to pack for his trip to Houston. Looking at his wardrobe, he said aloud, "I'm sick of all these clothes. I'm going to have Henri fix me up with an entire new wardrobe." Frederick came into his room, "Excuse me, Tony, but Maggie Weyland would like a word with you on the phone." His heart jumped into his throat, "Uh, thank you, Frederick, I'll take it here."

He sighed heavily as he picked up the receiver, "What a pleasant surprise! Good evening, Mrs. Weyland." "Hi, Mr. Cole. I hope I'm not interrupting anything, but I just had to speak to you." Tony smiled, "You're not interrupting anything…I'm packing to go to Houston tomorrow…is there anything wrong?" "Yes, I'm married to the wrong man…could you come over, please? Peter is still in California and won't be home until tomorrow and he's leaving for Houston Thursday morning. Please come over!" "No, but I'm hungry. How about going to eat with me?" Tony didn't dare go to her apartment; they both knew they couldn't control their emotions. "Okay, but only if we go to Gino's for pizza!" she laughed. "Gino's it is! "I'm always ready for that…I'll pick you up in an hour," he said happily. "Tony, please hurry! I want to see you terribly."

Maggie was waiting in the doorway when he pulled up; she ran to the car. He had the door open for her, "Hi Margaret, nice to see you." "Hey, what's with the Margaret!" she said as she closed the door. "You're such a sophisticated lady. I just thought you should be called by your sophisticated name," he laughed. "You know what you can do with your sophisticated bull," she leaned over and kissed his cheek as he drove away.

They sat in a booth near the back of the old pizza establishment and Tony ordered a large Gino's Special (everything on it) pizza and a pitcher of beer.

"So why the big desire for pizza tonight?" he asked. The waitress brought the beer as Maggie started to answer, "Well, I had the TV on, and there was a pizza commercial…and that's bull, too…I was thinking of you, how I haven't spent an hour alone with you for months…Tony, I can't do it this way…I, uh, I'm so unhappy!" Tony took her hand, "I know, I'm having problems with it myself…I find myself avoiding Peter; just because I think of you when I see him or talk to him." "Oh, Christ," she exclaimed "I've been doing the same thing with Roni. Do you know how hard it is to listen to her tell me what a great person you are, and how much she loves you, how she'd do anything for you; every time she starts, I want to tell her to shut up. I enjoy her so damn much!" Tony looked away then back at Maggie, "Well, if it's any consolation, she probably won't be making those remarks to you anymore. We parted ways a few days ago." "I didn't know, why?" she asked sincerely wanting to know. "Roni decided it was time for us to get married, and when I told her that I had no plans of marriage…she thought it would be best if we parted as friends. So, she stayed in California to work on her picture. We won't see each other again." Tony was outwardly upset. Maggie took a large gulp of beer, "It hurts you, doesn't it. You really do love her, don't you?" He pulled out two cigarettes, keeping one and giving one to Maggie, "Yes and no; <u>yes</u> to the part about it hurting me, but <u>no</u>, I don't love her…I'm very fond of Roni, I think she's a wonderful person, but I couldn't love her; and I tried. My feelings for her were nothing like my feelings for you. She didn't make my stomach do flip-flops…if you know what I mean." The waitress arrived with the pizza. "I feel terrible," Maggie stated, "If I would have stayed away from you, maybe you and Roni would have made it together. I'm sorry, Tony…" she put her hand on his cheek…"My dear, sweet Tony." He touched her hand and smiled, "The pizza is here!" Maggie sighed, and said, "You're right, let's eat!"

They engaged in small talk, laughed a lot, and drank three pitchers of beer. As Tony ordered the fourth pitcher, Maggie smiled at him, "I love being with you…you're so much fun; I never laughed with anybody else…Tony, I'm going to leave Peter…I can't live with him and be in love with you; I have no feelings for him anymore. I'm going to leave him this week, right after the Houston hotel opening." Tony shook his head, "No, not right now. I know how you feel, but I would appreciate it if you stayed with him for a while longer." She bit her bottom lip, "I thought you'd be happy, now that you and Roni have split, the only thing in our way is Peter! Now, I wonder if you really love me!" "Shit, Maggie," he was angry at her for talking that way." The other patrons were watching them…he grabbed her arm, "Let's get out here!"

Instead of going directly to the car, they walked around Rush Street. "Maggie, you don't understand, do you?" She frowned at him, "No, I'm sorry, but I really don't! Why don't you explain?" "Maggie, I want you more than anything; but right now, I need Peter." She broke in, "It's obvious you don't <u>need</u> me!" Tony stopped, "Look, I'm not going to spend the short period I have with you arguing. It's strictly business; I need Peter business wise…but you're wrong, I need you; I need you to know that you're going to be mine someday, but I won't have you unless I can have you morally right." He placed his hands on her shoulders and stared into her face, "I love you, Maggie; more than I ever dreamed I could love. Please understand!" She put her arms around his waist, and raised her head to look at him, "I really do…it's just, uh, I think about you all the time…Tony please kiss me, and tell me you'll love me forever!" He pulled her to him and kissed her hard, then looking into her tear-filled eyes, he whispered, "I love you now, tomorrow, and everyday for the rest of my life…and we'll be together someday, I promise." A young couple walked by as they kissed again, the man said, "It must be true love!" Tony looked at them as they passed, and replied, "You're right; it's true, wonderful love!" The couple applauded, Maggie and Tony bowed in acknowledgement of the applause, then began walking toward the car, laughing.

On the drive back to Maggie's apartment building, they didn't speak. Maggie just snuggled under his free arm. "Well, here we are," Tony said as he parked the car. I don't want to leave you…who knows when we'll be able to spend time together again," Maggie whispered in his ear, "Sure, you don't want to stay with me?" "What I want to do, and what I'm going to do is completely different," he replied stroking her hair. She sat up in the seat, "Tony, do you ever think about us, in bed, making love?" He grinned at her, "Only about 500 times a day and another 1000 times at night!" She kissed him, and said softly, "I can't stop thinking about making love with you…I just had an orgasm when you said you think of me that way…I'll make you happy that way, oh, God, will I!" Their kiss become animalistic; they devoured each other until Tony spoke into her ear, "We've got to stop…sigh…I can't take this…you drive me crazy!" She nibbled at his ear, "We don't have to…I'm well past the crazy stage…Tony, I want you inside me…I want you, darling…I love you so much but I understand and it makes me love you even more!" She opened the door and jumped out, "I'll see you in Houston, my dear sweet love. Good night!" He watched as she ran to the entrance. Maggie stopped and waved. He returned the wave as he disappeared into the building. He thought to himself as he started the car, "Now, I remember why I couldn't fall in love with Roni. I won't miss her anymore!"

CHAPTER TWENTY-NINE

Willie was waiting with the rented limo as he exited from the plane. The warm Houston air felt good; it was still a little cool in Chicago. Tony thought he might try to get in a round of golf while he was there. It had been a smooth flight, so he was able to sleep a while. He was in great spirits; anxious to get to the hotel.

"Stop, Willie!" Tony commanded. They were close to the hotel, and he wanted to take a good look at it from a distance. He and Willie sat on the fender of the limo, and Tony remarked, "That is one beautiful structure, don't you think?" Willie nodded, "Sure is, Tony. That Mr. Emerson and Mr. Krug know how to build a building." Tony sat and looked for a moment, then said, "Let's go, Willie Boy; I want to see the inside!"

There was at least one TV truck and two radio station cars parked at the entrance of the hotel. People with cameras were standing around with a lot of others. "Tony, it seems as though there is somethin' goin' on at the hotel; you better take a look!" Willie was slowing down to give Tony a chance to examine the situation. "What the hell? There shouldn't be any media people here…not today. Shit, I wonder what happened! We better get up there Willie."

As Willie rolled the limo to a stop, the reporters began shouting and sticking microphones against the window. Tony waited for Willie to open the door. Then amidst the barrage of questions, flashbulbs, and TV cameras, he stepped from the car. Smiling, he said, "Please, please, would just one person talk so I'll know what you want!" An extremely attractive female TV reporter jumped in front of the rest and asked, "Is it true, Mr. Cole, that your romance with Roni Scott has ended and that's why she quit the film she was working on?" Tony didn't know what to say...he was completely surprised...he spoke into the microphones, "I didn't know that Roni had left the picture...it's been several days since I've talked with her." Another reporter screamed out, "You didn't answer...has your romance ended?" He smiled directly at the first questioner...she popped the Mike into his face..."My romance with Roni Scott will never end. She's a wonderful, wonderful lady." "Then you are continuing your relationship?" asked another reporter. "You might say there's a snag in the relationship," he answered. Another question, "It's said that Roni is in a deep depression and is leaving the States. Can you confirm that?" Tony shook his head, "No, the last time I saw Roni, she wasn't depressed. We aren't mad at each other...I told you, there will always be a romance between us." He thought to himself, "What the hell has she done?" The attractive reporter asked him another question, "Mr. Cole, the studio says Roni walked out on her contract and they're going to take legal action against her because they stand to lose millions on the picture. Can you shed any light on this?" "No," he smiled. "Mr. Cole, it is common knowledge that you own Roni Cosmetics; would this be a publicity stunt to create business?" There was no smile when Tony answered, "I don't appreciate that accusation, but the answer is absolutely No." Another reporter started to ask a question, but Tony interrupted, "Ladies and gentlemen, let me say this, Roni Scott is the biggest star in Hollywood, she's at the pinnacle of her career. On the other hand, I'm at a very critical point in my own career...to put it simple... our careers have gotten in the way of our relationship. I have no answers for you other than that." He began to walk away, then stopped and said, "Why don't you all come in and see the most beautiful hotel in Texas?" He then walked hastily, toward the entrance where Mike Emerson, Paul Krug, and Carmen Lombardi were waiting; about half of the entourage followed him. He looked at Mike, "Give these bloodhounds a grand tour of the place. Paul and Carmen, let's go somewhere to talk!"

Carmen led them into the restaurant, "We can talk in the kitchen." Tony was livid as they slipped into the kitchen, "Why couldn't somebody warn me of that crap?" He pointed outside. Paul raised his hands and gestured, "They arrived here about an hour before you did. Mike called Chicago; you were about to land, so he called the airport but you left before you could get the message. Hell, Tony, we were as surprised as you." "I know,

I'm sorry. What the hell is going on anyway?" "I take it you didn't read the morning paper; your pictures and a big article is spread all over the front page," Paul informed him. "Do you have a paper here?" Tony asked. "I have one at the bar," Carmen said and went to get it. Tony smiled at Paul, "This is great for the hotel; free publicity." Paul returned the smile, "Yeh, especially since it's ready to open. The inspectors went through this morning; it only took about an hour. They were mad as hell. Who did you squeeze?" "A friend, the Mayor." Carmen returned with the newspaper. Tony read the article thoroughly, "Christ, you'd think we were married. They have blown this whole damn thing out of proportion. So what if Roni wants to take a vacation…hell, she deserves it." He threw the paper down and headed through the restaurant; Paul and Carmen right behind him.

The three of them were examining the lobby when the attractive female reporter asked if she could interrupt them. Tony agreed. "I just want to thank you for being so congenial, Mr. Cole. You were right; it is the most beautiful hotel in Texas." As she walked away, Tony stopped her, "Which station are you with…if I'm going to watch myself on TV…I want to watch the station that adds beauty also?" "I'm with KHTN-Channel 2; my name is Lana James," she blushed and turned to leave, but stopped, "Thank you, Mr. Cole. I agree with all I've heard about you. Good luck with the hotel!" She left.

"That's the best lookin' reporter I've ever seen! You could probably have that if you had a mind too!" Paul laughed as he slapped Tony on the shoulder. Tony just smiled.

After Mike had finished giving the reporters the tour, he joined Tony, Paul, and Carmen. They inspected everything. Tony was very particular, but so were the others.

When they had finished, they went up to the suite where Tony was going to stay. "Before we get into something, I want to see if I can find out what Roni is up to. He dialed her house in Palm Springs…no answer. He tried her apartment in Beverly Hills, no answer. He dialed Milton Schraff, "Hello, this is the Schraff residence." "Could I please speak to Mr. Schraff, this is Tony Cole." "Please hold for a moment, I'll see if Mr. Schraff is in." When his maid informed him that Tony Cole was on the phone, Milton sighed heavily, "I might as well talk to him now…I'll have to sooner or later." "Hello, Tony, so nice to hear from you!" "Nice to talk with you, Milton. Now, what's going on with Roni?" Milton rubbed his chin, "Tony, Roni is not doing well, you know women, love is very important to them, breaking up with you has saddened her tremendously. So, she just simply decided to go away for awhile. She'll be fine." Milton was trying to be pleasant. "Where did she go?" Tony asked. "She made me swear to secrecy...especially to you...she just wants sometime alone. Please, Tony, don't try to locate her; at least not now, give her some time. She needs it, Tony." "If that's what she wants, okay; but you keep my number handy and let me know how she's doing from time to time. Thank you, Milton." He hung up.

CHAPTER THIRTY

The Anthony Hotel was in its splendor; glittering in the Texas moonlight. The first guests started arriving around four o'clock. The acceptance was even greater than L.A….Cole Industries had another winner.

Tony had been talking in the lobby with a few of the guests when he realized he was supposed to meet Mayor Roberts and his party for dinner. As he headed toward the restaurant, the TV reporter, Lana James, stopped him, "Good evening, Mr. Cole!" Tony smiled, "Hello, I'm glad you could make it. Are you enjoying yourself?" She returned the smile, "Of course, how could you not enjoy yourself at a bash like this." He pointed toward the restaurant, "I'm meeting the mayor for dinner, would you join us?" "Well, uh, I, no, I don't want to intrude, thank you anyway." She hoped he would insist. He took her arm, "You're looking for news, aren't you? Where could you possibly get more news than having dinner with the Mayor of Houston? Come on, I would enjoy your company." She slid her arm in his, "You talked me into it. I'm sure I'll enjoy your company."

Maggie had tried to reach Roni all day, but couldn't reach her. "She left and didn't say a word. Damn her!" she said aloud. She looked at her watch…10:30… "I guess the party is at full throttle by now. I hope they all have a terrific time!" She said sarcastically as she poured herself a drink. Maggie had decided not to go to Houston. She couldn't bring herself to be that close to Tony, and act like a friend…not so soon after being with him. "God, if I would have gone, I could have been near him at least." She cried herself to sleep.

Lana James stayed at Tony's side throughout the evening. He introduced her to everybody they saw. She was having the time of her life. Tony Cole was the most impressive man, person, she had ever encountered. It was passed two a.m. and most of the guests were retiring. Tony thanked everyone he could. Finally, nearly all guests gone. Lana said to him, "Tony, I want to thank you for the most enjoyable evening I've spent in a long time. I really have to go now!" She put out her hand, he took it and said, "It was my pleasure; you're very lovely and quite nice to be around. Good night!" She turned away but stopped as Tony spoke, "Lana, would you stay with me tonight?" She didn't turn around…her heart was pounding like a drum…she didn't know how to answer. She definitely wanted to say yes, but was afraid he would think she's easy…but, then, how often does a girl get a chance to sleep with THE TONY COLE! He put his hand on her shoulder, as she turned around, he said, "Excuse me, I don't mean to be vulgar or disrespectful to you, but you excite me. I would love to make love with you!" She could feel her nipples harden, and the wetness between her legs; she put her hand in his and smiled, "Lead the way!"

Lana was leaning on one elbow, just smiling into his face; she said softly, "Why don't I fix us a drink?" "Great idea; I drink…" "I know, Jack Daniels on ice," she said as she grabbed his shirt and put it on. "Very sexy!" he said, and patted her bare bottom. He put on his pants and followed her out of the bedroom. He watched her fix the drink, and thought to himself, "She reminds me of her. I wonder if making love to Maggie will be that good…no doubt…it will be better…Christ, she even drinks scotch and soda…" "Here you are, Mr. Cole!" "Thank you, Lana," he said taking the drink from her. She sat next to him, with her legs curled up beneath her and one breast exposed from the shirt. "Tony, you are the most fascinating man I've ever met; I don't say that to make you feel good. I really mean it." Tony smiled at her, "I'll bet you say that to all the boys!" She smiled back, "No, just you. Tell me, how can you know so much about so many different things. I mean like the oil business, the hotel and restaurant business, the cosmetic business, land, movies, sports, God, is there anything you're <u>not</u> an expert on?" "You tell me," he said as he kissed her cheek and squeezed her exposed breast. "Yes, even that, you know exactly what to say, and when to say it, what to do, and when to do it…but in everything!" She kissed the back of his hand, "Tell me, please!" He picked up a cigarette, "I don't consider myself an expert – on any subject – I just try to be knowledgeable. I never know when I may have to make a quick decision, and if I wasn't knowledgeable, that decision could cost me millions." She smiled, "I have to confess to something; when I got the assignment to come here tonight, I did some research on you. I found some news magazines that ran stories on you, and a newspaper interview where you discussed your personal life. All of the ink you received was very flattering...I'm glad I wasn't disappointed." "So am I. Want another drink?" he said, getting up to fix another. "Tony, I realize this is not the time to ask you this, but I have to know. Are you in love with Roni Scott?" He didn't look back from the bar, "You're right. It's not the time!"

He handed her her drink and she asked, "Should I expect to ever see you again, or would you suggest I put tonight in my memory bank?" "That depends on you. If you want to ask a lot of questions about Roni, then count it as a memory. If you want to have a relationship that consists of having dinner, going to an occasional ballgame, and only seeing me when I'm in Houston, then, yes, I would say we'll see each other again. There is no other way. So you tell me." She stood in front of him and released the two buttons on the shirt, then dropped it on the floor, she smiled, "I'll take it. When you come to Houston, I'll come to you. Now, will you make love to me again?" He picked her up in his arms and carried her to the bedroom. In seconds, he was inside her. "Oh, Tony, I'm going to be like all the rest, huh, I'm going to feel in love with you!"

CHAPTER THIRTY-ONE

The next few months were hectic for Tony. He worked continuosly; he spent nearly twelve hours a day in his office when he was in Chicago... his time was split between Chicago, LA, and Houston; but he added trips to New Mexico, Arizona, Utah, New York, Philadelphia, and numerous other states and towns.

The Oklatex purchase was consummated quickly with no hang-ups. The Oklatex name was formally dropped and Five Star Oil took overall of their operating stations. Five Star also began – as Tony suggested – to move swiftly into Panhandle Oil territory. Newsweek, Business Week, and several oil industry publications ran feature stories on Cole Industries and Five Star Oil. Tony and Five Star was creating a lot of waves within the oil industry. Just as Tony had expected, Five Star was beginning to cause fear among some of the larger companies – especially Panhandle. They were called "rogues," going against normal policy the industry had long stood by such as, while everybody else made major ramifications to their buildings to set up "save yourself" type stations, which allowed them to sell at cheaper prices; Five Star added attendants and service plans; they increased the appearance of stations by adding plants, and painting the building with the bright orange and blue Cole colors. Five Star had seminars and training classes for their attendants. Actually, they turned the calendar back fifteen years. They make their stations enjoyable to enter, and while doing this, they kept their prices equal to their competitors. Wherever Five Star was located, they cornered the business. By early June, Panhandle was showing deep losses in the units where they met Five Star head-to-head. Panhandle wasn't the only competitors that Five Star was hurting. Mobil, Texaco, and Gulf Oil also expressed losses in the areas of Five Star.

Tony, Alvin Young, and Derek attended a government conference in New York along with the heads of the other oil companies, and the three of them were bombarded with questions and insults. The news media covering the conference had a field day with Tony and Derek answering any questions, as long as they wanted to ask. One government official even asked Tony, "What are you trying to do? You're upsetting an apple cart that has ran very smoothly for many years. Why do you want to upset it?" Tony answered simply, "The apple cart has been running smoothly for the big guys; but the little guys apple cart hasn't always ran that smoothly. Besides that, Five Star Oil is a subsidiary of Cole Industries, and Cole Industries is in business to make money!" One oil magnate remarked, "Tony Cole has given the oil industry a shot in the arm, a new excitement…although I don't agree with him, I admire his aggressiveness…he reminds me of the old days except for one thing…he's much smarter than any of us!" Tony and Five Star had definitely arrived to the oil industry!

The oil business was booming for Cole Industries, but the cosmetics were going out of sight. Irving Epps not only had added two shifts so they could operate 24 hours a day, but a shipping/storage warehouse was purchased to alleviate the space problem.

Since Roni disappeared, the orders had nearly tripled…by the first of June, the Cole Industries Cosmetics Division, reported just over four million dollars in sales from Roni Cosmetics and Perfume, and an astonishing $1.2 million in sales from Roni's Fashions. They were increasing the fashion line with hopes of equaling the sales of the cosmetics. Henri was totally immersed into the Cosmetics and Apparel Division. Although he was still the President of the Retail Division, he added an Executive Vice President to control the Cole Department Stores.

The Anthony Hotel chain opened their third unit in Chicago; and like the previous two, was experiencing phenomenal success. America's Favorite Restaurants, a national food service publication, ran a feature article on Carmen Lombardi and the King Cole Restaurants in which they referred to Carment as "a genius restauranteur" and the King Cole's were reported as "definitely one of the top 10 eating establishments in the country." Tony committed building hotels in New York, Philadelphia, San Francisco,

Dallas, and New Orleans. Peter Weyland was vigorously acquiring the land for not only the hotels but for shopping centers as well.

Every facet, division, of Cole Industries were growing at an alarming rate. They had taken over the entire Stuyvesant Building. Giving one whole floor to the most innovative computer system, one entire floor to Cole/ Emerson Architects, due to customers from outside the Cole empire.

By July, Tony Cole was seen on television interviews, heard on radio broadcasts, and read about in hundreds of newspapers and magazines. He could have spent the entire day, everyday, just giving interviews. He had become the most sought after male for speeches, interviews, and guest spots on talk shows. There was still no word on the whereabouts of Roni Scott…it was as though she disappeared from the face of the earth. Tony had explained their relationship a hundred times or more. Milton had assured him that she was alright…she was just taking an extended vacation. He continued the small romance with Lana James, which she used to further her carrer by accepting offers to interviews. She had become a popular figure in Houston.

The unrealistic love affair between Tony and Maggie had come to an abrupt halt. The last time they met. Maggie informed him, "This is going to be the last of our meetings like this. I'm moving back to my house in Palm Springs. I'm going to forget my love for you…I have to…I'm losing my mind. Every time I spend a few hours with you, I can't sleep for days after. I'm rotten to everybody I come in contact with…maybe it would be different if you'd make love to me. But, <u>oh no</u>, not the high moraled, high principled Tony Cole. You can screw every other woman, like that big-mouthed Lana James, but you can't seem to bring youself to climb into bed with the woman you say <u>you love so much</u>. Bull shit! At one time, I was so happy because I knew you loved me the way I love you; well, I don't think you love me now, or ever did. So, Mr. Cole, you can take your empire and sleep with it, eat with it, drink with it, and marry it…but don't expect to see me again…oh, the exception being, when I accompany my dear loving husband to one of the famous <u>Cole parties</u>! Tony, you're a wonderful guy, you'll do anything for anybody, but you don't know how to love. If you love me like you say, you wouldn't care if I was married. You'd make love to me anytime you could…it's simple, Tony. You're in love with Cole Industries, money, and power. You're obsessed with that stupid damn <u>challenge</u> that Jonathan Stuyvesant saddled you with. Well, you've got everything you want – all the money and power a man can have – you've met the challenge. I only hope you'll have an enjoyable life together." She was crying uncontrollably as she got out of the car, but she stopped and added, "Tony, the only thing I've ever wanted since I met you…is you. I love you so damn much!" She slammed the door and ran into the building. He sat for a long moment, debating with himself on whether to go after her and say the hell with everything else, or to let her go…even though he knew she was the only woman he would ever love… he drove away! Maggie left for California the next day. Peter never knew why, but agreed since he spent as much time there as he did in Chicago.

CHAPTER THIRTY-TWO

They were sitting in Tony's office, awaiting the arrival of Charles Reed, a Vice President of Mobil Oil Corporation when Derek asked, "Have you talked to her, or seen her?" A puzzled Tony said, "What and who the hell are you talking about?" "Don't act stupid, Tony; remember I'm your oldest friend – I know it's eating at you…Maggie, Goddamnit! Have you communicated with her?" "No, and I have no intention to do so. There is no reason to, nor is there a future in it," he replied matter-of-factly. "I don't fuckin' believe you," Derek exclaimed. "You're in love, both of you! Why the hell don't you go to her, tell Peter, and live happily ever after – instead of being miserable for the rest of your lives!" Tony lit a cigarette, "I could never do that, you know me well enough; I'd never be able to live with myself knowing I had broken up a marriage." Derek began laughing, "How can you be so damn smart in so many ways, and be so fucking dumb in others?" Tony was oblivious to Derek's accusations. Derek leaned on Tony's desk, "Peter Weyland fucks everything that wears a skirt. Christ, he's been keeping a mistress in some dinky town in California for years, plus, he's balled half the girls that work in the California shopping center, not to mention the waitresses, barmaids, and God knows who else at the hotels! And you think you would be breaking up a marriage? Huh!" Tony was dumbfounded. He had no idea that Peter was like that. He sat looking at his cigarette, speechless. "Hey, uh, I'm sorry. I had no right talking to you like that," Derek realized that Tony was shaken, "It's none of my business. Oh, hell yes it is. I love you. You're like my God damn brother, and I don't like you to be unhappy!" Tony walked around the desk, and grabbed Derek's hand, "Thank you! I don't know what I'd do without you; I appreciate your concern, and someday – maybe I'll do that, just go after her, but I can't right now. There are more important things to do…I can't let my friends down, now can I!" The intercom buzzed, it was Theresa, "They're coming now."

Theresa opened the door and two impeccably attired gentlemen entered as Tony greeted them, "Good morning. I'm Tony Cole, and this is Derek Hill. The larger man, apparently Mr. Reed acknowledged, "Godd morning, Mr. Cole, Mr. Hill. I'm Charles Reed and this is Arnold Friedberg." Theresa brought in coffee as they were sitting down. Tony didn't sit behind his desk, instead he and Derek occupied two of the leather chairs opposite the two that the Mobil executives had sat in. Tony spoke first, "Well, before we begin, may I suggest we be informal and address each other by first names?" "Very good, Tony." Charles Reed nodded. "Now, what could we do for you, Charles, Arnold?" Tony gave them the lead. Charles leaned forward, "Tony, your Five Star Oil had been the talk of the industry for the past couple of months. You're making quite a name for yourself. You've taken a small, quiet, family-owned oil company and done something with it. It's still small, compared to our standards, but it isn't family-owned and it sure as hell isn't quiet. In fact, it's become quite loud, loud enough to be heard all over the nation. A year ago, if you would have asked half of the large oil companies executives who Five Star Oil is, you'd have been lucky if 10% could answer. A year is a long time, because now if you would ask those same executives, 100% knows who Five Star Oil is. I congratulate you. You've done well." He leaned back in his chair. "We appreciate the compliments, but I'm sure you didn't come from New York to pay us compliments. What can we do for you?" Tony stated flatly. Mr. Reed wasn't prepared for that type of attitude. He was expecting broad smiles and a lot of I agrees. "Well, you're, uh, right. There is a reason for our requesting this little meeting. We, Mobil Oil, being aware of your success and presumably continued success, would like to present an offer toward the purchase of Five Star Oil." Derek could hardly sit still. Tony had been right all along. It was happening exactly as he said it would. Tony poured a cup of coffee, slowly so they could wonder what he was going to say. He smiled and said, "Well, we appreciate all of the thought that you, Mobil Oil, have give to our small oil company – but I don't think we want to sell." Derek almost fell over, "What the hell is he doing," he thought. Reed looked at Friedberg who licked his lips and said, "Uh, Mr. Cole, rather Tony – excuse me – Mobil is prepared to make you a very substantial offer. Being aware that Cole Industries is the sole owner, with no stock out, it can be very lucrative for you. What would you say to an offer of let's say $9 billion?" Arnold sat back, smiled at Charles; Derek stomach was turning flips, it was all he could do to control his excitement. Tony had said they could sell near six, but nine! "That's a very handsome offer," Tony said very softly, "But I guess you didn't understand. We enjoy the oil industry, hell, we're just getting the taste of it – and we like the taste. Oh, we're never going to be a Mobil, but we feel that we're going to continue to grow. We don't really want to sell...but everybody has a price." (Derek couldn't belive he was going to turn it down.) Tony continued, "We're no different; we have a price also. Being that we aren't pursuing to sell and would rather stay in the oil business, we would name our own price...say $13 billion." Their mouth dropped open, and so did Derek's (he was flabbergasted). "That's totally absurd. Five Star isn't worth six billion," Charles Reed sounded upset. "We figured the growth you'll experience over the next five to seven years and we added that in; that's how we arrived at the nine billion figure. You're trying to rape us. There is no way!" Tony leaned forward to express his next point, "You made only one mistake; you figured our growth rate wrong. You were absolutely correct when you said Five Star has begun making noise...well, gentlemen, right now, you're hearing one trumpet, but I can assure you that you will be hearing the whole orchestra very soon. Thank you for coming. I hope you enjoy your flight back to New York." He stood up and extended his hand. Derek and the two Mobil execs sat motionless. Finally the three of them stood. Tony smiled, "I'll have our driver take you to the airport. It's been a pleasure to meet you. I hope we'll have the chance to do it again." Reed accepted Tony's hand. "Good day, Tony, Derek. I must say that I'm impressed by your boyish enthusiasm, but you should realize that Mobil Oil is not Oklatex or Panhandle. Just keep in mind – Mr. Cole."

Derek watched them leave. He turned to Tony, but didn't know what to say. Tony put his hand on Derek's shoulder, "They were nice guys, weren't they?" They both laughed aloud. They laughed so loud that Theresa came in, "What in the world are you two doing?" Derek, trying to stop, said, "We just watched $9 billion bucks walk out that door!" He began laughing harder. Theresa stood with a very confused look on her face. Tony had controlled his laughter and said to Theresa, "Would you assemble the troops for me. I don't care what they're doing, or where they are. I want Underwood, Shapiro, Vachon, Krug, Emerson, and Lombardi here tomorrow afternoon for a meeting at two o'clock." She shook her head and started out, "You got it, boss!"

Derek was more confused than ever, "What are you calling a meeting for?" Tony grinned, a large grin, "We have to have a vote before we can sell our oil company!" Derek threw his arms up in the air, "Are you nutso? You just turned down their offer. We'll never hear from them again!" Tony lit a cigarette, "Right. I just turned down their offier. Their first offer… we'll accept their second!" Derek finally realized what Tony had done. "You mean…you think they'll make a counter offer?" Derek, my boy," Tony replied, "They came in here trying to build us up, telling us that they were offering us what we would be worth in the future. They shot us a low-ball figure, taking a chance that we might jump on it. I gave them something to think about, like we might expand further, at an accelerated pace. I then high-balled them. My prediction is that they will return later with the final offer of ten billion…which, I would reccomentd we accept. I want to present it to the rest of the board so you and I can make an on-the-spot decision." Derek smiled and shook his head, "If it happens, like you think it will, you will have then totally convinced me that you are the smartest fucker I've ever met!" "What will I be if I've predicted wrong?" Tony laughed. Derek just smiled, "I'll put my money on you!"

All members of the board were assembled in the conference room, awaiting Tony and Derek. "I wonder what Tony wants to buy this time?" Paul remarked. "Well, I've heard General Motors is on the market!" Peter said sarcastically. The rest laughed.

Tony entered the room in his normal manner; crisp walk, smiling face, impeccable dress, and always the "Good afternoon, my friends." Derek followed him into the room, said his hello's, and sat at his normal spot – at the right hand of Tony.

The expressions on their faces were as he had expected. They were curious as to why they had been summoned on short notice. "Are you curious?" Tony smiled. "Naw, Peter already told us…we're buying General Motors!" Henri added. They all laughed. "Well, we aren't ready to take on General Motors…but how about Mobil Oil?" Everybody's eyes lit up – they stared at one another, then at Tony…none of them really understood Tony's thinking…but each one of them was envious of his amazing success. "I'm sure you're all aware of the success we're enjoying in the oil business. It seems as though, we're stepping on some big toes. Those toes are what we've gathered to discuss; Derek will give some figures." Tony definitely had their attention. Derek went to the blackboard, "Gentlemen, Cole Industries first ventured into the oil business with an investment of less than $200 million. When Claude Benaforte passed away, we bought out the rest of Five Star Oil…I don't mean to bore you, but it's important you all know this whole story…, so at that point, we've invested nearly $350 million. Then we acquired Oklatex, and spent exactly $900 million which brings our total oil investment to less than $1.3 billion." Derek looked at Tony, "You have anything to add at this point?" "Nope!" He returned to the blackboard. "Okay. We all know that we stole the remaining portion of Five Star, and – as with Five Star, Tony's bargaining got us Oklatex for much less than it was worth. Our best calculations say that after the Oklatex acquisition, our oil interests were worth approximately $4.5 billion. Since then we have increased our share of the market and our worth is now nearer to $6 billion. I'll give it back to Tony."

Tony lit a cigarette, sipped at his coffee, then began. "I'll get back to the toes we're stepping on. It comes to our attention that we are operating our oil business unethically. That is, we're not plodding along like the other companies in the oil industry – they seem to want the consumers to think the oil business is going through a rough period, and that Five Star Oil is causing the consumer to think differently. They're exactly right. Wherever we have operating stations, we get the bulk of the business. We do better than Mobil, Texaco, Shell, Gulf, all the majors, and the smaller companies – such as Panhandle. To put it bluntly, we have scared the hell out of all of them. For them to regain their share of those markets – they are going to have to change their policies to be similar to ours. They don't want to do that – it would cut into their profits – which are higher than ever before. Okay, so much for that.

The reason I called this meeting is to take a vote. We are going to have to make a decision shortly on whether to sell our oil interests, or hang on to them. I mentioned Mobil previously. No, we aren't going to buy them… they want to buy us…our oil interests that is. Before we discuss selling or not selling, let me give you something to think about.

"One; our oil interests are far and away our biggest money maker – volume, dollars, and profits. If we stay in the oil business, we should continue to enjoy that. Two; if we stay, we quite possibly will see some trouble from the other companies. I have been informed that they are going to take physical action against us if we don't conform to their way of doing business. Three; if we sell, we stand to make a bundle. Derek and I met with Mobil yesterday – they offered $9 billion – I turned it down, but told them we might be interested if the offer was nearer $13 billion." He paused to look at the faces, then continued. Four; if we sell – I think Mobil will return with an offer of $10 billion – we would make enough profit from the sale to pay off the loans we have outstanding in the other divisions of the company. Cole Industries would have a worth of well over $5 billion and not owe a dime. Five, and finally; if we sell, $3 billion comes of the top – to <u>me</u>. Before you question that, I'll explain why. The initial investment was made by me personally – solely to enhance my own financial status. Cole Industries never reimbursed me for that, and $3 billion is the approximate worth of what my initial investment is today. If we were to sell at $10 billion, and I take $3 billion, Cole Industries would receive $7 billion, which is at least 1 billion more that it's worth. Now, let's have your questions, I'm sure there are many."

Each of the board members looked around, shuffled in their seats, lit cigarettes, sipped at coffee, and rubbed their chins. Finally, Henri spoke. "If we sell, will it allow us to further expand our present operations?" "Of course," Tony exclaimed, "Not only will we not owe anybody, we'll have money left over to divide among the divisions, and possibly start new divisions. For example, your division is the second leading division profitwise – the cosmetics and fashions. Peter has been contacted by and he contacted some cities about Cole putting a department store in their towns. We have five or six sites we could step into immediately. To answer your question – yes, that is the main reason for deciding to sell or not to sell." Paul Krug asked, "Do you really think they would try violence to stop our business practices?" "I know they would, Paul!" "Are you sure our profits would continue at the same rate? I feel the oil division is the main reason the banks will lend us whatever we want, is that so?" Mike questioned. "Can I answer that, Tony?" Bob requested. Tony agreed. "You're right, the banks we deal with, and there are about nine of them, look very hard at our profits from the oil, but with more and more oil being imported, they might not look so hard at oil in the future. Will our profits stay as high as they are now? Nobody can be sure, but it is possible." Nobody else had questions. "Anybody else? Peter, what about you?" Tony asked. "I'm for making our money now and let the <u>true</u> oil people have it." "Carmen, wha do you say?" He smiled, "Tony, I know noting 'bout that business. I jus know food. So I say, sell." "Henri!" "I agree, sell!" "Paul!" He shifted in his seat, "I would hate like hell to let them think they ran us out of the business; but we're businessmen, not street fighters. I vote we sell!" "Mike!" "Well, I like the prestige of the oil business. I like the thought of the high profits, I vote no to selling." "Peter!" "I would like to see Cole Industries debt-free. The banks would look at that much more favorably than owning oil and having a couple billion dollars owed. I vote sell!" "Bob!" "Peter has a valid point about the banks; but if we didn't turn around and spend some of that money – immediately – our taxes would be astronomical. At this point, my vote is to keep our oil interests, and not sell!" "Larry!" "From reading about the oil industry – which is all I know about it – I feel that the prestige of being in that industry is going to dissipate rapidly. I vote to sell." "Derek!" "I have mixed feelings. I, too, like the prestige and the high profits; but I lick my lips at the thought of the profit we'd make by selling – and profit now wins out over prestige – I say, sell!"

That left only Tony to vote. "If we do this democratically – we sell by a vote of 5 to 2 and one not voted yet. I feel the same as all of you; I truly enjoy the oil business, it is prestigious, and very profitable. Like Paul, I certainly don't want them to think they ran us out of the business. Larry hit the nail on the head; the consumers are beginning to have a negative view of the oil industry, and the Middle Eastern countries are going to become more and more influential in the very near future. Bob is also right, if we sell, we're going to have to expand quickly or get eaten alive at tax time. Taking all of this into consideration, I still feel we should sell, and since the majority went that way – we sell." He stood up and said, "One other thing, each of you will receive $5 million for you personally at the time of sale." They all clapped. "Well, I have to return a call to Mr. Reed at Mobil; he phoned before the meeting started – said he wanted to speak to me again. Thanks to all of you for dropping what you were doing and coming here."

CHAPTER THIRTY-THREE

"Maggie, you've never played as well as you are now. You're a shoe-in-to-win next weekend!" Angela exclaimed. "I just hope it's cooler; it's really going to blister today. I'm looking forward to playing in that tournament. There will be some really good players coming in." Maggie was wiping the perspiration from her face. "Will Peter be going to Vegas with you or will he meet you there?" Angela asked. Maggie ordered an iced tea, "I'm not sure; in fact, I don't even know if he's going. Who knows, he might even be in Chicago or Houston or who the hell knows where!" Angela had noticed a big change in Maggie ever since she returned from Chicago in the spring. "Mag, I don't usually stick my nose in my friends business, but, we've been friends for a long time. You just haven't seemed happy since you returned. Would you like to tell me about it?" "Nothing happened! Everything is just as wonderful and rosy as always!" Maggie spoke sarcastically, and Angela didn't miss the sarcasm. "Come on, Mag, why don't you tell me what's bugging you. Christ, you play tennis at least once everyday, you don't go out, Peter's never home – Maggie, are you and Peter having as many problems as it seems?" Maggie looked at her – she wanted to tell somebody about Tony, but Angela wasn't the one; hell, she had always been a friend, but she had always wanted to spread her legs for Peter; maybe she has already. "No, we aren't having any problems. It's just that he's always gone. I get jealous sometimes, that's all." Angela didn't pursue it any further, although she didn't buy the answer. "I better run, Angela. Peter should be home from Chicago by now – he had to go for a special meeting – I'll talk to you tomorrow." She left Angela sitting alone.

The phone was ringing when Peter opened the door. Maggie's Mercedes was gone, so he ran to get the phone. "Hello, Weyland's residence!" "Well, you sound like you're out-of-breath, been running?" Angela cajoled. "Oh, hi Angela; no, I just walked in. Maggie's not here; want me to have her call you?" Angela was smiling, "No, in fact, she just left me. We were playing tennis and she said she had to get home because you should be there. I called to talk to you!" Peter was curious, "What is it?" "Peter, could I see you sometime – without Maggie knowing – I have something to talk to you about; it's personal. Could you meet me somewhere?" "This is odd," Peter thought. "Well, I don't know – how important is it? Can't you tell me now?" "I can't talk over the phone. Could you please meet me?" She was very persuasive. "Uh, yeah, I guess so. How about tomorrow, Jilly's for lunch?" She beamed, "That would be super. I'll meet you at noon!" She hung up before he could say anything. "She must be having marital problems or some shit," he thought as he went into the kitchen.

"Peter! Peter! Are you here?" Maggie yelled as she came in. "I'm in the kitchen! Come on in!" She went into the kitchen, and kissed his cheek. "How'd your game go today?" "Good, I'm playing better than ever. How was the meeting?" He was opening a beer, "Fine. We're going to sell Five Star!" She was shocked, "Why? I thought since you bought out Oklatex, the oil division was growing faster than before!" He smiled at her, "It seems as though Mr. Cole has pulled off another coup!" Hearing his name made her heart jump. Peter continued, "Mobil Oil made an offer to purchase Five Star for much more than it's worth. Cole Industries is going to make a bundle, and so is Tony. If the sale goes through, he gets $3 billion right of the top!" "He's done it," she thought, "He's beaten the challenge!" She got excited, but tried not to show it. "Maybe, this means, he'll come for me now," she continued to think. "I guess, I shouldn't be jealous though. He's giving each one of the board $5 million immediately after the sale." Peter said. "Oh, that's, uh, terrific. You should be happy. It isn't everyday you make $5 million dollars that easy. When is the sale going to take place?" asked a curious Maggie. Peter shook his head, "I'm not sure. I think Tony will meet with Mobil in the next couple of days. Let's see, today is September 12th; I'd guess the deal should be consummated by the first of October. Tony moves pretty fast on these things."

She wrestled with her thoughts, "Should I call him? No, I'll wait until after the sale. Oh, God, please let this be all. Let me have him now. He will have beaten that damn challenge. I still love him so much."

She was standing next to her car as he pulled into the parking lot. Peter had always thought Angela was attractive, but she sure looked good standing there. Many times he had thought about trying to get her into bed, but figured it was much to close to home and she'd tell Maggie. He couldn't help but remember the times, especially when she drank too much, that she'd give him a friendly kiss and rub herself against him. "Oh, well, I'll hear her troubles, give her some stupid advice, and she'll be on her way," he sighed.

As he pulled into the parking spot next to her, she opened the car door and jumped in. "I don't really want to have lunch; would you mind if we just took a drive?" Peter shrugged, put the car in reverse and said, "No, I'm trying to drop a few pounds anyway." He couldn't help noticing her skirt being higher up than normal, exposing quite a bit of her dark-tanned legs. In fact, he was getting hard!

"So, what can I do for you, Angela?" Peter asked as he pulled onto the highway and headed toward the desert. She leaned her head back on the head rest. "It's not what you can do for me, but what can I do for you?" He looked at her, totally confused, "Hey, did I call you, or did you call me?" "Oh, I called you! Peter, it's obvious that you and Maggie are suffering through some problems, and I'd just like to help you during your troubled times." She smiled at him. "I don't know what you mean! Well, uh, yeh, I guess Maggie has told you some of the things we've been going through." "So, there are problems, and Maggie wouldn't tell me – and I am supposed to be her best friend," she tought to herself. "Peter, she did tell me some, but, I'd rather you wouldn't tell her I told you. Actually, I feel you're the one being deprived!" She was searching, but didn't think he would catch on. He didn't. "I'm glad somebody agrees with me. She just didn't like living in Chicago, so she takes it out on me. Christ, we haven't slept together in a month!" "Bingo!" she thought. "Peter, pull over for a second!" As he steared the car to the side of the road, she said, "I know, that's why I wanted to see you." When the car was stopped, shed took his hand and guided it up her dress, between her legs. She wasn't wearing underwear. "I think, I can take her place until you get it back together!" He was shocked, but excited as hell! "Angela, what the hell! Do you know what you're doing?" She spread her legs further apart, allowing him to maneuver his hand freely. "Peter, I've wanted to make it with, ohh, you ever since I met you – ohh, ohh, Peter…let's go to a motel – shit, we can talk about it later!" He sat up, and drove to the closest motel. They spent the next three hours together, and made plans to meet whenever he could find the time. Peter was very happy with the situation; he had his mistress in Indio, which he had been planning to dump; Angela gave him the reason he had been looking for. Angela had what she had wanted for a long time – Peter!

CHAPTER THIRTY-FOUR

Charles Reed and Arnold Friedberg were more than gracious – much different attitudes than when they left a couple of days ago. "Tony, Derek, so nice to see you again!" Charles smiled broadly. "Yes, Tony, Derek, I'm glad we're having another chance to talk!" Arnold pointed for them to sit down. "Would you care for a drink? I think you both drink Jack Daniels – Tony with ice, and Derek a little water!" Charles said with tongue-in-cheek. "I see you've done your homework, Charles," Tony acknowledged. Charles laughed, "I had to – after the way we misjudged you earlier. I congratulate you on your awareness, Tony!" Tony toasted him. As Charles sat down, he said, "You like to get to the point, right. Well, let's do just that. We don't want to waste your time – or ours." Arnold moved into the conversation, "Tony, Derek, now that you've had time to consider the generous offer we presented, we certainly hope you've had a change of mind!" Derek looked at Tony, Tony looked at Derek, then smiled at Charles, and turned to Arnold – the smiled disappeared – "You're full of shit!" Both Arnold and Charles were stunned. They looked at each other; obvious to both they had misjudged Tony again. "Uh, is that all you have to say?" Charles had to fight himself to keep from screaming.

Tony took a long sip of his drink, "No, I do have something else tosay. I think we will go now. I thought we ere perfectly clear during our last meeting – we weren't interested in your generous offer, as you call it, then, and we're a helluva lot less interested now. Good evening, genetlemen!" Tony stood; Derek followed. Charles jumped to his feet, "Now, hold on. Why don't we start over?" "What do we have to talk about?" Tony continued to leave. "How about another offer?" Charles blurted out.

Tony winked at Derek, who could hardly keep from laughing, "If you had another offer, why did you insult us by making the same offer again? I'm not sure we want to hear another one, or if we will be interested in doing business with Mobil Oil – you aren't the only one who, uh, the only oil company in the world!" Once again, the two Mobil executives shot looks at each other. Tony had almost said another company was interested, purposely, and his word play did its work. "Okay, let's quit playing games," Charles sighed, "Would you please sit down? We would like to make another offer." Tony and Derek returned to their seats, and Tony waved his hand toward them, "You have the floor, we're listening!"

Arnold fumbled through papers, and Charles got impatient, "Oh hell, Friedberg, forget it! Tony, Derek, we are prepared to offer you $12 billion! We cannot meet your demand of $13 billion." Tony didn't hesitate, and stated flatly, "We accept!" "That's it? You accept; just like that?" Charles didn't understand. "Yes. That's all you had to do, just make the offer and wait for our answer. It was that simple." Tony replied. "Fine! Fine! We'll inform the proper government agencies, and we'd like to get this finished as soon as possible; if that's okay with you?" Tony and Derek stood, shook hands with Carles and Arnold. Tony said, "Our lawyers will contact you for a meeting. We, too, would like it done quickly. Thank you gentlemen, maybe we can do this again! Charles laughed, "I'm sorry, but I'd rather not negotiate with you anymore – your good, Mr. Cole! Real good! Good night." As they opened the door, Arnold asked, "Who were the other bargaining companies?" Tony looked back and smiled, "There weren't any!" At that, they left.

CHAPTER THIRTY-FIVE

It was official; Five Star Oil (a division of Cole Industries) was sold for the astronomical price of $12 billion! A news conference was held following the signing of the purchase was over! The Mobil Oil officials had left! Tony Cole and Derek Hill had answered the media's questions! Bob Underwood, Vice-President of Finance at Cole, had deposited the check! Cole Industries would be debt free by tomorrow afternoon! Each board member of Cole Instries is $10 million richer! Tony increased each member's share due to the extra 2 billion. Tony Cole is $4 billion richer; he becomes one of the wealthiest men in the entire world! One-and-a half years ago, Jonathan Stuyvesant (who's worth was between 2 and 3 billion dollars) had left Tony with a fortune, and a <u>challenge</u> to become the next multi-billionaire.

The medias of the world had made Tony Cole <u>big news</u>. The story of the <u>challenge</u> was printed and reprinted. He was constantly being interviewed. Everywhere he went, he made news. Every business deal he was involved in, made news; his personal life – where he went, who he went with, and what he ate – made news. His romance with Roni Scott, the beautiful movie queen was constantly in the news. The ending of their romance was news. His next romance – a TV news reporter, Lana James – had been news – Lana James became an instant celebrity.

The <u>challenge</u> had thrown Tony Cole into the world of political figures, movie stars, and big business. He was called the world's most eligible bachelor – the world's most handsome multi-billionaire – the nice-guy billionaire – the man every man wanted to be – and the most-wanted man by women. He was the epitamy of America: poor orphan boy makes it big. Now, that he had met the challenge, he was to become even bigger news!

He sits alone, watching Lake Michigan's waves play tag with the beach behind his house. To any other man, this very moment would be the happiest moment in their lifetime; but for Tony Cole, it was only satisfying. He was happy about his success in business, but his personal life was sad. For here, on the day he actually became a multi-billionaire, he was alone. The woman he loves so deeply, is married to another man. The other woman, who he loved, but not in the same way as the first, had gone away – to forget him. He wanted Maggie to share his fortune with him; he would never be happy until they were together.

As he watched the water, he began to think of what it was like when he was a child. "The rain is coming in, Sister Carolyn! The rain is coming in through the roof!" "Yes, Tony; I see, but we don't have the money to fix the roof, so we'll have to live with it – go and get the large wastebasket and catch the rain in it." He was six years old then – the roof was never fixed! "Tell me, Tony, did the boy hit you first or did you start the fight?" "Well, uh, he started the fight – but, uh, I hit him first." "I think you'd better explain to us!" "I was walking with Jenny, and he – David – came up and started making fun of Jenny – calling her a cripple, a funny looking orphan cripple. I told him to stop and go away, to leave us alone. But he told me to shut up – then he shoved Jenny – that's when I hit him – he, sniff, sniff, made Jenny cry, Sister – he made my little Jenny cry – that's, sniff, why I hit him, and if he does it again, I'll hit him again – I don't care what you do to me – I just don't want him to hurt little Jenny!" "It's okay," Sister Carolyn wiped the tears from his eyes, "It was good that you protected Jenny. You acted like a man, instead of a twelve year old. Now, let's go home to Jenny."

Jenny died the next year; she was only eight years old. She came to the orphanage when she was three – her parents didn't want to be saddled with a crippled girl who had a bad heart. She was always so small, he remembered. From the time they got her, she clung to Tony. He treated her like a fine piece of jewelry – they loved each other more than brothers and sisters – Tony was holding her the night she died, and when the doctor took her away from him, he cried, "Now God will take care of you. Tony can't anymore. Goodbye, my little Jenny. Goodbye!"

Tony couldn't stop the tears when he thought about little Jenny. "God, she'd be 25 now!" he said as he ran his thumb under his eyes to wipe away the tears. He continued to reminisce as he watched the water. He remembered everything as though it were yesterday. It was after Jenny died that Tony became the <u>man</u> of the orphanage. He made the rest of the children do as Sister Carolyn said. He was their big brother and father all in one. Sister Carolyn depended on him more and more. He remembered Sister Carolyn's funeral. The Church was overflowing with people. He was in his early 20's and the priest asked him to do the eulogy.

He stood at the podium, wanting to be strong – the way she had taught him – but as he began to recall the past, he couldn't control the tears. "Sister Carolyn was, and always will be, the only mother and father we ever had. She nursed us when we were sick, she fed us when we were hungry, she sat up with us when we were afraid in the night, she scolded us when we were bad, she praised us when we were good, and – most of all – she loved us when we needed to be loved. Sister Carolyn was a saint! I remember the night little Jenny died. All of the children were crying, but Sister – who loved little Jenny more than any of us – didn't cry; she stayed strong for us. She always stayed strong for us. That night, when all the other children were asleep, I could hear her, in her room, crying. I'll never forget it. She asked God to hold little Jenny because she liked it so much. Sister Carolyn gave so much and received so little. She will be missed by all of us. I say this next statement, with no thought of being wrong; Sister Carolyn Kelly was the greatest woman this world has ever seen!"

"What do I do now, Sister?" Tony said aloud. The darkness was setting in, the white tops of the waves were all that could be seen off the lake. "Tony, have you forgotten about the time?" Frederick interrupted his thoughts. "Yes, Frederick, to be honest, I did." He went in to dress for the party.

CHAPTER THIRTY-SIX

The largest conference room at the Chicago Anthony Hotel was all decked out in the now familiar Cole Industries bright orange and blue colors.

The party was being given by the Cole board members, to honor their leader and to show their appreciation for what he had given them, plus it was his 30th birthday. It was September 26th. They had invited everybody who was of importance. They had attempted to contact Roni Scott, but she wasn't available – she couldn't even be found. Lana James flew in from Houston, after all she was the girl in his life – the media had decided anyway. What they didn't know was the one, and really only one, that Tony wanted to see at his party was Maggie Weyland' but she wasn't going to attend either. She was playing in the Nevada Women's Amateur Tennis Tournament. Her husband Peter would attend instead of going to his wife's tournament.

All the sppeches had been given, and the party was now well underway; the guests were milling around and discussing subjects, ranging from finance, to baseball, to sex. Tony put his hand on Peter's shoulder, "Peter, I want to thank you for attending this shindig, but don't you think you should have been at Maggie's tournament?" Peter sighed, and bit his lip, "No, Tony, this is where I should be. You see, oh shit, Tony, it looks like Maggie and I are going to split up." Tony couldn't believe it; now, he could go to her, the day they had waited for has finally come – but will she still want him. "Peter, what the hell happened?" Peter was unaware that Tony knew of his sexual exploits. She has never been the same since we moved to Chicago. I thought it would be better after she moved back to Palm

Springs, but it only got worse. I thought she might be, uh, having an affair, but Maggie isn't that way, she'd never do that. I'm the only asshole that continues it; but you know, Tony, no matter how many women I have – none of them will ever be the woman Maggie is. I'm really going to miss her!" Tony understood; he felt the same way. "I wish I knew what to say, but I really don't. I just hope things work out the way you want them to, Peter." "Oh, everything will be alright. Hell, look at you, you're doing fine as a bachelor. You know, when I look at you I get kind of anxious to be, uh, single." Tony took a moment to look at him, and thought, "You're in for what could be a rude awakening – but he'll do alright. He has no morals anyway." Lana James grabbed his arm, "Hey, did you forget about me?" Tony almost laughed, because he had forgotten her. His mind was filled with the thought that he and Maggie might be together soon. "Oh, hi Lana! Enjoying yourself?" "Of course, with all thse big name people around, but mainly because I'm going to be able to spend a few days with you instead of a few hours." She said as she snuggled her head against his arm. "See what I mean?" Peter smiled then walked away.

Stephanie Emerson took hold of Tony's other arm, "Hi ya! Damn, you get better looking everytime I see you!" She kissed him. Lana thought she noticed more than a friendly kiss, she put out her hand towards Stephanie, "Uh, hi! I'm Lana James, and who might you be?" Tony looked at Lana, then at Stephanie and smiled. Stephanie smiled back, then folded her arms and said, "The name is Stephanie Emerson, and I'm in love with this guy; after all we women always love the man that popped our cherry! I'm no exception." Lana was speechless and Tony blushed, "You see, Stephanie helped create the man I am today!" He squeezed her and they laughed – except Lana of course. "Well, I guess I've caused enough trouble I'd better mosey off," she kissed Tony's cheek and walked away without acknowledging Lana. "Was she putting me on?" Lana asked. Tony shook his head, "No, in fact, it was the first time for both of us. She's now a very dear friend."

The party lingered through the evening. Tony attempted to speak to everybody who had attended. Most of the guests thought Tony was a little special prior to the party, but they were positive when it ended.

The last to leave was Henri, and friend. Tony was walking out with them as Lana – who was sitting at a table near the door – said, "Do you think I might tag-a-long?" Tony had completely forgotten her. All he could think about was Maggie; on two separate occasions, during the evening, he had called other women Maggie. He had decided to call her – tonight. It had been months since they had talked. He took Lana's hand, "Yeh, of course. Let's go."

While the elevator made its way to the Presidential Suite, Lana was trying to talk to Tony, but he was oblivious to her chatter. He was going to tell her that it was over between them as soon as they got in the room.

Tony checked the time, as he closed the door – 3:10 a.m. Lana turned to him, and without speaking, unzipped her gown and dropped it to the floor. At that moment, the red light on Tony's private phone began to blink, and chimed. "That's my specialy phone. Frederick wants me to call, it is something important. Put your dress on; I want to talk to you when I get off the phone!" He picked up the phone, "Yes, Frederick! What is it?" A sleepy voiced Frederick spoke slowly, "Tony, a Mr. Milton Schraff just telephoned. He says it's very important he talk to you immediately. I didn't want to bother you but he said to tell you it pertained to Roni Scott." Tony felt numb. Roni, something happened to her – or she's back. "Fine Frederick. I do want to talk to him. Sorry your sleep was disturbed. Good night!"

Lana was sitting on the arm of the sofa, clad only in her panties, "Not bad news, I hope?" She walked to him. He was thinking to himself, for a moment, then opened his wallet and pulled out a business card – it had Milton's home phone number on it. Lana leaned against him, he said, "I thought I asked you to get dressed. Lana, please, this is very important and private. Would you mind waiting for me in the bedroom?" "Why not, I've been waiting for you all night!" She left her dress lay and stomped into the bedroom.

The phone rang nearly ten times before Milton picked it up, "Hello!" he sounded angry. "Milton, this is Tony Cole, returning your call." Milton calmed down, "Oh, Tony, thank you for calling. I'm sorry for disturbing you; but I felt I had no choice." Tony's curiousity was killing him, "Would you please tell me what's up. Is something wrong with Roni?" Milton paused, then said, "Tony, I promised her I'd never tell you, but I have to now. Tony screamed into the phone, "Tell me what, Goddamnit!" Tony's voice surprised Milton, "Uh, Roni's pregnant! She's due to deliver very soon!" Tony fell into the chair he was standing beside, "Why, why the hell didn't she tell me? Why?" "She wanted to marry you more than anything Tony – but she didn't want to force you or intrude into your life. She still loves you Tony," Milton was near tears. "Tony, she's having some problems. She has nobody, nobody who she really cares about but you!" "Where is she? I'm going to her right away!" Milton sighed with relief, "Geneva! Geneva, Switzerland; she's at a private residence, a Herr Minke; it's a farm outside of Geneva." "How the hell did she find that place?" Tony wondered. "The Minke's daughter had been in a film with Roni a few years ago and she week-ended with them once. She had kept in contact through the years. It was the one place she was sure to be left alone until after the baby was born. Tony, she never intends to make another movie – she says she just wants to raise the baby that you gave her." "Thank you, Milton! You're a true friend to both of us! I'm going to leave as soon as my plane can be ready. I'll be in touch Milton – and thanks again!"

He went into the bedroom. Lana was lying on the bed, now totally nude, but Tony didn't even notice the nudity. Lana, I'm sorry to do it like this, but I haven't got time to get into a big discussion – but, you and I, we're through. Like I said, I don't have time to discuss it. Hate me, or whatever, but I really wish you'd put your clothes on so we can get out of here. He handed her her dress. "Is this the way you dump your women, just throw them out in the middle of the night; what did I do wrong?" she was in tears. "Look," Tony ran his hand through his hair, "I'm really sorry to end it like this, but I must go away. I really liked you Lana..." She shrieked, "Liked me! You sound like we're back in grade school – I'm in love with you and you <u>like</u> me! What am I supposed to do? Just walk out that door, and say thanks and forget all about you?" Tony nodded, "Yes. I think that's the only way to do it. I'm sorry; but we didn't exactly have the most normal relationship in the world. Unless you call two or three nights a month normal." "To you, those nights meant only a good piece of ass – but to me, they were all I lived for – I couldn't wait until I saw you again – I wanted more, but I knew you didn't, so I took what you would give me – and, sniff, now I'm losing it all. Why? What did I do?" "Nothing, Lana, it's just that...I don't have time to explain. I have to take an emergency trip. I'll call you when I get back. You stay here tonight, my driver will be here in the morning to drive you to the airport. There'll be an airline ticket for you there. I'm sorry Lana, I hate to leave it this way, but I have no other choice. Goodbye!" He left her, still on the bed, still nude, and weeping violently.

He went to Derek and Theresa's room; they decided to stay at the hotel instead of driving home. When he got there, he decided to call them from the car. He called Willie's room, told him to meet him at the car. Tony used the office phone to call Chris Pike. He told Chris to get the plane ready for a flight to Geneva, as soon as possible. He would meet him at the airport. By the time he finished talking to Chris, Willie was waiting in the car. The first thing he did was pour himself a drink, then he called Frederick to inform him of his leaving and he wanted to be packed by the time he got there. He then called Derek's room at the hotel.

The phone startled them, they were fast asleep. Derek picked it up, "This had better be important!" "It is!" Tony said, "Derek, go in the other room. I don't want Theresa to hear what I'm going to tell you. You can tell her later, but just keep it quiet for a while." "Sure, just let me go in the other room, I don't want to disturb Theresa." "Okay, what's up?" "Derek, I'm going away for a while – I don't know for how long – but you are going to be the <u>only one</u> who knows where I am." Derek interrupted, "What the fuck has happened?" "I'm going to Geneva, Switzerland. I'm going to Roni. She's just about to deliver <u>my</u> child. I'm going to marry her. I'm using Chris and the company plane, I'm going to keep him there, he can use it as a vacation. Buy another plane and hire another pilot. I don't know when I'll be back. So you hold the fort down, old buddy." Derek sat in shock, "When did you come to this conclusion?" "Milton Schraff called me tonight. I'll call you at home in a couple of days to let you know where to reach me See ya later!" He hung up before Derek could say anything else.

CHAPTER THIRTY-SEVEN

Finally, the orange and blue jet was airborne. Tony sat by the window watching the ground disappear as the swift airplane glided through the early morning sky. His thoughts turned to Maggie. "So close…now, I'll never have her…she'll be free and I'll be tied to someone else…it isn't fair…I guess I shouldn't complain; I've done pretty well – except in love – Roni, why didn't you tell me…" Chris' voice came over the intercome, "Mr. Cole, we have to land in New York to refuel; we'll probably have a couple of hous wait before we can continue to Geneva. I just wanted to inform you ahead of time." Tony flipped the talk switch, "Fine, Chris. I understand. Thank you."

He shut his eyes, and instantly he envisioned Maggie – he remembered the first time he saw her, she was beautiful that warm California morning. She was in her white tennis outfit that made her tanned body glisten in the sun; she beat me in tennis, too! …then, he remembered that day in Chicago, she was standing on his homesite, the wind blowing her hair and the cold air turning her cheeks a rosy, childish red – then as she cried when he took her to the orphanage; she's so gentle and caring – he remembered the first time they kissed; oh, God, he wanted her, and he's wanted her ever since – he realized, no matter whatever happens, there'll never be anyone in his heart or mind but Maggie; his beautiful Maggie. The tears ran ever so slowly from his sleeping eyes.

The ride to the farm was beautiful; the snow-capped Alps always in sight; the little homes that looked like pictures. Tony was very impressed with what he saw. The farm house, where Roni was preparing to birth his child was now in view.

The farm house was gorgeous. Herr Minke was undoubtedly one of the more wealthy Swiss inhabitants. As the car stopped, a plump little man ran from the house. He jabbered something in his normal Swiss dialect, but Tony couldn't understand a word. She turned to the driver, who said, "Herr Minke is right behind me, Mr. Cole." Tony turned around to look at the doorway, Herr Minke stood there alone, he didn't speak to Tony, he said instead, "Roni, you have a visitor," he disappeared. Tony stood directly in front of the door with one foot on the first step. Roni looked out, she couldn't believe her eyes, it's Tony; it's really him. She burst through the door, "Oh, Tony! Tony!" She threw here arms around his neck, but her large tummy wouldn't allow her to get as close as she wanted. She kissed him passionately. He pulled away, "Let me look at you!" She blushed and tried to hide herself, "Oh, shit, I forgot, I was so excited to see you. I completely forgot how I look!" "You're still the beautiful, beautiful star I've always known you as. You really look ravishing, Roni."

"I suppose Milton told you where I was, and also about my condition?" "Yes, of course. He has been a very good friend to you." Tony said as he led her up the steps into the house. "Why didn't you tell me, Roni?" She smiled, "We'll talk about whys and why nots later, but I want you to meet my very good friends, Dr. Minke and his lovely wife Ulna." She turned to the Minke's and said, "This, this is Tony Cole, not only is he the father of my baby, but he is a well-known celebrity and I understand he is now one of the richest men in the world." "Dr. Minke, it is my pleasure to meet you." They both grinned, obviously honored to meet Tony. Roni explained, as they sat down, "Dr. Minke is my doctor, and Mrs. Minke is my nurse. They are also allowing me to stay here. Would you believe, you are the first person I've seen, other than the village people since I've been here. I'm beginning to learn the language." She was bubbling with excitement. Tony smiled, "Do you think we could talk for a moment?" The Minke's excused themselves and Roni just sat smiling at him, "I can't believe you're here; I can't believe we're here; it's so far away from what we're used to. You look good, Tony. I've missed you so much." "Why didn't you tell me, Roni? You knew about the baby the night you ran out – didn't you?" he interrupted her enjoyment. "Tony, you explained how you felt that night – I understood, really I did. I wanted you to say you loved me and would marry me instantly! I also knew, that if you were aware of the baby, you would have probably wanted to marry me. I didn't want that for either of us. So, I ran away, completely incognito, spys, and disappearance. I removed myself from the world, to have my baby." Tony was amazed at how exuberant she always managed to be. "Don't you think I should have had something to say about my – our – child?" "No. I gave you your chance and you said you had no intentions of getting married. So, I took that as not having a family, either. I told you I understood." "Yeh, but I don't!" he snapped. "Hey, I'm sorry. This is a tough situation for me. Uh, how are you feeling anyways?" She walked to him, put her hands in his, and said, "I really appreciate you coming clear over here. It's very gallant but I'm fine. Tony, I knew what our relationship was like, right from the beginning; I wasn't stupid. I knew I stood a chance of getting pregnant everytime you made love to me. Tony this (she patted her stomach) was the only way I could ever end up with part of you." "I want us to get married, right away!" he blurted out. Her beautiful face beamed, "After the baby's born, we'll discuss it. I love you, Tony!" She ran to his arms and sobbed, "Oh, I've missed you so much. Thank you for coming! Thank you!"

"How did you get into the country without being recognized?" "Oh you would have loved it. I dressed up; well, I really dressed down. I booked a flight on coach from L.A. to Switzerland. I went to an Army/Navy store and bought some hiking boots, an Army jacket, and jeans. I put those on with a flannel shirt, and I fixed my hair to fall all over my face, plus I added glasses and a cowboy hat. You'd have been appalled at my outfit. I only carried a back pack – you see, I looked like I was going to back pack across Europe. I had Milton send my other things to the Minke's in their name. Pretty clever, huh?" "Clever enough to fool the media of the entire world!" They laughed.

Tony entered Dr. Minke's study. Can I bother you, Doctor? Roni's asleep and I wanted to talk to you in private." "Of course, Mr. Cole" he spoke fluent English. "I was hoping we could have a chat alone!" "Would you like a brandy, Mr. Cole?" Dr. Minke asked as he walked to a rolling bar filled with different types of liquor, including a bottle of Jack Daniels. "I'd rather have some of that Jack Daniels, if you don't mind." The doctor poured himself a brandy and Tony a half of glass of his favorite drink. "I guess, you'd like to discuss Roni's condition?" "Yes, I would. Milton Schraff said there were problems, but she acts fine." Dr. Minke sat next to him, "Mr. Cole, Roni has told us everything about you. That's why I called Mr. Schraff and asked him to tell you of Roni's pregnancy. She was right. She said that if you were aware of the baby, that you would have never allowed her to leave. I'm very glad you came; she's going to need you. She could have a very hard time during delivery of the child. Se says she wants to have the baby here, but I've told her it would be better if she was admitted to the hospital in Geneva. You see, Mr. Cole, I've found a problem with her heart – I haven't told her – and I'm afraid – well, I'm not sure her heart can take a normal birth, much less, a breech birth!" Tony sat stunned; he didn't know what to say. "Do you understand what a breech birth is?" Dr. Minke asked. "It's where the baby is turned the wrong way, isn't it?" Tony replied. "Yes, basically, that's correct. It is much more difficult to deliver and the mother has to work much harder. Tony, this could be very dangerous for Roni. I haven't said anything to her yet, I just didn't want to worry her, but I think she should be told." "What are the alternatives?" Tony asked. "If she insists on having the baby here, she increases the possibility of problems. On the other hand, if she would agree to being admitted to the hospital, prior to the beginning of labor, it will allow us to be more prepared for complications that may arise." "You make the arrangements for her to enter the hospital, and I'll assure you that she'll go in. When should she go in, anyway?" Tony was going to make sure she did. "She's actually due on the 7th of October, so I'd like to admit her pretty soon, like on the 3rd of October." Tony waved his hand, "Do it! Make the proper arrangements; she'll go in on the 3rd." The doctor stared at him, "Even though this is a foreign country to you and Roni, she'll still be susceptible to the press, as you will." Tony smiled, "You worry about delivering that child and caring for Roni, and I'll handle the press." "You've got a deal," the doctor held his glass for a toast, "And Roni was right. She said I'd like you, Mr. Cole." "How about dropping the Mister and calling me Tony!" "Right, Tony it is."

CHAPTER THIRTY-EIGHT

"Do you think we could talk? I really think we need to," Peter said as he went into the bedroom where Maggie was lying. "Sure! I guess you've got a lot to tell me after your big party. Let's sit by the pool." She left the bedroom and went to the pool as Peter followed. She sat on the edge of the pool and dangled her feet in the water. Peter stood beside her. "So, tell me all about the fun you had at the big Cole Industries bash!" She said sarcastically. "I don't want to talk about that; I want to talk about you, uh, you and me!" Peter choked a little when he spoke. She didn't look up, "What about me and you?" He began to pace, "It's gone to hell, Maggie! Our marriage, it's gone straight to hell!" She turned to look a him, "What do you want to do about it, Peter?" He pulled a chair close to her, "Well, I'm not sure. I think we ought to separate for a while!" He waited for her to respond. She kicked at the water for a second, then said, "Peter, we're living as though we're separated right now. You're gone all the time. You don't even accompany me to the biggest tournament I'll ever play in – you're married to Cole Industries – I think you should have your freedom, we should get a divorce. That's what you really want, isn't it?" He was surprised that she was so point-blank, "You're wrong about my being married to Cole – I'm going to resign, in fact, tomorrow. I'm going to stay out here and return to my law practice. I've made the money I wanted Cole Industries to help me make."

Maggie listened closely to what he was saying. She thought, "If that is so, and they did get a divorce, there would be no reason Tony and her couldn't be together." She felt excited, "Are you sure that's what you want to do? Return to practicing law?" "Yes; I'd like to open an office in Beverly Hills.

Do you want a divorce, Maggie?" This was the question she had been asking herself for months. She looked at him, "I'm sorry, Peter, but I think I do. It just hasn't worked for us. I think you would be better off without any ties." He was glad and sad at the same time, "Well, if you've felt this way, why didn't you say so before. Hell, I could have left a long time ago!" "I didn't realize that's what I wanted until now," she said, "But I agree that our marriage is over. When or why or how doesn't seem to matter. You have always been aggressive and anxious to be wealthy – well, now you're wealthy, and I think you should do what you want with your life. We have drifted to far apart over the last several months." She took his hand in hers, "Let's end it on a friendly basis. I have no animosity or dislike for you – and I hope you have none for me – so, you tell me what you want and I'll agree to it." Peter wasn't sure he was hearing her correctly – he knew, but didn't really want to, "You've been thinking about this, haven't you?" He began to pace again. "Yes, I have, Peter! I'm sure you have, too." "Well, hell, yes, I wouldn't have brought it up if I hadn't been thinking about it! Okay, we'll get a divorce; what kind of settlement would you consider fair?" He was speaking more softly now. "I would never be unreasonable – I just told you to say what you wanted – so if you want me to make the first proposal, then fine. I think I should get the house – to do with as I please, and I think you should give me $1 million cash; at that, we can call it even. You'll never have to pay alimony. Does that sound fair? His lawyer's mind was beginning to work. It's not a bad settlement. If they went to court, she could end up with a lot more than one million. He could be paying alimony for years, which would be a pain the ass. He nodded, "I think that is a reasonable settlement. I'll get Ray Stark to handle everything; that is, unless you want your own attorney?" "No, Peter, I have no reason to have my own attorney. Just have Ray send me the papers, I'll sign them," she smiled. "Well, uh, I guess that's it! I really don't have much else to say," Peter sighed. Maggie stood up, and put her arms around his waist, "Thank you, Peter, for some great years. You'll take care of youself; promise?" "Yes, you too; if you ever need anything – you'll let me know?" He was near tears, as he stroked her long black hair – for the last time. "Yes, I will. Goodbye, Peter." She turned and walked into the house. He followed her, and said, "I'm going to pack my things and fly to Chicago tonight. I want to give Tony my resignation first thing tomorrow morning. So, I guess, this is it. Goodbye Margaret!" He had only called her Margaret once before – after he kissed her to end their wedding ceremony. "I'm going to take a drive so I won't be here when you leave. Goodbye Peter!"

She was headed towards L.A.; a Barbra Streisand tape was blasting, and the quiet desert terrain whistled by. Maggie was nearly jubilant – she wasn't upset at all; she only thought of one thing – she could be in the arms of the man she knew she would love to her dying day. "Oh, Tony, I can't wait – we'll be so happy…" she smiled to herself. She was going to call Tony from L.A. She couldn't wait until Peter resigned; she had to tell him the good news right away. She'd get a hotel room for the night and call him from there.

She walked up to the registration desk at the Beverly Hills Hotel, "Would you possibly have a room, no, a suite, available for tonight?" she asked the clerk. "I take it you don't have a reservation?" The clerk had no personality as he looked at her suspiciously. Maggie smiled at him, "No, I would just like to treat myself to an elegant night alone," she pulled a hundred dollar bill from her purse, "I'd really like a suite!" The clerk quickly put the money in his pocket, returned the smile, and said, "Uh, yes, uh. I'm sure we can accommodate you Miss, uh, Mrs…" "Maggie Weyland!" She gave no Miss or Mrs. "Okay, Maggie," the clerk didn't push "We'll put you in the Pacific Suite; I'm sure you'll be quite comfortable and elegant there. "He was right," she thought as she looked around the enormous suite, "I do feel elegant." As soon as the bellman left, she ran to the phone. "Tony, you're going to be surprised and happy…" she laughed as she dialed the number to Tony's Chicago office.

"Good afternoon, Cole Industries. Whom would you like to speak to?" The Cole operator answered in a monotone voice. "May I speak to Mr. Cole?" Maggie said gleefully. The operator connected her to Theresa, "Hello, this is Mr. Cole's office. May I help you?" Theresa was always pleasant. "Hello, Theresa, this is Maggie Weyland. How are you? It's been a long time since I've seen you!" Theresa was glad to hear Maggie's voice, she thought she was the perfect woman, "Oh, Maggie! It's so nice to hear from you! I'm fine! But, why haven't we seen you for such a long time?" "I've been doing some soul-searching, and playing lots of tennis. I'm sorry. I've been such a terrible friend. I promise I'll stay in touch much more often. Could I talk to Tony for a moment?" "You could, if he was here." Maggie felt a touch of depression, "Uh, could you tell me where I could reach him? It's kind of important that I talk to him?" Theresa replied, "Yes – if I knew! I have no idea where he is. He left in the middle of the night – and I have no idea where to. It's the first time since I've worked for him that he didn't tell me where he was going to be. I can put you through to Derek, maybe he can help." "Yes, please. Thank you, Theresa! I'll give you a call real soon." Maggie wondered why Tony didn't tell Theresa where he was; but Derek would know. "Well, hello, Maggie! God, it's good to hear from you. How are you, anyway?" Derek said smiling. "Oh, Derek, I'm fine! I hope that you and Theresa are getting along as well as ever?" Derek wondered why she was calling tony, "We're still love birds; hell, we haven't even been married a year yet. Is there something I can do for you, Maggie?"

Maggie could hardly keep the smile from her face – she didn't care if Derek knew; he had been the only one who knew about their feelings for each other anyway. "Yes, you handsome devil, you can tell me where I can reach Tony. It's very important that I talk to him!" Derek was in a dilemma. "I wish I could, Maggie. But I don't know where he is at this very moment. I'll be talking to him tonight, but until then, I can't help you. Is anything wrong? Is Peter alright? Can I help you in some way?" He was attempting to get something out of her. "Oh, Derek!" She decided to tell him about her and Peter (but she would let Peter break the news to him about resigning.) "Derek, Peter and I have separated! We're going to get a divorce; and I want to tell Tony." Derek didn't know what to say. His mind went crazy, "Should I tell her where Tony is – should I call Tony first – oh, Christ!" "Maggie, why? Are you sure it's over? She replied, "Oh, yes, it's over. Peter will be in Chicago tomorrow morning; I'm sure he'll tell you about it. Derek, you've known for a long time about the way Tony and I feel about each other – well, now we can do something about it – please find out where he is. I've just got to tell him!" Derek fumbled for a cigarette. He had to have time to think about what he should do. "Where are you? Are you at home? I'll have Tony call you, or I'll call you as soon as I know where he is." "No, I'm not at home; I've taken a room at the Beverly Hills hotel. I just wanted to be away from my own surroundings for awhile. I'll be here all night. Please hurry, I can't wait to talk to him." "Okay, I'll let you know as soon as I hear from Tony, and I won't mention this to him, I'll leave that to you. Goodbye Maggie, I'll talk to you soon," he wanted to hang up so he would have time to think. "Okay, thank you Derek, you're a good friend. Bye, bye!" She put the phone down and sighed, she would have to wait to tell Tony the good news. Maggie layed on the sofa, she suddenly felt exhausted, in no time, she was sleeping.

Derek stared at the Chicago skyline, thinking about his closest friend. He was well aware of the love Tony had for Maggie, he wanted him to be happy, but should he tell Tony or wait? He had not told Theresa where Tony had gone, he had never told her about the torches Tony and Maggie carried for each other, he could not make this decision alone, and who was better to help him than his own wife. She loved Tony as much as he did. He pushed the intercom button for Theresa, "Theresa, would you please come into my office?" "I'll be right there, Mr. Hill," she replied.

"Did you invite me in here for some afternoon delight, I hope?" Theresa asked as she closed the door to Derek's office. "I wish that's why," he said with a troubled expression. "What's wrong, honey, uh, I mean Mr. Hill, I forgot we're working." Derek commanded, "Sit down, Theresa; I've got to discuss something with you. I need your opinion!" She sat down facing Derek, "Is there something wrong with Maggie or Peter?" He slumped into his chair and lit a cigarette, "You might say that. Hell, I'd better start from the beginning if I expect you to help me."

Derek began, "Some time ago, about a year or so, maybe longer, Tony met "the" woman of his dreams. Only one problem, the woman was married to a close business associate. So, Tony being the high moralled, high principled ass, shyed away from this woman and struck up a long, lengthy relationship with Roni. During this time, Tony and the woman encountered each other on a fairly frequent basis, which, she ultimately fell in love with Tony. Are you following this so far?" Theresa frowned, "I hope I'm not, but I think I am. Tony fell in love with Maggie, who's married to Peter, so Tony took up with Roni, and sometime later Maggie has fallen in love with Tony and they've been carrying on an affair. Right?" Derek pointed at her, "Almost, you're right about everything except the affair. Tony would not hear of it, as much as he wanted Maggie, he never gave in because she was married to Peter." Theresa remembered how Tony had refused to share her bedroom, only because she was his secretary. Derek continued, "Well, as time passed and they had to see each other more and more, Maggie couldn't take it any longer. That's why she returned to California and refused to attend any Cole functions. Theresa, they're madly in love!" Nervously, he lit still another cigarette, "As we all know, Roni disappeared several months ago, apparently because Tony had broken her heart. She has been in seclusion ever since. Then came Lana James, beautiful newscaster. She filled a sexual void for Tony, but he continued to think only of Maggie. Now, you better hold on. After the party the other night, Tony received a call from Milton Schraff, right, Roni's agent, who informed Tony that Roni is somewhere in the world, and I don't know where yet, getting ready to deliver Tony's baby!" "Oh my God," Theresa shrieked. Continuing, Derek added, "Tony, upon hearing this, boarded the company plane and took off to be with Roni. He said he's going to marry her!" Theresa wiped her eyes, "Oh Derek, that's beautiful." "Oh is it?" Derek asked then moved on, "If you say yes, you're wrong, or at least I think you're wrong, I really don't know, but the rest of this damn soap opera is what I need your opinion on. As you know, I just talked to Maggie. Well, she informed me that she and Peter are separated and getting a divorce. She called to tell Tony. She was really excited. Theresa, I didn't know what to the tell her!" She wiped away more tears, "Derek, that's awful!" "Is that all you can say, oh Derek that's beautiful, oh Derek that's awful," he mocked her. "Well, what do you want me to say? Shit, I don't know what you want me to say," she roared back at him. He walked over to her, "I'm sorry. I have to do something and I'm afraid I'll do the wrong thing. I either have to get hold of Tony and tell him about Maggie and Peter before he marries Roni or I have to call Maggie and tell her where Tony is and why! What the hell should I do?"

Theresa just looked at him, and then asked, "What do you think you should do?" He threw one hand in the air, and said, "That's my dilemma. I want to do the right thing for Tony. I have to think like he thinks. Which is morally first, with my head second, and my heart third. Whatever happens, there is one of these three fine people going to be hurt, and that person won't be Tony, not if I can help it!" "We have to look at the choices and the consequences of each choice," Theresa explained. Derek ran his hand through his hair, "Okay, here are the choices; one, I call Tony, tell him about Maggie and Peter, he makes his own decision, and I'm off the hook. Two, I call Maggie, and tell her the truth, that Tony is with Roni. Three, I could tell Maggie that I can't reach Tony, put her off for awhile. How would Tony handle it? That's the big question. From a moral standpoint, he would stay with Roni, marry her, raise their child, and live unhappily ever after. From the head standpoint, I think he would do the same thing. Ah, but from the heart, he would give Roni a bundle of money and fly straight to Maggie!" Theresa touched his hand, "I think you just gave yourself the answer. I can't believe Tony would ever abandon his child, not after his own childhood. No matter how much he loves Maggie. I don't think you have any choice, you should tell Maggie where Tony is and if she wants to pursue it further, and I'm sure she won't, then that's up to her." Derek still puzzled, "Yeh, fine, but shouldn't I tell Tony about Maggie and Peter? He could make his own choice?" Now, Theresa put her arms around him,

"Derek, Tony isn't going to make any choice other than staying with Roni and their baby. You know that, so why torture him by telling him the woman he loves is free, now that he isn't?" Derek sighed, heavily, "Yeh, i guess you're right. I'll call Maggie a little later; I only hope Tony doesn't hate me when he finds out. Poor Maggie! Fuck! I wish i could hide right now!"

She jumped up, startled by the ringing of the phone, "Hello, Tony?" "Sorry to disappoint you Maggie, but it's Derek." "That's okay. Tell me where Tony is. You didn't tell him did you?" Maggie was very excited. In just a few minutes she could tell him how much she loves him and that they could now be together forever. "Maggie, how much do you really love Tony?" Derek was trying to be as gentle as possible. "You know, Derek, that's a very hard question to answer. How do I measure the nights of sleep lost thinking about him, or the tears i've cried reading about his affairs with Roni and Lana James, or those very special moments that we spent talking when we both wanted to be in bed, or how do I measure giving up a husband and a marriage. Oh Derek, I love him with every bit of my heart and soul. Tony Cole has never had the pleasures of my body, but he possesses me. Tony Cole is the only thing or person in the world that matters to me, and I know he feels the same about me. We were made for each other and now we'll get the chance to be together forever and ever, for eternity!" Derek pulled the phone from his ear and bit at his bottom lip. "Oh Christ, how can I do this, it'll destroy her," he said to himself, then returned the phone to his ear, "Maggie, uh, listen very carefully to what I'm going to say!" "What's wrong, Derek? Where is Tony? Please tell me!" She interrupted. Derek sighed, "Maggie believe me, and I'm the only one who knows, Tony loves you more than anything, you'll always be the only woman he truly loves. I know this but…" Maggie interrupted again, "But what? Derek you're trying to tell me something. Will you please just tell me? "Yes, yes, I will. Uh, Maggie, uh, Tony is with Roni, they're going to be married." "No!" She shreiked, "He promised me he'd never marry her, we were waiting until the time was right for us, now it's right for us, Derek you're lying to me. You're afraid Cole Industries will be hurt! He'll never marry Roni! He loves me, and I love him!" "Maggie, Maggie," he was trying to calm her down, "Listen to me. Maggie, Roni is pregnant! That's why she disappeared!" He waited for her to answer, but there was only silence. She was stunned and speechless. "I'm sorry, Maggie, but it's true. She's ready to deliver the baby any day now. I'm so sorry. Oh God,

I'm sorry!" She was sobbing, "It, uh, it, sniff, it doesn't matter, he loves me, we love each other, he doesn't love Roni, he never has!" Derek felt sick, "Oh Maggie, don't you understand? Yes, he loves you and always will, but don't forget, Tony is an orphan. He's gone to Roni for the child's sake, not because he loves Roni, only because of the child!" There was a long silence except for the sobbing. Then she asked, softly, "Tell me, Derek, what should I do?" "I can't tell you what to do, but I know that Tony will never give up his child, you know that too. Maggie, is it to late to reconcile with Peter?" She answered sternly, "Peter, I don't love him! He wants the divorce as much as I do, sniff, that part of my life is over, no matter what else happens. So you're saying I should forget about Tony, right?" "Yes, if you don't, you'll only get hurt worse. I'm sorry Maggie. Is there anything I can do?" He wanted to cry, they love each other more than he thought. "Okay, Derek, I guess I have no choice. Goodbye!" Uncontrolled sobbing was the last sound he heard before the click of the reciever being replaced.

Derek stood looking at the phone, hoping he had done the right thing, and wondering about Maggie. "I saw your light go out," Theresa said as she came into the room, "How did she take it?" As soon as she saw the look on his face, she knew she had asked a dumb question. "I feel sick," he said, "She loves him! Oh god, does she love him! I worry about her, she sounded terrible. Theresa, tell me, I did the right thing. Please tell me!" She pulled him close to her, "You did, darling, you did the right thing!" They held each other for a long time.

CHAPTER THIRTY-NINE

"Tony, boy, am I glad to hear from you! What the hell is going on?" Derek felt relieved to hear Tony's voice. "How are you, Derek? How are things at Cole?" Tony sounded tired. Derek grinned, "No, you tell me first. What's going on?" "Well, not a lot at the moment. Roni is definitely going to have a child. She looks terrific, but, uh, we're going to admit her to the hospital in the next couple of days. She's due on October 7th. Now, tell me what's happening there," Tony commanded. Derek wanted to tell him about Maggie and Peter's separation and upcoming divorce, but didn't, "Not a lot, just one large happening. Peter Weyland resigned yesterday. He says he wants to return to his law practice." Tony wasn't surprised, "That doesn't surprise me, I expected him to leave us when is wallet was filled. What do you suggest we do about his position?" Derek was prepared for the question, "I thought you might want to discuss that. I recommend we promote Clint Mackey to that position. He's done a terrific job under Peter, and we could use his name more if he was in a higher status. I mean, it's not every day we get one of the finest players in baseball attached to Cole Industries. What do you think?" Tony agreed, "I agree, his name will open a lot of doors. You can tell him right away." Derek felt that Tony's heart wasn't into talking business, "Tony, is there something wrong? You don't sound like yourself, and a minute ago, you said Roni looks terrific but, then you stopped. Is there something wrong with Roni?" "Uh, she'll be fine; she's carrying the baby in what they call a breach position, the babys upside down in other words. She'll be okay. Derek, you haven't by any chance seen Maggie, have you?" The question he was hoping not to hear was finally asked. He thought, "He asked if

I've 'seen' her!" Quickly he answered, "No, no Tony, I haven't seen her. If I do, should I tell her anything for you?" "No, she'll find out what's happened soon enough. I expect it will be in all the media as soon as Roni enters the hospital. The media will tell her, I guess." Tony paused, then added, "Let me tell you where I can be reached." He gave Derek Dr. Minke's phone number and the number to the hospital in Geneva, then told him to kiss Theresa for him, and that he was sending Chris home with the company jet. He said he would be gone for probably a month and for Derek to handle all business affairs.

"So, did you talk to Derek? Yes, of course, you did. You miss being there, don't you?" Roni smiled, she smiled all the time, now that Tony was with her. "Peter Weyland resigned. He's returning to his law practice in L.A.," Tony said. "You're kidding," Roni was surprised, "I thought Peter would die with your company. Why, I wonder?" Tony answered matter-of-factly, "He got what he wanted from me and Cole Industries, all of his debts cleared up and money in the bank." Roni walked towards the phone, "I've got to call Maggie. I've felt rotten about not talking to her through these months. Anyway, this is a good reason to…." "No!" Tony stopped her, "No, don't call her, not yet! Why don't you let things calm down for them first? You can call her after the baby is born." He didn't want Maggie to hear about this from Roni. "God, will I ever get her out of my mind?" He thought. "Yeh, you're right. I've waited this long, I'll wait till after," she stopped, patted her stomach, and continued, "Until our baby is born." Her beautiful face beamed with happiness.

"Roni, about the baby, or rather about you delivering the baby. I want you to have the baby in the hospital," Tony was strong, as though he was telling her instead of asking. Roni was adamant, "No, I want to have it here, just like always. I really don't want all of the media bullshit that would occur if I went in the hospital. I want us to have a nice private birth. Why do you want me to go to the hospital?" "Hell," he thought, "I'm going to have to tell her!" Before he could tell her, Mrs. Minke came in, "It's a beautiful evening. Why don't you two take a little walk, it will be good for Roni." "Oh, that's a great idea! Come on Tony!" Roni took him by the hand and ran towards the door. As she pushed the door open, she slipped, she fell end-over-end down the five steps leading from the house. "Roni! Roni!" Tony screamed as he ran to her. She was in a lot of pain. "Where does it hurt?" Tony was trying to help. Dr. Minke ran out of house, "Lay still,

Roni." "Ooohh!!!" she yelled. Dr. Minke looked at Tony, "The fall has thrown her into labor. We've got to get her into the house!" Tony picked her up by himself; he layed her on a large feather bed in one of the empty bedrooms. Dr. Minke told Ulna to sit with her while he called the hospital. Tony grabbed his arm, "Get her whatever she needs, don't worry about costs, just get it!"

The doctor shut the door to the bedroom, where Roni lay in pain, "There's no stopping it now. I just examined her, she's dialated to five centimeters and the pains are less than four minutes apart and regular as hell!" The whirling noise of the helicopter blades made the doctor smile, "Thank god! We're going to need all the help we can get!" "What's that noise?" Roni screamed. Tony picked her up, "It's a helicopter, we're taking you to the hospital in Geneva." "No, put me down, I want to have my baby here! Put me down, ooohh!" He carried her through the house and to the waiting helicopter. Her pains were now under three minutes apart and she was getting very weak. She quit trying to persuade them to let her have the baby at the house, practically as quick as she started. She was in constant pain. Her breathing was getting weak. She squeezed Tony's hand with each pain. He noticed that the squeezing was weaker also.

The helicopter landed amidst a horde of reporters and cameramen, and one lonely ambulance. "What the hell is going on down there?" Tony yelled. Dr. Minke put his hand on Tony's shoulder, "I had to tell them who she was, by doing so, we were assured of everything being ready. It was the only way. You take care of the reporters and I'll take care of Roni." Two attendants from the ambulance helped Tony lift her onto the stretcher. The reporters ran toward the helicopter. There was so much noise that Tony couldn't make out what any of them were saying. They were in the ambulance and gone without answering a single reporters question. Roni was rushed directly into a large delivery room, where they had set up heart monitors, oxygen, and anything else that might be needed.

Tony went to meet the reporters, he might as well; the doctors forbid him to go any further; he would just have to wait anyway. He looked through the window of the door before going through. "Vultures," he thought. They ascended on him like bees to honey. To his amazement, they knew who he was, as well as Roni. An American reached him first, "Mr. Cole, what is the condition of Roni Scott?" Before answering, he said, "I'll answer all your questions. Please ask them one at a time. Roni is going to have a baby any minute, that's all."

Question, "Are you the father of Miss Scott's child?

"Yes."

Question, "Is the child the reason Miss Scott went into seclusion?

"Yes. She wanted to have a normal pregnancy. Not one that was all over the news.

Question, "Were you aware of the baby? It was reported that your relationship ended when she disappeared?"

"No, I wasn't aware of it until a few days ago."

Question, "Does this mean you'll be married?"

"Yes, just as soon as Roni's able."

Question, "Will you be married here, in Geneva, or back in the States?"

"We haven't discussed that."

Question, "What about your affair, uh, romance with Lana James?"

"That's over."

Question, "What was the reason for the helicopter? Are there any complications?"

"We're just being cautious."

Question, "Since the two of you are world known, will you allow us to have some pictures of the baby?

That will be up to the doctor."

Question, "Will Roni return to making movies after the baby is born and you're married?"

"That's up to her."

Question, "How do you think the American public, or since she is known throughout the world, will accept what has happened?"

"You mean, having a child and not being married? Personally, I don't give a damn."

Tony raised his hand, "Please, if you don't mind, I'd like to return to Roni now. If you're still here, after the baby's born, I'll answer more questions. Thank you." The reporters waited as he disappeared beyond the doors.

CHAPTER FORTY

The house was quiet, except for the television, which was on, but she wasn't paying any attention to it. Maggie was sitting in a chair with no lights on. She had been sitting like that for hours, but she was oblivious to time. Her whole world, which only yesterday was so happy, had crumbled around her. She didn't want to talk to anybody or see anybody. She told the servants to take a vacation. The phone had rung several times, but she ignored it. She had not eaten, nor had she had a drink. She just sat thinking about Tony. She was mad at him, but understood him; she hated him, but loved him. Maggie was completely confused. She couldn't believe he would marry Roni. "He promised, he promised," she kept saying aloud. Her thoughts were never about Peter, except when she remembered how close she was to having Tony. Tony, he's all she could think about. He possessed her mind a year ago, and now he possesses her whole spirit. She was convinced that she would live in misery forever. "Maybe Derek was wrong," she kept hoping. She glanced at the television as Roni's picture appeared. She leaped from the chair and turned up the volume as the reporter said, "Nearly eight months ago, the news was filled with the disappearance of the academy award winning beauty, Roni Scott. She hasn't been heard of since, until today, she surfaced once again. The movie queen was rushed to a Geneva, Switzerland hospital, where she is apparently going to give birth to a child. The apparent father is none other than Tony Cole, the billionaire owner of Cole Industries, who had been romancing Miss Scott for more than a year. It was the break-up of the romance which triggered Roni's disappearance. Mr. Cole is at her side in Geneva. It is reported that he and Miss Scott will wed shortly after the birth of their child..." "No!

No!" Maggie screamed. She grabbed a vase from the coffee table and threw it into the screen of the television. The crashing noise frightened her as she fell to her knees and sobbed, "Oh, Tony, Tony! I love you so much and you're gone, you're gone!"

It was over an hour before she gained control of herself. She stood up, looked at the mess she created and thought out loud, "I've got to get away, get away from everything. I don't want to ever hear about this again. I'll go somewhere but where, I'll get a house on the beach, Monterey, no, Newport, yes, I'll get a house in Newport!" Within a couple of hours, she had packed some clothes, made sure he had her check book, and cut the cords to all the phones. As she lay on the bed, she said to herself, "In the morning I'll withdraw some money and go to Newport, where I can live alone without phones, newspapers, radios, or televisions. I'll literally escape from the outside world."

"Theresa," Derek yelled, "It was splattered all over the damn news. The whole world knows now, about Roni and Tony! Christ! Did you hear me?" Theresa was standing in the doorway; she said softly, "Derek, why don't you go to him? Be with your friend, he probably needs you." Derek was looking at her and smiled, "I love you, and you always know the right thing to do. Thank you!" She put her arms around him, "Poor Tony, tell him, well, give him my love." Derek assured her that he would pass along her love, and then said, "Call Bob Underwood and tell him he's in charge while Tony and I are away. Then call the other board members and explain our whereabouts, even though they surely know by now, and call Chris Pike and have him warm up the plane and he's headed back to Geneva."

CHAPTER FORTY-ONE

He lit the last cigarette in the pack. He looked at his watch. More than three hours had passed. There she was, Roni giving birth to his child, and the only person he could think of is Maggie, "She'll hate me forever and I'll always love her." "Tony," Dr. Minke was standing in front of him. His expression told Tony that all was not well, "Yes, doc, how did she do?" Tony hated to ask. Dr. Minke sat down beside him, "Tony, you are the father of a beautiful and healthy daughter, but i'm afraid Roni didn't fare so well." "What? Tell me, is she, is she going to be alright?" Dr. Minke put his hand on Tony's shoulder, his face showed strain, "Tony, the delivery was extremely hard. Roni had a coronary, a heart attack; we've done everything possible..." Tony interrupted, "Is she," he didn't need to say more. Dr. Minke then continued, "She's still alive, but only by a thread. We're keeping her alive with machines. Tony, I'm afraid there's no hope for recovery. I'm so sorry!"

He had been sitting there for hours, nearly a full day, looking at her. The blue line on the life support machine was nearly straight, only an occasional blip interrupted the continual moving streak. His mind was a total blank. He just watched her. He couldn't believe how beautiful she was, even now. He wanted to speak to her, but didn't know what to say. Then he remembered what Sister Carolyn had told him, "When your lost, and don't know what to do or say, look up, into the heavens, and ask God. He will always help you; all you must do is ask him." Tony looked toward the ceiling, "Sir, dear God in heaven, I ask of you, please give me the strength to endure, give me the words to say to her, please give her one more moment to hear the words you give me. Please, God, I beg of you to let her hear me. Oh God, I pray for her. She never hurt anybody. Please take care of her." He looked at Roni, God must have listened to him, for her eyes opened slightly. Tony was holding her hand, with tears streaming from his eyes, dripping onto their hands. He looked into her eyes and said, "Oh Roni, I'm so sorry, I've never told you, I'm sorry, but Roni, I love you, I love you!" Her eyes closed and the blips stopped on the blue line. She had waited to hear him say he loved her, then she was gone.

"Come on, Tony, it's over," Derek put his hand on Tony's. He had just arrived and was standing in the doorway watching. Tony looked upward and said softly, "Thank you!" He then stared at Derek, "She's gone, she's gone." As Dr. Minke switched off the machine, he said, "I'm so sorry, Tony."

Tony and Derek stood in the hallway, niether saying anything. Tony had his hands in his pockets, taking deep breaths, trying to regain his composure. Dr. Minke came out of Roni's room, "Tony, I have to tell the news people something. Is there anything special you want me to say?" Tony shook his head. The doctor headed to the elevator, but Tony stopped him, "Wait, Dr. Minke. I'll talk to the press. You shouldn't have to, it's my place. He stood at the door, looking at the reporters and cameramen. There must have been over a hundred of them. They were from all over the world. Derek and Dr. Minke were with him. He took a deep breath and pushed open the heavy doors. "There's Tony Cole! She's had the baby!" A reporter yelled out, "Is it a boy or a girl?" Tony began to speak, "Roni Scott has given me a new daughter!" Derek was amazed at how Tony could reach deep within himself to speak with authority, only he could speak with. Tony waited until the buzzing of the reporters died down, "As I said, Roni Scott gave me a daughter, but in doing so, she gave up something very precious, Roni Scott gave her life." Total quiet fell over the entire crowd. Tony then continued, "God has taken Roni Scott by way of heart failure during childbirth. While she was on this earth, she was always giving. She loved making movies; she loved her fans as much as they loved her." He was fighting to stay composed. "Please, I ask of you, write only the good things about Roni Scott for she loved life. God awarded her with a great gift, she brought enjoyment to everybody she came in contact with. Roni Scott has left us, but she didn't leave us without memories. The whole world loved Roni Scott, especially me. Thank you!" He turned to walk away and a reporter asked, "Mr. Cole, what name did you give your daughter?" He stood looking at Derek and said, "Name, daughter?" He then realized that he hadn't seen his new daughter. Before he knew why, he turned to the reporter and said, "Jennifer, Jenny! She'll be called Jenny!" The little crippled orphan girl who died in his arms flashed through his mind. He turned again, the tears softly falling, and asked Dr. Minke, "May I see my daughter?" "Of course, Tony, follow me," the doctor smiled.

"This is against hospital regulations, but under the circumstances, we'll break the rules," Dr. Minke explained, as a nurse handed the new born child to Tony. Tony held his daughter out in front of him, she was beautiful. Slowly he pressed the infants face to his shoulder, "Oh, Jenny, Jenny, I've missed you! Nobody will ever hurt you again! Tony will take care of you, I'll give you everything, I promise you'll never suffer again. Tony's here, Tony's here!" Derek had to walk away, his emotions had peaked.

The news of Roni's death filled the radio, television, newspapers, magazines, and any other possible types of media immediately. Tony's interview, in Geneva, had been seen all across America and throughout most of the world; Roni's fans mourned her sorrowfully. The U.S. President remarked, "This is a sad day, there are to few Roni Scott's, it is a true shame to lose her." The heads of television networks instantly ordered commentary's to be produced about Roni. Movie industry hierachy started considering "who" would play the lead in "The Roni Scott story." Her fans bought all of the Roni cosmetics and fashions available. Both divisions of Cole Industries were swamped with orders. This all happened within hours of the news of her death. By dying, she proved her greatness, she was an instant legend and many people compared her to Marilyn Monroe, but with much more talent.

Derek made the arrangements for Roni's body to be returned to California, he contacted Milton Schraff to make the funeral arrangements. Like so many celebrities before her, Roni was to be laid to rest in Forest Lawn Cemetary. The funeral was scheduled for October 5th.

CHAPTER FORTY-TWO

Tony was looking through the window of his hotel room, when he asked Derek, "Would you and Theresa take care of Jenny for me, just for awhile?" Derek was surprised, "Well, of course, Theresa will be so excited. Yes, Tony, we'll take care of her for as long as you want. What about Theresa's job?" Tony responded, "She can forget about her job while she's caring for Jenny, but she'll continue to receive her salary."

Derek attempted to cheer him up, "Hell, we don't need her salary; she's just working so she can keep tabs on me!" Tony didn't acknowledged that Derek was kidding around, "You know, all the time Roni was in the delivery room, giving birth to my child and dying, I was sitting in that damn waiting room thinking of Maggie! Do you belive that? Maggie!" Derek's mouth dropped open, for he never told Tony about Maggie and Peter. Instantly, he thought, "Maggie will bring him out of this depression." He smiled, "Tony sit down; I've got something to tell you. Maggie and Peter have separated, they're getting a divorce!" Tony sat motionless, "Thank you for not telling me before Roni, uh, you know." Derek grabbed the phone, "Call her, call her right now!" Tony shook his head, "No, not now. I'm sure she's aware of what's happened; I'll wait for her to call me." Derek raged, "What the fuck is the matter with you? I don't fucken believe this! You've spent the last year and a half wanting Maggie, now that you're both free to do what you want; you play stupid fucking childish games!" He dropped into a chair and threw his hands up. Tony reached for the phone and smiled, "I got your point." Derek shook his head, "Well, hallejujah!"

The overseas operator said, "I'm sorry sir, but the number in California of the United States has been disconnected." Tony put the phone down, "Disconnected. Her home phone is disconnected. She's probably moved somewhere else." Derek answered, "No, Peter said she was keeping the house and he was moving to Beverly Hills. There must be some mistake." Tony said, "I'll call her when we get to Chicago. Come on, let's go. We have to pick up Jenny and the nurse on the way to the airport."

The house faced the Pacific Ocean; the entire back of the house was glass, from the peaked roof to the sand. There were two balconies, one that was off of the two lofts bedrooms and one that ran the entire width of the downstairs. A spiral stairway led to the loft. There were three bathrooms, five bedrooms (including the loft), a game room, living room, kitchen, and dining room. The closest house was nearly a mile away to either side. It was completely furnished. No one had lived there before. Maggie stood on the balcony looking out at the sea. She had hardly looked at the house. She turned to the man who was showing her the house, "How much?" "Uh, $1800 a month plus utilities," he answered squeamishly. "I'll pay you $2000 per month and you pay the utilities," she offered. He scratched his head, "Well, I never pay the utilities myself, uh, I..." she interrupted him by pulling out a handful of large denomination bills, "Would it make a difference if I were to pay you a year in advance in cash?" He could hardly wait to get his hands on the money, "Yeh, I guess that would persuade me. You've got a deal Miss uh, I didn't get your name." She asked, "Do you have a rental agreement with you? I'll give you the money when you give me the agreement." He reached into his pocket, "Just so happens I have one on my person, Miss uh, I didn't get your name." Filling out the agreement, he said, "I must have your name, Miss." She looked around, she hadn't thought of her name, she couldn't use her name; she looked out at the sea, blue, "Blue, Margaret Blue!" It was an appropriate name. "Okay, Miss Blue, here you are. The place is yours, at least for the next year." She handed him $24,000 of the $50,000 she withdrew from the bank this morning.

After renting the house and getting rid of the rental agent, she decided she would sell her Mercedes that would be an easy way for somebody to find her. So, she drove to a nearby Mercedes dealer and sold her car for $40,000. It was worth much more and the dealer was ever so happy to pay her in cash. She then hailed a cab and went to a Pontiac dealer where she plunked down $12,000 cash and drove away in a brand new Firebird, purchased under the name of Margaret Blue. She started the morning with $50,000 cash, she has rented a house, paying a year in advance, sold her car, purchased another car, and now had $54,000. She figured she had enough cash to last her until she felt like rejoining the world of the living. She stopped at the grocery store and bought nearly $300 worth of food, and on the way home she bought a freezer. She hoped she wouldn't have to leave her house for anything. She even set it up with the grocer that she would send him her list and he would deliver it. Maggie planned on lying in the sun, and hiding.

CHAPTER FORTY-THREE

Willie met the plane at the airport and dashed them off to miss any of the news media that might be around. Jenny had handled the flight extremely well. Theresa was with Willie to meet them. She held Jenny all the way to Tony's house. Frederick was waiting for them when the car stopped, "Mr. Cole," he always referred to Tony as Mr. Cole whenever others were present, "It's so good to have you home. Please, Mrs. Hill, let me take the baby." Theresa handed him the small infant. "She's beautiful, Mr. Cole! Just beautiful! She'll be a welcome addition to this big house." Tony smiled at him, "Jenny's not going to stay with us, just yet. She's going to stay with Derek and Theresa for awhile, until I can sort things out. Then Anna (he presented the Swiss nurse he hired to Frederick) and Jenny will come here to live.

Frederick and Anna took Jenny upstairs so she could sleep. Tony, Derek, and Theresa went into Tony's office. Tony poured them drinks then asked Theresa, "Any word from Maggie?" Theresa was bewildered, "No, Tony, I can't find her anywhere. I've called her house, the tennis club, her friend Angela, her parents, everybody except Peter of which I didn't have to call him, because he called to give his condolences and he asked if I had talked to Maggie. He hasn't seen or talked to her since the day they agreed to separate. It's as though she's dropped out of sight. First Roni, and now Maggie; I'm sure she'll be at Roni's funeral, they were close friends.

Derek walked around the room, "Tony, I've got to tell you something." Tony glared at him, "What? Tell me!" Derek looked at Theresa then at

Tony, "I have to make a confession. I may have been the cause of Maggie's disappearance. You see, the day after you left for Switzerland, Maggie called for you, since you weren't in, Theresa asked if I could help her. Well, she was really excited to talk to you, I've never heard her so happy. She was happy because she and Peter had just agreed to get a divorce, and she wanted to tell you that the two of you could be together. Huh, well, I told her I didn't know where you were, but I was going to hear from you that night, and I would call her back so she could call you herself. Tony, the last thing in the world I ever wanted was to hurt Roni, Maggie, or you, especially you. So, I thought I would try to think like you. What you would do in that particular situation. I figured, with your morals and principles, that with Roni carrying your child, you would marry her and have to tell Maggie that it just wasn't in the cards for you and her. Right or wrong, I told Maggie for you. I told her that Roni was pregnant and you were with her and you were going to marry Roni. She didn't take it well; she kept saying no, you promised her. Tony, I'm sorry I blew it. I hope you'll forgive me. I really tried to save you from trying to live with a decision you didn't want. I'm truly sorry." Tony walked over and grabbed Derek's hand, "I'm glad to have a friend like you. It took a lot for you to tell Maggie. Forgive you, hell; you never have to ask my forgiveness for anything. You did what you thought was best, and so do I. Now, let's figure out a way to find her. I don't give a shit what the media or anybody else says about it, I want Maggie! I want her to be Jenny's mother. I'm worth over $4 billion and I'll spend every last dime to find her if I have to!" Tony motioned for Theresa to come to him. He put an arm around each of them, "I love you both, that's why I'm letting you take care of my little Jenny." Theresa kissed his cheek and ran from the room in tears.

Roni's funeral was said to have been "the largest wake in the history of mankind." The procession was limited to 200 cars, but 2000 would have joined if the law would have allowed. People lined the streets to get a glimpse of Roni Scott's final passing. The movie industry literally shutdown; when Walter Henshaw, the famous director, spoke at the funeral there wasn't a dry eye to be found. He said, "Roni Scott was more than a woman, she was a gorgeous woman. Roni Scott was more than an actress; she was "the" actress. Roni Scott was more than a star; she was the "only" star. When Roni Scott was near, you always felt better, you felt better because of her ever present smile, her effervescence that spilled out of her body like champagne flows from a bottle. She was rarely sad, or down, and she never said a bad thing about any other person, that I know of. Roni Scott was recognized as the most beautiful woman in the world. She very well could have been recognized as the most beautiful person in the world. Roni Scott is a legend, we movie people will make movies about her, authors will write books about her, and excuse the cliché, but it's very fitting, Roni Scott is gone, but Roni Scott will never be forgotten."

CHAPTER FORTY-FOUR

The snow was falling quite heavily. The large white flakes fell softly against the window, but melted immediately. "Such a short life!" Tony thought as he watched the flakes disappear against the window. "Short life – not only for snowflakes, but for humans as we..," he said to himself. He stood up to look down on the street, many floors below. "Where could she be?" As always, Maggie filled his thoughts. He had been working – but accomplishing nothing. "She's out there somewhere – but where? She must know about Roni!" He raised his head and looked at the sky, "Dear God, as always, I'm coming to you for help. I miss her God! I need Maggie! Won't you please help me find her? I'll never be right until I find her. Oh, God Almighty, I need you – I need your help. Please, please, help!"

"Tony! Are you alright? I've buzzed you three times," Theresa walked up behind him. "Yes, of course. I was just daydreaming, I guess. What is it?" "Clint Mackey is about to come through the phone; he want's to talk to you so badly. Can you talk to him?" Tony nodded, "Sure, what line is he on?" Theresa looked confused, "The only one blinking."

"Hello, Clint! What can I do for you?" "Tony, I didn't think I'd ever get through to you. I've got a line on something that could prove to be financially outstanding for Cole Industries!" "Like what, Clint?" "I heard through the grapevine that a heavy gambler has lost his shirt in Vegas and is in some deep shit with the mob. It so happens this loser owns a helluva lot of property around Newport Beach. It's being said that he's willing to unload it for quick cash – but when I say quick, that's exactly what I mean. He needs it within 48 hours." "Have you seen the property, Clint?"

"Yes. It's about four miles long and a mile wide and has four houses on it which he rents. I've checked with the assessor's and the property is worth about $10 million bucks as is, but if one was to add some more homes, the value would increase even more. I think we could get it for 2 million in cash." Tony looked back at the snowflakes, "Hang on a minute, Clint." He put Clint on hold and buzzed Derek. "Yes." "Derek , what's the possibility of you dropping what you're doing and catching a quick flight out to California to look at some land Clint is all hot about? He says we can make a quick 8 million?" Derek leaned back and smiled, "You better believe I'll go. I need a couple of days out this damn cold, snowy weather. I'll call Chris and have him fire up the plane." Tony got back to Clint, "Derek will be leaving very shortly. You meet him at the Orange County Airport. If he likes it, he can get the money from one of our banks out there immediately. Talk to you later, Clint."

As soon as he hung up, Theresa came in again. "Tony, can I talk to you for a moment?" He pointed to a chair, "Sure." She acted nervous. "Tony, uh, I'm concerned about you. You haven't been acting like yourself. Is there anything I can do?" He flashed the smile that had become his trademark – a smile that made men feel comfortable, and made women's heart beat faster..."Thank you, Theresa, for your concern; but I've just got to work some things out." She was wanting to say something else but couldn't get it out. Tony was very perceptive. "You're concerned about why I haven't been to see Jenny, right?" She smiled and nodded, "Yes, Tony, she's a beautiful baby. Derek and I are getting very attached to her; but you haven't seen her in over two weeks. I just wanted..." He interrupted her. "I know what you're saying. I realize how beautiful she is. I think about her – I think about her a lot. I know, I should be spending more time with her, but – Theresa – for the first time in my life, I'm confused – really confused. I can't stop thinking about Maggie; I should be thinking about Jenny, and of Roni – but my every move is centered around Maggie." "I understand! I really do." Theresa said. "I just don't want you to forget about Jenny- it's amazing at how much she looks like you." "Is this why you decided to come back to work this week?" She replied, "Yes. But it's taken me three days to get up the nerve to talk to you. Tony, has there been any word about Maggie?" He shook his head and sighed, "No, and I've offered three different detective agencies a million bucks to whoever finds her! You'd think with the three of them working on it, that they would come up with something – but they all come up empty-handed. Peter even reported her missing – but the police came up empty also. The last place she was seen was at a car dealer where she sold her Mercedes. From that moment on – she just vanished." "Do you think she went back to her folks?" Theresa asked. "No, they're as interested as we are to find her. They haven't seen her or talked to her in over four months. Oh, Peter got the divorce already. So she's free and doesn't even know it."

Theresa stood, "If there is anything I can do – well, you know!" She started out, but stopped when Tony said, "I'll come this weekend, it it's okay and spend some time with Jenny." Theresa ran to him, crying of course, "Thank you, Tony. I'm so worried about you!"

It was so quiet and peaceful – so different than what she was used to – the soft slashing of the waves coming in, the large bright moon, and just a whisper of a breeze. The air was a little cool, but she enjoyed it. Maggie walked along the beach, hands in the pockets of her baggy jeans. She kicked at the water as it rolled over her feet and ankles. As always, she thought about Tony. "They're probably playing with their baby right now – they're probably laughing – they're probably very happy – I wonder if they had a boy or a girl – a boy, and he looks just like Tony – gorgeous – but if it's a girl and looks like Roni, she's still gorgeous – Roni is in her glory, I'll bet – she always did love children – Roni, Roni – I'm so jealous of you – I want him, too – I want him more than you do – I want him, I want him – oh, Tony, Tony…!"

St. Michael's Roman Catholic Church seemed to be undaunted by the decaying city around it. The nearly century old structure loomed like a flower in a bed of thorns. It looks the same today as it did the first time he could remember seeing it – when Sister Carolyn marched all the children to mass. During the first fifteen years of his life, he spent every Sunday morning in this ominous house of God. As he stood looking at the large, heavy doors, he realized it had been a long time since he had been there – or in any church for that matter – so why was he going now? While going home, he thought about the orphanage, Sister Carolyn, Father O'Halloran, and the old neighborhood. He told Willie to turn the car around and directed him to Chicago's south side.

The snow was still falling. It was beautiful; it created a Christmas card image as it covered the church. Tony walked up the steps and opened the huge wooden door. The church was empty, except for the glowing candles by the altar. "It hasn't changed in all these years," he thought. He walked to the front pew – without realizing he sat in the exact seat he occupied every Sunday as a child.

Tony sat there for a long time, remembering his past more than praying. He stood up to leave, whe he saw Father O'Halloran standing nearby – he had been watching. Tony walked briskly toward the man who had taught him to swing a golf club and throw footballs. Father O'Halloran looked the same, although his hair was white; but time had been good to him. "Tony! It is Tony Cole, is it not?" The priest said with a smile. Tony put out his hand. He was excited to see the only man, other than Jonathan Stuyvesant who had any influence on him as a young man or child. He hadn't seen him since Sister Carolyn's funeral. "Yes, Father! It's so good to see you!" The priest held onto Tony's hand for a long time. "How good of you to come by, Tony! You look good; but troubled." "No, everything is fine," Tony smiled. Father O'Halloran frowned, "Tony, I never knew you to lie – why would you now? You didn't come here this time of night just to rest. You forget that I could always tell when you were troubled. I also read the newspapers. I know about Tony Cole. I know that you have become very rich and famous; but I also know that you have had some unpleasant personal things happen to you lately. Please, Tony, tell me about your troubles – like old times."

They went into his office and Tony told him of his need for Maggie, of his relationship with Roni, and about his daughter. Father O'Halloran listened quietly as Tony explained his feelings. "Father, I don't know where to turn. I'm one of the wealthiest men in the world. I can buy anything, anything I want. Yet, the only thing I want – is something I can't buy, and worst of all, I can't even find." "Yes, Tony, you do have all the money and material things a man needs. You have had the love of a beautiful woman, and now, you have the love of a little child; but you have forgotten that you have the love of God, as well. I would say you had forgotten; but I think you remembered today. Tony, if God wants you and Maggie to be together, then it will happen. God has been very good to you; but how good have you been to him?" Tony stood up, extended his hand to Father O"Halloran, "Thank you, Father. It's been very nice seeing you again." He reached in his picket and pulled out a check that he always kept for emergencies. He wrote out the check, payable to St. Michael's Parish, for $100,000. He handed the check to the old priest, "You're absolutely right! I did forget, and I have remembered. Please take this. I'm not giving it

out of guilt, but because I want to. Thank you again, Father. Goodbye!"
"Goodbye, Tony. And thank you for the generous contribution." He put his hand on Tony's shoulder, "Have faith. God realizes the love that you and Maggie have for each other. I'm sure you'll find her. Goodbye, Tony!"

CHAPTER FOURTY-FIVE

Tony sat at his desk, engrossed in computer print outs that he had ignored previously. Athough he personally had been somewhat out-of-touch with Cole Industries daily functions, Cole was not only making money, but each division was growing in leaps and bounds. He shook his head, in utter disbelief of the figures that were being generated. He went through each division separately.

Cole/Emerson Architecture and Design had become the most sought-after architectural firm in the country. Mike Emerson had been declared Architecht of the Year by his peers for his design of the Anthony Hotel Chain. They were not only designing Cole Industries buildings, but were also doing the designs for other major corporations – the new Volkswagen of America Headquarters in Pennsylvania; a new R. J. Reynolds office building in North Carolina' A Scott Paper Company office building in Missouri; and a public library in Seattle. Besides the commercial buildings being designed, they were also designing homes, shopping centers, and other hotels. Cole/Emerson Division would gross nearly $90 million for the year.

Cole/Krug Building and Construction was turning down more new business that most construction firms have. Besides their offices in Chicago, Los Angeles, and Houston, they added offices in Seattle, Philadelphia, and Atlanta. This division became the second largest construction firm in the states with a gross income for the year of nearly $700 million.

Cole Real Estate and Land Development had grown to unbelievable proportions. This division operated The Anthony Hotel Chain – which now totaled five, the management of the Cole Shopping Centers, the houses built by Cole/Krug and sold by Cole Real Estate, plus they owned more than six million acres of prime land located from California to Florida. This division was going to show gross income of just over $40 million – which would be much higher, except for the continued purchasing of land.

King Cole Restaurants and TC's Saloons were located in the five Anthony Hotels plus there were free-standing eateries and night spots in San Francisco, Dallas, Philadelphia, and Atlanta. Carmen Lombardi received all major awards awarded by the National Restaurant Association. The restaurants were all given a five-star rating for quality of food and service. The nightclubs (TC's) were full every night. Plans for the next year was to build six each free-standing plus the three new hotels planned. The division would gross $25 million.

Cole Department Stores, the smallest division with stores in the four Cole Shopping Centers and two free-standing stores in Chicago was very profitable while grossing $18 million.

Anthony Joseph Cosmetics and Designs made an impact to their markets like a jet airplane. The Roni Cosmetics line skyrocketed in sales after Roni's death and never slowed. Another manufacturing plant was purchased and distribution centers were established in New York, Chicago, and Dallas. Sales were going to top the $300 million mark. Anthony Joseph Fashions was also a surprise. After realizing the success from the Roni Collection – which was being made by a small French manufacturer, Cole bought out another clothing manufacturer and expanded the line. The sales from this division would top $15 million. Henri Vachon had relinquished the reins of Cole Department Stores to Eric Springfield so he could devote his full attention to Anthony Joseph Cosmetics and Design.

Cole Industries would experience more than a billion dollars in gross income for the full year. This was amazing to the entire business world, but nobody was more amazed than Tony himself. He sat back in his chair, shook his head, and said aloud, "Christ, if we continue, we'll double our gross next year!" He began to think. "We've got to diversify more – expand into other areas – but what – where?

"Ready to hit the skies, Mr. Hill?" Chris Pike asked. Derek smiled, "Let's hit it, Chris. I'm ready for some of that beautiful California sunshine!"

Derek sat back and watched the Chicago skyline disappear as the sleek orange and blue jet zoomed skyward. He loosened his tie, unbuttoned his vest, and lit a cigarette. Derek loved to fly; he insisted that flying was like a tranquilizer – he was totally relaxed in the air.

Derek began to think about Tony and how he wished he could help him; but he knew that Tony would be alright – sooner or later.

"We'll be landing soon, Mr. Hill!" Chris Pike bellowed through the plane's intercom. Chris' voice awakened Derek from a deep sleep; he pushed the intercom button, "Do I have time to freshen up?" Chris answered, "Yes, sir, Mr. Hill! I always leave you time." Derek went into the small bathroom and brushed his teeth, shaved, and fixed his clothing. He – as did Tony – always made sure he looked his best when he arrived to meet someone.

Clint Mackey was pacing nervously awaiting Derek's arrival. His contact was getting anxious to sell the property and Clint was afraid they would miss out on the deal if they didn't make the decision quickly. "It's about damn time!" he exclaimed when he saw the bright orange jet glide into the runway.

Derek stepped from the plane, and Clint was waiting. "Christ, I was wondering if you were coming!" "Don't get excited, Clint. We'll take care of business right away," Derek was learning to be calm from Tony. "I have a car, we'll run out to the property now – if that's okay?" Clint asked. Derek looked around, "No, I don't want to see the property from a car – not just yet anyway – but I would like to see it from the air; let's rent a helicopter – that way we can see what potential the land really has." "Why didn't I think of that?" Clint remarked.

The helicopter lifted up, and Derek looked out at the California terrain. "Damn, it's nice out here. It was snowing like a bitch when I left Chicago," he said to Clint. Within minutes you could see the Pacific Ocean with white capped waves on its bright blue color. The pilot maneuvered the bubbled aircraft along the shore giving Derek and Clint a majestic view. "We're coming up on the property now," Clint pointed ahead. "Okay, it starts at this intersection," Clint was directing Derek to look, "And goes from the western edge of the main road to the sea; it runs all the way to that fence just below us." Derek motioned for the pilot to turn around. "Does the seller own the four homes that are located on his property?" Clint nodded, "Yes, only two of them are occupied – both rented." "What a beautiful piece of property!" Derek exclaimed.

They flew over the same stretch several times, and finally Derek said, "Sit it down; I want to get out and see what it looks like on the ground." The pilot said to Derek, "I can sit it down to let you out, but I can't stay down – it's against the law. I'll have to get back in the air immediately." "Fine, take Clint back to the airport. Clint, get your car and pick me up here!" Derek ordered.

CHAPTER FOURTY-SIX

"Bob, I want to increase the building of hotels, restaurants, shopping plazas, and single-family homes and condominiums," Tony was acting like his old self, "I want us to pursue new areas. Are you and the accounting department aware of our current financial situation?" Bob Underwood wasn't sure why Tony was so hyped up. "Of course, we're very much aware of our finances. In fact, we're pretty damn proud of the success; uh – aren't you?" "Hell, yes – I'm pleased as hell that we're going to pay some damn astronomical amount in taxes this year. I'd like to know what you've planned to do?" Bob had never seen Tony in this type of mood. "I don't know what you mean. Tony, Cole Industries is making money faster than we can keep up with. Shit, the rest of us are patting each other on the back for the success we're experiencing. Why are you so damn upset?" Tony threw a handful of computer readouts into Bob's lap – very uncharacteristic of him, "I just finished looking at these! You're right; we are making more money than we can keep up with. Each division is doing phenomenally well; but if we don't do something quick, all the profits are going to be fed into the damn welfare system!" Bob squirmed in his seat, the spoke calmly, "Tony, you forget – you were gone for over a month, and you haven't had a lot of input since you've been back. Business has just rolled along. What did you expect us to do?" "I expected you to run your department as efficiently as Paul Krug or Carmen Lombardi, or any of the others. Their job is to make money for Cole Industries – your job is to see that Cole Industries ends up in a profitable situation! Do you need me to do that for you? The others didn't seem to need me!" Tony screamed at him. Bob sat speechless, wondering why Tony's personality had taken such a change. Tony lit a cigarette, "I want you to arrange to transfer $10 million to each of the Cancer Society, Birth Defects, the Heart Fund, the Northwestern Medical Center, and the University of Illinois, School of Medicine! That should create a better tax return for Cole Industries! I want it done immediately!" "Whatever you say. I'll get it done right away," Bob said as he started to leave Tony's office, but he stopped at the door, "Tony, we're all sorry about Roni. We know what you're going through; I'm sorry if we've let you down!" He shut the door behind him before Tony could reply.

Tony sat down heavily, and stared down on the city. He was shaking. He had never talked like that to any of his friends before. He felt terrible. He had hurt Bob. He took out his depression on him and Bob didn't even know why. "I've either got to get over Maggie, or find her – but how!" he said aloud as he snubbed out his cigarette angrily.

He opened the file of phone numbers on his desk. He found the number he wanted – Charlton DeGrand, President of General Distilleries. He dialed the number himself, instead of putting it through Theresa.

The female voice answered, "Good afternoon, this is General Distilleries." :This is Tony Cole of Cole Industries. May I please speak to Mr. DeGrand?" "I'll put you through to his secretary, Mr. Cole. Please hold!" The next voice was just as programmed as the first. "Mr. DeGrand's office; may I help you?" "This is Tony Cole of Cole…" The programmed voice changed, "Oh, Mr. Cole – I've read so much about you, uh, oh – I'll get Mr. DeGrand for you – just a moment!"

"Tony, Tony, so nice to hear from you!" Charlton DeGrand was exuberant. "Charlton, I'd like to meet with you sometime; the sooner, the better." "Whenever you say," Charlton almost jumped through the phone. Tony replied, "How about tomorrow morning? I'll fly down." "I'll be expecting you, Tony. Have a nice flight down." Tony hung up as soon as Charlton had finished.

He buzzed for Willie, who came in immediately, "Yes, Tony?" "Willie, you can make plans for tomorrow. I'm going out-of-town; but I'm going to drive myself." "Whatever you say, Tony," Willie said, then left.

He pushed the door open to Bob Underwood's office, "Can I interrupt you for a minute?" "You're the boss!" Bob said throwing his pencil onto the desk. Tony closed the door and walked to the front of Bob's desk, "I want to apologize for the way I talked to you. I'm sorry, really I am. You're doing a helluva job." "You don't have to apologize to me, Tony. You were right – I should have been looking for ways to ease our tax situation." Tony put out his hand, "Thanks, Bob." "Are you okay, Tony – uh, I mean – I've never seen you get angry before. What's wrong?" Tony squeezed his hand, "My mind is a little out-of-whack right now, but bear with me, okay?" He left without saying anything else.

Tony took a cab to a Chevrolet auto dealership, purchased a Corvette, and drove away; headed south to Louisville, Kentucky – the snow and ice didn't bother him. He just wanted the few hours alone – just him, the Corvette, and his thoughts of Maggie.

CHAPTER FORTY-SEVEN

"Hello, Tony! When did you arrive?" Charlton DeGrand greeted him to his office. "Last night – or rather early this morning. Nice to see you, Charlton." Tony smiled as he shook Charlton DeGrand's hand. "Sit down! Sit down!" Charlton insisted.

Charlton DeGrand had been the president of General Distilleries for more than thirty years. He took over the operation when his father, Charlton DeGrand, Sr., passed away. This Charlton was now in his seventies, and had a massive heart attack couple of years ago, which all but retired him. During his absence, General Distilleries suffered great llosses, while the Controller of the company acted as president. Even though Charlton was told not to return to work, he dismissed the Controller and once again took over the reins of the company.

Charlton DeGrand was a strong domineering person. He had been involved in some business dealings with Jonathan Stuyvesant over the years, which is where Tony first met him. When he became president, his company was known as Kentucky Distilleries and sold only Old Kentuckian Bourbon. The company was financially solid, but was losing its share of the market slowly. Charlton saw what was coming, so he acquired two smaller distilleries in Kentucky which gave them the broader product mix to share in the market. Within five years, Kentucky Distilleries had grown to five times its size and had changed their name to General Distilleries.

Charlton's first born son, Devereaux – his mother's maiden name – was being groomed to follow in his father's footsteps, but was killed when he was thrown from a horse. Charlton DeGrand III, now 25, has been preparing to take over from his father, but isn't ready – at least his father says he isn't.

Charlton's secretary had brought them coffee; they reminisced about Jonathan; they discussed Charlton's health, and also talked about Tony's metoric rise to extreme wealth. Finally, Tony got to the point of his visit.

"Charlton, your company has suffered some great losses during the past year. I know that you're not physically capable of running the company – and that you don't trust anybody else to do so." Charlton interrupted, "Who the hell else is there? The only one I would consider trusting is my son, but hell – he's just a baby; he doesn't have the guts yet – and I'm not sure he ever will!" Tony shut him off, "That's what I'm getting at, Charlton. I would like to buy General Distilleries!" Charlton's expression didn't change, "Tony, this company has been in my family for nearly 100 years – and l would like to keep it in my family for another 100 years – but thank you."

Tony walked over to the coffee, poured himself another cup, then said, "Charlton, if you died today – what would happen to the company?" "God forbid! Why, the whole fucken thing would go under!" Charlton was sure he was the only person that could save his company. "Would you rather kill yourself trying to rebuild the company, or sell it and give us a chance to rebuild it?" Tony asked. Charlton toyed with an unlit cigar, "Tony, I realize I could go the the great-distillery-in-the-sky if I continue working, but I have to – uh, I have to leave a solvent company for my son; just like my father did." Tony returned to his seat, "If your son was assured to be taken care of – would that ease your mind about selling?" Charlton rubbed his forehead, "What did you have in mind?" "Look, Charlton. Nobody in my company has any expertise in operating a distillery, but we have proven we know how to operate different types of businesses efficiently. I would like to put your son in the President's seat and let my people work with him." Tony was sure Charlton would go for that dimension. Charlton laughed, "If I thought Charlton could handle it, I'd hand it to him now. He's not ready yet!" Tony rose to his feet, "If you sell General Distilleries to me, I can assure you that we will make it run profitably; I'll also assure you that if for some reason it does not turn around – Charlton DeGrand III will always have an executive's position with Cole Industries." "Why do you want to buy a floundering whiskey dealer?" Charlton suddenly became inquisitive. Tony smiled, "I could say because I personally drink a lot of whiskey, or I could say it would be a tax write-off for this year, or I could say I need a new challenge – the last is the reason. Charlton, I would enjoy the challenge of rebuilding General Distilliries – hell, I'd have you as a consultant, wouldn't I!"

Charlton grinned, "Christ, you remind of Jonathan! How much; how much are you willing to pay?" "Are you willing to sell?" Tony responded. "It's down to how much you want to pay!" Charlton was entering a game that Tony never loses. Tony smiled at Charlton, "If we have a deal, my finance man will come down," he extended his hand," "If we don't have a deal, then, I've enjoyed our visit, Charlton." Before Charlton took Tony's hand, he asked, "Aren't you interested in how much you pay for a challenge?" "Do we have a deal?" Tony asked without expression. "Yeh, by God, yes, we do – but only if my son is taken care of as you said?" He grabbed Tony's hand. "Thank you, Charlton – it will be as I said. Bob Underwood, my Finance V.P. will be down next week to consummate the deal – and by the way, he'll know how much to pay." He turned to leave, but Charlton's remark stopped him. "Just like him, just as if you were his blood son' just like Jonathan Stuyvesant!" Tony looked at him, "Thank you!"

The northbound expressway was fairly quiet during the afternoon. Tony was guiding the Corvette, instead of driving. Normally, after making a good business deal, he felt exhilarated; but today, he felt no different than he had felt any other day for the past few months. He was depressed; depressed like he had never experienced before. It was Maggie – it was always Maggie. "I've got to find her; I've got to find her!" he said to himself, as he slammed his fist against the steering wheel. When he hit the wheel, he accidentally jerked it – the car was speeding faster than he had realized – the rear of the car suddenly spun – Tony fought to gain control, but the light sports car was out of control – the left rear tire slid into the snowy grass of the median – Tony could not keep the bright yellow Corvette from spinning wildly through the median – as quickly as the car began to spin, it came to an abrupt stop, smashing into a guard rail! The car split in half – Tony was thrown from the car; face down in the snow!

The snow was cold on his face; his first thought was that he was dead – he lifted his head, rolled over, then moved each arm, leg, and finger; he felt his face, looked at his hands; there was no blood – he smiled to himself – he was alive, and apparently unhurt.

An elderly man rushed to Tony's aid. "Lay still! Don't move; something might be broken!" The man was trembling, as Tony stood up. "Oh, God, I thought you were killed! Look at your car; it's demolished!" Tony began to laugh, and laugh, and laugh. The poor, scared man was confused, "Why, why are you laughing? You were close to being killed!" Tony stopped laughing but smiled at the little man, "But I wasn't!"

The police arrived shortly, and after the proper questions were asked, and Tony had refused to go to the hospital for a check-up, he asked the old man to drive him into Lafayette – a city in northwestern Indiana. The man agreed.

The old man, Roscoe Davis, pulled his battered pick-up truck in front of the small airport terminal. Tony opened the door, and said to the man, "Mr. Davis, I truly appreciate your kindness. Thank you very much!" "I was just glad you weren't hurt. Good luck, Mr. Cole – it's obvious that God is in your corner." Tony shut the door and Roscoe Davis drove away – Tony watched him until his rusty old truck was out-of-sight.

CHAPTER FORTY-EIGHT

"Damn, I'm glad I'm out of that egg-beater! They scare the hell out of me anyway!" Derek said to himself as the chopper flew out of sight. He began walking along the road that bordered the property. "God, this is beautiful!" He walked a short way by the road, then headed toward the water. He slung his sport coat over his shoulder, and when he reached the water, he couldn't resist pulling off his shoes and socks, rolling up his pant legs, and wading in the soft white suds. Derek completely forgot about his world of high finance and big business; he was in another world; and enjoying it immensely. He had been strolling slowly and didn't know for how long; when he noticed a shapely bikini-clad female lying on a blanket in front of one of the rented houses. He picked up his pace as he approached the dark-tanned woman.

"Good morning!" Derek said standing over her. The woman wore sunglasses and a large hat to shield the sun. She removed the sunglasses as she sat up in reply to the stranger standing over her. Her mouth flew open as she stared at Derek. "Maggie? Oh, my God, it's you!" He dropped to his knees and put his hands on her shoulders. "Derek, is it really you?" She threw her arms around his neck and sobbed.

"We've been searching the world over for you! Where have you been?" Maggie pulled away, jumped up, and started to run. Derek grabbed her arm, "Maggie, why are you running?" "Please let me go! Please, Derek, please!" He wouldn't let her go. "What is it? Just tell me why you disappeared?" Realizing he wasn't going to leave without her explaining, she took a deep breath, "Let's go in the house, and have a drink; we might as well talk."

She fixed them a drink, and they took a seat on the balcony overlooking the sea. Maggie had not talked to another person in over a week, and the last time she spoke to anyone was the clerk at the bookstore. She had become accustomed to her life as a hermit. She didn't own a clock, radio, or TV; she had not seen a newspaper or magazine since the day she became a recluse. She didn't even realize Christmas was nearing. "How have you been Derek?" she said as they sat down. "Hell, I've been fine; but how have you been – that's what I'd like to know?" "Fine, terrific, just super!" Maggie insisted. "Maggie, Tony has had three top detective agencies, police, and even some unsavory persons trying to find you," Derek said questioningly. She bit her lip to keep from crying, "That's great! Why would he want to find me? Afterall, he should be worrying about his new bride and child – don't you think?" Derek stood up, threw his hands in the air, and exclaimed in complete shock, "You don't know? Christ, you don't, do you?" Confused, she asked, "Don't know what? You told me he was going to Roni; he was going to marry her, and raise their child. Isn't that what you told me?" Derek looked at her for a moment, then told her, "Roni had the child – but she and Tony never married; Maggie, Roni died delivering the baby!"

She threw her hand to her mouth, "Oh, Derek, no! Oh, my God, no!" Derek pulled her up and held her in his arms for a long time. "He needs you, Maggie. Tony and Jenny need you – that's his daughter's name, Jenny. How could you not know? It was in all the papers and magazines for weeks. It was considered the largest funeral in the history of Hollywood. How could you not know?" She leaned on the railing, rubbed the back of her neck, and said, "I was so hurt – Tony had promised me he would never marry Roni – he would wait until our time was right – Derek, I loved him so much; I was so excited that Peter wanted a divorce, and to leave Cole at the same time. When you told me about Roni, I just couldn't face anybody – so, I changed my name, rented this place, and became a hermit. Derek, you may not believe this, but I haven't heard or seen any type of news since the day I talked to you – Jenny, the baby was a girl? Is she okay? Does Tony have her?" "Yes, she's a beautiful girl; she's healthy and well, Tony has her – in a matter of speaking!" "What do you mean?" Derek shrugged, "Theresa and I have been taking care of her, and Tony has not seen much of her. Maggie, Tony can't think about anything but finding you – he's obsessed with it – he loves you so much!" "Where is he now?" she asked with her eyes twinkling. Derek grinned, "He's in Chicago." "I've got to go to him – oh, Derek, I love him!" "I'm flying back in a couple of hours; pack your things and you can go with me – you can surprise him, it can be his Christmas gift." Derek was excited. "Is it Christmas time?" Maggie had lost complete sense of time. "Yes, boy, have you been out-of-it!" She kissed him and said, "Let me throw some things in a bag, and then take me to Tony!" She stopped for a second, and once again, rubbed her neck. Derek questioned, "Are you okay?" "I think I was in the sun too long. I have a slight headache; but it'll be fine – now that I'm happy again," she smiled as she left him.

CHAPTER FORTY-NINE

Tony hired a private plane to fly him to Chicago; then took a cab to his house. He realized he had brushed death's door once more; he wondered how many more times he could come that close!

He phoned his office, "Theresa, Tony here!" "Hi, ya, boss man! What can I do for you? Where are you?" He replied, "I'm at home, and I need to speak to Bob Underwood right away!" Theresa transferred him to Bob's secretary, "Arlene, Mr. Cole is on the line and would like to talk to Mr. Underwood." She buzzed Bob without saying a word, "Mr. Underwood, Mr. Cole is on the phone for you!" Bob grabbed the phone, "Hello, Tony!" Tony got right to the point, "Bob, I want you and Larry Shapiro to come out to my house – right away. I have to discuss something with you; oh, you better plan on taking a short trip." Bob would never get used to Tony's quick maneuvering, "Whatever you say – but can you tell me what's up?" "I'll tell you when you get here!" Tony hung up.

Bob Underwood left his office, slightly disgusted. "I'm leaving Arlene, and I'm not sure when I'll be back. I'll call you later." He walked into Larry Shapiro's office, and asked Larry's secretary, "Is the Counselor busy?" The attractive blonde smiled, "No, Mr. Underwood! Go right in." Bob walked in, "Ready to take a ride, Larry?" Larry looked up from the desk with his eyes only, "What the hell are you talking about?" "Haven't you talked to our leader?" Larry shook his head, "No, Bob, I haven't. I don't even know where he is. So what's up?" Bob smiled, "Tony wants you and I to come to his house and to be prepared for a short trip! Right now!"

Larry threw his hands in the air, "Just like that; drop what you're doing – no matter how important – and run to the master's beckon call!" Bob was laughing uncontrollably. Larry shouted at him, "What the hell are you laughing at? You don't like this drop-everything bullshit, either!" Bob controlled himself, "I know, but it is so funny – you get really Jewish when you get mad!" He began to laugh again. Larry threw a pencil at him, "Come on you financial fuck-up; let's go see what scheme the master has dreamed up this time!"

Aren't you ready yet? Clint will be here anytime with the car!" Derek bellowed from the balcony. Maggie came out – she was as lovely as ever; she put on black slacks with a beige satin blouse – her dark-tanned skin glistened – she was happy for the first time in months. "Well, I'm ready!" Derek turned to her, "Maggie, you look great! I think I'm a little jealous of my friend." They both laughed. "Derek, who's Clint? You know you didn't even tell me what you were doing on this particular beach! What are you doing here?" Maggie questioned. "Damn!" Derek exclaimed, "You're right. How ironic that I'm here. Clint Mackey has taken over Peter's position with the company – oh, Christ! I'll bet you don't know that either!" Maggie looked puzzled, "Know what; that Peter left Cole Industries? I knew that." Derek smiled at her, "Maggie – Peter has already gotten a divorce! You're free, free to marry Tony!" She hugged him, lauging and crying, "No, I didn't know!"

Derek said, "Let's you and I take your car; we'll go to the bank, and Clint can go directly to the seller." Maggie was very confused. "What are you talking about?" He shook his head, "That's why I'm here – on this particular beach – we're going to buy four miles of this beach area, and the four houses on it. Clint is returning to pick me up." Derek saw Clint walking toward the house. "Here he comes now, come on let's go."

"General Distilleries! Tony, I'm not sure I've ever heard of them! Who are they?" Bob Underwood asked. "They manufacture medium to low priced booze. At one time, they were the most profitable distillery in the country. They have declined rapidly within the last three years. Bob, it will be an acquisition to help this year's tax problem; but next year, we'll rebuild it into a higher stature," Tony was very deliberate. Larry had become accustomed to special <u>deals</u> that Tony arranged. "What are the special arrangements in this acquisition, Tony?" "Only one! That Charlton DeGrand III comes with it as President of Cole-General Distilleries." "That's it? What concessions did you ask for?" Larry asked again. Tony replied, "That was my concession." Larry looked at Bob, "Well, we'd better go. One thing's for sure, I'll bet we get a free drink on this trip!"

CHAPTER FIFTY

The white-haired man looked through the window. There was a green pick-up truck coming up the driveway. "Somebody's coming, Sarah!" he yelled to his wife. "I don't know who; I've never seen the truck before. Better put the coffee on!"

Roscoe watched as a large black man pulled the pick-up to a stop, and got out. He watched him as he came onto the porch, and knocked heavily. Roscoe opened the door, "Hello, may I help you?" The large man asked, "Are you Mr. Roscoe Davis?" "Yes. Yes, I am," he replied. "May I come in for a moment, sir? I have news for you." Roscoe stepped aside, "Oh, of course, please come in. Sarah, bring the coffee!" Roscoe pointed to a chair as his wife brought in a tray of coffee, cream, and sugar. "So, what kind of news have you brought us? I'm sorry, but did you tell me your name?" The black man smiled, "No, sir. I didn't tell you, but my name is Willie – I work for Mr. Cole, Tony Cole." He waited for a response from the old man. "Oh yes; the young man who had the accident yesterday – nice man – sure was lucky – the car was destroyed but he never had a scratch – lucky, really lucky." Willie spoke clearly, "Mr. Davis, I was sent here to present you with that new pick-up truck outside; a gift of thanks from Mr. Cole." Roscoe looked up at his wife, "I, uh, well I can't accept it – my gosh, I just gave him a ride – shew, that truck must have cost 6, may $7,000 – no, I can't accept it – but you tell Mr. Cole I appreciate the thought." "I'm sorry, Mr. Davis, you have no choice. The truck is already paid for and is in your name. It's yours whether you want it or not; and Mr. Cole would be extremely hurt if you didn't accept it," Willie said convincingly. "Well, I guess I have no choice. You tell Mr. Cole that Sarah and I will pray for him – and that we thank him so much," Roscoe was very sincere. Willie flashed a broad smile as he handed the keys to him, "There is only one catch; you have to drive me to town so I can get my car." Roscoe laughed as he grabbed his jacket and led Willie to the door.

While driving towards town – and Roscoe looking like a kid with a new toy – Willie asked him if he wouldn't mind stopping at the bank. "Sure, Willie; I'll stop at the bank where I do my business."

They entered the bank, and Willie asked Roscoe who the manager was. "Mr. Hyatt, right over there. What do you want with the manager of this bank?" Roscoe was beginning to wonder why Willie wanted to go to the bank. Willie walked over to the manager. "Mr. Hyatt, my name is Willie, acting for Mr. Tony Cole." The bank manager practically leaped from his chair, "Yes, sir. I have everything right here; just as Mr. Cole requested." Willie took the papers from his hands, "Mr. Davis, could you come here for a moment?" Roscoe came over to the manager's desk; he was totally bewildered at why they were in the bank.

"Mr. Davis," Willie smiled, "Here is something else Mr. Cole would like you to have." He handed the papers to Roscoe. The bank manager was smiling from ear-to-ear. Roscoe thumbed through the papers, then raised his head, "This is the deed to my farm, and the bank note I owe – both say paid-in-full – I, uh, I…" "Mr. Cole telephoned me from Chicago," Hyatt said, "Your farm and bank note has been paid in full by Mr. Cole. You don't have to worry anymore, Roscoe." He couldn't control his emotions as he attempted to thank Willie. Finally, he said, "Who is Mr. Cole? Is he crazy – he's doing all of this just because I gave him a ride – he must be a millionaire that doesn't know what to do with his money." Willie put out his hand to Roscoe, and replied, "He does have a lot of money, Mr. Davis, and he has a heart as big as the Pacific Ocean. When you told him about your fear of losing your farm, he was touched. These are the things that make him happy. It's been nice meeting you, Mr. Davis; I have to go now." Roscoe and the bank manager watched Willie as he left. "This Tony Cole, uh, he must be one of God's chosen people!" Roscoe exclaimed.

"Oh, Derek, I'm a nervous wreck! What if he's changed his mind – what if he doesn't want me now?" Maggie carried on as the jet eased onto the runway at Midway Airport in Chicago. "Would you settle down, Maggie! I assure you, he still wants you – oh, God, how he wants you. Theresa will be excited when she sees you – I called and asked her to meet me here; I told her I had a surprise for her," Derek said. "Terrific!" Maggie grinned, "You know, I've missed her, too. Do you think she'll have Jenny with her?" Derek shook his head, "No, I'm sure she left her with the nurse. It's really cold here, you know."

The jet finally came to a stop, and the door opened. Theresa was standing just beyond a glass barrier; Derek stepped through the door – he told Maggie to wait until he met with Theresa, and then come out – he waved to Theresa; she came out to meet him, "So, where's my surprise? It better be good, since I came out in this cold." Derek turned to the plane, "Just watch the door."

Theresa shrieked as Maggie stepped through the door; she ran to her and Maggie practically flew to the ground. They hugged each other and cried. "My, God, I can't believe it – you're here, you're really here!" Theresa cried, then hugged her again. Derek came out to get them, "Hey, don't you realize how cold it is?" Theresa turned to him, threw her arms around his neck, and said, "You wonderful human being. This is the greatest surprise of all times. I love you!" She kissed him. He took both women by the arm and headed toward the Executive terminal. He smiled, "Since I've given you such a nice surprise, does that mean you're going to give me what I love most?" Maggie laughed and Theresa squeezed his arm, "Honey, I'll give you so much of what you love most that you won't be able to get out of bed!" Derek stopped, and with a frown said, "Do you mean, I'm going to have to eat all that ice cream in bed?" Theresa punched him in the arm, as they all laughed.

"Are you going to spend the day at the Hill residence, Tony?" Frederick questioned. Tony was sitting in the large winged-back chair in his office. "Uh, no, Frederick. I'm not going until tomorrow; I'm going to the Northwestern basketball game with Henri today. Why?" "I was just curious," Frederick shrugged.

Tony watched the flames jumping from the logs in the fireplace; he always enjoyed a fire; it felt homey to him. Since it was Saturday, he started earlier with his Jack Daniels. He wasn't sure he wanted to put up with the crowd at the basketball game. It had become necessary for policemen to escort him into any event; they also sat next to him and escorted him out. It really wasn't much fun anymore. Tony Cole had become more than a celebrity – he was a billionaire who declined to be surrounded by body guards or to give up doing normal things that normal people do – but he had promised Henri he would attend.

He could see her face in the dancing flames. He always remembered Maggie at a certain time they had spent together – especially the time at the orphanage sight; he had told her about what it was like to grow up there – and she cried. Tony loved her emotional personality. She could cry at the drop of hat. He also loved her femininity; she always dressed like a queen; but he laughed at how she played her heart out to beat him at tennis. She was so tender – he loved her tenderness – he loved everything about her – and was beginning to realize that he'd probably never see her again!

They didn't stop laughing until they had reached the car. The chauffeur was waiting as they approached. When they were finally tucked into the limousine, Theresa asked, "Maggie, where in God's name have you been?" Maggie explained the whole story to her on the trip to their house. Theresa explained what happened to Roni, then told her about Jenny. "Maggie, she's beautiful, and such a good baby – she never cries, just coos and eats – you're going to adore her." "I can't wait to see her," Maggie grinned.

"Your house is beautiful, Theresa!" Maggie said as they entered. "Thank you!" Theresa accepted the compliment, "Would youlike to see Jenny or freshen up first?" Maggie smiled, "Are you kidding; let me see Jenny – please!"

Maggie took the sleeping child from the comfort of the nurse's arms. "Oh, Jenny, Jenny; you're so beautiful – you look just like your Daddy." She hugged the infant tightly as she sobbed – Maggie knew she would never experience giving birth to her own child, but at this very moment, she knew that she wanted to be Jenny's mother. She held her for a long time, just watching the baby sleep.

Theresa was downstairs waiting for Maggie; how good she felt that now Tony could be happy – he would have the only thing that had ever eluded him. She was startled as Maggie said, "You were right – she's a gorgeous child." Theresa stood up, "Would you like to freshen up now?" "Yes, I feel crappy. I have a nagging headache. Would it be alright if I take a shower?" "Of course. Come on, I'll show you where."

"Here you go, it's all yours. I'll wait for you downstairs," Theresa hugged Maggie. "Why don't you stay and talk to me while I'm showering – I bet I haven't said more than 50 words to another human being in the last few months – please?" "I'd love to – in fact, I have something to tell you that no one else knows yet," Theresa closed the door behind them.

Maggie stepped into the shower, "Well, go ahead, what's the big news?" Theresa puffed on a cigarette, "Derek and I have become very attached to Jenny – and we have discussed how we're going to feel when Tony comes to get her. I thought it would be just terrible – but things have a way of working out – not that we won't miss Jenny, for God's sake, we'll always love her – but, Maggie, I'm pregnant!" "Oh, Theresa! Oh, that's great. Wonderful!" Maggie was elated. "How far?" Theresa handed her a towel, "About two months. I found out yesterday. Maggie, I'm really excited." Maggie wrapped herself in the towel, then hugged Theresa, "I'm so happy for you! What did Derek say?" "I haven't told him yet – I'm waiting for the right moment."

As Maggie dressed – she put on a dark green dress – she and Theresa planned a congratulations party.

Maggie and Theresa both felt like children again – they had never been happier.

"Hello, this Derek Hill." "Mr. Hill, this is Frederick; Mr. Cole informed me that he intends to go to a basketball game with Mr. Vachon today," Frederick was enjoying his role in the surprise. He was excited when Derek phoned him earlier. He so wanted Tony to be happy again. "Fine; thank you, Frederick. I'm going to phone Henri; but in case I miss him, you find a way to keep him there; you have him call me before he sees Tony. Okay?" Derek commanded. "Yes sir. I'll see to it Mr. Hill," Frederick assured him.

Derek dialed Henri's number. He was just about to hang up when Henri answered, "Hello!" "Henri, Derek here!" "Yes, Derek, what can I do for you?" "You can cancel your plans to attend the ballgame with Tony today!" Derek practically insisted. Henri was surprised at Derek's statement, "What? Why should I do that?" "Believe me," Derek was pleading now, "Henri, it will be in the best interests of Tony! Please call and cancel. I'll explain later. Please!" Henri was still confused, but said, "Sure, hell; I can go to a ballgame anytime; but let me know what the hell's going on…I can't handle all of this suspense!" "I promise; and thanks, buddy." Derek hung up the phone.

"Tony," Frederick said as he entered Tony's office. "Mr. Vachon just phoned; he said something has come up, and he must cancel the plans for today. He said he was very sorry." Tony wasn't the least bit upset, "Fine, thank you Frederick. I'll catch up on some work, and watch a game on TV." Frederick nodded and left the room.

Derek knocked on the door, "Are you decent? Can I come in?" Theresa answered, "Yes, com in; the lady is decent!" He seemed nearly as excited as Maggie, "Everything is set. Tony is going to be home all day! Are you ready to see him?" Maggie sighed heavily, "You bet I am – but, God, I'm nervous." "Well, you look absolutely gorgeous!" Derek exclaimed. Theresa stood up from the bed she was sitting on, "He's right; you look gorgeous – now, go. Would you like our driver to take you?" She shook her head, "Oh, no, no. But I would like to borrow one of your cars. I still remember how to get there." "Of course; why don't you take Theresa's; I'll have Robert bring it out front for you," Derek said as he kissed her cheek. "Thank you, Derek. Thank you so much!" Maggie hugged him tight. He knew she wasn't thanking him for the use of the car.

Derek and Theresa watched her from the bedroom window. After she was out-of-sight, Derek said, "Well, I doubt if we'll have Jenny much longer." Theresa felt the same as he did. They would both miss her terribly, but Theresa had something to tell him – and the time would never be better. "Yeh, Tony will probably come and get her shortly. I guess we'll just have to have one of our own!" Derek looked puzzled, "Would you? I mean, I'd really love to have our own child. Hell, if we started trying right away, maybe we could have one by next Christmas." Theresa was about to laugh, and said, "I think I'd rather have a baby in July or August, but preferably July." "But that would mean we'd have to wait another year and a half. Theresa, I don't want this house to be without a child for that long!" She had to turn away to keep from bursting. Then she turned to him, "I could have a child by this July!" He shook his head, "Oh, since when did women start having six or seven month pregnancies?" Her smile was wide, "Oh, they didn't – but if I was pregnant right now, and was a couple of months ago, then I'd be due in late July. Right?" "Yeh, right; but you aren't…" He clapped his hands, "Yes, yes, you are, aren't you? You're pregnant!" Theresa nodded, "Yes, darling!" They held each other for a long while. This day had turned out to be the happiest in their lives.

CHAPTER FIFTY-ONE

Maggie's hands were sweating as she steered the silver Cadillac Seville up Lake Shore Boulevard. She didn't know if she was anxious, nervous, or both. It was just hours ago that she still longed for him and yet knew that she would never have him – and now, she was on her way to meet him, and be with him forever. "What if he's changed his mind?" she thought. Derek said he hadn't, but what if he's mad because she disappeared – no, he'll be happy as I am…"

She visualized his beautiful smile, his dark hair, his sincere eyes, and his soft touch. She thought about what it would be like to be Mrs. Tony Cole; she loved the sound of it. She said aloud, "Mrs. Tony Cole – Mrs. Cole – Mrs. Margaret Cole – Maggie Cole – I love it. Mrs. Tony Cole!"

Maggie was enjoying the drive; she couldn't help but look out at cold, blue Lake Michigan; she could see a ship far off in the lake. She was sure she would enjoy residing in Chicago – this time.

She flipped on the windshield wipers, as it began to snow very hard. She could hardly see the car in front of her. The traffic had slowed considerably. Suddenly, Maggie felt a sharp pain in the back of her head; she rubbed it then another sharper pain – she grabbed at her head, "Oh, God!" Maggie felt herself getting weak from the pain; she began to breathe heavy and quickly when a third pain, much worse that the previous two, struck. She let go of the wheel and grabbed her head with both hands. The car swerved to the right and slammed into a parked police car. The policeman sitting in the car shook his head in disgust as he stepped from his car. When he reached Maggie's car, he noticed that she slumped over the wheel – unconscious!

"Mr. Hill, you have a visitor; a policeman," Derek's maid said. "Thank you, Helen!" He looked at Theresa, "What the hell does a cop want with me?" Theresa followed him downstairs. The officer was standing by the door. Derek approached him with his hand out, "Hello, officer. What can I do for you?" "Are you Derek Hill, sir?" "Yes!" The policeman sighed, "Mr. Hill, do you own a silver Cadillac Seville?" "Yes!" Theresa threw her hands to her face, "Oh, my God, Maggie!" Derek grabbed her arm. The policeman then asked, "Do you know a Margaret Weyland who resides in California?" Derek was upset, "Yes, hell, yes. We know her – what's happened?" "She's in the hospital, Northwestern Medical Center. She passed out while driving. She hit my car. There's very little damage to you car…" Derek yelled at him, "I don't give a damn about the car – what about Maggie?" "I'm sorry sir, I can't answer that. She was taken to the emergency room. I'll be glad to drive you there."

Derek turned to Theresa who was in a state of shock, "Honey, honey," he shook her, "Theresa, you go with the policeman to the hospital, I'll go get Tony!" Theresa asked the policeman, "Was she conscious by the time they reached the hospital?" He shook his head, "I don't know, Mrs. Hill."

Derek watched the snow fall as Robert drove slowly towards Tony's. "How can I tell him what's happened?" he thought out loud. "Christ, how much more is Tony supposed to take? If anything happens to Maggie, oh, shit, Tony will die." He opened the bar and poured himself a full glass of Jack Daniels.

Derek walked right by Frederick, "Where's Tony? I must see him right away!" Frederick answered, "He's in his office. What is it Mr. Hill? What happened?"

He sighed before opening the doors to the office. Tony looked up as Derek walked through the door, "Well, hi ya ol' buddy! What do I owe this surprise? Don't tell me you ran out of booze so you came to borrow some. Sit down, you look like hell!" Derek couldn't smile, "Tony, I want you to take a ride with me. I'll explain as we go, but you must come now, immediately!" It didn't take the brain of a billionaire to realize something horrible had happened, so Tony said, "Sure, Derek, let's go."

As Robert shut the car door, Derek said, "Let's have a drink!" As he poured, Tony asked, "What the hell is wrong, Derek. Has something happed between you and Theresa?" Derek stared at Tony, "I don't know how to tell you; I don't know where to begin." He took a long drink. Tony didn't say anything, but Derek knew by the look on his face that he didn't want anymore skirting around the issue. Derek rubbed his forehead, "Tony, it's Maggie! She's in the hospital! That's where we're headed!" Tony tried to be calm "How did you find her? What's wrong with her? Has she been in Chicago all this time? Does she want to see me?" "I'd better start from the beginning and tell you the events of the past day or so!" Derek then explained the way he found Maggie, their plan to surprise Tony and the visit by the policeman.

CHAPTER FIFTY-TWO

Tony and Derek leaped from the car as it stopped at the emergency room entrance. Tony walked up to the desk, "I want to see Margaret Weyland! She was brought in a short time ago!" The nurse behind the desk looked up at him, "Are you her husband or a relative?" "No!" "Then, I'm afraid you'll have to wait to see the doctor. Just have a seat over there!" Tony didn't want to hear any of that, "I want to know why she was brought in here, and what her condition is!" The nurse replied, "She was brought in because she passed out while driving. They're performing some tests. Now, would you please have a seat!" Theresa came through another door, "Oh, Tony, Tony. Could you find out anything?" He held her hand, "No, but I'm going to," "Ma'am, may I use your phone for a moment? I want to call Dr. Gessell!" She looked at him, wondering why he wanted to speak to the Chief Administrator of the hospital, "Dr. Gessell is going to say the same thing as I did, sir. Please have a seat, we'll call you when we hear something." Tony was getting angry, "Have you seen the new research laboratory that is being built about a block away from here?" The nurse nodded, "Of course; why? "Do you know what the name of that building is going to be?" She thought for a moment, then said, "Yes. Cole Research Laboratories." She wondered why he asked those questions. Tony took out his driver's license, "Read the name on this; it says Tony Cole. Tony Cole happens to be the benefactor of that building. Now, I want to talk to Dr. Gessell. The nurse quickly dialed his number.

Within minutes, a doctor representing Dr. Gessell arrived. "Mr. Cole, I'm Dr. Berenson, Chief of Surgery. I apologize for any problems you've had. Let me help you, come with me." Tony, Derek, and Theresa followed him to the elevator where they all rode quietly until they arrived at a lounge. Tony could wait no longer, "Okay, doctor, thank you for rescuing us, but now, what about Maggie, Margaret Weyland?" The doctor pleaded "Please sit down, Mr. Cole, please." Tony just stared at him. "Mr. Cole, Margaret Weyland had an aneurism in her brain. She's in emergency surgery right now!" Theresa began to cry, Derek dropped his head, and Tony calmly asked, "What are her chances, Dr. Berenson?" The doctor shook his head, "I can't answer that, but I can tell you that she's in the hands of one of the best brain surgeons in the country, Dr. Sweeney." That didn't satisfy Tony, "Please doctor, what can we expect?" Dr. Berenson looked at Tony, then at Derek and Theresa, "Normally, uh, I mean, these things, uh, look Mr. Cole, I have to be honest – it doesn't look favorable – I'm sorry, but we'll have to just wait until she's out of surgery." Theresa ran to Tony's side, "Oh, Tony! My God, how can this be!" Tony held her as she sobbed.

It was one-thirty in the afternoon when they had arrived at the hospital. It was now three-forty-five – Maggie had been in surgery for nearly four hours – and still no word.

A word had not been spoken in over an hour. Dr. Berenson and the three – very worried friends sat speechless – waiting in fear; fear of the worst.

Finally, at five-o-five, a doctor wearing perspiration stained greens, and looking totally drained came into the lounge. Theresa could hardly catch her breath as the tears swelled in her eyes; Derek clutched her hand, and Tony stood quickly – his face showing no emotion. The doctor wearing greens looked at Tony, "Are you Mr. Cole?" Tony nodded. "Mr. Cole, Margaret has survived the operation." Both Derek and Theresa ran to Tony. "Uh, I didn't finish!" The doctor interrupted their joy. The smiles vanished as quickly as they appeared. "I said she has survived the operation, but that's all." "Tell us the truth, doctor; what now?" Tony was pleading. "Mr. Cole, it's very simple; if she regains consciousness, there's a possibility she'll recover." "How many survive this thing?" Tony asked. "I wish I could say that the majority survive; but it is actually a very low percentage. I'm sorry. I really wish I could do more, but Margaret Weyland's life is out of my hands and God's the only one who can save her now. Pray, that's all any mortal man can do." Tony walked up to the doctor, "Thank you, doctor, for everything you've done. Can I see her?" "I'm afraid not. She's being kept in in the recovery room for a couple of hours, we'll take her to the neuro-surgery intensive care unit – you'll be able to see her then," he answered. Derek tugged at Tony's arm, "Come on, let's get something to eat; there's nothing we can do, you can't see her for two hours." Tony smiled at Derek, "No, you and Theresa go on home. I have some place to go. Thank you both." He left the lounge as Derek, Theresa, and the two doctors watched.

CHAPTER FIFTY-THREE

The hospital chapel was empty, except for Tony; kneeling alone in the front pew. He began to pray, "Dear God, please talk to me; tell me why this has happened to Maggie – she never hurt anybody – please tell me you'll make her well. Lord, I can't help but feel you're punishing me for something – you took my parents from me, you left me to grow up alone, then you took Jenny, a poor little orphaned cripple, then it was Sister Carolyn, Jonathan, then Roni, and now, oh, God, please don't take Maggie – let me have her. I've never asked you for much, but I'm begging you, Lord – I'm begging you for Maggie's life. I won't promise you that I'll do anything different, except one thing, I'll attend Mass every Sunday – I also ask for Maggie's life so that little Jenny will have her for a mother." Tony stayed until the two hours had passed.

As the elevator door opened, Tony's heart began to pound. He had dreamed about seeing Maggie again, but he never dreamed it would be like this. The nurse met him immediately and led him to Maggie's room. "Any change?" The nurse replied, "No, Mr. Cole, not yet." As they approached the door to her room, the nurse said, "You can only stay for two minutes, Mr. Cole." She opened the door for him then walked away.

The room was dark, except for a dim light on the table next to Maggie's bed. Tony stood in the door way; when he first saw her, his heart nearly jumped through his chest. "Oh, my God, Maggie!" Before he realized it, tears burst from his eyes and streamed down his face, his pulse quickened, his knees almost buckled, and he trembled uncontrollably. At that moment, all the love that Tony had for her doubled. He walked slowly to her side.

His eyes couldn't believe how she looked. He tried to force his thoughts from his brain, "She looks dead!"

Her head was bandaged; the sterile hospital sheet was tucked under her chin. She lay totally motionless; she looked so frail and helpless. To Tony, she was still beautiful – in fact, more beautiful than ever.

Tony pulled a chair next to her bed, he crossed his hands on the rail, and laid his chin on his hands – he sat completely still, the only noise – loving tears falling softly on the pure white sheets.

The nurse entered Maggie's room and spoke softly, "You have to go now, Mr. Cole." Tony was oblivious, he heard nothing. "Mr. Cole, you have to leave now!" Without looking up, he said, "No, I'm not leaving – I'm not leaving until she wakes up, not you nor anybody else can change that – now, please, leave us alone!" The nurse slipped out as quietly as she entered.

"It's alright, Millie. I'll take care of it," a young doctor told the nurse. He picked up the phone, "Dr. Gessell please, it's important!" "Hello, this is Dr. Gessell." "I'm sorry to bother you sir, this is Dr. Anson on three-west; we have a slight problem. Uh, it's Mr. Cole, he doesn't want to leave Margaret Weyland's room, and the rules say…" Dr. Gessell interrupted, "I know the rules, doctor! You leave Mr. Cole alone; I'm sure he's not going to interfere with your duties; and Dr. Anson – you give Mr. Cole anything he wants, anything! Do you understand?" "Yes, sir, I sure do! I'll pass the word," the young resident definitely understood.

The night dragged on – minute-by-minute, hour-by-hour – but to Tony, time was suspended. It was after 7:00 p.m. when he entered her room. It was now midnight – still Maggie lay unconscious.

As Tony sat watching her, his thoughts were reminisces of the past. He visualized little Jenny, dying in his arms; he could still remember the terrible hurt, sick feeling he felt that day. He remembered Sister Carolyn consoled him, telling him that God didn't want Jenny to suffer anymore, that he wanted to take care of her himself. He remembered moments with Jonathan, Derek, Sister Carolyn, and many of the moments he had spent with Roni, especially the last few moments of her life. Tony wondered why everybody he ever cared about had been taken away from him. Maggie, the one person he's loved most, is now on the brink of being taken away, too.

Tony felt a hand touch his shoulder; he turned his face to see who was intruding on his time with Maggie. "Tony, may I talk to you for a moment?" Father O'Halloran asked softly. "I can't leave her, Father. She might wake up; I can't leave her!" Tony replied. The old priest smiled, "I understand, Tony, let's go over by the window, just for a moment?" Tony stared at Maggie; then rose from the chair for the first time in nearly twelve hours. The sun was attempting to rise, and the dull winter light creeped through the drapes. Tony reached behind his head and stretched, then stood in that position for a couple of minutes. Father O'Halloran said nothing. Just as Tony started to speak, the doctor who had operated on Maggie entered the room. He nodded to Tony and Father O'Halloran, then began to examine Maggie. Tony watched the doctor check her pulse, listen to her heart, and look at her eyes. He inspected the machines and the IV needle that were attached to Maggie.

The doctor turned to Tony, "Mr. Cole, we weren't introduced yesterday. I'm John Sweeney." Tony squeezed his hand, "Dr. Sweeney, this is Father O'Halloran, an old friend of mine." As Dr. Sweeney shook hands with the old priest, he said, "There is still hope, Mr. Cole. These cases are never the same. Her vital signs are still at acceptable levels; waiting is still all any of us can do; any of us, that is, except you Father and your Boss." "What in your professional opinion are her chances?" Tony asked. He looked back at Maggie, "If she regains consciousness, she stands an excellent chance of complete recovery." "What about regaining consciousness?" Tony prodded the doctor. He shook his head, "I honestly don't know; but you, Mr. Cole, you shouldn't stay here. Why don't you go home; you have my word that we'll call you the minute there's any change!" "Thank you, Dr. Sweeney, but I'd rather stay' I won't get in the way," Tony smiled. "Sure, Mr. Cole, I understand. I'll have some breakfast brought in for you. Nice to meet you, Father." Dr. Sweeney checked the machines once more before he left.

"Well, Father, if you've come to persuade me to leave, I'm afraid you've wasted a trip. I'm not leaving!" "Tony, I've come only to be with you, in your time of need. Dr. Sweeney said it – only my Boss, God, can do anything for Maggie; but you, Tony, you need somebody, whether you'll admit it or not," Father O'Halloran said. "Yes, Father. I would appreciate your staying for a while. Maggie needs all the help she can get." They stood in silence for a moment, then Tony asked, "By the way, how did you, uh, how did you know I was here?" "Your good friend, Derek Hill; he thought I might be of some help," he answered. Tony smiled.

Tony just looked at the breakfast Dr. Sweeney had sent in. He continued to watch the parade of doctors and nurses coming in to examine Maggie. "Mr. Cole, are you still here?" the evening nurse who attempted to get Tony to leave the night before came in. Tony manages a weak smile. "Hello, Father! Mr. Cole, did you call in a recruit?" she joked. "Yeh, I guess I did," he answered. As the nurse left, she stopped at the door and looked at Tony. She thought to herself, "I wonder if the lady realized what kind of a man he is; I should be so lucky."

Tony was leaning on the rail of the bed, his eyes were slightly open. He didn't realize how tired he was. Suddenly, he snapped his head back. He stared into her face – his heart began to pound – his breathing became heavy – he stood up quickly – Father O'Halloran quickly went to his side – Tony continued to stare into Maggie's face. It happened again – there was a twitch in Maggie's face – the first movement of any kind – then her lips parted – Tony's heart was pounding so hard, you could almost hear it – then one of Maggie's eyes twitched. "Maggie, Maggie, can you hear me?" Tony pleaded. Slowly, her eyes opened – the first sight she saw was Tony's face, with tears streaming down his cheeks. Finally, her eyes were open wide, and she managed to utter his name, "Tony! Tony!" He bent down, kissed her forehead, and said, "I'm here, Maggie; I'll always be here. In the background, Father O'Halloran was saying "thanks" for the answer to his prayers.

Tony Cole had found his love – and met his challenge.

The End

Tommy has two more books that will follow *An Orphans Empire.*